SHADOWS IN THE STONE

Book 1

SHADOWS IN THE STONE

Book 1

Castle Keepers

DIANE McGYVER

Quarter Castle Publishing

where imagination is magic
New Scotland, Canada

Lady Diane McGyver's first novel *Shadows in the Stone* was almost 30 years in the making. The second book in her fantasy series, *Scattered Stones*, took a lot less time to get from first draft to publication. She's written a few short stories that reveal the history of some of the characters in the novels, and she's completed books 3 and 4 of the series. She is currently working on book 5, *Gathered Stones*.

Diane fell in love with the fantasy genre when an awesome dungeon master introduced her to **Dungeons & Dragons** at the age of 13. From there, she landed into the worlds created by Terry Brooks and Mercedes Lackey. By 19, she was truly lost to the *other realm*.

Her future goals are to complete the 10-book series and to live in a peel tower near the Atlantic Ocean where she'll raise chickens, tomatoes and Trouble.

To learn more about McGyver's books, visit her website: https://dianelynnmcgyver.com

Text Copyright@2019 Quarter Castle Publishing

Second Edition
Paperback ISBN: 978-1-927625-32-3
eBook ISBN: 978-1-927625-33-0

Cover and Interior Design: Quarter Castle Publishing
Originally edited by Jay Underwood
Originally Published May 2012
2nd Edition Published January 2019

Quarter Castle Publishing
Nova Scotia B0N 1Y0 CANADA
quartercastlepublishing.com

0212QCP0004

Please Note

This book was written using Canadian spelling.

Shadows in the Stone, Book 1 of The Castle Keepers series, is a work of fiction. Names, characters (regardless of race), horses, places, events and incidents are either the products of the author's vast and wild imagination or used in a fictitious manner. Any resemblance to actual persons and animals, living or dead, or actual events, past or future, is purely coincidental. Many locations thought to exist in Nova Scotia—Glen Tosh, Wyvern, Goshen, Shulie—truly exist in this novel.

If you share a name with one of these fictional characters, the author apologises; there are only so many unique names on the planet. If you really like the character, then you're welcome.

Direct enquires to Quarter Castle Publishing:
quartercastlepublishing.com

Quarter Castle Publishing bore the complete cost of publishing this book and received no financial assistance from outside sources.

S

Be-still Spell

Bored by the conversation, Joris tickled Isla's side. "How is Liam? Has he stolen a kiss, yet?"

Isla grinned. "Why would he kiss me?"

He leant near her ear. "It's what boys do."

She pushed him away. "Liam won't. He's my best friend."

"He will. One of these days, he's going to lean in to look at dirt on your cheek." He glided past her defences. "He'll flash his eyes and cast a Be-still Spell so you can't move and before you know it, wham!" He kissed her on the forehead. "He'll steal the first kiss."

"What if I push him away?"

"He'll try again. If a boy likes a girl, he'll keep trying for years. And Liam is sweet on you."

"What if *I* steal the kiss first?"

"Then I'd say you're nothing like your das."

Dear Readers,

The 2nd edition of *Shadows in the Stone* was necessary for several reasons. I won't bore you with too many details, but here are a few in a walnut shell.

I've grown as a writer since 2012, when the book was first released. I'd like to show off these new skills by improving your reading experience.

I failed to include a character list in the back of the book, and I've had several requests for one.

The print version of the 1st edition had smaller text, and I wanted to enlarge it slightly to improve your reading experience. The 2nd edition also has a prettier layout, which is more appealing to the eye.

The cover for the 1st edition was okay, but the 2nd edition cover is amazing.

The second book in the series, *Scattered Stones*, is 22,000 words longer, which bumped it into a more comfortable 6 inches wide by 9 inches tall format. Originally *Shadows in the Stone* was 5.5 inches by 8.5 inches. I wanted all books in the series to be 6x9.

So there have it. I hope my goal—to give you a more enjoyable reading experience—is reached.

Enjoy.

Diane McGyver
October 3, 2018

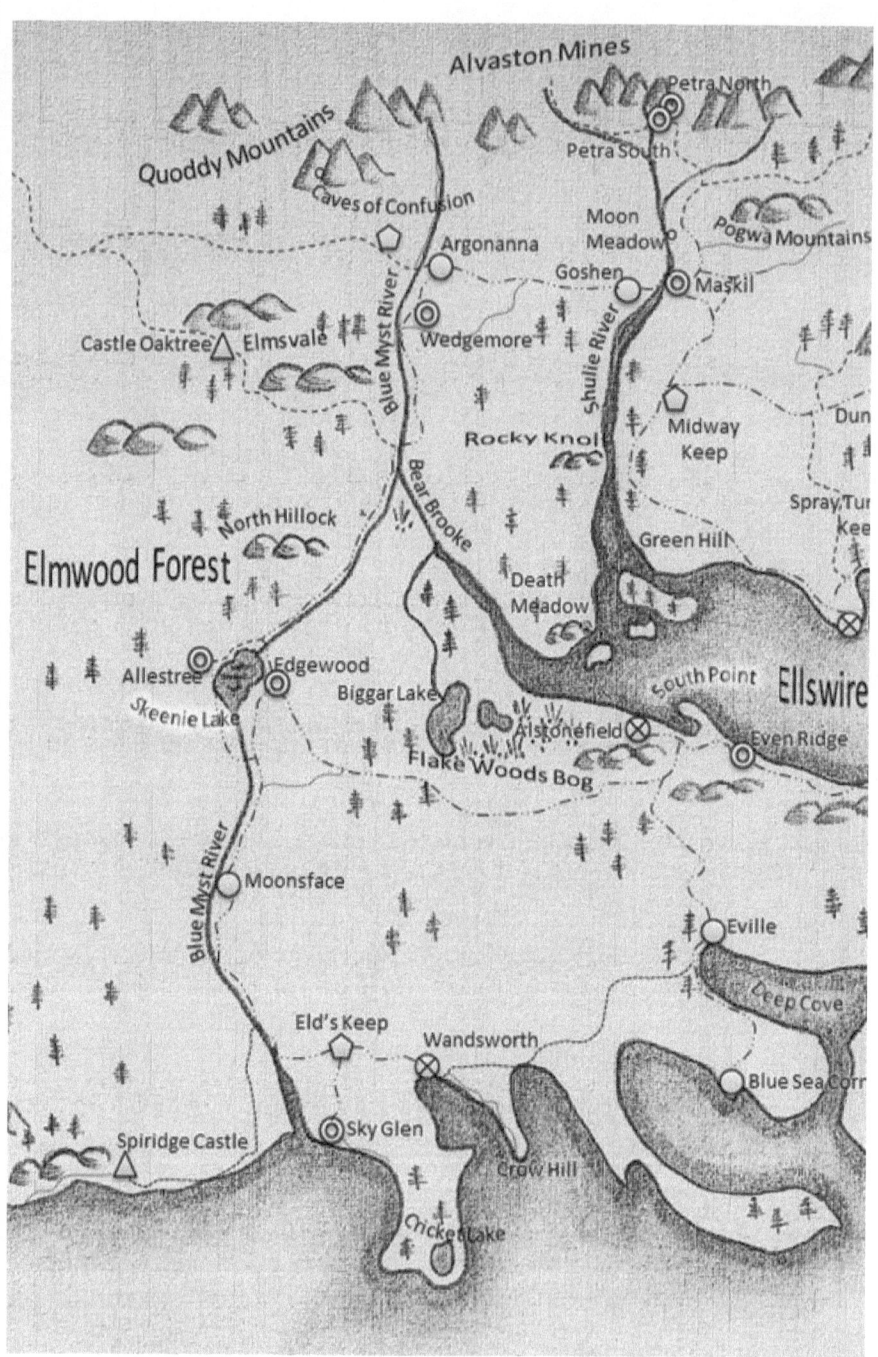

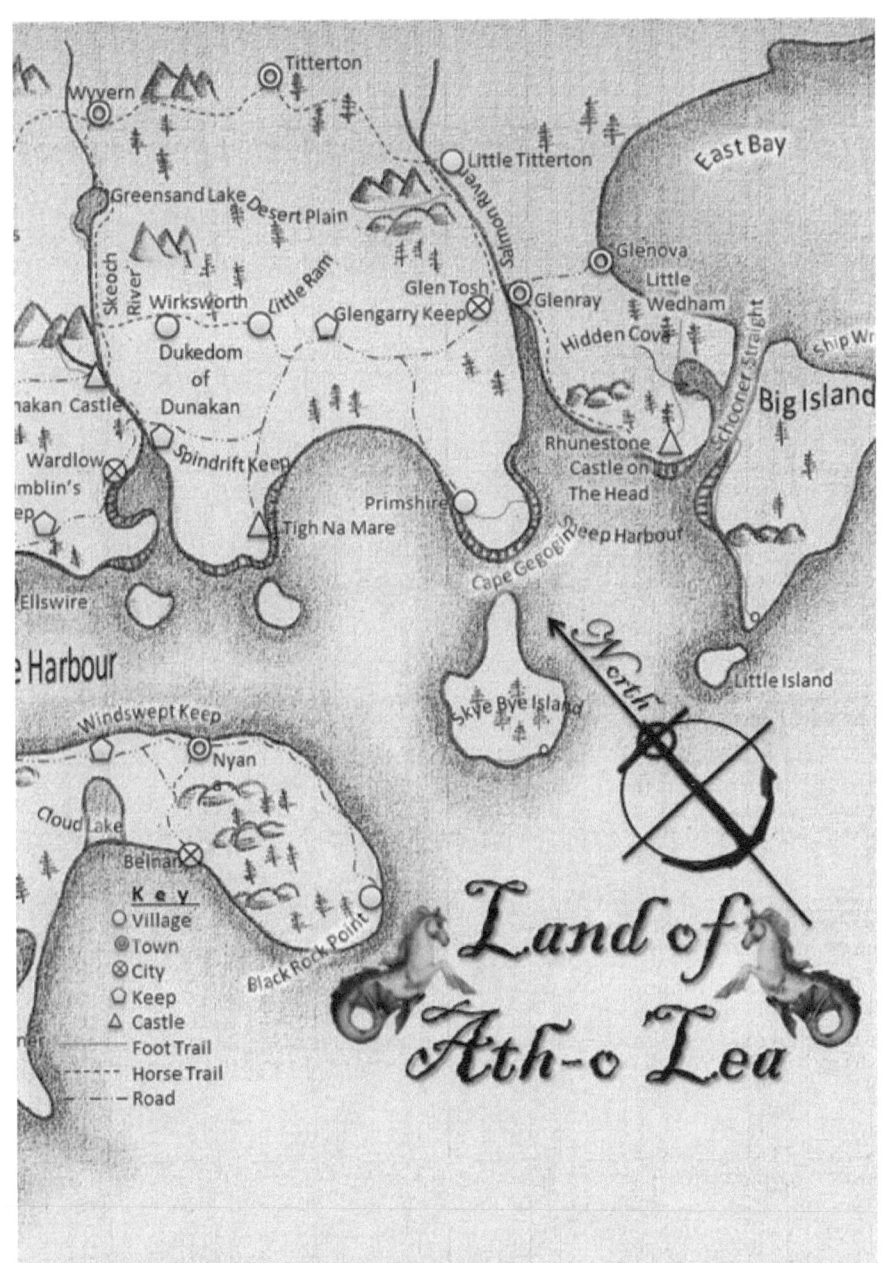

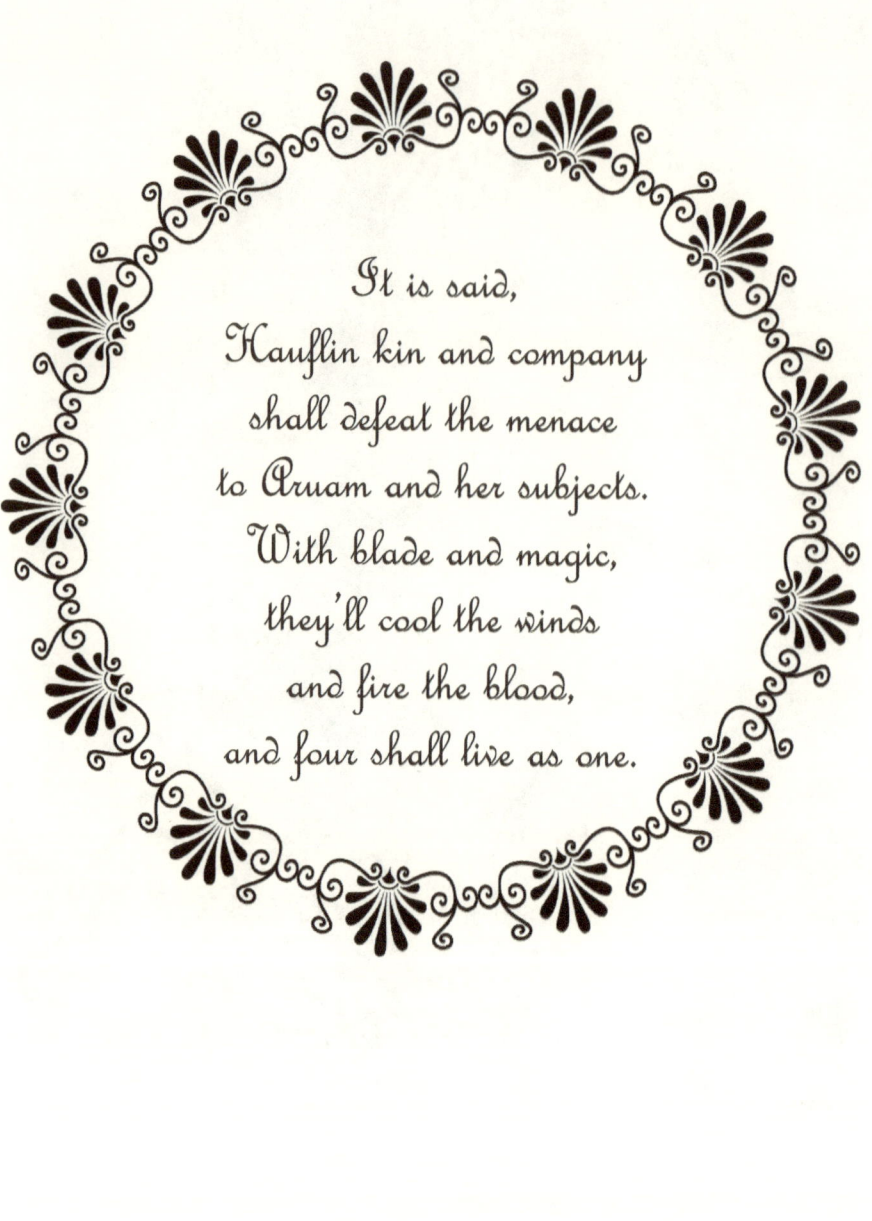

It is said,
Hauflin kin and company
shall defeat the menace
to Aruam and her subjects.
With blade and magic,
they'll cool the winds
and fire the blood,
and four shall live as one.

Dedication

Although many hands helped bring this book to publication, my journey to the land of Ath-o'Lea would not have started without the wisdom, dedication and humour of one man: Peter Mortimer.

I met Peter first as a dungeon master on a warm summer day as I raced through the Boys & Girls Club lounge. The next time I met him, he was the new director of the youth club. He stayed for about five years and created the club I'm glad I didn't have to live without.

Those few precious years between being a kid and becoming an adult are volatile. During this time, I was fortunate enough to discover the world of fantasy through a roll-playing game.

Peter introduced me to Dungeons & Dragons and to Argon (who would become Bronwyn) and encouraged me to explore the land of fairies. He has impacted my life in ways I can't even explain.

D

Shadows in the Stone

1

Maternal Instincts

ALAURA OF Niamh twiddled the small ring on her finger and drew shallow breaths. She glanced around the one-room dwelling and tried to identify the source of a lingering odour that renewed itself whenever someone moved. Was it the smell of decomposing food or drying afterbirth?

The small home appeared like many others in the town of Maskil except this one had no glass windows. Instead, the occupants had boarded-up the openings with scrap wood. The lantern Alaura had lit upon arrival at Maura of Ealasaid's home provided the only light. It illuminated the bruises on Maura's calves and wrists.

Alaura surveyed the half-naked hauflin; she was slim for a woman at full term. She quickly averted her eyes when Maura caught her staring. Alaura didn't want to be here, but Catriona Wheatcroft, her teacher, had insisted. She had made an excuse, but Catriona ignored it, saying, *I need you. Maura needs you.*

Although a stranger in Maskil, Alaura had been accepted as one of Catriona's apprentices. Her teacher had told her she'd be capable of great deeds if properly trained in magic. Those deeds included helping others in their time of need. Though Alaura believed a more experienced apprentice made a better choice to assist in the birth, she felt compelled to fulfil Catriona's request.

Maura cried out, making Alaura jump. Pain ripped through the small hauflin's body, renewing the beads of sweat drenching her skin. She clenched her teeth and gripped the frayed blanket beneath her.

"Push, Maura!" Catriona glared at the pregnant woman. "One great push for your baby!"

Alaura watched Maura. She lay on a dilapidated bed, staring at the ceiling. *She* didn't want to be here either. Her tattered dress, hiked up past her swollen belly, appeared unfit for washing a floor.

"I see the head!" Catriona's expression eased. "It won't be long now. Support her."

Alaura gripped Maura's hand and gazed into her face; the worry etched deep lines. "One more," she whispered, forcing a smile.

Maura clasped her hand tightly and stared into her eyes as if to gather strength for the final push. "You're like me."

She spoke faintly, but Alaura heard every word.

"Hauflin child."

Alaura gasped. Maura detected her hauflin origins! No one, not even Catriona, suspected her race to be anything other than full-blood human.

Maura held her breath. As if forces of their own making worked upon her body, the baby emerged from the womb. The excruciating pain subsided, and she fell limp against the mattress.

"It's alive!" Catriona wrapped the baby in a blanket and gave it to her apprentice.

The infant wriggled in Alaura's arms. Its large brown eyes circled the room, then swept over her face. A toothless grin lit up its dark complexion, making Alaura giggle. She opened the blanket. "It's a girl." She held the baby for the new meeme to see. "It's a girl, Maura. A beautiful, healthy girl. Now you have one of each."

"Shhh!" hissed Catriona.

Alaura clamped her mouth shut. Only the three women and a newborn occupied the room. What had triggered Catriona's uneasiness? The baby kicked the blanket away. "She has strong feet. She'll be running before long." Hauflins had thicker skin than humans on the bottoms of their feet and walked barefoot easily. Before arriving at Maskil, she had spent most of her time without shoes.

"Ignorant hauflins go shoeless in town." Catriona removed a silver necklace from a chest and draped it around the baby's neck. The cold jewellery on bare skin made the baby purse her lips in surprise. The five blue stones imbedded in the medallion sparkled.

"She's a dear." Alaura gently tickled the baby's belly. "Full of happiness."

"She's not meant for happiness."

She stared at Catriona. Why would she say this? Maura's horrid condition meant she'd expire soon, but her child had hope for a better life, not misery. A tug on her arm made her turn to the frail woman on the bed.

"Keep her safe." Maura's weak voice trailed off into almost inaudible words. "You're one of us. A woman. A hauflin. Upon my death, she becomes your duty."

Catriona hadn't heard the last few sentences, but Alaura's hauflin ears caught every word. "I'll keep her safe. You have my word."

"Your *word*?" asked Maura, her eyes growing wide.

Alaura caught her breath as the woman's grip tightened; she hadn't meant *that* word. She glanced at Catriona, who focussed on cleaning the birth mess at Maura's feet. The sorceress had warned her not to get personally involved. The baby had been assigned a home, and she'd never see it again. Giving her *word* meant she would be bonded to Maura's daughter. The new meeme couldn't see Catriona's negative expression, but she'd feel the pain if Alaura obeyed her.

Only eighteen years old, Alaura had problems of her own, which forced her to hideout in Maskil. Still, Maura's eyes begged her to accept the covenant, and the soft smile of the baby cradled in her arms tugged at her maternal instincts. How could she deny a dying woman's wish for her newborn to be kept safe?

"I give you my word," said Alaura.

"Your word is your bond." Maura presented the covenant.

"My word is my bond." A strange sensation stirred in her stomach and moved into her chest. It entered her throat and caused a small burp.

Satisfied, Maura released her and sank into the worn pillow. Her daughter safe, she appeared to welcome the journey to the Plane of Peace. She lifted her hand and gently touched the baby's cheek. "Isla of Maura."

"A beautiful name." Alaura gazed upon the bright child full of innocence and bliss, then saw her teacher frowning while she covered the young mother with a warm blanket. Although an apprentice for only two months, she had an idea of what Catriona might have been thinking: *It's senseless to think of protecting the child when it's destined for a family in Petra.*

Alaura gave her word to protect the child until then. Her bond dissolved when Isla arrived at her new home in the northern town. At the very least, giving her word eased Maura's concerns.

"Tend to her as a garden throughout the seasons," whispered Maura in Hauflin.

"I'll do my best." Alaura cradled the baby, rocking it gently.

Pain gripped Maura, and she cried out.

Catriona ushered her apprentice from the bed. "You know what to do." She pulled the blanket over the baby's face. "May the night fairies see you safely to your destination."

Alaura held the baby close and marched to the exit. She reached for the door knob and it swung open, smashing into her knuckles. Drawing back to assess her hand, she froze when she saw the man who entered.

"What's going on?" Keiron Ruckle, Maura's mate, cast a scowl around the room, taking in the scene.

"Maura lost the baby," said Catriona. "Alaura, take away the remains."

Alaura attempted to pass, but he grabbed her arm.

"Show me the body."

"Allow her to proceed out of respect for the deceased." Catriona deepened her voice and furrowed her brow. "Your mate needs your attention. She'll soon join your child."

Keiron drew a dagger from his belt and held it to Alaura's side. "It's my right to witness the passing."

Alaura's hands trembled, but she held the baby tightly. This man of the same race as her das had a scowl that conjured nightmares. She looked to Catriona for help while twisting her body away from the weapon. The grip on her arm grew stronger, and Keiron used the dagger to flick the blanket from the baby's face. He grunted in disgust, but the sight of the jewelled necklace stifled him.

"Maura is a breath away from death!" Catriona stood strong, but the shakiness in her voice betrayed her. "It's your duty as her mate to grant her your time!"

"If she's that close to death, she ain't needin' me but the undertaker." He stared at the necklace and his eyes grew shiny.

"She's a helpless child." Alaura tried to pull away but ceased struggling when the dagger poked her side.

"If yew know what's good for yew, ye'll hand over the bairn and run as if the harpies are at yer heels."

"Keiron, allow the girl to pass." Catriona kept her distance. "The baby will be taken care of as Maura instructed."

"The bairn's mine!"

"You can't have her!" Alaura planted her feet and held the baby tighter.

"Maura gave the baby to me!" lied Catriona.

"If it's the necklace you desire, take it!" The smell of meat and sour rum on the man's breath filled Alaura's air passages. "But leave the baby!"

"No!" Catriona stepped closer. "Alaura, we can't—"

"The Law of the Land grants me right to my child." In a flawless motion, Keiron struck Alaura in the jaw with the butt of the dagger and snatched the baby from her arms. He pointed the dagger towards Maura. "I expect this mess cleaned up and yew hags gone by the time I return." He left the dwelling, slamming the door behind him.

Alaura got to her feet and rubbed her jaw. "You should have given him the necklace! It's what he wanted!"

Catriona clasped her hands in front of her. "The Law of the Land grants him the claim to his child. We can't challenge that. As for the necklace, it must remain with the girl."

"Keiron will sell it!"

"I believe otherwise." She remembered Maura and went to her side. The hauflin lay still with a serene expression. She had completed her trip to the Plane of Peace.

FIVE YEARS LATER

The events of that night haunted Alaura still. She had promised Maura to protect her baby, and after Keiron Ruckle had snatched the child from her arms, she'd promised herself to never again be that vulnerable.

Slipping into her hiding place near Keiron's backdoor, she thought about the first time she came to spy on Isla. It had taken two days to convince herself to do it. When she did, she discovered the overhang of the adjacent building created a cubby, and she pressed herself into the hiding spot. It became the perfect location to watch the backdoor and the fenced-in pen where a Cotswold ewe tended to her lamb and Maura's baby.

She had been tempted to snatch the child and run, but she had nowhere to hide with a baby in Maskil? Returning to her hometown of North Ridge, Petra, proved too dangerous. Truth be told, she wouldn't have gotten far. If Keiron reported the baby missing, guards at the town gates would have remembered her with the child. They'd have thrown her in the dungeon or worse.

Night after night, Alaura watched the hauflin child. She brought food and drink and when the cold winds blew, she cuddled the orphan to her breast. During her long hours of vigil, she prepared for the day when she would escape with her.

Over the years, she sought spells to aide her task. She mastered the Cloaking Spell, which hid Isla from anyone who ventured into the yard. Combined, the Bubble and Warmth Spells created a small space that maintained the conjured heat where she and Isla stayed warm and dry throughout Forstig and Wintertide. These and many more had served them well.

The spells hadn't come from her teacher. Catriona may have convinced her to explore her powers, but another magic-maiden gave her the knowledge to sharpen them. The added confidence and skill level made her ready to face the challenges of travelling alone to Petra with a child.

She'd take the journey in a fortnight.

Alaura had befriended the guards at the town entrance gates. They knew her by name and that she pulled a small cart behind her, one large enough to carry several garments she crafted and sold to those living in surrounding settlements or large enough for a hauflin child.

She planned to deliver Isla to her brother Pym, who'd claim her as his own. Then she'd return to Maskil as if nothing happened and continue with her life in the limited capacity available to her.

The plan contained one irritation: Corporal Darrow. Unlike other Aruam Castle guards, he checked every cart, every sack and every waggon entering and leaving Maskil, including his dad's delivery waggon. Alaura had observed his steadfastness to regulations and while he worked the gates, she avoided passing through. While he patrolled the castle wall, guards at the entrance felt his presence and carried out their duties accordingly.

Corporal Darrow had to be off duty to improve her chances of escaping with Isla.

The corporal didn't appear rotten. In truth, he seemed amiable. His mum, Maisie Darrow, owned and operated the Forest Bakery and Herb Shop where she purchased many of the herbs to work spells and create potions. His family had become known to her, but she avoided him for the potential trouble he could cause and for the feelings he stirred when he smiled at her from a distance. The handsome, well-built man appeared unlike the dwarfs in the settlement north of Petra; miners everyone, they were gruff and scruffy. Corporal Darrow looked anything but scruffy. Nevertheless, she couldn't become acquainted with anyone serving with the castle because of the dangers it created.

Alaura pushed these thoughts from her mind and thought instead of Isla, who played with her stones beside the woolly ewe. A quiet child, she seldom spoke unless Alaura gave permission. Despite her living conditions and the lack of personal contact, Isla had grown into a generous and easy-going girl.

Removing a biscuit from her sack and placing it on her palm, Alaura cleared her mind and focussed on the food. It rose, moved across the yard and dropped into the straw before Isla. The child looked towards her hiding place but remained still. She withdrew another biscuit and repeated the Levitation Spell.

Isla gathered both biscuits, fed one to the sheep and ate the other. She did the same with the oatmeal raisin cookies and apples Alaura delivered. Then she cuddled into the ewe's warm wool and fell asleep while the sun set.

To pass the time, Alaura went over her escape plan. Her solitary vigil meant no one would suspect her of taking the child. After a five-day journey, Isla would be safe in North Ridge. Although she felt guilty about using her friendship with Maisie to commit an unlawful deed, she wouldn't hesitate when the woman complained once again about her youngest child's infrequent visits. *Is your son working days this week?* Though a casual question passed between a regular customer and a shop owner, the answer dictated when she would leave Maskil.

With Isla protected by the Cloaking Spell, Alaura snuggled into her blanket and fell asleep.

2

Searching the Darkness

ALAURA AWOKE to movement within the sheep stall. In the dim light, she saw Isla staring in the direction of Aruam Castle. She turned and looked in the same direction but found nothing unusual.

Isla slipped between the stall rails and entered the dwelling. Her increase in wandering away from the backyard was one more reason, Alaura had decided it was time to rescue the child. She couldn't keep Isla safe if she strayed from the yard in her absence.

A crash inside the dwelling startled Alaura. The once-dark interior exploded with light, but she couldn't see the source of the noise.

"Where is it?"

She didn't recognise the deep voice. After several loud bangs, another voice echoed on the night air.

"Maybe he already has it."

"Darnacles!" The first voice growled.

"Maybe it's outside."

Alaura froze when a large human flung open the back door. Two men followed him outside. All three brandished swords and wore dilapidated chainmail armour over rugged clothing of The Trail. They searched the backyard, kicking aside empty crates and tossing an old sack filled with garbage.

"This'll show Keiron how we deal with traitors!"

The leading man stepped over the rail, sliced the ewe's belly from neck to tail and flung it against the back door. The ewe squealed in terror until it struck the ground.

The three men marched down the alley looking for another innocent victim to murder.

The image of the slaughtered ewe sent a shockwave down Alaura's spine, and she squeezed her eyes shut. Gasping for air, she told herself she had to move, escape this place before the ruffians returned, yet she couldn't leave without Isla. Drawing strength from her mentor's lessons, she forced her eyes open. She half climbed, half fell from the roof and landed with a solid thud on the ground. One glance at the dark liquid seeping from the sheep told her she couldn't bear to move the animal to get inside. Instead, she sneaked to the front of the dwelling where she found the door broken down.

Once inside, she scanned the small dwelling but couldn't see Isla. Hearing movement in the backyard, she dived into the nearest hiding place, a closet, and scrambled behind the hanging clothes. One gasp for air made her cringe from the stench, and she tried to hold her breath. Her head swooned, and she was torn between passing out and vomiting.

"Damn!" Keiron spoke in a hushed voice. "They've been here."

"I guess that message is for you." Another man's voice seeped through the door opening.

"And yew, my friend."

Alaura heard a dragging sound—the ewe—and then footsteps inside the dwelling.

"Let's get the scroll and get out of here," said Keiron's companion.

She sensed fear in his voice. Peeking between the clothing, she watched Keiron move a small table by the front door and slide a stone from the wall, revealing a small opening. He extracted an item, then returned the stone and table.

"What are you waiting for?" The stranger paused near the door.

Keiron hesitated and looked around.

Did he sense her presence? A bizarre expression radiated in the limited light. What did he think of? He almost appeared sincere with a yearning for a dear memory.

He walked with determined steps towards a small window boarded-up on the outside and covered with a faded curtain on the inside. He flung open the material and half smiled at his discovery. "Yer as crafty as yer ol' man." He pulled Isla from her hiding spot.

"Why are you bringing that?" The man at the door threw his arms into the air.

"They'll kill her if I leave her here." Keiron walked out the back door with Isla under his arm and disappeared down the alley.

Their footsteps faded, and Alaura crept to the back door to watch their shadows disappear in the distance. Though tempted to follow, she held back. Hauflins had excellent hearing, and she had much to learn when it came to following in silence. She gathered her courage and stepped forward. Then she remembered the other dangers awaiting a young woman alone in the alleys of this part of town at night. She felt unprepared to face them. She shuddered, realising she had lost Isla. Her shaking hands went to her lips. There had to be another way. Turning, she went to the front door, peeked outside and slipped from the dwelling.

Catriona folded down the blankets on her bed. She looked forward to a good night's sleep after a full day instructing her apprentices. The large amount of energy drained from her body while practising spells always surprised her. Magic had never come easy for like others she'd known.

A soft noise in the alley compelled her to look towards the door. *Probably the stray cat I fed earlier.* She leant towards the taper and prepared to blow out the flame, but a rap on the thick wooden door startled her. The unidentified visitor tapped again.

She crept towards the door. No one came to her dwelling this time of day. Surely it wasn't anyone she knew. She stopped. Strangers were not welcome in her home. They knocked harder, forcing her body towards the sound. Her trembling hands opened the tiny peep hole, and she peered out, searching the darkness for the source of the knocking.

"Open up." The man gave the order in a hushed tone.

"Who are you?" She tried to mask the fear in her voice.

"Keiron Ruckle. Open the door."

"What do you want?"

"It ain't what I want. It's what yew want."

She cautiously opened the door. Keiron and his partner rushed inside, forcing her to step back. She gathered her flowing nightdress around her for protection from the cool air and her visitors.

"I need yew to keep Isla safe." Keiron sneered. "Can yew do that?"

"You're giving her to me?" She caught Isla as he shoved the girl into her arms.

"I ain't giving yew nothing. Consider it a loan. Keep her out of sight. People are looking for her. Bad people."

"Wha...what do they want with her?" She fought to control her shaking hands as she cradled the child in an awkward position.

"Her life." Keiron glared at her. "Don't look so surprised. They want mine, too." He ushered his partner towards the door. "If yew know what's good for yew, yew'll forget yew saw us. It might save yer life." He stalked into the darkness and disappeared.

Catriona heaved the door shut and snapped the deadbolt into place. She leant against the cool wood and braced her racing heart. Looking down at the child in her arms, every nerve came alive. "What am I to do with you?" If she sent Isla away to safety and Keiron returned, he might... She needed to think. She needed to calm herself and analyse the possibilities. She needed an herbal tea.

She crossed the room and set Isla on a cushioned chair. No sooner had she turned from the child when a frantic knock came at the front door. Petrified, she imagined the trouble Keiron had spoken of had arrived awaited on the other side. She considered escaping out the back door, but... Again, the front door was assaulted with quick knocking, and a muffled voice cried out. It didn't sound threatening. She picked up her magic staff, bit her bottom lip and swallowed hard. A quick peek, and if she didn't like the looks of the visitor, she'd pretend she was not home. Before approaching the door, she flung a blanket over the chair, hiding the young hauflin from view.

The voice spoke again. It sounded female.

"Who is it?" She held the staff at the ready.

"Alaura."

She cautiously opened the narrow peek hatch. A small figure dressed in black with a hood over its head stood on the other side of the door. "Alaura?"

"Yes, Sorceress, it is me." The woman removed her hood. "Please, may I enter?"

Catriona opened the door and ushered her inside, then closed it and secured the lock. "Why are you dressed like this? I didn't recognise you."

"A terrible tragedy has struck."

"What sort?"

"Ruffians were searching for Isla. When they didn't find her, they killed the ewe. Then Keiron came." Visibly shaken, she appeared smaller than usual. "He and another man took her away. I fear Isla's in terrible danger."

Catriona tilted her head and watched her apprentice through narrow eyes. How did she know this? "Have a seat and tell me everything."

"I can't sit." She paced the floor with her arms on her hips. "I have to act."

Catriona pulled the blanket from the chair.

Astonished, Alaura dropped to her knees in front of the child. "How did she get here?"

"Keiron brought her for safe-keeping. He's on the run. He must be in big trouble." She smiled. "Let's hope it catches up with him."

3

Kissing the Air with Each Leap

THE NIGHT had almost passed before Alaura departed her teacher's dwelling. Although she wanted to tell Catriona every detail of what had transpired during the night and about her vigil over Isla, her instincts warned her to be selective. Instead, she implied a guard had alerted her to a dramatic event at the castle. Together, they had sneaked into the alley near Keiron's dwelling and watched the action from afar.

Catriona had believed every word. Alaura had watched the fear wane and ebb in her teacher's eyes as she spoke of the intruders, the dead ewe and Keiron. Over the years she had come to realise the older woman talked more than she acted. Catriona spoke of challenging deeds, creating magic to fight evil and defending the innocent but in truth, she did little. She seldom left her dwelling.

It was this realisation that had prompted Alaura to secretly further her studies with another magic-maiden. Twice a week for the past four years, she had left the protection of the town walls and travelled to a cottage at Moon Meadow where Beathas of Ailsa, a hauflin in her mid-90s, shared her wisdom. Beathas had many sources of magic, including stones. Catriona believed stones made great paper weights and decorations but nothing more. Alaura believed otherwise.

Although far from completing her training, Alaura felt a sense of power, both driving and calming, from Beathas' lessons she had never experienced with Catriona's tutoring.

These thoughts played in her mind as she crossed the deserted street and followed the lane to her home. She slipped inside her small living space, locked the door and tossed her hood on a chair. Her meagre possessions scarcely dented the space of the one-room dwelling. They were the basic items needed to survive: clothing, dishes, a bunk with bedding, a rucksack and a small number of supplies to work incantations and to fashion the clothing she sold at the market. Her philosophy remained simple: the less kept, the faster travelled. Belongings weighed down the body and mind.

With sleep beckoning, she snuggled into her pillow and fell into a deep slumber.

ಬಿ ❖ ಗ

After Alaura left, Catriona made a comfortable spot on the chair for Isla to sleep. She extinguished the smoky taper and crawled into bed. For a long time, she lay awake thinking about the night's events and Alaura's intriguing yet frightening story. She'd never consider leaving the security of her home at night to hide in an alley to watch Keiron's dwelling.

She closed her eyes and tried to rest, but every noise sounded louder than usual. Several times she wondered if intruders meddled with the door lock. She listened for footsteps and voices but heard none.

Finally, she fell into a restless sleep. Maura's pleading eyes swayed in and out of her dreams like a breeze moving a curtain to-and-fro. Soft wings brushed her cheek, and she woke with a start.

Sitting up, she scanned the dwelling. The sun peeked in from around the closed curtains, creating shafts of light in the room. Dust particles danced in the shine, falling and rising in rhythmic spirals. Her eyes settled on the chair in the corner. It sat empty.

She sprang from the bed, ran to the chair and pulled away the blanket. Isla had vanished. She raced to check the doors and found both secure. The child had to be here.

She searched beneath tables and chairs, opened cupboard doors and rooted through the many sacks and boxes tucked into every available space. She rummaged through the garment closet and the water closet without success. In exasperation, she dropped into the chair.

A quick rap sounded on the front door. Catriona bolted upright and ran for her staff. She held it firmly as she peeked out the viewing hatch.

"Open up!" said Alaura.

She fumbled with the lock, then barely had time to step aside before her apprentice pushed the door open.

"What are you thinking?" Alaura dashed to the front window.

"What's the panic? I had—" Catriona froze, dumbstruck as the young woman pushed aside the curtain and pulled Isla from the window sill.

Alaura turned to face her teacher. "Why did you let her sit there for every passerby to see?"

"I didn't put her there!"

"She hid from you?"

"She did." She glared down at the shorter, slim-built human. If she didn't know better, she'd swear the girl possessed dwarf lineage because of her lack of height and her occasional rude demeanour.

Alaura's expression softened. "I'm sorry for accusing you."

"You should be. It's improper for an apprentice to speak to her teacher in that manner." She slammed the door shut. "I busied myself looking for her when you attacked my door. A moment more and I'd have found her and removed her from public sight."

Alaura cast her eyes to the floor. "It surprised me to see her in the window. It's her safety which concerns me."

Catriona evaluated her apprentice, approving of her submission. "I'm not asking for the impossible, Alaura. Only respect." She released the sternness. "You're forgiven for your outburst. The next time think before you react."

"Of course." Alaura pulled the child closer. "Let me care for Isla while you prepare yourself for the day."

Alaura bathed and dressed Isla, then disposed of the soiled water while Catriona sat the child at the table to break the fast. The little one slid from the chair and darted into the garment closet. She dug in between the sacks and boxes, burying herself from view.

"I think Keiron has the child terrified stupid," said Catriona. "There's no other reason to explain it."

"What shall we do with her?" asked Alaura.

"Send her to Petra."

"But what if she doesn't possess magic? She may be refused after all this time."

"Then we'll test her." Catriona pulled a black book from a shelf and flipped through the pages until she found the recipe. "The Tell-tale Powder will reveal her abilities." She made a list of required ingredients. "Stay with the child while I step out for supplies." She put on a sweater and took a shoulder pouch from a hook. "I won't be long."

After Catriona closed the door behind her, Alaura sat in the chair and looked towards the garment closet. She reached into her sack and withdrew a pear. Taking a deep breath and slowly releasing it, she focussed on the fruit. The pear rose and floated towards the closet. When it neared the spot where Isla hid, it dropped and landed on a stuffed sack. A small hand reached up and snatched it.

A short time later, Isla poked her head from beneath the closet contents and inched her way closer. Seeing only Alaura, she ran the rest of the distance, jumped onto her lap and snuggled into her arms.

Alaura hugged the young hauflin tightly and kissed her cheek. Reaching into her sack, she pulled out a small leather pouch. She opened it for Isla to see the contents. Inside, beneath a false bottom, lay the child's stones. In the light of day, she had returned to Keiron's dwelling to collect them. She believed the girl had gathered special stones, perhaps ones with unique powers. One gem appeared similar to the blue stones in the necklace that had disappeared the night of her birth. Undoubtably, Keiron had sold the jewellery.

~ 17 ~

"These are your stones, Isla." She spoke in Hauflin. "And this is your pouch to carry them in."

"Mine?"

"Yes, these are Isla's." She pulled her to her breast and kissed the top of her head. "With or without magic, there will always be a special place in my heart for you."

Catriona reviewed the recipe for the Tell-tale Powder. She and Alaura had set out the ingredients and prepared to mix them together.

"The difficulty with this spell is not the exact measurement of ingredients," said Catriona, "but the order and manner in which each ingredient is added to the recipe. The first item, cumin seed, is ground into a powder."

Alaura assisted in silence. She had created many mixtures and knew the proper procedures but making suggestions or correcting Catriona would create tense moments. As an apprentice, she listened; she didn't teach.

"The birthwart is next."

Alaura passed the brown powder to her teacher and watched her circle the wooden bowl twice with the ingredient before sprinkling it over the cumin seed. Although she'd never made the Tell-tale Powder, it appeared easy. She'd never known the sorceress to make it either.

An hour passed before Catriona announced the powder ready. "All we need to do is sprinkle Isla's exposed flesh with the powder, then we'll see the strength of her magic abilities. The brighter she glows, the stronger her power."

Isla looked up from a picture book.

"She's preparing to dart. You should hold her." Catriona waited until her apprentice sat on the floor and placed the hauflin on her knee.

"She knows you're up to something." She held out Isla's bare arm.

"Maybe she's not as dumb as she appears." Catriona leant over the pair with a tablespoon of the Tell-tale powder. As she prepared to sprinkle it, Isla pulled her arm away. "Hold her steady."

She held the child tighter, but Isla pulled and jerked to escape. "Hurry. She's stronger than she appears."

Isla mercilessly pinched the sensitive skin on the inside of Alaura's thigh and drove her heel into the back of her knee. Alaura squealed in pain and twisted her legs to escape the agony. Her right leg struck Catriona's foot, knocking her to the floor. The bowl flew into the air, spilling its contents over the three females. Alaura took control of the bowl's flight, stopping it from hitting anyone. She glanced at her teacher; her ability to cast the Levitation Spell went unnoticed.

Catriona had her own problems with the powder on her skin. With quick, rough strokes, she tried to brush away the brown substance, but the magic had already taken flight, and she glowed. The wan green shimmer upon her skin emerged like transparent waves of heat emanating from a rock under the hot afternoon sun; it flickered when looked for but could easily be unnoticed.

When Catriona focussed on her, wonderment filled her eyes. A radiant glow enveloped Alaura. Soft eruptions of various shades of effervescent green danced in the air and frolicked in the locks of her dark blonde hair. Whispers of yellows and blues revealed themselves near the skin, kissing the air with each leap. It enchanted Catriona.

"Now we know," said Alaura in a low voice. "I mean, we know Isla has no great magic." The child emitted a glow like that of the sorceress.

Catriona got to her feet and picked up the bowl. Slowly, she walked to the table, unable to stop herself from glancing back at the brilliant glow that continued to surround her student.

"I'll clean up the mess." Alaura went for the broom.

"I'll contact those in Petra." Catriona's voice sounded weary and laced with jealousy. "If they don't want her, I'll place her in the Maskil orphanage." She grabbed a damp rag and washed the powder from her skin with rough strokes.

Alaura whirled. "You can't do that! She doesn't belong in an orphanage."

"What am I supposed to do with her?"

"You always said you wanted a child." She spoke the words as if she meant them.

"A *human* child."

"I gave Maura my word I'd keep the child safe."

"That's right! *You* did. *I* told you not to get involved." Catriona glared at her.

"I must honour the covenant. Just because Isla doesn't live up to the expectations of the ridiculous prophecy, it doesn't mean she's worthless." Remembering Beathas' teachings, she drew a deep breath and tried to keep anger from clouding her thoughts. Still, it infuriated her that Catriona deemed hauflins insignificant. It had been wise to keep the race of her das secret. With a human mother, she was smaller than the average human but appeared to be of the same race.

Catriona crossed her arms. "Then what do you propose we do?"

"Isla should go to Petra."

"But she has insufficient magic like her brother, so they—" The sorceress slapped her hand over her mouth.

Alaura stared in disbelief. She had heard no news of Isla's sibling since the night the twins were born. Barely a few minutes old, another apprentice had taken him from Maura's dwelling to safety, the same place Isla intended to go before Keiron Ruckle intervened. She leant near and whispered, "What did they do with him?"

Catriona dropped her hand slowly as she glanced at the doors and windows. In a low voice, she said, "They found him a common home to live out his life."

"That's all I'm asking for Isla."

"She lacks the required magic, so they won't send the messenger. How will she get to Petra?"

"I'll take her."

Catriona huffed, then chuckled uneasily. "You wouldn't dare."

"I'll take her...tomorrow."

"Tomorrow? Are you daffy? Certainly, you can't think to reach Petra alive? It's a five-day journey. Who'll protect you from Lindrum's henchmen and the other monstrosities in the forest?"

"Who said I'd go alone?" She would of course, but Catriona didn't need to know this. She would deliver Isla to her brother Pym as she had planned and not to the designated family which would treat her only as a student of magic.

"If you're convinced you can reach Petra alive, take her." Catriona spoke as if to challenge her bravery.

"I'll return in the morning for her."

"Why not take her now?"

"I need time to prepare." And she had to visit Moon Meadow later today. If Catriona learnt about the lessons with Beathas, she'd be furious. No rules restricted additional training, but most apprentices had only one teacher. Beathas understood; Catriona would not. Alaura picked up the hauflin child. "It'll be an honour to transport you to safety, Isla of Maura."

The girl snuggled into her arms. "Alaura of Niamh, I want to be with you."

"You will, sweetie. I'll be back for you soon." She caressed her cheek. "Magic dust can't see you're special, but I can."

Catriona's anger faded, and she reached for the child. "We are all special in our own way."

Alaura picked up her sack and started for the door.

"Before you go," said Catriona, "is there anything I can prepare for your journey? Maybe a Protection Against Evil potion or similar spell? I don't want harm to reach either of you."

"I'll be fine." She smiled at Isla and left.

ಐ ❖ ೞ

Catriona spent the remainder of her day turning away apprentices, faking an illness and attempting to communicate with Isla. By evening, exhaustion had claimed her. She made sleeping arrangements on the chair for the girl, then checked the door locks again. She slipped into bed and pulled the blankets to her chin.

Her mind replayed the events of the day. Maybe she should have agreed to keep the child or find a good home in Maskil for her. Then Alaura wouldn't risk her life to reach Petra. Perhaps Isla did have enough magic ability to please those in the northern town.

Magic, she grumbled. *It has brought this trouble into my life.*

Old memories surfaced and danced in her head like sparks from a fire. As quickly as one burnt out, another took its place. To find peace, she had to extinguish them.

A whisper of wind brushed against her skin, and she found herself home with her family. They laughed and talked without noticing her. Her mother filled the table with food, and her father ruffled the hair of his youngest son as he showed him a map he had completed.

Catriona spotted Rod, the middle child. Young and full of energy, he often hopped around as if barefoot on a hot rock. But Rod appeared subdued as he stared at her. She gasped as grey fog seeped over his shoulders. No one else noticed the fog consuming Rod. Although she screamed, no sound came from her mouth. Rod cried for help, but she sat frozen, powerless to save her beloved brother. The ache in her heart expanded because she had created the fog.

Ripped from her sleep, she pounded the mattress with her fist. She'd thought time would fade the memories but on dark nights like this, it felt as if her brother had disappeared only yesterday. Her head hit the pillow hard, and she forced herself to think of other things.

Isla waited in the darkness, watching the woman until she lay still in bed. Then she slid from the chair and picked her way across the floor to the cupboards where she hoped to find food and drink. She climbed onto the counter and found it bare of food. She eyed bottles containing colourful liquids, picked up one and removed the cork. It smelt different than the liquids her das kept. Her thirst impelled her to drink until she emptied the bottle, then she returned to her makeshift bed.

A tingling sensation, like the reaction her das' liquids created, stirred in her tummy. She pushed the feeling aside and snuggled beneath the blanket. As sleep overwhelmed her, the downy softness of wool caressed her cheek.

4

Links of Chainmail

THE TOWN of Maskil nestled south of the Pogwa Mountain Range on the Shulie River. Fertile fields and rich forest surrounded it and its Aruam Castle, a sprawling, ancient structure located in the northern part of town. When the castle clock gonged to mark the midnight hour, most of the inhabitants slept in peaceful dreams.

Inside the small dwelling on Horizon Lane, even breathing created a smooth rhythm. Both, human and hauflin lay in deep slumber. Neither heard the steel tinker with the lock on the back door or the three human fighters dressed in rugged Trail clothing and chainmail armour rush inside.

A light from an unknown source lit up the room. Catriona didn't have time to scream before one of the men dragged her from the bed and forced her against the wall. She blinked under the bright light and tried to regain her balance as a large man shook her and rammed his forearm under her chin. The glint of steel near her cheek made her gasp.

"Whither is the child?" The man's breath reeked of meat and onions.

Catriona heard her belongings being thrown about but didn't take her eyes off the dagger blade. She had no doubt this man would use it to extract information from her. "Wha... what child?" The force on her throat made speaking difficult. The cold, rough steel of the man's forearm bracer pushed harder against her neck until she feared she'd cease to breathe.

"Keiron's," he hissed, spraying spit in her face. His dark eyes bulged with excitement.

"What's this?" Another fighter approached the chair in the corner. His short, blond hair, dirty from sweat and travel, stood on end.

Catriona stretched her neck to watch the stout man rip the blanket from the chair. She blinked in disbelief. Isla had transformed into a marmoset?

"I see the family resemblance." The fighter chuckled and held up the small monkey. "But I always thought of Keiron more as a spineless snake."

"Stop foolin' and bring it here." Unlike the other two, the fighter restraining Catriona wore a dark yellow bandana around his neck. "Tell me where Keiron's child is, or I'll kill your pet."

She swallowed hard. The pressure on her throat increased, bringing tears to her eyes. If he continued to apply force, she'd faint.

"Where's the child?" The man who had snatched Isla from the chair held her by the scruff of the neck and shook her in Catriona's face.

She closed her eyes to absorb the pressure and block the dizzying motion of the marmoset. "I sent her to Wandsworth."

"Wandsworth?" The fighter spat.

"Is that where Keiron's headed?" asked the man restraining her.

"I can't breathe." Catriona wheezed.

He relaxed his hold but didn't set her free. "Why did you send the child to Wandsworth?"

"Time!" The third fighter watching the back door drew his sword. The artificial light glinted off a ring on his left hand.

"Time's up." The fighter leant closer. Dirt stained his bandana, and it emitted a pungent odour.

His meat and onion breath fell upon her cheek while his eyes darted across her face, then settled upon her bosom. In the scuffle, her nightdress had twisted, leaving one breast fully exposed. Her nipple pricked when he deliberately brushed his cold armour against the tip. His face brightened as the veins swelled in the areola and the breast skin tighten. The arm which had once crushed her neck pulled her near. His large, rough hand caressed her buttocks through the thin material of her gown, then reached for the gap between her legs. Her throat tightened, and she gulped for air. She tried to pull away, but he held her firmly.

"Maybe you'll show me the way to Wandsworth." He grinned, revealing sparkling white teeth. A short, deep scar cut into the corner of his mouth and ran into his beard.

"We're here for the child, not your pleasure." The man holding Isla scowled.

"One should always mix business with pleasure." He slowly licked Catriona's cheek from jaw bone to eyelid.

Her head swooned at the thought of what might come next. She recognised the raiment they wore as those associated with Lindrum's henchmen. No doubt these men had committed nasty deeds. "Please," she begged, "go. I'll only slow you down. I'll give you a map."

The three fighters laughed as if she told the best joke they'd heard in years.

"We can't leave empty handed." The blond fighter held up Isla. "We'll take this monkey as our reward. It'll make a great playmate for my desert cat."

Catriona again tried to break free, but her assailant held her closer, pressing the links of his chainmail armour into her bare breast. "Please, leave my pet. He has done you no harm."

"Unfortunately," the fighter breathed in her ear, "you could." He nibbled her lobe as he lifted his hand holding the dagger.

The fighter watching the door hollered. "Guards!"

Half a dozen Aruam Castle guards burst through the open door with swords drawn. The henchman flung Catriona to the floor, drew his sword and rushed at the guards.

Catriona rolled out of the way and crashed into a wall. She turned to watch the fight and saw Isla had also escaped her captor. The monkey scurried beneath the feet of the men, trying to find a safe place to hide.

"Come." She motioned Isla towards her, being careful not to call her name. Dodging the many feet and swords, the small monkey finally leapt into her arms. She embraced the child as she cowered in the corner, hoping the castle guards would quickly dispose of Lindrum's men.

One guard had already fallen and was sprawled across the floor with blood seeping from his side. His eyes stared at the ceiling as if studying the wood pattern. Another guard fell under the heavy sword of the fighter with the yellow bandana. Then he struck a second man who dropped, clutching his side and screaming in agony.

The blond-haired fighter who had seized Isla fought an agile dwarf who wielded his sword with skill and agility. Catriona stared in awe as the short guard overtook the larger fighter. The sword found its mark, and the man stumbled backward into the table and crashed to the floor. The dwarf turned his focus on the fighter who had guarded the door. After several powerful blows, the intruder met the same fate as his companion.

The man with the yellow bandana struck one guard across the chest and another in the shoulder, bringing both to their knees. Seeing his chance to escape, he dashed out the back door and into the dark alley.

One of the fallen guards stood and ran to the door.

"Farlan, no!" The agile dwarf stepped in front of the man.

The human guard ground to a halt. "He's getting away."

The two men wore the standard blue uniform of the lowest class, but a yellow triangular badge on the dwarf's lapel signified he held a higher rank.

"I know." The dwarf pushed his sword into the scabbard. "Return to the castle and inform Sanderson of what happened. Tell him to send a search party to find the henchman and eight men with stretchers to gather the fallen."

"Yes, sir." Farlan opened the front door and rushed from the dwelling.

From the corner, Catriona watched the dwarf check his men. It appeared two were dead and two were severely injured. She grimaced when he pulled a sheet from her bed and ripped it into strips to bandage the wounds. Within a few minutes, stretcher bearers arrived to remove the bodies and escort the injured men.

As they prepared to take leave, the dwarf settled his attention on Catriona. "Did they harm you?"

She shook her head.

He placed his index finger to his lips and cocked his head. "I know you." He pointed his finger at her. "You've visited the Forest Bakery and Herb Shop."

She remembered seeing him there several times. "You're the shop owner's son. I'm Catriona, a regular customer." The knot loosened in her stomach, and she eased herself up onto shaky legs. When she stumbled, he guided her to a chair.

He prepared to speak, but his attention fell upon her breast, and he quickly divert his eyes. "Perhaps you should..."

She gulped, and her face warmed. Her breast still lay exposed. She quickly pulled a blanket around her and Isla, shivering as she recalled the feeling of the henchman's rough hands on her body.

When his attention returned to her, a deep shade of red coloured his neck. He cleared his throat and glanced as the last guard carrying a stretcher left the dwelling. "I'm Corporal Darrow with Aruam Castle. I must ask you a few questions. You're not accused of anything. This is procedure." He grabbed a stool and sat in front of her. "Your name is Catriona. Correct?"

"Yes, Catriona Wheatcroft. How did those men get inside the walls of Maskil?"

He ignored her question. "What did the henchmen want?"

She hesitated, unsure if she should tell the truth.

"I can't help if you don't help me." He waited, but she remained silent. "Whatever you say will be held in strict confidence. It'll be shared with only the lords of the castle." When she still didn't answer, he furrowed his brow. "We both know they were Lindrum's men. If they didn't find what they came for, they'll be back."

She closed her eyes, resolving to share the secret. He spoke the truth. Lindrum's men would be back for Isla. The evil wizard who wanted to capture Aruam Castle would never stop until he had terrified every Maskil citizens into submission and vanquished the lords. She ensured the room was empty, then narrowed her eyes at him. "You must promise to tell no one."

"Only the lords and the captain of the guard will hear. I promise."

She held Isla tighter. "They wanted a child."

"Whose child? Yours?"

"Keiron Ruckle's."

He scratched his head. "Obviously, they didn't find it."

"No, they didn't." She looked away.

"What do they want with the child?"

"What does Lindrum want with any hauflin child?" Over the years dozens of hauflin children had fallen victim to Lindrum's henchmen. She could use this history to protect Isla. Although the girl didn't possess enough magic to make her the hauflin child of the prophecy, she deserved to be safe. She sighed. Everything entangled itself in the foretelling of Lindrum's doom. It either consumed her past or controlled her future.

Memories seeped into her mind, and once again she remembered the series of dreams that had sparked her search for Isla's mother five years ago. Those nightly images had since lost their intensity, and she'd forgotten specific details completely. Why had she taken them so seriously?

Each dream had drawn her further into the darkness of a thick, lush forest. Along the way, emotionless faces stared at her from the shadows. The faces changed each night except for one: Maura's. The young hauflin followed Catriona on her journey through tangled weeds and long branches that obscured the view of what lay ahead. When fear threatened to overwhelm her, Maura offered guidance. Maura's determined eyes willed the human to continue the journey.

After more than a week of dreams, she broke free of the dark forest and entered a meadow with wildflowers bursting with blooms. In the centre of the clearing sat a large green orb. Someone had draped two silver necklaces embedded with blue stones over the top. Colourful butterflies fluttered about. A faint yellow glow shimmered around the orb. Inside, an image of two small figures took shape. The small creatures curled together in sleep. Stepping closer, she saw them to be hauflins, one much like the other.

An overpowering peace flowed through Catriona. She became part of the tranquil state that consumed the meadow. When she regained awareness in the dream, she didn't know how long the peacefulness of her surroundings had enchanted her. The woman who had followed her in the dreams gazed upon the pair within the orb. A single tear slid down her cheek.

The pair may not have been sleeping after all. Perhaps, they rested in the Plane of Peace. She recognised the emotions a mother had for her children. *Her* babies lay inside. The woman closed her eyes and faded from Catriona's view, disappearing in the breeze as if smoke from a smouldering fire.

She watched over the hauflin pair within the orb until morning arrived. When it did, she woke and gazed around her room, seeing things as if with new eyes. While compelled to act, she didn't know what to do.

That night marked the end of the dreams. In the days immediately following, she felt duty-bound to replicate the necklaces with the blue stones which had hung around the orb in the meadow. During her outings, she searched for the woman whose face she had seen in the dreams. Although ridiculous to believe she existed, she couldn't shake the feeling she had to find her. Discovering Maura at the market had astounded her, and she followed the pregnant hauflin from one stall to the next. She returned the next day to spy on Maura again to reassure herself that she hadn't imagined the encounter.

But what significance did the dreams hold if Isla did not possess magic? She couldn't be the hauflin Lindrum sought, so why had his henchmen searched for her? It had to be because of Keiron. They wanted Isla's life because of the misdeeds he had committed. They wouldn't stop until they accomplished their deadly task.

Although dangerous to suggest to the guard the child played a role in the prophecy, it had to be done for her protection. Keiron should pay for his own debts, not Isla.

"The prophecy?"

The guard's voice shook her from thought, and she nodded.

He cursed under his breath. "Always the prophecy." He rested his elbows on his knees and clasped his hands. "Do you know where the child is located?"

"I told them I had sent her to Wandsworth."

"Was it the truth? We can't protect her if we don't know where she is."

"She's a helpless child. I can't understand why they'd want to hurt her."

Corporal Darrow released a sigh and rubbed his eyes, then placed a strong hand on the back of the monkey. "Is this the child? Did you disguise her as a marmoset?"

She nodded reluctantly.

"How long will she remain like this?"

She glanced at an empty bottle on the counter. "About three days." Isla wriggled in her arms and leant closer to the guard. "Lindrum feels threatened by her, so he sent his henchmen to capture her."

He stood. "The prophecy speaks of a pair of hauflins. Does this child have a sibling?"

She shook her head, unwilling to divulge that fact.

"Then Lindrum has nothing to fear. She's not part of the *infamous* prophecy." Sarcasm laced his voice. "If you'd dress and gather a few things, you can stay in the castle 'til morning. A crew will be along soon to gather the bodies of the henchmen." The two lifeless men sprawled in their pool of blood, broken furniture and dishes.

She rose and sought a place to set Isla while she dressed.

"I'll hold it—her." He held out a hand for the monkey.

She hesitated, but Isla peered closer at the dwarf.

"She'll be fine." He eased the marmoset into his arms, and large brown eyes stared up at him. "How old is she?"

"Almost five." Catriona sifted through her closet, pulled out a dress and went to the water closet to change.

Corporal Darrow studied the small fingers wrapped around his thumb. Her warm touch made his skin tingle.

"Alaura?"

He leant closer. "What did you say?"

Catriona stepped from the water closet, pulled a few items from a drawer and stuffed them in a sack. She reached for Isla, but the child clung to the guard.

Corporal Darrow removed the monkey's clawed fingers from his dark blue vest and placed the creature in her arms. He stepped outside and led the way to the castle.

5

A Pleasurable Customer

CORPORAL BRONWYN Darrow waited in a small room inside Aruam Castle. Butterflies in his belly made him squeamish as he thought about attending his first private assembly with the lords. Although versed in meeting protocol, he'd be relieved when the official business ended.

The events since yesternight replayed. By the time he'd returned to the castle and gave a short report to the guard on duty, the sun had risen above the horizon. He secured a room on the third floor of the castle for Catriona and posted a guard at her door. Then he went to his shared quarters and fell into bed, exhausted.

He had slept past the usual wake-up call and into mid-day. When he awoke, he filed a more detailed report on the overnight events, then went to the Throne Room where a large crowd had gathered. Worried citizens packed the enormous room, and guards struggled to keep the mass orderly.

Pandemonium had grown amongst the citizens since the castle break-in and the theft of research papers and maps two nights before. Rampant rumours maintained Lindrum had used the stolen material to uncover the location of Lilja, the sacred dragon. Already his army had advanced to capture her. The brazen attack on a private dwelling by Lindrum's henchmen resulting in the death of two guards added to their fears.

Bronwyn had learnt Lindrum's history at an early age. The wizard, who had once associated with the Lords of Aruam Castle, declared war against them decades beforehand. He had attempted to capture Lilja and use her to destroy the town of Maskil.

Lindrum had failed, yet the exhausted lords had been unsuccessful in their bid to protect Lilja. Desperate and near death, the dragon attacked the wizard and sent him spinning into a portal to an unknown destination. Lilja and her fertile egg also disappeared without a trace.

The prophecy began about thirty years later when an old man stumbled into Maskil, half-blind and half-starved. He claimed to have been lost for years in a labyrinth of caves in the mountains west of town. While there, he had met a creature of mixed races who recited the cryptic message predicting Lindrum's demise. Then it gave him a scroll and instructed him to take it to the Lords of Aruam Castle. Upon receiving the message, the lords dispatched a company of soldiers to explore the mysterious Caverns of Confusion, but they never found them.

Bronwyn remained unsure if he believed the prophecy. It annoyed him more than anything because many citizens used it to explain strange behaviour and to make bizarre requests. If the prophecy turned out to be true and one day a pair of hauflin siblings and their companions destroyed Lindrum, he'd happily sing its praises. Until then he'd be practical.

While watching the mayhem in the Throne Room, he caught a glimpse of Sanderson, the captain of the guard. He tried to get the man's attention to update him on his overnight activities and ask his advice on Catriona and the monkey, but the turbulent atmosphere in the room made it impossible. Sanderson stood in the middle of the chaos, and citizens packed around him too tightly for Bronwyn pass.

Instead, Bronwyn watched from the sidelines as the citizens, full of fear and doubt, fired one question after another at the lords. The lords' calmness amid the insanity impressed him. Finally, the shouting, accusations and scuffling in the crowd prompted them to end the day's session two hours earlier than scheduled.

He took advantage of the early closing and asked a guard on duty to take a message to the lords requesting to speak with them in private.

After receiving the message, Lord Valmour Elfren glared at him from across the room. The lord's expression confused him. Instead of answering his request, he waved him off and followed the others from the Throne Room. A short time later, Bronwyn received a summons for him and the surviving guards who had taken part in the overnight confrontation at Catriona's dwelling to attend a meeting immediately following the evening ration.

Worried about who might be present at the discussion, he wondered how to approach the lords with a second request for a private meeting. He'd promised Catriona to divulge the identity of the marmoset only to them. What if they refused to grant him privacy?

The story circulating throughout Maskil had the child of the thief who had raided the castle on her way to Wandsworth. Bronwyn believed the report he'd filed was confidential, so how had the details become public? He assumed the lords had taken this false information as fact.

He smoothed the yellow badge on his lapel. The sewn-on triangle separated him from the lowest rank. It had taken four years as a soldier in the Royal Army and three years as a castle guard to earn it. Now only a month after the promotion, he worried he'd lose the badge for distorting the truth. He hadn't lied on the report, merely wrote what Catriona had told him. Depending on the interpretation, it might be misunderstood.

While he waited for the meeting to begin, he studied the large tapestry hanging on the opposite wall. It measured from ceiling to floor and from one corner of the room to the other. He'd never seen the incredible artwork depicting a magnificent golden dragon upon a turret of Aruam Castle. The rays of the setting sun cascaded across the tree tops and spot-lit the dragon as it smiled upon the small town below.

A figurehead appeared in each corner of the tapestry. He easily identified them as human, elf, dwarf and hauflin. Did they illustrate the original Lords of Maskil and Aruam Castle? Although he'd learnt the names of the lords during his educational years, he'd never seen images of them.

After Lilja had disappeared, the sitting lords increased their number from four to six for security reasons. The diversity remained with the four races being represented. Two additional worthy individuals, regardless of race, filled the extra positions.

Peering closer at the tapestry, he pondered the significance of the green orb located in the centre of the lower border. Three unfamiliar symbols, perhaps creating a word, were scrolled through its midsection. A faint yellow glow surrounded the orb and butterfly wings sprouted from its sides. His history studies hadn't contained information on such an orb.

The door opened, and he jumped to his feet. A tall, broad-shouldered human wearing a dark blue uniform with four yellow badges on each lapel walked in. Sanderson held the highest rank amongst Aruam Castle guards. Only the lords possessed higher authority.

Bronwyn stood at attention and saluted. Over the years his body had become straight and lean from training, and he fantasized of one day trading his light blue uniform for the dark one standing in front of him.

"At ease, Corporal." Sanderson unceremoniously waved and sat at the table.

Bronwyn resumed his position on the bench, and the door opened again. The royal scribe, Wilhelm, entered accompanied by Blomidon, the royal sage. They took seats at the far left of the table, across from where the lords would sit.

Wilhelm, a human of small stature, dressed in black and, unlike other scribes, wore a short sword. "Have you had word of the child?" he asked the captain of the guard.

Sanderson looked up from his papers and raised his black bushy eyebrows. "None." He returned his attention to his work.

"Is it possible the sorceress is hiding the child? Maybe hiding Ruckle?"

"As possible as it is for one to be thrown into the dungeon for irritating the captain of the guard."

Wilhelm fell silent.

The three guards who had accompanied Bronwyn to Catriona's dwelling the night before entered the room. They appeared in good health with their wounds dressed and uniforms cleaned. An empty chair—Bronwyn's—remained between Sanderson and the privates.

He had no sooner settled in the chair when the narrow door beside the tapestry opened. Everyone stood as the six lords entered and took their seats. Lord Val motioned for them to sit, then sat in a seat directly across from Bronwyn.

"Good evening, everyone." Lord Val, an elf, spoke in a smooth voice, his enunciation succinct and precise with every consonant pronounced. A single braid secured his long, green-streaked blond hair. His forest-green robe contrasted sharply against his pale green skin. "We know why we're here, so I won't waste time with formalities."

Bronwyn sat up and focussed on the lord. Occasionally Wilhelm's pen caught his attention. The scribe recording his words for future reference unnerved him.

Lord Val's gaze swept over the faces of those seated on the opposite side of the table while he spoke. "First, the man reported to be with Keiron Ruckle during the theft was apprehended this side of midnight. Guards recovered his body north of Edgewood. They found him with his feet melted to a stone. It appears he died several hours beforehand. There was no sign of Ruckle or the stolen material." He took a deep breath. "Corporal Darrow."

Bronwyn shivered when the lord spoke his name. "Yes, My Lord."

"I have read the report you filed when you returned to the castle this morning. It was"—Lord Val hesitated, staring at him—"brief. Please elaborate?"

His neck warmed, and he clasped his hands in front of him on the table. "I returned to the castle in the wee hours of the day and made a quick report. Later, after resting, I filed a more detailed account of events."

"I didn't receive the second report." Lord Val glanced at Wilhelm. "Do you have it there?"

"No, My Lord. No one alerted me to its existence. Perhaps the corporal will provide a verbal report now."

Bronwyn felt everyone's attention upon him. He wished he had brought the report, then he'd be able to read it without fear of making mistakes. "The second report contains a description of the henchman who fled the Wheatcroft dwelling. I also added details of our movements before the confrontation and about Miss Catriona Wheatcroft. The human female stated her age to be 33 years. The sorceress has practised magic for about sixteen years. She has five—no, six apprentices under her charge." He took a deep breath and tried to remember more.

"Is there anything further?" asked Lord Val.

"Not at this time."

The lord glanced at the paper in front of him. "Although this has yet to be confirmed, it appears Miss Wheatcroft's father, Emerson, was our chief cartographer fifteen years ago. His only daughter caused the loss of a son. He worked for a year afterwards, then relocated his family to Wandsworth. Obviously, Catriona didn't accompany them."

The elf rubbed his forehead as if trying to soothe a sharp pain. "Her apprentices are being questioned along with anyone with whom she has had personal contact." He turned his attention to Bronwyn. "Corporal, has she given any indication of Ruckle's whereabouts?"

Before Bronwyn could answer, a knock came at the door.

Lord Val grumbled. "Blomidon, see who it is. If not urgent, send them away."

The sage went to the door, opened it a crack and spoke with the person on the other side. After a brief conversation, she turned to address the lords. "Guards bring an acquaintance of Miss Wheatcroft. She makes a Right of Visitation and claims to be the nearest to next-of-kin. With your permission, I shall grant her entry."

"I wish to meet this nearest to next-of-kin," said Lord Val.

Blomidon opened the door, and two guards escorted a woman into the room.

The elven lord scrutinized her. "State your name."

"Alaura of Niamh, My Lord."

"What is your relationship with Miss Catriona Wheatcroft?"

"I have known Catriona for five years, first as her apprentice and then as a friend."

"You understand your friend has family in Wandsworth. They'd be the first granted Right of Visitation?"

"I do, but Catriona... How can I explain? Catriona and her family aren't close. Their relationship is strained by emotional stress."

"Is that so?" He leered at her.

"Yes, My Lord." She stood straight, feet slightly apart, hands clasped behind her back and her chin out. "I would like to make a Right of Visitation as is stated in the Laws of the Land so my own eyes can see my friend is well."

"How do we know you speak the truth, Miss...?"

"Alaura."

Lord Val gave a slight nod. "Alaura; and that you are naught but a stranger to Miss Wheatcroft?"

Bronwyn had watched the woman enter the room. Although the castle guards towered over her, it did not weaken her appearance. Instead, her demeanour created a stronger image. He recognised her as an apprentice who occasionally accompanied Catriona to his parents' shop, the Forest Bakery and Herbs. She had listened quietly to the instructions of her teacher as they chose the herbs needed to work their recipes.

Sometimes, she came alone. During those visits, she spoke discreetly with his mum, enquiring about certain herbs and their properties. Once he asked his mum about her, and she simply said, *A pleasurable customer who knows what she needs.*

Alaura had often worn a shapeless knee-length dress with a black leather belt. Her dark blonde hair hung loose, obscuring half her face. Still, her brown eyes caught his attention on many occasions as he went to and from his parents' dwelling above the shop. They flickered brightly even when the sun didn't shine.

Today as she entered the Private Audience Room of the lords, she wore tan trousers, a white shirt and knee-high brown boots. The fitted clothing revealed her subtle curves and firm bosom. Her hair surprised him more. Pulled back in a single braid, it revealed delicate features kissed by the sun. His gaze moved to her lips, slender and still, before rising to her slightly tucked nose. His eyes followed her cheek bone to her ears which appeared not as rounded as other human ears. When he found her eyes, shimmering in the evening sun shining through the window, he found them focussed on Lord Val.

Alaura of Niamh. He rolled the name over in his head. While he hadn't personally spoken with her, he believed it to be her name. Was she the Alaura the marmoset had asked for?

He recalled she often made trips outside Maskil, but he had never worked the gates when she passed through. From his guard position on the wall, he watched her come and go. When the guards inspected the small cart she pulled, she never fussed and willingly revealed the items inside. Walking away from the gate, she headed towards Linden Woods and Moon Meadow. He wondered which of the two places she visited, or did she continue on The Trail to the foothills?

Alaura looked directly at him and pointed a finger. "Ask your own guard."

The comment took him by surprise. Immersed in his own thoughts of Alaura of Niamh, he failed to follow the conversation. Unsure of why she singled him out, he swung around. Lord Val stared at him and waited for an answer.

"Well, Corporal, do you know this woman?" asked the lord.

"Yes...well...she visits my parents' shop. She's pleasurable... I mean...a regular customer." His face flushed, and he swallowed hard.

"Was she in the company of Miss Wheatcroft?" Lord Val's voice tightened.

"Yes, My Lord... Many times." He cursed himself for letting his thoughts get away from him. To regain his composure, he focussed on the lord.

"Thank you." Lord Val considered his words. He opened his mouth to speak but Lord Tasgall interrupted.

"One question, if I may, Alaura of Niamh?" said the hauflin lord. "I sense you are more than can be recognised by the untrained eye. Please, share with us your parentage."

"Yes, My Lord." Alaura hesitated. "My meeme is human, my das hauflin."

Several in the room caught their breath at the announcement.

"My Lord, a human and hauflin mix is rare, extraordinary." Wilhelm spoke in a hushed voice. "Pregnancies end prematurely, often claiming the mother as well."

"I'm aware of the fact." Lord Val eyed Alaura.

Although he tried to fight the urge, Bronwyn couldn't resist taking a second peek at Alaura. Her mix of two breeds explained the subtle differences. Maybe her skin wasn't well-tanned after all but naturally coloured. It certainly explained her lack of height. She stood shorter than the average human female but much taller than a hauflin.

"Permission granted for visitation." Lord Val waved her on.

"Thank you, My Lord." Alaura bowed, then turned on her heels and followed the guards to the door.

Her silent, graceful walk captured Bronwyn's attention. Where had she learnt to move like that? Alaura of Niamh glided across the floor effortlessly, as if a breeze carried her. When she reached the door, she glanced back at him, nodded and stepped into the hall.

He assumed the gesture to be a small thank you for vouching for her. He didn't mind saying he knew her, though he didn't know her well. She appeared to be an honest citizen. His mum approved of her and nothing escaped Maisie Darrow's attention. Satisfied the space had become empty of her existence, he turned towards the table.

Silence hung in the air. The door had closed several seconds beforehand, and everyone had returned their attention to the meeting table. They waited for him to do the same. Glancing at Lord Val, he found him watching with one eyebrow raised sharply.

"Now that the air has cleared of feminine distractions, we can proceed." Lord Val frowned.

The snickers and grunts compelled Bronwyn to sit straighter. Although he cringed with embarrassment inside, he wouldn't allow those around him see him cower. Stealing a glance at Lord Mulryan, the dwarf glared at him. He imagined his thoughts: *Dwarfs were the pillar of self-control, and your lack of it is shameful.* Alaura had distracted him and confused his thoughts. Everyone in the room knew it.

Lady Dasia caught Bronwyn's attention. She smiled pleasantly, giving no indication his behaviour had disappointed her. His embarrassment faded as he tried to understand the message she sent. Before he looked away, she winked at him. A smile played at the corner of his mouth, and he struggled to keep it from spreading across his face.

"Corporal Darrow, during the events of the previous evening, was there mention of Keiron Ruckle or his whereabouts?" Lord Val disturbed the air that had settled.

"There was no sign of him at Miss Wheatcroft's dwelling and no mention of his whereabouts." Bronwyn focussed on the business. He'd think more on Lady Dasia and Alaura of Niamh later.

"Wilhelm, have you found record of the child in the archives?" Lord Val turned to the scribe.

"Yes, My Lord. Isla of Maura was born at Maskil five years ago. Her mother is recorded as dying shortly after giving birth to her, her first child." Wilhelm consulted a paper in front of him and added, "It appears Ruckle has cared for the child alone since his mate's death. I found no further union agreements."

Lord Val returned his attention to Bronwyn. "You stated in your report Miss Wheatcroft came into possession of the child but sent her to Wandsworth. Did she say who gave her the child and to whom she then gave the child for delivery?"

Bronwyn had waited for this moment. Now he wished it hadn't arrived. "Yes, My Lord, Keiron Ruckle gave the child to Miss Wheatcroft." He paused, giving great consideration in the placement of his next words. "At this time, I humbly request a private audience."

Lord Val stared at the dwarf in disbelief. "This is a private audience."

"My request is for a private session with the lords only. I made a promise." His words lost their strength under the scrutiny of the eldest lord, an illusionist who had the authority to reduce his duties to cleaning the bailey.

"Corporal, to whom did you make this promise?"

"Miss Wheatcroft."

"Were you bonded by your word?"

"No, I didn't sign a covenant. But I honour my promises equally." He wished he had gone to the lord this morning instead of sleeping. He'd have avoided this awkward moment.

"I release you from your promise, Corporal. Answer the question. Did Miss Wheatcroft say to whom she gave the child for delivery to Wandsworth?"

"I'm sorry. I wish to honour my promise an...and seek a private audience." His mouth went dry. He had promised Catriona to tell only the lords of Isla's whereabouts, but making a second request went against protocol.

"Corporal." Lord Val wrung his hands as if ready to savour a delicious ration or twist someone's neck. "The information you divulge will not be shared with the public." His face twisted in anger, and he stared intently. "Answer the question."

He swallowed hard. Although he wished he didn't have to answer, he felt impelled to do so. "The child is not on her way to Wandsworth. She is...here."

The room fell silent.

"The marmoset in Miss Wheatcroft's care is not a pet. It's Keiron Ruckle's child."

Lord Val slammed his fist onto the table.

Dumbfounded, Bronwyn feared a more dangerous outburst followed. The lord acted out of control. Did these actions occur regularly behind closed doors? Glancing at Sanderson, he guessed from his startled expression they didn't.

Lord Val clenched his teeth and gave the impression he struggled to gain self-control. After a few calming breaths, he spoke. "We have men scouring the road to Wandsworth searching for this child. Why is our manpower being wasted?"

Bronwyn gulped. He'd written in his initial report Isla had been sent to the city to the south. He couldn't put the truth in writing if he wanted to protect her. "I had hoped to inform you of the truth before this. It's why I waited in the Throne Room and requested a private audience with you."

"The search party had set out earlier in the day." The corner of the elf's top lip curled. "The child, this Isla of Maura, what is her importance? Besides being the issue of Keiron Ruckle, why does Lindrum want to capture her?"

He felt a little less intimidated as the edge left the lord's anger. "Miss Wheatcroft believes she has ties to the prophecy. Since Isla has no siblings, this is impossible. I think the sorceress said so only to get protection for the child."

"Obviously, Lindrum senses an importance."

"I think Lindrum wants to use the child to control Ruckle." He became more assertive. "Or maybe they want her life as a payback for his misdeeds. There is no other logical explanation." He doubted the prophecy and couldn't pretend the child held any significance to it.

"But she is hauflin?" Lord Tasgall leant forward. "A full-blood hauflin?"

"I'm told so, but I haven't seen her in hauflin form. She drank a potion and will remain a marmoset for several days."

"I'd like to meet Isla of Maura," said Lord Tasgall.

"Because she's hauflin?" Lord Mulryan frowned. "I trust the corporal's judgement. She's not part of this *prophecy*." The last word rolled off his tongue as if it tasted like burnt fish.

"Because she's a citizen of Maskil," said Lord Tasgall. "Every citizen deserves protection, particularly the most vulnerable: our children."

"Defence of the castle and the town is our top priority. It will ensure the safety of the children." Lord Mulryan's deep voice filled the room.

Lord Val ignored the disagreement. "Corporal Darrow, has Miss Wheatcroft said anything to indicate the child possesses magic?"

"We didn't discuss magic."

"What is the connection betwixt Miss Wheatcroft and Keiron Ruckle? Why would a respectable sorceress have anything to do with a notorious thief?"

"I don't know. She may be a former friend to Keiron's mate."

Lord Val rubbed his chin. "Corporal, fetch Miss Wheatcroft and the issue. I wish to interview this woman myself and judge the child."

"Judge her?" Lord Mulryan's voice echoed off the walls. "For what? Magic? What if she does possess magic? Then what? Build our defences around her? The prophecy is a rumour! We can no sooner control it than the weather."

"Corporal, bring them to me now."

Bronwyn stood. He obeyed the eldest lord though he felt strong ties to the dwarfen lord who oversaw the castle guards and the army.

"My Lord, may I accompany Corporal Darrow?" Wilhelm set his ink pen on the table and prepared to stand. "Miss Wheatcroft may cause trouble if she feels the child is threatened."

Lord Val nodded.

"Shall we bring Alaura of Niamh as well?" asked Wilhelm.

"Yes. We may have more questions for her."

Bronwyn dreaded the idea of Alaura of Niamh being questioned further. She might reveal he didn't know her well enough to vouch for her identity.

Could this day get any worse? Since his promotion he had faced one ridiculous request after another. He felt as if an invisible force undermined every task. To add insult to embarrassment, a scribe had been assigned to protect him from two women and a child.

6

A Thousand Times in the Past

ALAURA FOLLOWED Catriona down the stone steps. Her teacher cradled her so-called pet monkey—Isla—in her arms. If events had gone as planned, Alaura would have departed for Petra with the child by now, but when she arrived at the sorceress' dwelling earlier in the day, she found guards searching inside. After several hours of surveillance, she enquired at Aruam Castle's gatehouse. There, she learnt about the overnight break-in.

The guard who had secured Catriona's room followed Alaura down the stairs. Wilhelm, the peculiar scribe, walked behind him. She disliked the way the scribe regarded her. Certainly, he couldn't be interested in a relationship. She cringed at the thought. His interest might stem from her mixed race. Regardless, her birth had dictated her future union, and no one could change the course chosen for her.

Corporal Bronwyn Darrow, the chestnut-haired dwarf she had hoped to avoid at the town gates when she made her escape with Isla, led the procession. He reminded her of his mum. Maisie Darrow, a kind and knowledgeable soul, who filled orders for special herbs. Though not a magic user herself, she possessed great wisdom about herbs and other plant material. Her son, a polite and respectable guard, behaved unlike many other guards she had encountered.

Knowing Maisie, she felt guilty putting her son on the spot in the Private Audience Room. She believed Bronwyn had paid attention to the conversation and knew how to properly answer her request. Unfortunately, his mind had wandered elsewhere, and she felt embarrassed for his twisted tongue. *She is pleasurable?* She smiled at the unexpected remark. What had he been thinking when he blurted out that? His dark brown eyes had danced for her until the lord forced him to speak the jumbled words.

Realising her focus drifted, she tried to shake the scene from her mind. Bronwyn remained a simple acquaintance who had vouched for her identity, nothing more. She had already wasted too much time thinking of him. Nevertheless, she wondered about his expression when he arrived at Catriona's room to escort them to meet with the lords. Why had he appeared reluctant to speak with her? Was he angry because he thought she had placed him in an awkward situation? He wore the blame for failing to pay attention, not her. Unlike the willing smile she'd received when they passed each other at the shop or on the street, he seemed ready to growl at her.

Enough! She had to plan what she'd say when the lords questioned her further about Isla and Catriona. Taking a deep breath, she cleared her mind.

A heavy weight struck her back, knocking the air from her lungs and slamming her onto the stairs. The castle guard slumped lifelessly over her small body. She shouted to alert the others though she couldn't see past the large uniformed shoulder.

Catriona's scream penetrated the material, and Alaura struggled to break-free of her baggage.

Shaken from brooding thoughts, Bronwyn reeled to see Wilhelm standing over the guard's body with his sword sullied with blood. Stunned, he felt unsure if the scribe had killed in self-defence or had ruthlessly attacked an innocent man. Alaura struggling to free herself from the burden of the body, and he stepped forward to help.

"Seize her!" Wilhelm thrust his finger at Catriona. "They plotted to kill us and escape with the child! I'll take care of this one!" He raised his sword to strike Alaura.

Bronwyn and Alaura exchanged glances. In the split-second connection, doubt attacked and killed the order. He raised his sword and deflected the scribe's weapon. Reaching down for the young woman's hand, he jerked her to her feet and into his arm.

"You're protecting a traitor!" Wilhelm advanced. "We must kill them both!"

"Alaura?" The ease of her name rolling off his tongue surprised him; it felt as if he had said it a thousand times in the past. He searched her eyes. They appeared kind and gentle, frightened but not those of a traitor. Every instinct advocated her innocence.

She clung to his arm. "I could never hurt you."

He raised his sword and defended her against Wilhelm's attack. The scribe had the upper hand being higher on the stairs, but he drew him down to the level hallway.

Catriona shrieked. Bronwyn turned to see a large, uniformed human grab her by the neck and throw her against the wall. He recognised the man as the one who had fled her dwelling the night before. The henchman struck the woman several times, then snatched the monkey from her arms.

A sharp tug at Bronwyn's waist made him look down in time to see Alaura seize the dagger from his belt. His heart shuddered. Had his instincts failed him?

Alaura charged at the henchman. As she prepared to plunge the dagger into his back, he swung around and struck her shoulder with his massive fist. She hit the floor but kept her grip on the weapon. She jumped to her feet and charged again. The human's large size permitted him to kick out and catch her in the knee before she reached him. He punched her face, and she flew backwards into the wall.

"What's the meaning of this?" Lord Landis' booming voice bounced off the stone walls.

"Wilhelm is a traitor!" shouted Bronwyn.

Lord Landis rushed forward with his sword drawn. "I'll take care of him. Help the women." The lord's sword clashed with Wilhelm's and drove the scribe up the stairs.

Catriona dragged herself to a seated position, tried to stand, then collapsed to the floor.

Bronwyn jumped in front of Alaura as the henchman drew his sword and prepared to strike her. With renewed strength, he attacked the intruder. For several moments, they exchanged blows, the fighter matching his skill.

The henchman withdrew a small flask from his pocket and threw it onto the floor. It exploded, sending Bronwyn crashing into the wall. Spots danced before his eyes, and he shook his head to clear it. The henchman raced towards him, and he struggled to rise, but the dizziness sent him spiralling.

Alaura leapt in front of him, danced her fingers in the air and mumbled foreign words he didn't understand. He gasped when the henchman swung his sword, then braced himself for the impending horror. Yet it didn't come. The sword bounced off an invisible barrier. He rubbed his eyes and stared at the empty space the sword couldn't pierce.

"Your sword!" Alaura jerked her chin in the direction of his weapon.

He shook the dizziness from his head and grabbed his sword.

In his effort to break through the invisible shield, the henchman lost his grip on the marmoset. Isla hit the floor and darted down the hallway. The henchman chased her with Alaura in pursuit.

Bronwyn rose on shaky legs and staggered after them. With each step, he shook the dizziness from his head until the shock of the explosion faded into his memory.

It took several minutes before the henchman caught up with the racing marmoset. When he did, he grabbed it by the back of the neck. Isla squealed and scratched and bit the human.

Bronwyn slid to a halt, swinging his sword before the henchman had a chance to make a proper stance. The sword struck his shoulder and the man reeled in pain. Isla dropped to the floor and again ran from her captor.

Catriona caught up to them, then slipped past to follow Isla.

The henchman made several attempts to connect with his sword, but his wound had weakened his swing. Bronwyn gathered his strength and delivered blow after blow, backing his opponent against the stone wall. He focussed on each swing and anticipated the next. Years of practice in his backyard and his training as a guard had prepared him for this battle.

As the confidence in his enemy's eyes slipped, the hunger to serve the final blow invigorated Bronwyn. He attacked relentlessly, delivering the lethal strikes that dropped the henchman to his knees.

He paused, his adrenalin waning as his opponent's eyes roll into his head. The body swaggered a moment before collapsing to the floor. He eased the death grip on his sword. It unnerved him to take a life, but he understood the necessity of it.

Alaura stared in awe, then a peculiar expression appeared, and she shuddered.

Bronwyn caught her studying him as he regained his breath. Besides her frazzled appearance and cut below her right eye, she was fine. Her deep breathing caused her bosom to gently rise and fall, drawing his eyes to the soft hollow between her breasts. A button had broken off in the scuffle, revealing soft curves of delicate skin. His blood warmed and the tiny hairs on his ears pricked. He swallowed hard, realising his gaze lingered too long. He quickly diverted his eyes. "Thank you for casting the spell to protect me." His voice sounded gentler than he expected. Her presence once again drew his attention. "You risked your life for mine."

"It's I who must thank you for seeing the truth. I'm not a traitor." She pulled the top of her shirt closed and fastened a button.

"I know." Though her eyes attempted to hold his gaze, he braced his jaw and looked away. "I knew you couldn't kill me." He glanced at the dagger in her hand. "But you almost had me doubting." He held out his hand for his weapon.

"Don't." She returned the dagger. "I spoke the truth."

"It's not wise to stake your life on blind trust."

"But you're not blind."

He nodded and sheathed the dagger. Until today, he had never stood within twenty feet of Alaura of Niamh. The details he'd missed surprised him. Inspecting her now, he saw the subtle features that suggested her parentage: the curve of her cheek bone, the upward angle to the outside of the eye, the sharpness of her ears and the defined shape of her lips.

He thought back to the first time he'd seen her. He had been passing through the bakery to his dwelling upstairs—he lived at home then. As he entered the backroom, he thought he had seen a person talking with his mum on the far end of the shop. He stepped backwards and craned his neck to learn their identity. For a moment he stared at the woman. She appeared new to Maskil or at least not from this end of town.

She must have felt his stare because her eyes left his mum and settled on him. Her expression softened, and her mouth curved into a gentle smile. A light he'd never seen before shimmered in her eyes. It triggered a sensation in his chest, which until then lay dormant.

From that moment onward, he watched for her in the bakery, on the street and at every place he visited. Strange how she possessed the ability to capture and hold his attention.

Pulling from his memories, he noticed Alaura uncomfortable under his stare. With her lips slightly parted and her brow in a quizzical angle, she watched him.

"I'm sorry for putting you on the spot," she said. "I thought you had paid attention to the conversation. Lord Val had asked you to verify the fact I knew Catriona. I assumed you could since you had seen us together in the bakery."

He could have easily answered the question if he had paid attention. "You're not to blame. I should have followed the conversation. I was thinking of someone—something else."

"It's been a trying twenty-four hours for many of us." She pointed down the hallway. "We should see to Catriona and Isla." She stepped over the pool of blood seeping from the body sprawled at their feet.

He followed in silence. Fortunately, he *had* blindly trusted her. His blood ran cold when he thought of what Wilhelm had ordered him to do. The murder of Alaura of Niamh by his hand would have created a pit of guilt too large to fill.

Catriona, flushed and anxious, rushed from a doorway. "Is he dead?"

Alaura nodded and steadied her teacher. "Where's Isla?"

"She's in here, but it's too dark to see."

Bronwyn walked past the women and entered the room. "Alaura, go along the wall. I'll search this side." The cavernous room dwarfed all others in the castle. He'd not entered it before but knew it to be the quarters of Lilja, the missing sacred dragon.

Expansive tapestries depicting scenes around Maskil draped the walls. The large doors leading to the outside balcony where Lilja entered in years gone by and a tall window remained locked from the inside. The single torch by the door illuminated only a small space. Once Bronwyn's eyes adjusted to the dim light, he saw only one place to hide: behind a large stone orb in the far corner.

As he approached, he looked from one side to the other, hoping to catch a glimpse of the monkey. He stopped when he saw a hairy foot. Kneeling, he whispered in Hauflin, "Isla, the danger has passed." When the foot didn't move, he edged closer until he saw a pair of large brown eyes staring at him. He stopped near enough to touch but made no motion to do so. Instead, he lay on his stomach while she crouched in the shadows. "You're safe. No one will harm you." The henchman's blood soiled his blade because of her. Take a life to save a life. He killed for only one reason.

He found it hard to imagine this monkey as a child. The transformation appeared perfect. Still, he sensed she understood every spoken word as if an intelligent being. He slid his arm towards her. As he did, he hummed a melody he often hummed to his sister's child.

Isla mimicked him.

He rested his hand beside her foot. She touched one of his fingers, and he relaxed as the monkey explored the palm of his hand. She circled a large callus, then traced a deep skin line to his thumb.

"Come to me." He spoke soft and low. "You can trust me."

Isla stopped humming and stared at him. He made no quick moves, no attempts to grab her. She inched forward until she rested in his palm. He pushed himself to his knees before cradling her in his arms.

Turning, he saw Alaura and Catriona watching intently. He flushed, embarrassed at his display of tenderness designed to wheedle the child from the shadows.

Catriona squinted past him to the object in the shadows. "What's this?" She stepped forward. The object stood almost as tall as she did.

"It shaped like an egg," said Alaura.

"I think it's a stone orb," said Bronwyn.

"Whose room is this?" Catriona reached out to touch the orb but hesitated. Her hand hovered above the stone as she gazed at it as if she'd fallen under a spell.

"This is Lilja's room."

"The sacred dragon's room? Her orb?" Catriona spoke in a hushed voice and placed her open palm on the stone.

Bronwyn remembered seeing a similar orb on the tapestry in the Private Audience room. This orb didn't have a yellow glow or butterfly wings but otherwise, it looked the same.

"It's cracked." Catriona sounded disappointed.

Alaura drew closer for a better view of the cleft. She guided her finger along the jagged edge running from the top of the orb to about the mid-way point. It spread wide enough to accommodate her slender finger and just as deep.

Bronwyn placed a hand on her shoulder, and she turned to him. "Only authorized guards are permitted to enter this room," he said. "We must leave."

"Don't you wonder what this might be?"

"I do, but my orders are clear."

"What is this?" Catriona moved to where Isla had hidden. The others joined her, and she pointed to markings on the orb. "It's too dark for me to read but perhaps you can?"

He and Alaura examined the three symbols scrolled across the mid-section of the orb. It exhibited the same symbols as on the tapestry.

"What do you make of it?" he asked her.

"Don't be silly," said Catriona. "She can see no better than I."

He raised questioning brows at Alaura. In cant, a voice inaudible to humans, he asked, "Can you read it?"

"I think I can see enough," said Alaura in her normal voice. "It's not written in a language I'm familiar with. It might be Dragon."

Bronwyn leant forward to see if more etchings appeared in the stone. At the same time, Alaura laid her hand on the orb. The three symbols glowed with soft green light.

Catriona pulled her apprentice's hand away, but the symbols continued to glow.

"It's not me," said Alaura. "It's Isla."

The three stared at the child who remained mesmerized by the illuminated symbols.

A noise in the hallway prompted Bronwyn to remove the monkey's hand from the orb. The glow disappeared. "Not a word. Follow me." He crept towards the door with Isla tucked into the crook of his right arm. With his left hand, he withdrew his sword from the scabbard.

"Bronwyn!" Farlan spotted the dwarf as he entered the hallway. "Is everyone okay?"

Lord Val and two castle guards followed close behind. They stopped at the body sprawled across the floor.

"We're fine, Private." Bronwyn walked clear of Lilja's room. Alaura and Catriona followed.

"Was he the only intruder?" Lord Val twisted his face in disgust at dead man.

"I believe so, My Lord." Bronwyn glanced around to ensure his assessment was correct. "He wanted the child. It appears he and Wilhelm worked together."

The lord rubbed his temple, squinting as if absorbing a sharp head pain. "It is in these days of strife we require loyalty, yet we find only traitors."

He sheathed his sword and covered Isla's eyes as he passed the corpse.

"Guards, search the body to see if anything useful can be discovered." Lord Val gave the order, then turned to Bronwyn. "Corporal, is this Keiron Ruckle's issue?"

"It is."

"Let me hold her."

When the lord reached for Isla, she darted up Bronwyn's sleeve and curled around his neck. She clung to him with all her strength.

"Ouch!" Bronwyn clenched his teeth as her sharp claws pierced his vest and entered his flesh. "She's terrified." He stepped away to see if Isla would ease her grip. To his relief, she withdrew her claws.

With wide eyes, Lord Val studied the marmoset intensely. Bronwyn thought he'd reach up and snatch it from his shoulder. Then as if a cloud sailed across the sun, the lord's expression relaxed.

"Are we to return to the Private Audience Room, My Lord?" asked Bronwyn.

"We will reconvene at first light. The castle is being searched for additional intruders." He licked his dry lips. "Return Miss Wheatcroft and her nearest next-of-kin to their temporary quarters. Post a guard inside the room and two to secure the door. Every precaution must be taken for their safety. I'll leave the duty to you, Corporal."

"Am I not permitted to leave?" asked Alaura.

Lord Val peered down at her. "You, Miss Alaura, are a witness to this evening's events. You'll remain and give your account at the inquest."

Bronwyn spoke up. "Given the circumstances and the time of day, you'd be safer if you stayed." He knew if she refused, she'd be held in the dungeon 'til morning.

They exchanged glances and after a moment's consideration, she spoke. "I will stay."

"The sword!" One of the guards shouted in disbelief.

The men searching the body sprang away from it. The blood surrounding the weapon foamed and hissed. Small eruptions sent puffs of warm fousty gas into the air. The odour spewing from the blood smelt of pus from a festering sore.

Alaura stepped closer. "The sword possesses wicked magic." She glanced at Bronwyn as if to re-evaluate his skill.

Bronwyn had witnessed a similar blood reaction, but what had caused it eluded him. During that incident, a dagger used by a henchman to kill a guard had foamed and hissed with the same stench when it had fallen into the killer's pool of blood.

"Corporal, remove the women from here," ordered Lord Val. "Assist him, Private. The rest of you, take care of this mess." He waved his hand in disgust over the bloody scene.

"Private." Bronwyn gestured for Farlan to lead the way. He motioned for Catriona and Alaura to follow as he carried Isla. Glancing back, he watched the lord step past the body and into the threshold of Lilja's room. The elf looked in the direction of the orb and raised one hand as if pushing open a door. Before turning a corner, Bronwyn swore he saw a flash of light emanate from the lord's palm and disappear into the shadows.

7

Or Else What?

BRONWYN STRETCHED and yawned as he walked towards his quarters. He had sat awake all night watching over Alaura, Catriona and Isla. Under the circumstances, he thought it best to guard the room himself. Time had passed without incident, but he ached from sitting in the hard chair, watching and waiting.

The women had talked little, unwilling to discuss anything of importance in front of him. It suited him fine, considering he didn't have anything to say. As expected, the evening assault had caused them great distress. The prospect of sleeping in an unfamiliar bed while a male stranger watched over them didn't help matters.

The monkey had put to rest any fears it had about the bloody fight and settled with ease. When he had sat in a chair with it still in his arms, it curled into his neck and fell asleep. Although he offered to place it beside one of them, both women agreed it was safer with him.

She's the one you're protecting, Alaura had said. She covered the marmoset with a small blanket, kissed it and went to bed.

Bronwyn's discomfort at having a hairy creature sleeping on his chest passed, and he settled in for the night with the rhythm of its breathing counting away the seconds.

With another guard watching the room as the women prepared for the early morning session, he had a few moments to freshen up and grab a snack.

The appearance of Lady Dasia leaning against the wall when he rounded the corner to the military offices surprised him. The elf smiled at he approached.

"My Lady, can I offer you assistance?" Her deep green eyes swept across his face. He hoped she didn't want to discuss his embarrassing distraction at the meeting the night before. He wanted to forget about it; pretend it never happened.

She placed her nimble hand upon his shoulder. "Do you have a minute?"

"I do." He grew uncomfortable with her nearness but felt obligated to remain still. She measured six inches taller than he, putting him eye level with her slim neck and the plain, silver chain she wore. Lady Dasia, an elder lord, had served for almost as long as Lord Val. She tended to the basic needs of the citizens of Maskil, and she visited them in their dwellings and shops and often strolled with one by her side.

"Bronwyn, I see in you a spirit missing amongst the guards lately." She took a step forward and positioned him between her and the wall. The light from the nearby window made the highlights in her mossy blonde hair shimmer. "Do you notice the disturbance in the energy, the unrest amongst those within the castle walls?"

What energy? He didn't see unrest. "Could you be more specific?"

"I sense an unbalance, a separation from the true ambition of our founders. Do you? Do you feel its pull on your spirit?"

He shook his head. Her wide delicate ears pricked forward as if she listened for not only his words but the breath he drew.

"It's there. I feel it." She looked down one hallway, then the other before re-establishing eye contact. "It wishes to claim you as well, but...you are different."

"I don't feel threatened."

"And there lies the danger. No one *feels* the threat." She gripped his shoulders and nudged him against the wall. "The castle has become stagnant. It resists change. Without change, there can be no growth. Beings cease to live, things cease to exist. Do you understand?"

"No... Yes... I don't." His mind raced to understand the confusing statements. How could a castle, a structure, become stagnant? It didn't grow.

Lady Dasia peered closer, gazing deep into his eyes. She traced his brow and jaw line with her long index finger. She acted spellbound, weaving her way closer until her breath fell upon his cheek. Her serene voice filled his ears, capturing his attention with every sound. "Bronwyn, you have much to give, yet you hoard your compassion."

He swallowed hard and his breath became short. Her intimate stance made his pulse race and the heat grow around his neck. He had never stood this close to Lady Dasia, nor to any other worthy woman. The scent radiating from her skin made him dizzy. What did she mean to accomplish by flaunting her charisma?

"The influences in your life are unbalanced. You need others to guide you." She lowered her brow as if to chastise him. "You have distanced yourself from family, and you've avoided others for the potential complications they create." Her jaw tilted, but her eyes remained fixed on his. "Alaura of Niamh is an enchanting creature, one capable of capturing the attention and admiration of the strongest of wills. Though many men try, only one will succeed in winning her loyalty. Her charms are seeded but need...nurturing."

He cleared his throat and sought a fresh breath unburdened by the elf's scent. "It's best those in the service of the castle remain single."

She huffed. "That philosophy hasn't served Zipporah Sanderson or the castle. It has only caused heartache for him and many others."

"Still, I'm not interested." He diverted his eyes. "I prefer to be single."

"If your life doesn't change, there will be no growth." She forced him to look at her. "Change is painful but what grows is fantastic. At times, it is the smallest of beings which kindle new growth. Once it starts, there is no going back."

He drew a deep breath and tried to steady his nerves. He had become claustrophobic with her closeness, pressing him against the wall, trapping him so he couldn't leave.

"Embrace the change, Bronwyn. Great matters are not viewed as such at first. They can be elusive until they reveal the truth. You are a brave and honourable dwarf. I have faith in you."

"Does this have anything to do with yesternight?" He grasped at the only possibility he could think of and leant away to snatch breathing room. "I'm confused if it isn't." Then again, he didn't know how it applied to the events of yesternight either.

Lady Dasia smiled. "It is about yesternight and what happened before then...and what will happen every day after this moment." She released him and stepped away. "Do not let me down, Bronwyn Darrow, son of Maisie Kintale. Do not forsake those who need your protection most. There is no better reward than knowing you have done your best by them."

The space she put between them offered relief. "If I do my job, My Lady, then I protect our citizens. I hope I haven't disappointed you with any shortcomings I have."

"You have never disappointed me, nor do I believe you could." She folded her arms and stared at him. "There are a few individuals who need your especial consideration."

He felt she sized him up for a specific duty, but what could she ask of him?

"Never believe a small task is not worthy of a great swordsman." She turned and walked away.

He watched her go, flabbergasted by her words. What did she want him to do? All the small tasks others ignored? But he didn't see himself as a great swordsman though he strived to be one. He always protected those who needed protecting.

With Lady Dasia's conversation still fresh in his mind, he passed Sanderson's office. Through the open door he saw the captain of the guard sitting at his desk.

"Corporal!" Sanderson's disgruntlement shot through the air. "I want a word with you."

He stopped and braced his tired body for the reprimand for last evening's conduct. Turning, he walked into the office.

"Close the door." Sanderson leant on his desk, a heavy piece of wood that supported his bulk, several stacks of paper, a few books, an oil lamp and writing utensils. His dark, bushy brows gave him a haggard appearance this morning. With one large hand, he brushed the greying hair from his forehead. "Sit."

Bronwyn obeyed.

"Your conduct in the Private Audience room was inexcusable." Sanderson's dark eyes pierced the air between them. "When a lord asks for information, your duty is to provide it without hesitation. Promises or no promises. And when the same lord turns down a request, you don't make it again. Do I make myself clear, Corporal?"

"Yes, sir." He disliked protocol when it got in the way of getting things done but kept this fact unspoken. "But there are exceptional circumstances—"

"No buts!" Sanderson leant forward. "Understand this, Corporal; my guards stay in line or they find themselves planting potatoes with the soldiers. Is that what you want?"

"No, sir."

Sanderson sat back in his chair and rubbed his chin as he eyed the dwarf. "I'm not supposed to do this, but I'm going to make an exception this one time." He tossed a small handbook onto Bronwyn's lap. "Keep it. Commit it to memory."

The corporal read the cover: *Protocol - The Foundation of Civil Organisation.* He had read it several times and could recite most of it already. The handbook became mandatory reading for every soldier on entering the castle's service. However, all copies had to be returned at the end of each day.

Sanderson eyeballed the dwarf further and spoke in a somber tone. "Do you have any idea the number of corporals in service at the castle when I became a guard?"

"No, sir." Both the question and the unexpected change of subject confused him.

"Fifty." Sanderson paused. "Do you know how many there are now?"

"Twelve?"

"Ten. Do you know why?"

He shook his head. "Why?"

Sanderson studied his office, taking in the sparsely decorated walls. For a moment, his thoughts consumed him. When he finally spoke, his words sounded distant. "I don't know."

This confused Bronwyn further. As captain of the guard, he should know.

"Over the years, corporals died or retired. Guards weren't promoted to fill the empty positions and eventually their numbers dwindled." Sanderson ran his callused finger along the curve of the desk. "As captain of the guard, it's my duty and pleasure to promote men worthy of a higher rank. Early in my career, I had the power to do so without question or authorization. I didn't need the approval of the lords."

He sighed. "In the past fifteen or so years, procedures have changed. I have dozens of men who deserve higher ranks, but none of them will see it. Corporal, do you have any idea how this affects command?"

Bronwyn had an idea, but he remained silent.

"I have ten corporals to command more than seven hundred privates. Pity help us if we come under serious attack."

Being new to his rank, Bronwyn hadn't realised the state of the castle guards.

Sanderson frowned. "Do you know why you received your promotion?"

He swallowed hard. The answer didn't appear to be one he wanted to hear.

"I *insisted*. I thought of you as worthier than any of the men who wore the uniform. I believed you had the leadership qualities and the skills to help me do my job and take care of my men. I badgered Lord Mulryan until he had to approve your promotion." He eyeballed him long and hard. "Did I make a mistake?"

"No, sir!" Bronwyn sat straighter and spoke with confidence. "I'm sorry I let you down. It won't happen again."

Sanderson leant back in his chair, resting his weary bones. "I'm not going to keep this post forever. I'll need a good man to replace me, one who will follow protocol to the word but more importantly, take care of my men and this castle."

Does he mean me? Was Sanderson preparing him to be the future captain of the guard? Impossible!

Sanderson chuckled despite his exhaustion. "You look surprised. You didn't think I wanted Captain Tibbins to replace me? That nut doesn't give a damn about my men or this castle. He sees only the power. He's itched for years to take over this office, but I'm not leaving until I trust the person wearing this uniform will think of the men beneath him first."

Bronwyn breathed again. He never imagined Sanderson marked him to be the next captain of the guard. "I'll do my best to live up to your expectations, sir. I offer no excuses for my behaviour, but I'll say this past week has been wearisome with many unexpected challenges."

"Every week will be similar from here on. It's part of the process. Get used to it."

"Yes, sir." He paused before asking the next question only Sanderson could answer. "Sir, about last night. Lord Val's anger surprised me. Does he often lose his temper?"

Sanderson shook his head. "It was indeed unexpected. He's a bit agitated lately."

"What is the cause?"

"I don't know. I sense a force, but..." He stopped short of sharing his thoughts about the lord. "It's not my place to judge."

"I thought it was."

Sanderson considered the comment but left it unanswered. "The meeting will begin soon." He straightened his vest and picked up several papers. "It won't take long to sort out this hauflin nonsense and send the women on their way."

Bronwyn stood and turned to leave.

"Before you go." Sanderson spoke in an even tone. "It's wise not to clutter your mind with fascinations that distract from duty."

"Yes, sir." He had hoped to avoid a discussion about the confusion Alaura of Niamh had caused.

"Don't let women steal your senses like the half-breed did. When it comes to women, it's better to bed 'em and forget 'em." Sanderson's gaze fell upon his bare hands. "Women and offspring hinder duty. If you want this office, avoid them as you would charging troglodytes."

"Yes, sir." To reassure his superior, he added, "I have no intentions of uniting." He had made the promise to himself many years ago on a starry night after the betrayal of a woman who he thought had loved him. Regardless of what Lady Dasia said, he'd keep the promise.

☙ ❖ ❧

Bronwyn changed into a fresh uniform, washed his face and combed his hair. He grabbed a quick snack, then returned to the Private Audience Room. Sanderson, Farlan, Blomidon, Catriona and Alaura had already arrived. The marmoset rested on Alaura's lap, half hidden behind her arm. A stranger, a male human, sat at the end of the table in Wilhelm's former seat.

The door near the tapestry opened, and Lord Val entered the room. Everyone stood as he took his seat. Once again, Bronwyn found himself directly across the table from the elven lord.

"I'll conduct the meeting alone this morning." Lord Val glanced at the paper in front of him. "The investigation into yesternight's incident is complete. The details on both men have been gathered and filed. There will be no further discussion."

"Over? The man broke down my door and assaulted me!" Catriona's sharp voice shot through the air. "He held a dagger to my throat! How could he gain entry to the castle? In a guard's uniform, no less!"

"Catriona's correct. He was the henchman who escaped," said Bronwyn. Sanderson's large hand on his shoulder quashed his next comment.

"Silence!" Lord Val glared at Catriona. "You're to remain quiet unless requested to speak. Castle security is not your concern."

"How can there be a discussion if everyone is not permitted to speak?" Catriona flung her hand in the air to stress the fact.

Bronwyn thought the same but remained hushed.

"One more word from you, Miss Wheatcroft, and you'll spend the night in the dungeon."

Catriona balked at the warning.

Lord Val moved a paper to the top of the pile. He paused, reviewing the next issue before reading it aloud. Surprise ripened in his greyish-green eyes and spread across his face like a dragon's wing unfolding before flight. The lord tugged at his shirt collar, then leant towards the paper and took a deep breath. Bronwyn thought he smelt the document.

In a calmer voice Lord Val continued. "To the business of this orphan. After sorting through the information on this...creature, we have decided it is not the child in the prophecy. Her only significance is her relationship with Keiron Ruckle, a notorious thief."

Sanderson placed his pencil on his papers and sat back in his chair.

"We believe the orphan is in no significant danger. She simply requires a caregiver to provide her basic needs until she's old enough to fend for herself. It's a small task but a worthy one." Lord Val moistened his lips. "We have appointed Corporal Darrow as her legal protector."

"There must be a mistake!" Bronwyn gawked at Sanderson for help, but he appeared more stunned at the announcement than he.

"Corporal, you were not asked to speak." Lord Val cleared his throat. "The lords have discussed the options and have decided you are the ideal person to provide care for this orphan."

"I disagree!" Alaura raised her voice. "Isla needs a hauflin family who will love her. I have found such a family in Petra."

"Silence!" ordered Lord Val. "She is a citizen of Maskil, and here is where she will remain!"

Alaura stood. Holding Isla in one hand, she rested the other on the table and leant forward to challenge the lord. "With all respect due to Corporal Darrow, he's in no position to provide a loving home for this child. He's not united!"

Lord Val flicked his fingers in Alaura's direction. She closed her mouth and sat down. An unknown force trapped her, and she struggled against it. Bronwyn glanced at Sanderson; his facial expression spoke volumes. With his eyes and every muscle in his face, Sanderson urged him to refuse the appointment.

"My Lord, I agree with Alaura." Bronwyn swallowed hard and thoughts of planting potatoes crossed his mind. "The child needs a mum. I'm dedicated to duty. I don't have time to play nursemaid."

Lord Val raised his hand to hush him. "The decision is final. Corporal, you will take immediate charge of this orphan."

"I don't want it!" He rose from his chair. "How clear must I be?"

The lord folded his hands on the table and spoke in an emotionless voice. "If you refuse to care for this orphan, you will be charged with neglect. You will be stripped of your rank, dishonourably discharged and sentenced to two years in the dungeon. Do you accept this appointment, Corporal Darrow?"

The expanding lump in Bronwyn's throat made swallowing difficult. He had dedicated his life to mastering the sword and the past seven years to the service of Aruam Castle. Despite his accomplishments and commitment to duty, he teetered on the verge of losing everything. Flabbergasted, he slid into his chair.

"Corporal Darrow, answer the question."

The two years in the dungeon weren't as damaging as the dishonourable discharge; that would sully his reputation, making him ineligible to re-enlist as a castle guard after serving his sentence. All his life he'd dreamt of wearing a uniform. If he had to relinquish it, he'd be lost. He had to keep it at all cost.

"I accept."

"Speak up."

"I accept the appointment." He scowled at Lord Mulryan's empty chair; why had the dwarf lord done this to him? Did he punish him for the lack of control he displayed the night before? He wished he'd never laid eyes on Alaura of Niamh and her monkey.

"It is settled then. You are removed from duty for the next three days to familiarize yourself with your ward. Then you are expected to fulfill your duties as usual. You will be assigned new quarters to accommodate you both." Lord Val rose. "The meeting is over. May you all be well." He picked up his papers and exited the room.

Damn you! How in the Caverns of Confusion am I supposed to care for a bairn and fulfill my duties? Impossible! He hoped the potion never wore off. He'd cage the monkey with food and water and walk away. Sanderson rose and left the room. The ownership of a child spelt the end of a promising career. No one with a bairn rose above the rank of corporal. Blomidon and the new scribe also left.

Bronwyn sulked as he thought about his future. The lords had no right to force a ward into his life. He'd always be a single man. What would he do with a child? He slouched in his chair, rested his head in his hand and tried to come to grips with what had transpired.

"Sir, shall I escort the women out of the castle?" Farlan waited for his orders.

He signalled for Farlan to remove them. He wanted to be alone.

"Perhaps an element of good will come from this." Alaura rose from her chair. She hugged the monkey and placed it on Bronwyn's lap. "I'll drop by this afternoon with her personal items."

"Whatever." He sank into a brewing storm. "Bring only what it needs. Dispose of the rest." He didn't want junk cluttering his quarters.

"That shouldn't be a problem." Alaura's sarcasm churned in the air. "Make sure she remains safe."

"You're going to threaten me, too?" His voice grew with his frustration. "Fortunately, you can't do more damage than what's already done!"

"You selfish rogue." Her eyes flashed. "You've forgotten there's an innocent child who has to live with the outrageous ruling of that lord!"

"I made it quite clear I didn't want it! I don't give a damn what happens to it!" As a final jab, he said, "Maybe I'll sell it to the theatre. They're always hiring new acts."

She erupted and slapped him across the face. "Your mum would be ashamed if she witnessed your behaviour! You're nothing like her!"

Startled by the slap, the monkey ducked beneath Bronwyn's vest. It wriggled until it tucked its small body into the warm confines of the uniform.

Taken by surprise, Bronwyn had no time to defend himself and received the full strength of the slap on the cheek. Her hand left a burning sensation that fueled his anger. He'd have struck her down with one solid punch if she'd been a man. "Farlan, escort this half-bitch and her two-bit witch out of the castle!"

"Yes, sir!" Farlan ushered the women towards the door.

Alaura glared at Bronwyn. "If anything happens to her, I'll hold you personally responsible."

The door closed, and Bronwyn released a long sigh. His anger waned, and his thoughts cleared. As minutes ticked away, he replayed Lord Val's words, searching for a loophole to rid himself of the monkey. His mind worked forward through the meeting until the end when Alaura had threatened and slapped him. He cringed recalling the words he had spoken to her.

He couldn't believe it. He had never spoken so harshly to anyone. Why to Alaura, of all people? Although they barely knew each other, he admired her. But the look she gave him, the one that said he had better do what she said or else, ignited his anger. *Or else what?* She had taunted him, lured him into saying his worst.

It confounded him that the woman could make him lose his senses, first with her grace and then with her spite. She must have used magic.

He wanted to fall into a deep sleep and forget about Alaura and his new unreasonable responsibilities, so he closed his eyes and let his head fall against the chair. This could be a nightmare and when he woke, everything would be as it should. He breathed deeply, trying to cleanse his mind.

Movement in his vest disturbed his thoughts. If he kept his eyes closed, would it disappear? He squeezed them tighter and wished it away.

The animal moved off his lap, and its claws clicked on the surface of the table. It soon returned, its paws slipping on his trousers.

"Ah!" He jumped when icy water splashed against his face. The monkey, a glass and the chair went flying. Water soaked his fresh uniform, and his anger resurfaced. "Can this day get any worse?" He searched for the creature and found it hiding beneath the table.

"Get over here!" He clenched his fist and glared at it.

The monkey backed away, staring at him with glossy eyes.

He shoved aside chairs, marched around the table and caught the marmoset before it darted away. As he prepared to yell insults at it, he felt its rapid heartbeat. Its large, round eyes gawked at him, and its appendages flailed. It sensed imminent pain in his grasp. Last night, he had soothed the monkey's fears. Today, he provoked them.

He calmed his anger. He had no intentions of harming the strange creature though it caused his troubles. It really hadn't purposefully robbed him of his freedom; Lord Val had woven their lives together. The monkey had as much say in the matter as he did. As Alaura had said, the ridiculous ruling affected him and an innocent child.

Or did the blame sit with Lord Val? The early morning conversation with Lady Dasia replayed in his mind. She had told him to embrace change, to take care of those who couldn't protect themselves. A child fell under that category, but raising a child made no small task and certainly not one for a swordsman.

The door flew open, and a female servant rushed in. "Is everything as it should be?"

He drew the monkey near. "I made a small mess. I'm sorry."

"No worry. Accidents happen." She smiled at the animal in his arms. "What's its name?"

Not wanting to connect the monkey with his future ward, he said, "I'm minding it for a friend." He eyed the colourful buttons on the woman's blue dress. "Its name is Button."

"Well, Button, you're as sweet as a button. Don't worry about the mess. I'll take care of it."

Bronwyn nodded to the servant and left the room. He glanced at the monkey in his arms. Carrying it this way felt unnatural. "Maybe you should ride up here." He lifted it to his shoulder. Its claws dug into his vest but didn't reach his skin.

8

Stone Collector

BY MID-MORNING, Bronwyn had completed the business that couldn't wait until he returned from his three-day leave. Now he needed to attend to his personal business and change into civilian clothes.

On the way to his quarters, he passed the captain of the guard's closed office door. He thought about speaking to Sanderson, then changed his mind.

"Excuse me, sir." A private called to him from behind. "I'm to give you this." The guard placed a key in his hand and provided directions to his new quarters. "Your belongings have been delivered."

Bronwyn didn't know what to say. Those in charge had surprised him by taking care of his relocation. He thanked the private, then proceeded towards his new quarters. When he neared his room, he found youngsters of various ages and races playing and lingering in the hallway. A pair of human boys scooted past, one shouting at the other. In his effort to avoid them, he bumped into a female dwarf backing out of her doorway.

"Sorry." He moved aside.

The expecting mother rested one hand on her large, round belly and grasped the small child clinging to her leg with the other. "Cute monkey. Does it bite?"

He shook his head and placed a gentle hand on the monkey's side.

Reassured, she picked up her child and strode down the hall.

Bronwyn, single and childless, didn't belong in this area. He'd never get used to the noise or being around so many united couples and their bairns. Several doors later, he arrived at his quarters. He entered the small room and closed the door behind him. The thickness of the wood thankfully blocked most of the sounds emanating from the hallway.

Natural light shining through a three-foot by four-foot window lit the end of his new home. A rough-looking double bed with a tattered mattress occupied the far-left corner.

On the opposite side sat a small wood stove for warmth and cooking. Beside it, a short countertop adorned the wall. Above this hung two shelves holding odd dishes. A small round table rested to his immediate right. The remains of a chesterfield with more board showing than cushion lay on the left. Next to it a door, he guessed, led to the water closet. The trunk with his personal items sat nearby.

He didn't recognise the small brown sack lying on top of the trunk. Picking it up, he went to the bed to sort through it. The sack contained Isla's possessions. He'd left instructions at the guardhouse for Alaura to leave the child's things there instead of giving them to him personally to avoid another confrontation with her.

One-by-one, he pulled the items from the sack, promising himself he'd keep to his word and discard anything unnecessary. The monkey would live with the essentials as he did. The low number of items in the bag—two dresses, two pairs of socks, a sweater, two pairs of panties, a pair of shoes, a child's book, a hair brush and a small leather pouch—surprised him. Keiron Ruckle's issue, if this monkey turned out to be the child Isla, needed all of this.

The monkey crawled from his shoulder. It sat beside the leather pouch and struggled with the clasp. He reached forward and unfastened the oval, wooden button. When the monkey peered inside, it appeared disappointed. With big round eyes, it stared up at him. Uncertain about what it expected him to do, he waited.

Then, in a flash, the monkey's expression changed, and it dove into the pouch. With only its rump exposed, its thin brown tail twitched back and forth. When the monkey emerged from the bag, it held a blue stone.

Bronwyn peeked inside the pouch and saw the false bottom pulled open. "You're a stone collector?"

It tugged on the outside of the pouch and with his help, emptied the remaining stones onto the mattress. Although small, each stone filled the marmoset's hand.

The monkey hadn't answered him. It had spoken only once when it had asked for Alaura in a small, frightened voice. "The potion didn't steal your ability to speak. I heard you say *Alaura*."

The monkey's eyes grew wide, and it slapped its hand over its mouth.

"It's okay. You're allowed to talk." He spoke in Hauflin, hoping to hear more, but it remained silent. Strange for a child of this age; his four-year-old nephew never shut up.

The monkey returned to the stones, rolling them across the mattress, matching them in groups of two. When it finished, every stone had a mate except for one, the heliodor. The yellowish orange stone, similar in colour to goldenrod, sat alone. The marmoset picked up the translucent stone and dropped it into his chest pocket.

Bronwyn reached in and removed the rectangular stone. He fingered it for a moment, then set it on the mattress. The monkey picked it up and put it in the pocket again. When he reached to retrieve the stone, the creature clutched his little finger to stop him.

"You're giving it to me?" He watched for a sign to indicate an agreement, but it only stared. He let it guide his hand to the mattress.

The dwarf sat up straighter and scrutinized his new quarters. "If we're going to sleep here tonight, we need food." He searched the cupboards but found nothing provided for his convenience, not even a canister of tea. "Come on, Button." He swung the monkey onto his shoulder. "Let's go to the Keep and pick up supplies."

The pair returned a few hours later with a sack of food. Two older boys carrying a new mattress followed. Bronwyn removed the old one and instructed the youths to put the other down in its place. He handed a coin to each of the boys, then held open the door as they carried away the discarded mattress.

After organising the food in the cupboard, he turned his attention to the bed. He had almost finished making it when the monkey sat on the counter and stared up at the food cupboard. "Hungry?" He tossed the pillow onto the bed. "You and me both." He pulled a loaf of bread from a cloth sack and cut three thick slices. On these, he spread a generous layer of fenberry jam.

Button sat on the counter and watched him prepare the ration. Although its stomach growled, it didn't complain. He placed one sandwich on a plate and set it on the counter in front of the monkey.

"It's not fancy, but it's good." He took a large bite and savoured the taste. He seldom made his own meals; instead, he opted to eat in the great mess hall. Other times, he ate at the Glenelg Inn or at his parents' dwelling. "I hope you like sandwiches. We'll be eating a lot of them."

The monkey broke off a piece of bread and ate it. The food quickly disappeared, and it stared up at him.

"At least you don't mess with your ration." He set the plate near the wash basin, bagged the bread and cleaned off the counter. Though only late afternoon, his body ached for sleep.

"I'm going to take a nap. Button, you can do...whatever it is you do." Then he remembered the monkey had no place to sleep. He reached into the bottom cupboard and pulled out a shallow wooden crate. He dumped the contents into the cupboard and placed a small blanket on the bottom.

"Button, this is your bed." He placed the crate on the tattered chesterfield. "You sleep here." He sat the monkey inside. It could lie down easily.

He stripped to his shorts, picked up a small sack of mixed nuts, then slid beneath the blanket. Laying on his back with his head propped up by a thick pillow, he dropped a few nuts into his mouth. He scanned the room as he chewed and thought about tomorrow. He could visit his parents, but how would he explain the monkey? Maybe he'd take a walk and see where his feet took him.

Button climbed out of the crate and onto his bed where it eyed the bag of nuts.

Bronwyn set two nuts in front of the monkey. It took a bite of one, then, without looking at him, passed the other back.

He shrugged. "I guess you're not hungry." He popped the nut into his mouth.

Button finished chewing and looked for more.

"Another?" He gave it two more nuts. Again, it ate only one and returned the other. "Button, you're a strange monkey. But then rumour has it, you're not a monkey at all." As he ate, he wondered if the creature would change into a hauflin. Had Catriona played a trick on everyone? Had he heard it say *Alaura* or had his weary mind fooled him? Deep down, he hoped so. He preferred a pet monkey over a hauflin ward.

After they ate half the nuts, he set the bag on the bedside table and snuggled into the blanket. With one eye, he watched the monkey curl beneath the corner of the pillow. "Your bed is over there." He pointed at the crate. When Button didn't move, he nudged it with his hand.

"Where's Alaura?" The marmoset crouched low, cowering under its hairy hands, with its rump stuck in the air and tail curled beneath.

"You do speak!"

The soft voice sounded frightened. He placed a gentle hand on its back and felt it tremble. He released a heavy sigh; this was no ordinary monkey.

"Isla, Alaura's not here right now. But you're safe. I'm not going to hurt you." He tried to imagine how it must feel, removed from its familiar surroundings and put in the care of a stranger. "Maybe you'll see Alaura tomorrow." He smiled, hoping to ease its fears.

Pulling the monkey near, he covered it with the blanket. "You can stay here tonight. But tomorrow"—he tickled its belly—"you get your own bed." He rested a reassuring hand on the creature and hummed the melody to a bedtime lullaby, the same one he'd used to calm the child the evening before. He closed his eyes and possibilities started to surface. If the creature had an emotional attachment to Alaura, he might be able to give it to her. She came better equipped to handle it. The monkey moved, and he opened an eye to spy on it.

It slid from beneath his hand, crawled under his chin and snuggled into his neck. It yawned and before long, its breathing slowed into a restful rhythm. He copied the yawn and before long, he too fell asleep with a protective hand on Isla's back.

9

Debris Flew Everywhere

EARLY THE next morning, Bronwyn explored a part of town he didn't often visit. Button, perched on his shoulder, looked from one scene to another, taking in all the activities.

He crossed the bridge leading from the castle and walked along George Street. When he reached the Scintillate Theatre, he paused to read the billboard. The latest play starred Breckin Dole. He scowled at the name: it stirred dreadful memories. On a night long ago, too many mugs of ale had numbed his senses whilst the woman he loved clouded his mind. Her betrayal of his innocence left a deep scar. He'd never forgive her.

Button reached to touch the billboard, and he pushed it back to his shoulder. "No. Don't dirty your hands. I did and have regretted it since." He walked on.

Farther ahead, the bustling Maskil Market with its tempting venues beckoned him. He couldn't recall the last time he had browsed through the stalls. Dozens of vendors crowded the marketplace, and he soon became lost in a sea of people. He then remembered petty thieves frequented the market. Although he didn't have many coins, he slipped his hand into his trousers pocket to guard the few he carried.

The sound of music permeated the air with merriment. Bronwyn enjoyed the atmosphere as his eyes swept across the many displays of food, clothing, weapons and other wares. He picked up a side pouch that fastened to a belt and, after bartering with the vendor, he walked away satisfied he had snagged a bargain. At another stall, a woman tried to sell him a cloak, but he had no need for one. When he came to a fruit stand, he stopped to gaze upon the many varieties on display.

As he bartered over apples, Button leant too far. Fearing for the monkey's safety, he pushed it back onto his shoulder.

"No monkey on my stand." The middle-aged vendor shook his crooked finger. "It'll soil the fruit."

"Button, stay still." He reached into his pocket for a coin and found it empty. "The Orc's Curse!" Who would be so daring to steal from him, a corporal with the Aruam Castle Guard?

"No money! No apples!"

"A thief stole my money!"

The vendor reached for the sack. "You should be more careful."

Button stretched towards the apples, but Bronwyn pushed it back. It attempted to reach in another direction but again his hand stopped it. Button leapt from his shoulder and onto the table.

"No! No!" said the vendor. "No monkeys on the table!" He swung the sack of apples at it, and Button darted.

"Button! Come back!" Bronwyn raced after the monkey as it jumped from one table to the next. He bumped into several people, knocking items from their hands. "Sorry. Sorry," he blurted and kept running. His eye on the monkey, he didn't see the female in his path, and together they tumbled to the ground. As they struggled to separate, he realised he had tackled Alaura.

"Watch where you're going, you clumsy imp." She pushed herself up using him as a crutch, then gave an extra shove to throw him off balance. As she brushed dirt from her dress, he regained his composure and jumped to his feet.

"Thanks a lot." Sarcasm sharpened his words. Of all the people he could have bumped into, why did it have to be this face-slapping wench. "If I lose it, it's your fault."

"Do you always blame others for your misfortune?"

He rolled his eyes. "Are you always so crabby?" She turned to leave, and he grabbed her arm. "Aren't you going to help me catch it?"

"Catch what?" She yanked her arm from his grip.

"The monkey." He pointed at the hairy-armed creature swinging on the overhang of a stall about a hundred feet away.

"Oh, my! How could you lose her?"

"I've been busy tripping over people and being pushed around by you."

She frowned. "You're a sad excuse for a castle guard. You can't hold onto a five-year-old child. Don't just stand there. Let's go." She sprinted through the crowd.

Her attitude irritated him. Still, he followed.

The pair ran through the market and burst into the open street. Button ran well ahead of them, almost out of sight. Alaura didn't hesitate; she appeared to know the monkey's destination and dashed into an alley. Her speed and agility as she manoeuvred around objects strewn about impressed Bronwyn. He had difficulty keeping up and pushed himself harder, until she came to an abrupt stop. He halted beside her, bending over to rest his hands on his knees to catch his breath.

"You should run more." Her expression remained intense. "Around things. It improves dexterity."

He ignored her jibe. "Where are we?"

She pointed to a shoddy building. "Isla's dwelling."

He surveyed the area with renewed interest. The dwelling nestled in the poor part of town that harboured the low-life of society. Garbage littered every corner. Broken furniture, rags and old dishes lay scattered around the trash pile near the back door. The small fenced-in stall, which had obviously housed an animal, was strewn with droppings and various pieces of matter he didn't care to identify. The whole place smelt more like a stagnant swamp than a home. "Isla's dwelling," he repeated under his breath. "It's amazing anything could live in this."

The monkey stopped near the back door next to what appeared to be a large blood stain. "What's it looking for?"

"*She's* looking for her meeme."

"Didn't *her* mum die in child birth?"

"Not Maura." Alaura grimaced. "The ewe that tended her."

"The ewe?"

"As a newborn, Keiron put Isla outside with the sheep. The ewe had a lamb and she tended to Isla, too."

"That's..." He caught Alaura's stare; she spoke the truth. "Crazy." He put his hands into his pockets and reconsidered the area. He couldn't imagine living in this vile place.

"You see, Corporal Darrow, Isla didn't have the luxury of an adoring family who coddled her near a warm fire. She didn't have fresh food or clothes lovingly stitched by a mum's hand." She turned to face him. "Her life is nothing like yours. She's a child of neglect."

He swallowed hard. His upbringing contrasted sharply to Isla's. "So, she's here looking for the ewe. Where is it?"

"The men who broke into Catriona's dwelling killed it."

"How do you know?" He stared at the monkey as it ran a finger through the dirt.

"I watched over Isla that night."

He eyed her suspiciously. "You stayed here by yourself? Spying?"

"My duty is to tend to Isla." She avoided eye contact.

"Your duty?" While distracted, he inspected her. She wore her usual shapeless brown dress that hid her delicate curves. Her long hair hung loose, concealing her pointed ears and slight features. If he didn't know better, he'd swear she cloaked herself. But who would seek Alaura of Niamh?

"You can stop staring. I stayed only for Isla. I had nothing to do with the theft at the castle." She glared at him. "I'm not a thief."

"I didn't say you were."

"They came hunting Keiron. When they didn't find him, they searched for Isla. They killed the ewe to send a message to Keiron."

"Where was Isla? Catriona's?"

"No. She remained hidden inside."

"She saw the dead ewe?"

Alaura sighed. "I don't think she realises it's dead." Her voice lost its sharp edge. "She misses the ewe, and because she doesn't know it's gone, she'll look for her."

Bronwyn stared at the monkey. He found it hard to imagine a five-year-old child beneath all the hair. "I didn't know." A pang of guilt erupted in his chest. "This is no life for a child. She deserves better. You know, she misses you, too."

She glanced at him sideways.

"She asked for you. I did what I could to ease her fears, but she wanted you not me."

"Isla trusts few people."

Observing the monkey, trying to see the child, he found the small figure blurry. He lifted his hand to shield the sun from his eyes, but he continued to see an undefined image. Was the nauseating stench making him ill? He viewed the back door of the dwelling: the image appeared sharp, clearly defined. His eyes returned to the monkey. He squinted, attempting to bring its shimmering aura into focus.

His peculiar expression piqued Alaura's interest, and she turned to see what he watched. "Goodness! Do you have her clothes?"

"What clothes?"

"Take off your jacket."

He disliked her domineering tone. Why did she want his jacket? He ignored her and continued to stare at the marmoset. It shimmered with an odd light, then slowly transformed into a naked child. He quickly removed his jacket and held it open. Alaura placed the hauflin in his arms and wrapped the jacket around her.

"She's bigger than I thought," he said. Isla filled his arms as much as his four-year-old nephew.

"Marmosets are small, much smaller than a hauflin child."

He gazed upon the girl. The same brown eyes that had followed his every move for the past two days stared up at him. When he'd awoken this morning and found the monkey hiding in a cupboard eating from the bag of nuts, he had chuckled at its shenanigans. He had lifted it out of the cubby and sat it on the bed to eat while he dressed. In spite of the predicament in which he found himself, he enjoyed the short time they had spent together.

Now, as he took in each feature of Isla's innocent face, he released his negative feelings. The monkey he had carried for two days had always been this beautiful little girl. His paternal instincts awakened, and he held her near. The overwhelming desire to protect her caught him off guard. He shivered, remembering the danger she had experienced. If the henchmen had seized her, no telling what they'd have done. Did Lady Dasia mean for him to protect Isla?

A large piece of wood crashed through the boarded-up window near the backdoor. Pieces of debris flew everywhere. Bronwyn and Alaura jumped.

A crooked old woman, a dwarf, poked her head out of the opening and eyed the strangers. "Get or I'll fetch the dog fer yew! This be my dwelling now!"

Bronwyn placed a protective hand over Isla's face; at the same time, he positioned himself between Alaura and the woman. "We mean no trouble." He tightened his grip on Isla, then ushered Alaura from the alley and led her to his quarters. Once inside, he placed the child in her arms. "I'll get her clothes."

"Can you get warm water, too? She needs a bath. She smells like you."

He smelt under his arms. "I don't smell."

"I didn't say you smelt bad. She has your...odour. Anyways, she hasn't had a bath for a few days."

He searched the room for bath supplies, then lit a fire in the stove and placed a kettle of water on top to warm. "I think I saw a small basin in the water closet." He added tinder to increase the flame.

Alaura found the basin and placed it on the floor near the wood stove.

As he waited for the water to heat, he listened to her talk to the child. Her words about odour replayed in his mind. "These are fresh clothes I put on this morning."

She scrutinised his outfit. "You look different when you're not in uniform. If I didn't know better, I might mistake you for a civilian."

He tugged on his shirt. "I suppose. I'm not used to wearing regulars."

The water warmed, and he poured it into the basin. Alaura removed the jacket from around Isla and lowered her into the bath.

Bronwyn placed the kettle on a trivet. Turning back, he saw red marks on Isla's buttocks and lower back. He grimaced. "Where did they come from? It looks as though she's been beaten with a stick."

"Her das. Keiron abused many."

His shame came immediately when he remembered the incident in the Private Audience Room when Isla had spilt water on his clean uniform. She had good reason to believe he'd strike her. He inwardly vowed to work harder to control his anger. He didn't want the child to fear him.

When she finished bathing Isla, she wrapped her in a towel, then scanned the room, seeking a place to sit. She frowned at the chesterfield.

"Here." He pointed to the bed. "The mattress is new."

She hesitated.

"It's okay." He sensed sitting on his bed made her uncomfortable. Nevertheless, she settled on the edge near the foot and dried Isla.

"What's the crate for?"

He shrugged. "It's an old crate." He stepped into the water closet to dispose of the bath water.

When he returned, she frowned at him. "Did Isla sleep there last night?"

A sheepish grin spread across his face. "I'll get a more appropriate bed. I didn't think she'd be this big." In fact, he had only bargained on caring for a monkey, not a hauflin child.

"There's a shop on Masonry Lane that sells beds for children of all sizes."

He nodded.

"You'll have to train Isla to sleep in her bed. She's never had one of her own."

He glanced at his pillow. Was this why she had curled up next to him instead of going to the crate? He released a heavy sigh as he thought about the special attention the child would need. "I'm not sure... No, I'm not the right person to care for this child. She needs more than I can give her." Overwhelmed, he sat on the bed next to Alaura, folded his hands together and rested his elbows on his knees.

"I agree," she said. "Isla needs a caregiver with a passion for children to make up for the years of neglect."

He could see she didn't think him to be that person. Sadly, he agreed with her. His gaze fell upon the floor. "I'm a single man. I can't do this by myself."

"No one said you had to."

He looked at her. The sparkle in her eyes held his attention. What did she offer?

"Families don't exist in bubbles. Families with both a meeme and a das get outside help. Teachers, grandparents, aunts and uncles and friends lend a hand. It's the collaboration of all these individuals which help a child grow and prosper."

"Will you help?"

She smiled and embraced the child. "I'd take her every day if I could. Certainly, I can manage several days a week."

"That'd be great. Do you think Catriona will volunteer, too?"

"You'll have to apologise a hundred times on your knees with a dragon patty on your head if you want *her* help."

He cringed, recalling what he had said yesterday. Alaura of Niamh had brought out the worst in him. He had to mend the hole in their relationship if he expected her help. "I'm sorry for what I said to you. My temper got the best of me."

"Apology accepted. I'm sorry for striking you. It's not my usual method for dealing with frustration." She glanced at the small bruise on his cheek. "I hope I didn't hurt you."

"No," he lied. She appeared weaker than her slap dictated. "People with less beauty have hit me harder." He smiled to make light of it. "You caught me off guard is all. I'll try to not let it happen again." The pleasantness with which he had become familiar with over the years returned to her features. He believed this face to be lovelier than when her stubbornness and overbearing side dominated.

"I hope we can put our differences aside. For Isla's sake, we should be congenial."

"How about friends?" They could only be friends; they lived very different lives.

"Friends. Sounds nice." She coddled the child and caressed her cheek. "Isla, you have a new das. He's much nicer than the old one. This one is in training, so you'll have to forgive his mistakes." She winked at her. "This is going to be your home, but you'll still see me every day. Okay?"

Isla wrapped her arms around Alaura's neck. "Isla safe?"

"Isla is safe."

"It feels like you're her mum," he said.

"Meeme. Hauflins call their mum meeme. Dads are called das." She reached for Isla's clothes. "On second thought." She handed the clothes to him. "Isla's new das should dress her." She plopped the child on his lap, catching him off guard.

"I don't think this will be where my problems lie."

Isla sat quietly, gazing up at him while he dressed her. When he put her shoes on, she tried to kick them off, but he tied them tightly so they'd stay on.

"Isla has fine clothes," he said. "Did you buy them?"

"I made them."

"They're beautiful."

"Thanks. I make items—shirts, vests, pouches—and sell them at the market."

"My sisters own a dress shop. Maybe you could sell items there."

"Your mum introduced them to me a few years ago. I buy many of my supplies from them, and they sell my items on consignment."

"I didn't know." How did Alaura know so many members of his family, yet he had never spoken with her?

"I suppose you wouldn't. Your mum says she seldom sees you."

He hadn't realised so much time had passed since he last visited his parents' dwelling. But his mum knew. The youngest of her brood of seven, she considered him her baby. Surely, he had outgrown the humiliating title by now.

"I must go." She stood and walked to the door. "I have an appointment."

He followed with Isla in his arms. "An appointment? Outside of Maskil?"

She turned. "Why do you ask?"

"Curious." He didn't want her to think he watched her movements. "I'm often on the wall when you pass through the gates. I wondered where you went. Linden Woods? Moon Meadow? Or perhaps the Foothills?"

"Moon Meadow. I have a friend there."

Searching his memories, he imagined the most likely dwelling she'd visit. "Beathas of Ailsa?"

"How did you know?" She eyed him suspiciously.

"Beathas is an old friend of my parents. But you probably know this. I visited her many times when I travelled with my dad in my youth. Given your craft, she'd be the most likely person you'd visit."

"In your youth? You make yourself sound old."

He grinned. "There are days, I feel as if I've kicked around a hundred years instead of twenty-five."

"Then you should concentrate on enjoying life more instead of wearing out your uniform."

"Maybe you could teach me how." His face flushed, and he clamped his lips shut. His words hadn't come out right. This beautiful woman wouldn't be interested in him. She probably had a dozen men trailing her, vying for her attention.

She gazed at him sideways with one eyebrow raised. "I'm sure you'll manage on your own." She opened the door and paused to look back at him.

He sensed she once again sized up his qualities as a caregiver. A gentle smile creased her lips. She leant forward, kissed Isla on the forehead and patted him on the arm. "I'll see you both tomorrow. In the meantime, introduce your mum to her new grandchild." She winked, then slipped from the room.

10

The Forest Owned Her

ISLA DOVE beneath the large fern. Her heart pounded against her chest as she struggled to hide from view. The cool moist ground kissed her cheek, stained her bare feet and knees, and soiled her clothes, but she didn't notice. She waited here to catch her breath before setting out for the safety of the great oak.

A bird screeched high above in the canopy of the trees. Eight, nine, ten. Isla slipped from beneath the fern and wove around a boulder in her path. The great oak grew nearby. Her eyes darted left and right, looking for the hunter. If he found her... She shuddered at the thought.

A shadow leapt from the depths of a leafy bush, driving her into soft moss. She rolled several times before crashing into the trunk of a tree where she lay on her back, gasping for breath and realising once again today, she had lost.

Liam lay beside her, wearing a big grin. "That makes two weeks' worth of oatmeal raisin cookies!"

She laughed and slapped her friend in play. "I'm taking to the trees the next time." Liam had grown faster, stronger. Alaura said he would, being a boy, but Isla still had a few tricks. It pleased her that his meeme had allowed him to join her and Alaura at Moon Meadow after the session hall closed for the day. Out here in the forest, they ran and played freely without the watchful eyes of adults. At twelve, she didn't need constant supervision.

"You should be sneakier, less honourable," said Liam.

"Sneakier, yes, but less honourable is not an option."

He grinned. "At times life, not the person, dictates the level of honour. No use being honourable and dead." He jumped to his feet and put out a hand to help her up. "Let's cool off in the pool."

"I'd race you, but you've had the rest from waiting in the bush." She playfully pulled on his shirt. "You'd win, and I've lost enough today."

The two hauflins had known each other for about seven years, since Bronwyn hired Liam's meeme, a former teacher, to tutor Isla. Since then, they'd become best friends.

They made their way along the thin trail towards the river and their favourite swimming pool. Within minutes, they dove beneath the cool water. After splashing about, chasing an otter and scaring a mother duck, the youths climbed onto the grassy bank to dry.

Isla lay on her side, watching clouds drift by. Her gaze fell upon the calm water of the pool and skipped across the surface to where the shortest of the waterfalls cast rainbows into the air. Beathas' home grew on a ledge surrounded by several waterfalls of various heights. Green outcrops of ferns, bushes and blossoming trees that reached out to catch the rising mist, divided the walls of water. A narrow but sturdy bridge joined the jut of land to the forest. If not for the bridge, the journey to Beathas' would be both wet and dangerous.

Beathas had once said the forest owned her home and by its grace, permitted her to dwell there. Isla believed her. The forest grew around the wooden structure, cradling it in its arms as a meeme embraced a newborn. At certain times when Isla hunted for the cottage, she couldn't see it; the lush foliage and rich colours that painted the seasons fooled the eyes into believing it didn't exist. During these times, she found her way from memory, surprised each time she stumbled upon the bridge which appeared out of nowhere.

Isla sighed, closed her eyes and rolled to her back. She felt at home here, nestled in the heat and humidity of the forest. The smell of dampness and green growth filled her pores and ignited a curious energy. If not for returning to Maskil soon, she'd have dozed off. Hearing Liam rustle the grass beside her, she opened one eye. He dug for her leather pouch, the same one Alaura had given her years ago.

"Any cookies left?" He unfastened the clasp and peeked inside.

"A few." Liam always felt hungry these days. *I'm a growing boy*, he often said when she rolled her eyes at his need for extra food. She disagreed. He simply loved oatmeal raisin cookies.

"What's this?" He pulled a small leather-bound book from the pouch and read the title. "A *Trail of Hope*."

"Alaura gave it to me."

"What's it about?"

"This girl gets lost in the forest, and all she has to mark her trail are the pages from the book she's reading."

"Sounds silly." He found the sack of cookies. Only two remained. He lifted the secret flap on the bottom of the pouch to see if she had hidden any there. She hadn't. Only her special stones she took everywhere rested inside.

"No; it's good. There are dragons, friendly fairies and naughty brownies in the water. I'm at the part where she has only one page left. She can't decide if she should use it to mark her trail or carry it with her."

"Why would she carry it with her?"

"She thinks there may be an important spot farther along the trail where she could use it. She also thinks since it's the last page, she should keep it; it's the only thing to remind her of home and the book she loves."

"Is anyone following her trail?" He finished the first cookie and started on the second.

"Her das and older brother."

"Then why doesn't she go back and pick up all the pages. Eventually, she'd find them."

"She doesn't know they're following." She put out her hand. "May I have the last bite?"

He looked long and hard at the small chunk of cookie, then placed it in her hand. "If you need it, but I *am* a growing boy." He leant close to watch her pop it into her mouth.

She ruffled his hair. "I'd do the same for you."

He smiled widely, his brown eyes shining. "Even if you were starving?"

She nodded and his gaze sweep across her face. He was a handsome boy, and she knew he thought her to be beautiful though she believed otherwise. He'd let that secret slip one day after he had tackled her in the snow. All the same, she wouldn't tell what she thought of him.

Liam rolled to his belly and propped himself up on his elbows. He pulled two thick blades of grass from their roots and tried to make a horn sound by blowing on them while pressed between his thumbs.

His most recent challenge was grass blowing. Last week, whistling with two fingers pressed against his tongue had been his obsession. He failed at that, too. The deep blue stone swinging from his neck reflected sunlight into her face. She had fashioned a necklace from the translucent cube years earlier. Since then, he always wore it.

After she heard enough raucous sounds from the grass, she sat up and gathered her things. "We should return to the cottage. Alaura will look for us."

He stood. "Are you coming again tomorrow?"

"No. Alaura won't be able to bring me." She walked along the edge of the pool towards Beathas' cottage. "But I'll be here the next day. Ask your meeme if you can come, too."

"I will." He followed her through the undergrowth along the water's edge. "Do you think Alaura will let us ride Clover?"

"I'm sure she will." As long as they stayed within the perimeter of Beathas' covert they remained safe. Though Beathas had never explained, Isla knew forces other than the breath of nature made the wind chimes hanging near her cottage door sing. She believed they alerted Beathas to approaching danger.

She climbed the ridge until she could go no farther by herself. Liam hoisted her up to the next level. Once there, she pulled up him.

Before long the hauflins crossed the wooden bridge to Beathas' dwelling. The cottage, speckled with dandelion yellow, lilac purple and rose red hues, blended in with the blooming foliage surrounding it. Sumortide neared, and every plant wore its formal attire.

Alaura's head rose from the basket of herbs on her lap. "Goodness, look at you both! Did you roll in mud?"

Isla and Liam grinned. Although they appeared in their usual state after a day at Moon Meadow, Alaura acted surprised. Isla guessed adults had to express such thoughts this way.

"Go put on fresh clothes. If I take you home like this, your parents will never let you come again." Alaura shook her head as the hauflins entered the cottage.

಄ ❖ ಬ

Bronwyn pushed the silver pin through the lapel of the guard's vest. Although officially still a private, the triangular pin indicated recommended for promotion. The guard, a corporal in training, would take charge of ten men, making him the forty-fifth junior corporal unofficially promoted in the past two years. His own promotion to sergeant fourteen months earlier had better equipped him to instruct his men to respect the junior corporal rank.

He had tried to promote men officially, but the lords had declined all but a handful of his recommendations. Sanderson agreed with most of his referrals but couldn't grant them all. Still, the captain of the guard saw the benefits of junior corporals and supported his efforts to gain control over the privates who desperately outnumbered the officers.

"I know you'll respect this pin, Junior Corporal Cronin." Bronwyn stood back and saluted the guard.

Sawney Cronin turned to the ten privates who stood at attention, watching the formality. These men were now his responsibility. They saluted him in unison.

"You may take possession of your men. Serve them competently." Bronwyn nodded at Sawney and let him lead the men from the courtyard.

"I think he'll do well." Farlan stepped up behind Bronwyn. "Sawney is tough, but he knows when the men have had enough."

"I'm sure you're right."

"Have you spoken with Tibs?" The human pulled several pumpkin seeds from his pocket and popped them into his mouth.

"I've arranged to meet with him at day's end."

"I wonder what he wants." Farlan crossed his arms and surveyed the empty courtyard. "I hope it doesn't have anything to do with the drills. The last change was ridiculous."

Bronwyn put his hands in his trousers pockets. His left hand fingered the small rectangular stone Isla had given him years before. Though he had planned to return it to her pouch, he never did. Instead, he carried it with him every day. When considering matters of importance, he liked to hold the stone. It cleared his mind.

"I don't know what he wants. He gave no indication."

"Let me know if it's anything serious."

"Will you be in your quarters this evening?"

"No, I'll be busy." Farlan smiled mischievously. "After I visit the castle gate, I'm off duty."

"And Selina?" He grinned. "Will she be busy, too?" Farlan had dated Selina for about two years. He thought they made a perfect pair; Farlan enjoyed a good joke, and she loved to laugh.

"She might be." He winked and backed away. "You'll have to tell me about Tib's meeting in the morning."

The two waved good-bye and headed in different directions.

Farlan walked through the guardhouse and headed for the front gates of Maskil. Along the way, he saluted fellow guards, waved to friends and stopped to help a young elf tie his shoes.

"Corporal Burkenshaw." The privates saluted Farlan as he approached the gate.

He returned the gesture. "Any troubles or concerns?"

"No, sir." A tall blond man stepped up to make the report. "Bored all day. It'd be nice to get a little excitement now and again."

"Excitement costs lives, Macky."

A warning blast alerted the guards of an approaching traveller.

Alaura led Isla and Liam towards the town gates. The hauflin children raced and skipped, playing tag from what Farlan could judge.

"Good afternoon, Alaura." He gave a slight bow to acknowledge her arrival. The attractive woman presented herself unlike any he knew. She had an inner strength he respected.

"It's a fine afternoon, Farlan. I mean, Corporal."

"How are the two rascals?" He flicked Isla's nose, and she made a funny face. When she became Bronwyn's ward, he took on extra responsibilities. He and Bronwyn spent a lot of their leisure time together; Isla naturally tagged along. He enjoyed the days and nights passed entertaining her while her das patrolled.

"As active as ever." Alaura smiled. "Have you seen Bronwyn?"

"He's at the guardhouse," he said. Her eyes lit up as they always did when she spoke of his friend. He'd have considered this lovely woman himself if not for her relationship with Bronwyn. She befuddled the otherwise rigid sergeant like no other. She also ignited a smile for no reason or sent him on an uncontrollable tantrum. This surprised Farlan at first, but over the years he came to understand why: Bronwyn's blood burnt for Alaura.

Farlan pointed in the general direction of the castle. "He's in a meeting but shouldn't be long."

"I'll wait for him at the bakery." Alaura gestured at the children. "Let's go."

As they passed, he grabbed Isla and tickled her sides. She giggled and wriggled until he stopped. "Little Sprite, that's payback for the lizard in my boot." She laughed harder as he kissed the top of her head and sent her on her way.

11

Magic of the Night

BRONWYN SAT in a chair opposite Captain Tibbins. The captain's thick wooden desk separated them, and tapestries, weaponry, plaques, flags and awards filled the walls. Each time he entered the room, the elaborate decorations overwhelmed him. He remembered his first visit several years ago; the dazzling display of military memorabilia had enthralled him to the point he'd have missed the conversation if not for Sanderson nudging him constantly.

Today the items had lost their lustre, and he couldn't wait to leave. For the third time in as many months, Captain Tibbins offered him the opportunity to earn valour by accepting a quest. It wouldn't be a difficult mission, but one valuable to Aruam Castle.

He felt compelled to accept simply because the captain had asked. Captain Tibbins insisted the journey contained little danger.

The assignment sounded safer than the previous two quests, but why had Tibs selected him; Sanderson needed him here. A warning from the captain of the guard nagged at him: *Quest? If they offer one, turn it down.* He had asked why, but Sanderson only said, *Don't throw away your career for a ridiculous quest of honour.*

Captain Tibbins finished his speech, and Bronwyn cleared his throat. "Sir, I appreciate the fact you personally solicited me for this quest, but I graciously decline."

"Sergeant, I don't understand. I offer you a chance to prove to yourself as well as to others you're a worthy fighter, that you place the security and well-being of this castle and the citizens of Maskil before anything else, but here you are, denying me your services once again."

"I understand this is an important quest, but I believe there are others who could handle this business."

"I could order you to accept the mission." The corner of Captain Tibbins' mouth twitched.

For a long time, he had feared this type of order. He, however, had one advantage over other sergeants. "Sir, I bring to your attention I have a child, and that I'm the sole provider for her well-being."

Tibbins scoffed at the idea. "Surely, you have family who could tend to this child whilst you're away."

"It's not while I'm away that concerns me. If I don't return, she'll be an orphan." He braced himself. "Captain Tibbins, with all due respect I decline your offer on the grounds of being a single provider for a child."

Captain Tibbins drummed his fingers on the desk and stared at him with cold blue eyes. "Dismissed."

Though lucky this time, Bronwyn's gut forewarned another imminent request. He'd visit Sanderson's office to see if he was there. Given the time, the captain of the guard probably enjoyed his evening elsewhere. His hunch proved correct; Sanderson's office sat empty. He'd meet with him in the morning.

Turning abruptly, he bumped into Riagan, a dwarf who worked in the military records office.

"Excuse me." He caught her arm before she stumbled to the floor.

Riagan giggled as she steadied herself. She slipped her hand into his and pulled him near. "No harm done."

He tried to pull away, but she held him firm. "I didn't see you there. My thoughts distracted me."

She leant near. "Thoughts of a woman or work?"

The attractive woman flattered him with her attention. "Work."

"I thought you might be thinking of me." She winked.

"Business. You know me. Always business."

"What does a woman need to do to get your attention?" She slid her hand to the back of his neck and pushed her fingers into his hair.

He held her at bay. Though pretty, he had no feelings for her. "Riagan, I'm on duty."

"Later then?" She smiled and softened her eyes.

He forced her hand from his hair and held her at arms' length. "I have other commitments."

A frown knotted her face. "With that human?"

She didn't like Alaura; he saw it in her eyes when the women passed each other in the hall. Alaura felt indifferent to her jealousy. While not his mate, his thoughts dwelt on the enchanting half-breed, part human, part hauflin. Since Isla had become his ward, his daughter, Alaura had become a constant presence in his life. She helped him through the stages of childhood and often tended to Isla while he patrolled. He didn't know what he'd have done if she hadn't stepped forward to help him.

"Alaura is my friend, a best friend. But tonight, I'll be with my daughter."

Riagan dropped her hands. "Maybe another time."

"Have a good evening," he said, slipping out of range and leaving the office area. He almost reached the exit of the guardhouse when he saw Lady Dasia staring out of a window overlooking the courtyard. Though already late to pick up Isla at the bakery, he felt compelled to stop and enquire about the woman's well-being.

"My Lady, is there anything you need?" He stood off to the side and waited for her to acknowledge him. She appeared sad, as if yearning for a lost love.

Lady Dasia closed her eyes and spoke in a subdued voice. "There is." A tear slipped down her cheek.

"What is it, My Lady?" He stepped forward. "Should I summon Lord Nevell?"

She shook her head as a gentle smile creased her lips. "Healing is not what I seek." Again, she gazed out at the courtyard. "Do you see what I see?"

He stepped closer to the window and considered the view: stone walls surrounded the workout area for his men. "What am I to see?"

"It's empty." Her smile grew. "Everyone has gone home or is on their way to loved ones."

"Training is over for the day, My Lady."

"Emptiness can be more moving than anything else. Yet, it is what many fear." She eyed him. "Do you?"

He cocked his head. "I don't fear an empty courtyard, an empty room or anything else which doesn't contain people."

"Because you carry those you love in your heart." She touched his shoulder. "The growth of that love started small and has grown quite large. I'm proud of you."

He assumed she talked about Isla. He had never asked, but he held little doubt she had orchestrated his taking possession of the child.

"You bring life to the castle with your open show of emotions. The castle looks kindly upon you three."

Three? She meant Alaura, too. "I hardly think a stone structure is watching us."

She leant close. "Don't be so sure." Returning her attention to the courtyard, she sighed. "We all must make sacrifices to initiate change; occasionally what we surrender is life altering." She fell silent and played with an item in her hand and although he couldn't see it clearly, he thought it to be a coin or other round object.

"I have a favour to ask, Bronwyn." She spoke without looking at him. "Are you up for a challenge?"

"Whatever you ask, My Lady. It's my duty to serve."

"No." She turned on him. "This has nothing to do with your duty or this castle! This is personal. I ask you as Bronwyn Darrow to help me, Glynn Dasia of Moonsface."

The urgency in her voice startled him. "What is it you wish, Glynn Dasia? I'm honoured you asked me."

"I'm sorry. I should not speak to you in this manner. It is..." She opened her hand and stared at the object resting on her palm.

The decorative belt buckle puzzled him. It appeared ancient. "My Lady, I mean, Glynn, you seem upset." His temperature rose as he ventured into unfamiliar territory.

"It will pass." She placed the buckle in his hand and wrapped his fingers around it. "I wish for you to give this to someone."

"Who?"

She grinned. "And there lies the challenge."

"I don't understand."

"I cannot give you a name. You'll know the person when you meet them. I can tell you this individual is elf, like myself. They are not in Maskil, but they might visit." She bent near. "You have never met them, but you'll know it is they when you see them. Give this to them and answer all their questions."

"Am I to leave Maskil and search for them?"

She shook her head. "They'll find you. Wear it as your own for everyone to see."

"I'll affix it to my belt this evening." He slipped the buckle into his pocket.

"Thank you, Bronwyn. I can never repay you for your kindness in this matter."

"Payment isn't necessary, My...Glynn. I'm honoured to help." He leant close to her ear. "Do *you* know the person I'm to give this to?" Her expression filled with doubt.

She wrapped her arms around his neck and whispered in his ear. "They are the dearest to my heart, ones I've not had the pleasure to embrace in many years." Her breath caught. "I trust you more than many in this castle and now, I entrust my greatest gift to you. Give them my love and share me with them."

He felt dizzy as her voice and hot breath consumed his ear. If not for her embrace, he might have stumbled. Though he didn't know the spell she casted, a rush of energy surged into his body. He felt her heart breaking, but he could do nothing to ease her pain. When he steadied, she released him and turned back to the window.

"Glynn, I promise I'll do everything you ask to the best of my ability."

"And that sets my heart free." She paused, and her eyes glistened. "Go to the ones who love you. Both young and old await your arrival." As he turned to leave, her distant voice stopped him. "You are a fortunate man, Bronwyn Darrow, though there will be times you think otherwise."

He felt fortunate to have good friends and family. "And you are loved by many though at times you might feel alone." The surprise in her eyes made him chuckle. "We all forget the obvious now and again."

He walked away from the guardhouse with lighter feet. Serving his favourite lord made him proud. Though unsure of how or when his task would be completed, he felt positive he'd succeed.

❀ ❖ ❀

Bronwyn entered the Forest Bakery and Herb Shop and found Alaura waiting for him.

"You're still here." He slid his hands onto his hips and straightened his back but at his tallest, he still stood shorter than her. Maybe if she wore no shoes they'd be the same height. "I thought you'd have left by now."

"I was talking with your mum and Finola." She smiled and clasped her hands behind her back. "We made plans for two days from now. Isla and Liam wish to come to Moon Meadow for the day."

"Will it be a problem?" He caught her scent, fresh from the forest, and couldn't rein in his smile.

"It's fine." She tucked her loose hair behind her ears. "We're going to have a picnic on the ridge."

A *picnic*? He'd love to go. His mind mapped ways to get himself invited.

The door to the back room opened, and Maisie Darrow and Isla entered the shop.

"Das!" Isla ran to him and jumped into his arms. "You're late." She wrapped her arms around his neck and squeezed.

~ 97 ~

He hugged her warmly. Since becoming a family, they had had their battles but for the most part, they enjoyed life. Their routine made them both happy, and they had grown closer than he had imagined possible.

"Things must be busy at the castle," said Maisie.

"Not really." He thought about his meeting with Captain Tibbins; his reasons for refusing the quest and staying in Maskil surrounded him.

The bell over the front door rang and his sisters, Rhiannon and Loran, entered.

While the girls said hello to Alaura, Maisie discreetly spoke to Bronwyn. "You should stay for the evening ration. I've cooked extra."

"I'd love to, Mum." He released Isla from his arms, and she went to his sisters.

Maisie tugged on his sleeve and whispered, "Ask Alaura to stay, too."

"What?" He hadn't heard her words clearly, but when she repeated her request, which sounded more like an order, and pinched his arm, he jumped into action. "Alaura, would you like to stay for the evening ration?"

Alaura shook her head. "Thank you, but I don't wish to inconvenience your mum."

"Nonsense. Stay. There's plenty of food." Maisie placed a hand on her son's forearm. "I should have asked myself. Leave it to Bronwyn to think of you going home to your lonely room."

He gave his mum a side-ways glance.

"I shouldn't," said Alaura.

"Yes, you should," said Loran and Rhiannon together.

"A fantastic material arrived at the shop today." Rhiannon's voice rose with excitement. "I want to tell you all about it."

"You can tell me tomorrow." Alaura stepped back. "Your mum already has plenty around the table."

"One more never hurts." Loran looped her arm around Alaura's and guided her through the bakery.

"Rhiannon, flip the sign and lock the door." Maisie tossed a mischievous glance at Bronwyn, then followed the girls upstairs.

"Look what Loran made." Isla held up a dark blue vest with diamond embroidery. "It's like yours."

He held out the bottom of the jerkin for a better view. "Did you ask her to make this for you?"

She nodded. "I'm going to be like you and wear it everywhere." She slipped her arms into the holes of the jerkin, fastened the three buttons and danced around the bakery.

He smiled at her happiness but before he could say anything, a force on his arm propelled him towards the back room.

"You should have changed your clothes at the castle." Rhiannon's nose crinkled, and she eased her grip on him. "You look and smell as if you've hung out in the stables all day."

"I did." He glanced at his uniform and saw the dirt that until now had avoided notice. "It's only a ration."

"Men!" Rhiannon rolled her eyes. "Isla, come upstairs with me. You," she pointed a finger at her brother, "clean yourself up. We have a guest."

ℝ ❖ ℞

By the time Maisie and her mate Gaven completed the preparations for the evening ration, Loran and Rhiannon had the table set. Loran guided Alaura to the seat at the end, next to her dad. Bronwyn sat directly across from her.

Moments earlier, when he had attempted to leave his former bedroom, Rhiannon had stepped in to inspect him. Without asking, she removed his uniform vest and threw it on the bed. He fussed about it, but she ignored him and unfastened the top button of his shirt. When she went for the second button, he stopped her.

"Fine." She tugged at the scabbard belt.

He pushed her hands away but finished what she had started and placed the sword and scabbard beside the vest on the bed. "Satisfied?"

She stepped back and scrutinized him from head to toe, then tucked a hair into place, straightened his shirt over his shoulders and adjusted his trousers. By the time she finished, the nerves in his neck twitched and his face warmed. She kissed his cheek and gave him a hug.

~ 99 ~

"You were a cute little brother, but now you're a handsome man. Alaura likes you. Don't worry."

Only two years in the age difference, they had grown up together. They had shared secrets, and she knew about his bashfulness better than most. He tolerated her nit-picking more than their older sisters' because they shared the same mind set; shyness afflicted her, too, but she hid it better.

"Now that you've primped and preened me, you tell me not to worry?"

"Bronwyn, be yourself. You're a sweetheart. You don't have to worry about Alaura liking you; she does. I can see it in her eyes when she talks about you."

"You talk to Alaura about me?" He swallowed hard.

She rolled her eyes. "We talk about everyone. But when you enter the conversation, her voice softens, and I see she's thinking sweet thoughts about you."

He endeavoured to hold in the smile but couldn't. It quickly faded, and he turned serious. "Can't we enjoy the ration and forget about all this stuff?"

"Is it what you want?"

He nodded.

"Fine." She grabbed his hand and pulled him from the bedroom.

Now, with Alaura sitting directly across the table, he felt on display. He shouldn't have combed his hair. She'd think he'd done it for her. While he had, he didn't want her to know it. Cursing himself for his lack of confidence, he agonized about all the stupid things that had worried him as a teen during his attempts to impress girls at the study hall. His parents and sisters watching his every move only intensified his self-consciousness.

Beside him, Isla nibbled on a biscuit while waiting for the ration to begin. He placed a hand on her shoulder to steady his nerves. She smiled up at him and slid closer, fitting under his arm pit. He kissed the top of her head, pinched a corner from the biscuit and popped it into his mouth.

He glanced at Rhiannon and Loran, who sat to the left of Alaura. His sisters chatted and laughed with her. Their skills with needles and thread had them looking their best.

"It's good to see so many happy faces around my table." Maisie sat at the end and smiled the warm smile of a mum pleased to be surrounded by family. As she prepared to grant permission to begin eating, footsteps sounded on the stairs leading to the second-floor dwelling.

ೞ ❖ ೞ

"Joris. Isn't this a surprise?"

Although his mum smiled, her voice sounded as though she wasn't happy to see him. He glanced around the table and saw his dad, younger siblings and Alaura of Niamh, the woman his brother drooled to have but couldn't build up the courage to claim. Releasing a low snicker, his mind worked on ways to entertain himself at his brother's expense. "The surprise is mine; look at this fine ration." He plopped down in the empty chair between Isla and his mum. "How is my little nymph?" He tickled Isla's neck and pretended to reach for the biscuit.

She grinned and stuck out her chest to show off the jerkin.

"That's the prettiest jerkin I've ever seen."

"Vest."

"Of course." He glanced at Bronwyn and winked.

Maisie retrieved a plate for her older son and filled it to the edge.

"Mum, you're certainly generous tonight." He gawked at the mound of food on his plate.

"Remember *not to talk* with your mouth full. We have a guest." She patted him on the forearm sternly and lowered her brow. "You may begin the ration."

Joris ogled the guest. She was pretty by hauflin standards, but her human features dulled her beauty. She appeared too delicate for his liking, and her reserve manner told him she'd be a boring date. However, these shortcomings hadn't stopped his brother from becoming infatuated with her and tonight, he'd stir the embers to see if a flame erupted. "Alaura, you add more beauty to this table than a hundred bouquets of delicate flowers."

She tried to suppress a smile. "I'm sure the flowers would do the ration more justice."

"I could argue the fact but don't wish to disagree with one so enchanting." He glanced at Bronwyn. "I'm jealous; little brother has the best view."

A reddish hue grew on Bronwyn's neck. He dug his fork into a slice of potato and put it into his mouth, keeping his eyes on his ration.

"Joris, you should eat before it gets cold." Maisie gripped his arm. "You look unwell. Have you been eating properly?"

"I'm fine, Mum. Never felt better." Joris stabbed a carrot and propelled it into his mouth.

Between the clinking of silverware, Rhiannon and Loran told Alaura about the new material at their dress shop. Their discussion changed to designs they wanted to try and gossip about a nasty customer who refused to pay full price for anything.

Bored by the conversation, Joris tickled Isla's side. "How is Liam? Has he stolen a kiss, yet?"

Isla grinned. "Why would he kiss me?"

He leant near her ear. "Because that's what boys do."

She pushed him away. "Liam won't. He's my best friend."

"He will. One of these days he's going to lean in to see dirt on your cheek." He glided past her defences. "He'll flash those eyes and cast a Be-still Spell so you can't move and before you know it, wham!" He kissed her on the forehead. "He'll steal the first kiss."

"What if I push him away?"

"He'll try again. If a boy likes a girl, he'll keep trying for years. And Liam is sweet on you."

"What if *I* steal the kiss first?"

"Then I'd say you're nothing like your das." Glancing at Bronwyn, he bet he hadn't stolen his first kiss from Alaura. But why did she wait; most women would have moved on by now. Could it be bashfulness had claimed her, too?

Bronwyn grunted and frowned at him. "Isla's only twelve; too young to think of that stuff."

"*That stuff* brings dreams to life." Joris raised his voice. "It makes you feel alive in all the right places; a sensation you can't get from an immaculate uniform."

Beneath the table, Maisie discreetly kicked him in the shin and smiled. "Leave room for dessert. I made lemon pie."

Joris jumped from the surprise as much as from the sharp pain and stared at his mum. "Lemon pie? I love lemon pie." He bent towards Isla and chuckled. "So much, I think I'll kiss it."

He watched Bronwyn steal glances at Alaura. His obsession with the enchantress couldn't be more obvious. Alaura appeared less transparent. His brother could catch her for a mate if he set his mind to the task, but he never used his good looks to his advantage. If *he* had those features, he'd flaunt them. Regulations and duty filled Bronwyn's thoughts, and he didn't live for the moment. He looked sharp and secure in his uniform, but he couldn't hide behind it forever.

Joris slid his leg out of his mum's reach. "Alaura, it'll be dark by the time we finish the ration. I'll walk you home to ensure you arrive safely." He saw his mum make the kick, but she didn't make contact.

"Never you mind, Joris." Maisie glared at him. "Bronwyn invited Alaura to stay. He'll see her home."

He didn't look at his mum. She had always protected her baby, but Bronwyn needed a type of courage he couldn't get from wielding a sword. "It'll be no problem, only my pleasure. And Bronwyn can get this little nymph home and into bed." He patted Isla's head.

"Thank you for the offer," said Alaura, "but I'm capable of walking home alone."

"Nonsense. Bronwyn will escort you." Maisie eyed her son. "Bronwyn?"

"Of course." Bronwyn rested his silverware on the table and furrowed his brow. "Alaura, it'll be an honour to protect your virtues from the fiends who roam the streets as well as those with whom we share our ration." He grinned at her, and she gazed back with her hand over her mouth to hide her smile. Her eyes sparkled, and his gaze lingered.

Joris put a forkful of food into his mouth. He loved his brother and would give his life for him, but he wouldn't coddle him.

Bronwyn held Isla's hand as they walked along the street towards Alaura's dwelling. He took in a full breath of night air and savoured the taste. It swallowed easily unlike the sticky air usually found within the town walls during Springan. The crisp, clean air had an unmistakable energy which heightened his awareness, making his calloused hands feel the tenderness in Isla's.

Alaura pulled her dark cloak snuggly around her. Yet she didn't appear to mind the coolness. With each new breath, her smile deepened and her features softened. She felt the energy in the night as well.

Isla slipped from his grip and skipped the remaining fifty feet to Alaura's stoop. She slid on one of the rails as she awaited their arrival. Not willing to abandon the night so soon, Alaura and Bronwyn rested against the rails and gazed off into the distance.

"It was kind of you to invite me to the evening ration." She broke the silence, but he didn't mind. Her voice sang on the breeze and added to the magic of the night.

"I'm glad you stayed. I enjoy your company." When she noticed his stare, her breath caught. He held her gaze and saw the start of a smile on the corner of her lips before she diverted her eyes.

"Bronwyn, you've changed since becoming Isla's das. You're not the same rogue you appeared to be that day at the castle. I mean...you appeared gruff."

"I don't think I've changed as much as I've returned to who I used to be in my youth." He smiled with an easiness he hadn't felt for a long time. "I guess in the struggle to advance in the ranks, I had lost sight of the important things in life. Isla and...and you helped me see the missing pieces." For the first time, he felt truly satisfied. He needed only one more thing to make his life complete. Taking a deep breath, he gathered courage from the night air.

"I wondered," he began as he always did when faced with this dilemma, "if you would... I mean... Are you free tomorrow evening?"

She pulled her cloak tighter around her.

"We could enjoy the food and entertainment at the Glenelg Inn. I can come by..."

She shook her head. "I have lessons with Beathas. I won't be back in town until late."

"I'll wait—"

"No! I mean... I don't want to inconvenience you. I'll be busy with my studies and work." She cast her eyes to her hands, then her door.

"Another time maybe." He tried to brush it off but once again, he regretted taking the chance to see if she'd accompany him on an outing. He had to accept the fact she didn't think of him as he thought of her. Rhiannon had presumed wrong. Alaura considered him a friend, probably because of his different race. It didn't help that he lacked magic. She needed a slim-built human, a man taller and experienced at satisfying a woman like her. If the human possessed magic, he'd be the perfect mate. She had avoided other offers for her time, and though he promised himself he'd never ask again, realising the way he felt, he knew he would.

"I should..." She pointed to her door. "I should go in. It's cool outside. Isla needs her sleep."

He glanced at Isla who quietly sat on the bottom step, looking into the night. "I suppose you're right. Isla." The sooner he got on his way, the sooner he didn't have to worry about the expression on his face.

Isla jumped up, climbed the stairs and wrapped her arms around Alaura's waist. "Thank you for taking me to Moon Meadow today."

"You're welcome." Alaura hugged her and kissed her cheek. When she rose, she rested her hand on Bronwyn's upper arm. "Thank you again for inviting me to the evening ration. It was thoughtful of you. Your mum is an excellent cook."

"I'll let her know. She always likes to hear she pleased the appetite." He placed his hand over hers, and she gently drew it away.

"I'll see you again." She opened the door.

"Have a good evening." He guided Isla down the steps and towards the castle. He glanced back to see Alaura slip inside and close the door. He sighed. Maybe the time had come to move on and give this whole

Alaura thing a break. He'd beaten around the bush for a few years without success; she probably thought him desperate, pathetic.

When they had almost reached the castle, Isla spoke. "Das, did Alaura make you sad?"

"I understand she's busy." Disappointment stirred in his heart more than anything. The time had come to accept the fact she held no special feelings for him.

"Maybe you should have stolen a kiss." She giggled. "I stayed quiet so you could cast a Be-still Spell."

"Isla! Don't listen to your uncle Joris. At times he says things he shouldn't." Then again, he hadn't thought of stealing a kiss.

"But didn't you want to?"

"No." He sighed. Even a child could tell he lied. "It wouldn't be right. Friends don't steal kisses."

"I'll ask Alaura if you can have one. Then it wouldn't be stealing. She won't mind because you make her happy."

He didn't want to ask but couldn't help himself. "What do you mean?"

"I've seen her smile at you when you're not looking. She thinks nobody sees her, but I do." She ended in a whisper. "She likes you."

He smiled. His daughter remained innocent to the ways of men and women, but he wished she spoke the truth. Alaura often smiled. It didn't mean he ignited it.

"I'll tell Alaura you want a kiss, and she—"

"Please, don't." He didn't need a twelve-year-old begging a woman to give her das a kiss.

"Why? We talk about you all the time. I can tell Alaura anything."

Again, he couldn't resist. "What does she say about me?"

"I can't tell you. It's against the rules."

Rules? Girls and women had rules when talking about men? He stopped walking and bent to face her. "Isla, it'd make life less awkward if you didn't tell Alaura I wanted to kiss her."

"So, you *do* want to kiss her." She cupped his face with her small hands.

He gave up. How could he convince her he didn't want to kiss Alaura when he honestly did? "Let's keep this our little secret, okay?"

"Okay, das. I won't say anything." She threw her arms around his neck.

"Time will sort out the things we don't understand." He hugged her, lifted her into the air and tossed her onto his back. The rest of the way home, she rode piggy-back.

ಙ ❖ ಐ

After Bronwyn left, Alaura stepped inside her dwelling, shut the door and set the lock. Turning to face her small room, she rested her weight against the door and released the breath she'd held since he had asked her for an outing. She had almost accepted the invitation. Common sense stopped her.

There, with the night air preying on her senses, she had felt the attraction for the dwarf emerge stronger than ever before. Three steps away, his playful eyes had teased her, beholding her as a mate admired the one his blood burnt for. Those eyes hid nothing from her; he held only honest and true intentions. His moist lips, smiling to reveal his easy-going nature, appeared perfect for the kiss her mouth craved to impart. The breeze teased her, beckoned her to reach out and wrap her arms around him. She imagined his strong arms embracing her, and his gentle hands exploring her body like no other man had.

She drew deep calming breaths. Bronwyn remained only a friend. She told herself this every day to make herself believe it. The alternative held too many dangers for them. She swallowed hard. If anything happened to him because of her, she'd never forgive herself.

Realising the position in which she had put herself, she should have declined the invitation for the evening ration. But the Darrow family reminded her of her family at North Ridge, and her desire to stay had won over the need to keep her distance.

Bronwyn expected more of her, but she could never be with him. She had to stay pure. Thankfully, he hadn't forced the matter. His bashful nature kept him from saying and doing things other suitors would have tried. Still, she regretted hurting his feelings each time he gathered enough courage to ask her for her company. She wanted to say yes but duty bound her.

She should have taken Beathas' offer to accompany two other magic-maidens to Moonsface to attend an herbal training session. When asked, she had declined because she didn't want to leave Isla for three months. In truth, she didn't want to leave Bronwyn. But she should have. She needed to distance herself from him—maybe leave Maskil for good—if she wanted to remain loyal to her pledge and guard him against harm.

Staring into the darkness, still feeling Bronwyn's warm hand upon hers and still savouring his scent, she feared it to be already too late.

12

A Cloud of Confusion

❧◦❧◦❧◦❧◦❧

NOT MUCH had changed in Sanderson's office over the past seven years. The addition of a hand-drawn portrait of his likeness given to him by Isla appeared to be the only noticeable difference. The captain of the guard smiled in the picture. When he asked the young hauflin why she had drawn him in such a manner instead of with an authoritative expression, her answer surprised him: *Because I remember you smile, but occasionally you don't. This will remind you.*

This picture held Bronwyn's attention as he waited for Sanderson to complete the report in front of him.

Sanderson put down his ink pen. "What's on your mind?"

Bronwyn told him what had transpired the day before in Captain Tibbins' office. "I believe he would have ordered me to accept the quest if he had the authority. I declined the offer by exercising the single parent clause."

Sanderson listened intently. When Bronwyn finished, the captain sat back in his chair and rubbed his chin. "And his reaction when you refused?"

"Outrage. He suggested I leave Isla with family."

"He has no right to commandeer my guards for his pleasure." Sanderson scowled. "If he asks again, refuse his order. I'll deal with him. I want you here." His thick index finger struck the desk.

"Yes, sir." Relieved, he relaxed; he'd remain in Maskil with Isla and his family.

A knock came at the door, and Sanderson motioned for him to answer it. Startled, he found Lord Mulryan on the threshold. The captain of the guard stood.

"Have a seat." The lord stepped inside and closed the door. The dwarf's vivid blue eyes, a sharp contrast to his charcoal-black hair, scanned the sparsely decorated room. "Captain Tibbins requested a number of recruits for an important quest. I gave him permission to choose whom he pleased. It appears, however, not everyone feels honoured to be selected."

Bronwyn held his breath. He couldn't refuse if the lord ordered him to accept the quest; it went against protocol.

"Are you insinuating my men are cowards?" Sanderson stood to challenge the lord. His calm, authoritative voice filled the office.

"Coward isn't the appropriate word. It's lack of respect for the captain's generous offer."

"My men have the right to refuse any quest offered them. It's the Law of the Land." Sanderson picked up a heavy book and dropped it on his desk. "I challenge you to say otherwise."

Lord Mulryan grunted. "Every man should be honoured to be given the opportunity to prove themselves worthy of Aruam Castle. No brave dwarf would refuse the challenge."

"Brave dwarfs are needed at the castle. Take the sergeant for example." Sanderson gestured towards Bronwyn. "If he left for several weeks on a quest, it'd bring our re-organization plans to a standstill. Sergeant Darrow is responsible for engineering and implementing the junior corporal rank, giving structure and order to the companies. He's only one. There are many others. Each has the sense and the courage to do what is best for the castle, Maskil and her people. They won't abandon their duties simply for the sake of personal honour."

The silence in the room threatened to choke Bronwyn. His future, his very life, depended on how Lord Mulryan responded to Sanderson's speech. Quests were different than what they appeared to be. Too many times he saw good men leave and never return. He expected a certain degree of danger in a mission but a good chance of survival, too.

The dwarfen lord nodded. "You have trained your men well."

"I'd like to think I've given them every opportunity to acquire the skills needed to perform their duties to the best of their abilities, My Lord."

Lord Mulryan glanced at Bronwyn with what appeared to be more curiosity than disappointment. He turned to leave but stopped, his hand on the door knob. "What I don't understand is why a brave dwarf requested custody of a ward in the first place? Had he planned to use her in his defence of refusal?"

Bronwyn and Sanderson exchanged glances, both confounded by the lord's comment.

"My Lord, this sergeant didn't choose the ward. The lords appointed him as her guardian. Against his will, I might add."

A cloud of confusion shadowed the lord's face.

"Piffle. I'd never have agreed to such nonsense." Lord Mulryan pulled open the door and left.

Bronwyn's jaw dropped. He remembered the day as if yesterday. Lord Val had said *all the lords* had agreed upon the best guardian for Isla: him. The lord had to have known the details.

"It appears Mulryan has difficulty recalling facts." Sanderson sat in his chair. "No matter. He'll put the good captain in his place, leaving you to carry out your duties."

"Yes, sir."

When Bronwyn didn't immediately stand, the captain of the guard pointed to the door. "Your duties await."

Bronwyn stood. Before he left the office, he saw the beginning of a smile on the corner of Sanderson's mouth. Isla proved right; he did smile when the right moment presented itself.

13

The Enchanting Woman in his Bed

THE SUN drooped towards the horizon. Its rays left the heat of the day simmering on the stone walls of Aruam Castle. A fresh company of guards relieved those who had patrolled for twelve hours. Worn weary from the unusual heat of Springan's End, they stumbled from their posts, seeking the coolness only the bowels of a stone structure provided.

The sweltering temperatures made it unbearable inside Bronwyn's office. With no ventilation to permit fresh air, he struggled to concentrate on the work at hand. His thoughts drifted to images of cool water and damp moss beneath trees. The ink pen slipped from his grip. His clumsy fingers, swollen from the heat, pushed back his damp hair. A bead of sweat glided down his cheek to the rim of his chin, hung there a moment, then fell to the paper below.

To cool himself, he removed his vest, unfastened the top three buttons on his shirt and rolled up his sleeves. He appeared dishevelled, but no one would see. He planned to head to a cooler location as soon as he finished the last report in front of him.

He glanced at Isla curled up on a chair in the corner. She had spent the afternoon with Farlan. A short time ago, his friend had delivered her to the office, so he could prepare for his evening patrol.

When Isla first arrived, she had bounced around and talked non-stop about the horseback ride she, Farlan and Liam had taken along the Shulie River. For the past twenty minutes, she'd lain quiet and still. He leant to get a better view of her face to see if she slept. She stared off into the distance as if mesmerized.

He wiped sweat from his forehead and picked up the pen. He tried to read the report, but his attention drifted. Forcing himself to focus, he struggled through the last page. He placed the report in a folder with several others.

Footsteps at the door drew his attention and through hazy vision, he saw Riagan from the records office sashay in. She eyed Isla on the chair but seeing no interest from the child, moved closer to him.

"Sergeant, are the reports ready?" She slipped behind the desk and leant against the edge, blocking his exit.

"I just finished."

She rested her hand on his shoulder. Seeing the opening in his shirt, she slid her fingers along the collar and down to his exposed chest. "It's certainly warm today."

He grabbed her hand. "Stop."

"Did you say, don't stop?" She moved closer and sat on his lap.

"Ahem." Farlan stood in the middle of the office, watching.

As she rose, Riagan ran her fingers along his arm. "I wanted only the reports."

Bronwyn thrust the collection of papers into her hand. He stared in confusion as she sauntered from the room.

Farlan considered his friend with one eyebrow raised. "To say she's interested would be an understatement."

"I wish she'd leave me alone."

"She might get the hint...eventually." Farlan glanced at Isla. "Is she sleeping?"

"Resting. Riding must have tuckered her out." Bronwyn straightened the pile of papers on his desk and placed his writing utensil in the holder.

Farlan knelt beside the chair. "Hey, Little Sprite." He placed his hand on her shoulder and shook her gently. "Isla." He raised his voice to get her attention. When she didn't respond, he shook her harder.

"Why isn't she responding?" Bronwyn rushed to his side. He lifted Isla and supported her in a seated position.

Farlan put his hand on her forehead. "She's burning up. Let's remove her vest." Between the two of them, they stripped off the dark blue jerkin.

"Isla?" He cupped his daughter's face. "Can you hear me?"

She remained still, her eyes gaping into space. The men stared at each other.

"Sunstroke?" Fear shot across Farlan's face.

"Would she gawk like this?" He put his hand beneath her nose and detected shallow exhaling. He swallowed hard; children died of sunstroke.

"I'll get Alaura. She'll know what to do." Farlan started away but stopped. "Where will I find her?"

The heat and the worry for Isla confused Bronwyn's thoughts. Where was Alaura today? At Moon Meadow? The Market? Or would she be at her dwelling at this hour? He anguished over the possibilities. She had left before he picked up Isla at the bakery two days beforehand.

"Moon Meadow." The words tumbled out. "She has to be there. Choose the fastest horse. Bring her to us."

"Take Isla to your quarters. It'll be cooler there," shouted Farlan over his shoulder as he raced out the door.

Bronwyn hoisted his daughter into his arms. Within minutes, he shoved open the door to his quarters and indeed found the air cooler. He laid Isla on her bed, removed her trousers and shirt, then dressed her in a thin nightshirt. Throughout it all, she remained unresponsive.

He flung open the window but found the outside air warmer than that already occupying the room, so closed it. He filled a basin with cool water and patted Isla's forehead with a damp cloth. Her faint breath brushed his skin as he peered closer at her transfixed eyes.

A noise sounded in the hall. He turned at once, hoping to see Farlan and Alaura. No, not enough time had passed. It took fifteen minutes of hard riding to get to Moon Meadow. Judging by the time that had elapsed, he believed Farlan would be only arriving at Beathas' cottage.

He dipped the cloth in the water and dabbed Isla's face and neck. He applied the cool liquid to her arms, legs and feet. Goose bumps formed, and he feared she might be too cool now. He covered her with a thin blanket and held her hand. Lowering his head close to her face, he watched for signs of awareness.

"Isla." His voice cracked. "You'll be fine. Alaura's coming. She'll know what to do." He stared at the door. Where were they? What if they arrived too late? No! He wouldn't let negative thoughts invade his senses. Isla would recover. He caressed her forehead, cheek and hair. "I'm here, Isla."

The door flew open, and Alaura and Farlan rushed in. Bronwyn stood, giving her his spot on the bed. "Thank you for coming."

Alaura felt the child's skin. Leaning close, she peered into her eyes, gently drawing down the lower lids to examine the edges. "Farlan told me she appeared to be sleeping, but her eyes stared into space, and she couldn't be stirred. Has her condition changed since moving her to a cooler room?"

"No. Nothing."

Alaura dug into her satchel and extracted several cloth pouches and a shallow porcelain dish. Into the saucer, she poured two different types of fine powder: one orange, the other rich yellow. "Her breathing is faster than normal but shallow. Her skin is hot and dry, but I don't think she has sunstroke." She spooned a small amount of the powder mixture near Isla's nostrils. "I think it's much worse." She glanced at Bronwyn who sat on the opposite side of the bed.

His face twisted with anguish. "What then?"

"Poyson."

"Poyson?" He shot a look at Farlan. "Did she eat anything unusual today?"

Farlan shook his head, astonished. "She ate an apple. Nuts. We had strawberry tarts from your mum's shop. She's eaten all those things before. I ate them, too!" He flopped into a chair and rubbed his hands against his lap. "I don't know where she came in contact with poyson."

"Farlan, you're not to blame," said Bronwyn.

"But I feel as if it's my fault." His voice trembled.

"It's not. We can't predict every danger."

With gentle nudges, Alaura directed the powder into Isla's nostrils. Once she had pushed a sufficient amount into the naval cavity, she asked Bronwyn to hold open Isla's mouth. Then she sprinkled a light dusting of the fine powder on her tongue.

"What's that? Magic?"

"It's an herbal remedy." She slid his hands from the mouth and used her own to close it. "Her body will absorb the powder; draw it into her lungs and blood. It'll seek out the poyson and remove it."

"How is it removed?"

"The way a body always releases unwanted material." She scanned the room. "We'll need a bucket."

Farlan jumped up and went to the water closet. He returned with a pail and handed it to her. "Do you need anything else?"

"No. Thank you. If Isla's body accepts the remedy, she'll take care of the rest."

The three patiently waited as the minutes ticked by. The still air added to the silence that ate at Bronwyn's nerves. Trying to calm his speeding pulse, he scanned the room, taking in the familiar surroundings and the worried expressions on his friends' faces. On any other given night, a gathering like this would have put a smile on his face.

All at once, Isla heaved. At first, her body appeared in control, but it quickly turned violent.

"Hold her on her side. She'll choke if she stays on her back." Alaura held the bucket, ready to catch whatever came from her mouth.

Convulsions seized the child's body. Bronwyn had difficulty holding her near the bucket. A repugnant smell escaped her mouth, making his eyes water and triggering his gag reflex.

"Look away and take a breath."

He heeded her advice and gasped for clean air. Isla shuddered, then threw-up into the bucket. The wretched stench spread quickly throughout the room. He didn't want to look but couldn't resist. What he saw in the bucket made his stomach pitch. The black gelatinous substance danced and hissed. Little eruptions spewed forth puffs of gas.

Isla took a deep breath and flopped down onto the bed.

"Farlan, dispose of this." Alaura handed him the bucket and leant away to catch a breath of fresh air. She wiped Isla's mouth clean of vomit with the damp cloth.

Farlan started towards the water closet, but Bronwyn stopped him. "We'll never get rid of the smell. Throw it outside."

Eager to find relief from the nauseating substance, Farlan opened the window and flung the bucket into the air. It fell two storeys before hitting the ground. When he turned, Alaura stared in disbelief. "What?"

"You threw away the pail." She flinched and put her hand on her abdomen.

"There must be another in the closet." Farlan hesitated to abandon the fresh air entering the window but went in search of another bucket.

"Will she be better now?" Bronwyn cradled Isla in his arms.

"She released the poyson. It's a good sign." Alaura placed her hand on his forearm. "She needs sleep and warmth. Give her a moment, then we'll see if she'll drink."

"Where do you think it came from?" He had a hunch but hoped it to be wrong.

"I don't know. If I had accompanied her today perhaps..."

"I've smelt the stench before," he said. "The night the henchman tried to take Isla from us; his blood smelt of it. You said it contained evil magic."

"I remember, but I don't see how the events of that day connect with this event." She caressed Isla's cheek.

"Is it Lindrum's black magic?"

"Possibly. I've smelt the distinct odour a few times."

Farlan exited the closet with a small pail. "This is all I could find."

"Das." Isla spoke in a weak voice and stared up at him, her eyes wet with tears.

"Isla." He kissed her forehead. "You're going to be okay."

She buried her face in his white shirt and cried softly.

Holding her tightly, the moisture rose in his eyes. "It's going to be okay, Isla. The worst is over." He glanced at Alaura for reassurance. "Right?"

"I believe so." She took a deep breath and rubbed her forehead.

Farlan glanced at his watch. "I hate to leave, but I'm already late for patrol." He knelt beside the bed and stroked Isla's hair. Tears streaked her flushed face, and hair matted against her skin. "Be well, my Little Sprite. I'll see you in the morning." He took one last look, then left the room.

"Bronwyn, may I have a glass of water?" Alaura eased the child from his arms.

When he returned with the water, she held the glass to Isla's lips. "Sip it, honey. Your throat may be tender." The child drank eagerly. By the time the glass emptied, Alaura's hand shook. She shoved the glass at Bronwyn and wiped her brow. "Shut the window."

"What about the stench?" He preferred the warm air over the smell.

"Close it!" She rubbed her forehead with trembling fingers, then tucked her hair behind her ears. After pulling the blanket to Isla's chin, she kissed her cheek. "Rest, my sweet Isla."

Bronwyn studied Alaura as he closed the window. "Is anything wrong?"

"I'm warm." Her shaky hands fumbled with the pouches of herbs, then rammed them into her satchel. She struggled to fasten the flap. Grabbing a book from the small bedside table, she fanned her face and neck. She placed her palm over her belly and became lost in thought.

"Are you sure?" He knelt on one knee beside her and took her hand in his. "You don't look well."

"I'm fine. Really. I am." She pulled her hand free. "I need cool air. Fresh air."

"Will you come back later and check on Isla?"

She nodded and gingerly pushed herself from the bed. When she rose to her full height, her eyes rolled, and she blinked several times. She stumbled, and he caught her.

"I don't think you're as well as you say you are." He helped her sit back down on the bed. "Why don't you stay?"

"Here? With you?" She shook her head awkwardly as if drunk. "I can't stay."

"I don't bite." He smiled to make light of the situation but in truth, he worried about her. She appeared ready to burst into tears. "If you stay, you'll be here for Isla. You can sleep in the bed, and I'll sleep—"

"No!" Her eyes grew wide and fear painted her features. "I can't stay with *you*!"

Taken aback by her insistence, he didn't know what to say. She knew him to be a good person. Why didn't she feel safe with him?

"Help me up," she demanded, reaching for his hand. "I'll rest at my dwelling."

Pulling her to her feet, he waited for her to steady herself before letting go. He felt grateful she had come to help Isla, and if she didn't want to stay, he respected her decision. He wished things to be different, but...

She released his hand and took a few steps forward, forcing one foot in front of the other. It didn't appear she'd make it to the door, let alone her dwelling. Her hands grabbed at her stomach, and she stumbled. He caught her before she hit the floor, then lifted her into his arms and carried her towards his bed.

"Let me go!"

"I won't. You're staying." If he needed to use force, he would— sparingly. Though her words sounded strong, her body fell limp. "Alaura, you're too weak to walk alone to your dwelling, and since I can't leave Isla, you have to stay."

"I can't. It's not safe for me or you." Her body flopped against him, and she pressed her face to his shoulder.

"Nonsense. You're safe here. I promise." He sat her on his bed and took off one of her boots. She protested when he attempted to remove the second boot, but her strength faded, and he quickly removed it.

He prepared to rise from his kneeling position but stopped abruptly when her hands applied pressure on the top of his shoulders. Her gaze travelled down his face to his partially unbuttoned shirt. She slipped her hands into the opening, and as her fingers caressed the skin on his shoulders and neck, her facial features softened. His pulse raced when she pulled him to her breasts and danced her hands over his back, drawing his shirt tail from his trousers. A loud grumble erupted from her stomach, and she winced in pain. Though he wished to enjoy the unexpected closeness, he sensed she didn't control her actions, so pushed her away.

Terror sped across her face, and she pulled her hands free, wrapping them across her stomach.

"Alaura, you have fallen ill."

She nodded, avoiding eye contact. "I must have caught Isla's illness. No, I couldn't have. I felt troubled the moment I passed through the gateway of the castle." Her trembling hand went to her temple. Her body swayed from side-to-side. "I want to lie down."

She gave him a weak smile, but she attempted only to mask the pain and worry and stall the tears welling in her eyes. She didn't resist when he removed the belt holding her dress snug or when he guided her beneath the blankets. Laying her head on his pillow, she breathed deeply and closed her eyes.

"Alaura." He shook her and breathed a sigh of relief when she looked up. "I'm worried you..." He glanced at Isla in her bed, watching and listening. He bent close to her ear. "Do you need to ingest the herbal mixture? The same you gave to Isla?"

Lost in thought, her fingers traced the outline of his chin from one ear to the other, then crossed his cheek to settle upon his lips. They felt soft upon his skin like a whispering wind on a warm day. He wanted to kiss them, but remained still, trying not to move, hoping they wouldn't fall away. When their eyes met, she shook her head. "Sleep." Her soft voice trailed off, and she withdrew her hand. Slowly her eyelids closed and relaxed.

He hoped she was right, and that she needed only rest. Sitting upright on the bed, he glanced between Isla and Alaura. He had to watch over them both. To make things simpler, he lifted Alaura to the inside of the bed, then placed Isla next to her. He set the lock on the door and extinguished the lantern. He wanted to strip to his shorts, but instead kept on his trousers and lay next to Isla.

When he settled, Isla reached up and touched his chin. Her small hand climbed to his cheek. "Das, I'm scared. It feels like a hundred ants are marching through my belly, stomping their feet and shouting."

He pulled her near. "The worst has passed." He kissed the top of her head. The females falling ill from a similar but unusual ailment puzzled him. Had others fallen ill in the castle? If so, was Lindrum's evil magic responsible? Here in his quarters, all was under control. To reassure himself, he glanced towards his sword hanging on its hook near the bed. He could find it in the dark if need be.

For a long time, he lay awake listening to the steady breathing of his bedmates. Watching over them gave him a sense of his real duty: to care for and protect two of the most important women in his life.

Tonight, his quarters felt more like home than they normally did. All the familiar sounds came to him: the ticking clock, the soft footsteps in the outside hallway, the closing of a door and the distant sound of the bell tower chiming at every hour. But two new sounds whispered in the darkness: Alaura's gentle breathing and occasional movement. Her scent added a distinct flavour to the air, yet it blended with his and Isla's to create a pleasant aroma. Calmness settled over him, and the warmth of his small family filled his heart.

He touched his lips and wondered what Alaura had thought before she dozed off. An unpredictable woman, she could be one moment full of delight, enticing him to come closer, and the next, distant and cold, pushing him away as if she didn't wish to know him.

He occasionally wished he hadn't met her. Her stern manner of instructing him on the proper upbringing of Isla got out of hand. It caused many arguments between them. Alaura found him too strict with his teaching of right and wrong, but too lenient when he turned almost everything else into fun.

Still, he couldn't imagine life without Alaura. Over the past seven years, he had grown to know her in ways he hadn't known a woman and to respect her like no other. Their casual friendship had grown into more than she would admit. Though she refused a lone outing with him, he sensed she had feelings for him.

One day while fishing along the Shulie River with Isla and Farlan, she had hooked a large, energetic fish. He helped bring in the sea trout. As he held it up for her to admire, she had thrown her arms around his neck in triumph. He hugged her with his free hand, savouring the closeness. Then, as if realising the intimacy of her actions, she pushed herself away. Her shove came so quick and strong, he fell backwards into the river, losing the fish in the fall. He clung to moments like this, hoping with the passing of time, their friendship would evolve into a fulltime relationship.

But Alaura had become more than a potential mate; she spanned the gap between him and Isla. When Isla had come home crying from study class one day, his attempts to calm her failed. Alaura arrived, took Isla aside and had her smiling within minutes. She explained Isla's classmate had teased her about Liam, and she punched the other girl in the mouth. Isla felt afraid to tell Bronwyn because she knew he'd be disappointed in her. *She's a little girl. She'll make mistakes,* Alaura had told him. *She needs to know you still love her when she does. It's you she wishes to please most.* He and Isla discussed the incident, and he put her mind at ease.

He touched Alaura's cheek. She felt warm, too warm. He pulled the blanket off her shoulder and folded it over her hip. He touched her forehead; the fever gripped her. He ran his finger along her chin and crossed her cheek to her lips, warm and soft.

Then, without warning, he fell asleep, dreaming of the ones he loved. The strong feelings ignited a fire in his blood and incinerated any illness the poyson inflicted on him.

∞ ❖ ∞

A loud, rapid knock came at the door, stirring Bronwyn. He rolled to his back, stretched and rubbed his eyes as the rising sun poured rays into the room.

The knock sounded again.

He stumbled from the bed and grabbed his shirt. He pulled it on and fastened a few buttons before opening the door.

"Sergeant Darrow." The private saluted him. "Your presence is requested in the Throne Room."

"What's this about?" He rubbed the sleep from his eyes.

"I wasn't told, sir. You must report to the Throne Room immediately for an urgent announcement."

"I'll go as soon as I'm dressed." He dismissed the private and closed the door. Scratching his head and yawning, he walked back to the bed and found Alaura had awakened.

"What is it?" she whispered, not moving from beneath the blanket.

"I've been summoned to the Throne Room."

"Why?"

"He didn't say." He glanced at Isla, still sleeping. "Can you stay with her?"

She nodded. "How long will you be?"

"I don't know. Help yourself to food, to whatever you need." He pulled a clean uniform from a drawer, then stepped into the water closet to wash and change.

Before leaving he stood next to the bed and belted his scabbard and sword around his waist. Alaura's skin appeared pale and her eyes dull though sunshine lit up the room. Her hair lay lifeless and flat.

"How do you feel this morning?" he whispered.

"Much better."

He wished he didn't have to rush off so early. "You can take Isla to Mum. She'll care for her until my shift ends."

He gazed upon the enchanting woman in his bed, her head lying on his pillow as if she woke there every morning. But she would be gone when he returned at the end of the day and might never venture this far again. Putting one knee on the mattress, he bent forward and kissed Isla's forehead. Though pale, her temperature felt normal. He paused for a moment, hovering over Alaura, longing to check her temperature using the same method. But his courage faded. She lay frozen beneath him, as if holding her breath until he left, so he moved away.

"Bronwyn."

He halted and looked back at her.

"I wish..." She paused, struggling to find the right words. Then, as if giving up, she said, "Be careful."

He smiled. He'd be careful for her.

14

Life Force of All Beings

QUICK FOOTSTEPS caught Bronwyn's attention. He attempted to question the guard running past, but the man didn't stop. He didn't even salute.

Muffled sounds drifted down the hallway leading to the lobby. Inside, about three dozen guards lingered in the spacious entrance hall, chatting in small groups. The air, still heavy from the heat of the previous day, carried a spicy odour that mixed with the smell of men who had rolled out of bed and those who had patrolled for twelve sizzling hours.

When he approached, the guards fell silent and saluted.

"Sergeant, why are we here?" The dark-haired human tucked more of his white shirt into his trousers and pulled at the base of his vest to straighten it.

"I thought you could tell me, Private."

"The lords ordered everyone from their quarters. Most are in the guardhouse and courtyard, but we're to wait here for further instructions."

He looked towards the Throne Room entrance. "Are we supposed to go in?"

"You are, sir." A large-framed human near the door gestured for him to proceed.

Bronwyn stepped past the rest and entered the Throne Room. All officers and several individuals important to the castle, including the archivist who seldom emerged in public, waited inside. The elf who tended the archives and library clutched a note pad and rocked back and forth in his chair in a methodical motion. Bronwyn noticed the misaligned buttons of the elf's untucked shirt. Strange for a man who supposedly organised every record held at the castle for the past seventy-five years.

In the far corner of the room, he spotted Farlan speaking with Sanderson. Farlan's face appeared flushed and anxious. Sanderson poked a finger at the corporal's chest, yet Farlan didn't flinch. Hoping to save his friend from whatever mess he'd gotten himself into, Bronwyn moved through the crowd until he stood next to him.

"Where in Knavesmire were you?" Dark shadows accentuated Sanderson's scowl.

Stunned by the tone of voice and question, Bronwyn had no answer. Like most off-duty guards, he had slept away the night.

"I'll speak with you later. Here come the lords." Sanderson strode away and took his position near the thrones.

Bronwyn leant near his friend. "What's going on?"

"I don't know. Sanderson dragged me off the wall—literally, dragged me off the wall—and interrogated me." Farlan talked out of the side of his mouth in a low voice. "It has to be serious. I've never seen the ol' man so short tempered, so quick to judge." The natural colour of his face returned. Still, he appeared shaken. "My men, the ones on overnight duty, are in one miserable state. Several fell asleep. Others retched over the wall. They had the same odour as what Isla put in the bucket. After midnight, Junior Corporal Parnell stared off in a daze and asked where could he find his mother, *his momma*? The elf is one of my strongest men, and two guards had to escort him to the Infirmary."

Bronwyn knew Parnell and couldn't believe what his friend said. It sounded incredible. Whatever the illness, it affected men as well as women. Although he hadn't felt sick, he'd slept well, too well. He doubted if anything could have wakened him. "It sounds as if everyone suffered from some degree of poysoning. What about you?"

"I was sleepy but chewed pumpkin seeds to stay alert."

"Did you feel ill?"

"My stomach felt unsettled, but I blamed it on the ride from Moon Meadow and the odour from your quarters." Farlan's expression grew concerned. "And the worry for Isla. How's she doing?"

"She's fine."

"Where is she?"

"My quarters."

"Alone?"

"Alaura's with her."

Farlan raised an eyebrow. "Alaura spent the night in your quarters?"

"She did." He reined in a grin, but a fragment lingered at the corner of his mouth. His friend knew how he felt about Alaura and might make certain assumptions. The glint in Farlan's eyes held his gaze. Though he tried to cloak his feelings, his blood warmed. A bit more of the smile escaped.

Farlan folded his arms as a mischievous grin lit up his face. "Good. She watched over Isla. She should move in and tend to her full time. At the very least, I'd eat well when I came for a ration."

Bronwyn's untethered joy spread across his face, but when he found Sanderson glaring at him, he promptly removed it. To appease his superior, he straightened his shoulders and pasted a solemn expression on his face.

Everyone stood as the lords approached the thrones. Lord Mulryan led the way. He moved a little peculiar, but Bronwyn couldn't identify the reason why.

Farlan leant close to his ear. "Mulryan wasn't here last night. He left shortly after I started my shift and didn't return until about an hour ago."

He reassessed Mulryan. Where had he spent the night? That's it! He wore the same clothes he had yesterday.

Lord Layne Nevell, a healer, sat next to Lord Mulryan. The ashen-haired human, the youngest lord, supervised the Infirmary serving the inhabitants of the castle, the castle guard and the army. He also trained others in the craft and visited the healing stations within Maskil.

Sitting in a rigid position, Lord Nevell pleated a small piece of cloth on his lap. With the folding completed, he flicked it straight and began again. His usual pale skin shone with a lighter colour. The cloth slipped from his hands, and he grasped the edge of his robe and played with the hem. His eyes darted about the room, settling on Bronwyn. A peculiar expression clouded his features, and he silently solicited his help and implored him to step forward. Then, his face relaxed, and he eased into a peaceful state.

Lord Val moved sluggishly. His somber expression revealed little about the announcement to come. He placed a comforting hand on his stomach and drew a deep breath.

Bronwyn's mind drifted to Isla and Alaura. Had they recovered completely from their illness? A sudden urgency sparked in his gut and a chill ran down the back of his neck. The desire to race away and confirm their safety overwhelmed him, but duty grounded him.

Next, the hauflin, Lord Peadar Tasgall, slid onto his throne. Tasgall's eyes explored the room. The lord folded his hands on his lap and continued to search, not settling on any particular object or person.

The next throne sat empty. Where was Lady Dasia? Had she fallen ill from the heat? The elf never missed a session in the Throne Room. Bronwyn had seen her only yesterday from atop the castle wall. She walked with a citizen towards the Maskil Market. They laughed together. But he hadn't spoken to her since their meeting in the guardhouse, when she had given him the belt buckle. His hand went to the decorative object. He wore it proudly, hoping to find the person to whom it belonged. Later, he'd seek out Glynn Dasia to find the reason behind her absence.

Lord Dirck Landis took his seat last. The human measured almost as tall as Sanderson. A ponytail pulled his dark hair from his sallow face, revealing the square edges of his jaw. Bronwyn didn't speak to him unless necessary. The lord, who governed over both the justice system and dungeon, spoke down to the dwarf, making him feel unworthy of his rank. The tone of his voice, not his words, implied his dislike.

Bronwyn had mentioned it to Sanderson, but he said not to worry; *Lord Landis talks like that to everyone.*

Lord Val held up his hand for silence.

Bronwyn straightened and Farlan did the same. He had met this guard, who would become his best friend, at a similar meeting many years ago, when an attack by a small force of Lindrum's henchmen had penetrated the castle walls. The efficiency of the lords and how quickly they settled the matter had impressed him. Watching Lord Val now, he didn't see the same urgency or confidence marking his features as on that day.

Lord Val cleared his throat. "It'll take all our strength to see the day through and maintain the confidence of the noble citizens of Maskil." He gazed around the room, making eye contact with several individuals. "It's my duty to inform you of the horrible events that occurred within these walls yesternight. Whilst we slept, a ruthless murderer entered our castle, our home."

He paused. With a small cloth he wiped sweat from his brow and pallid cheek. "It's with a grievous heart I inform you our beloved Lady Dasia has been taken from us."

Bronwyn gasped. Who had taken her? Did he mean murdered? Impossible! Lady Dasia, a noble wizard, ranked superior in her craft. Who could have done it? Who would dare?

Lord Val raised his hand to quiet the rumblings in the audience. "It's unbelievable but true; Lady Dasia was murdered as she slept. The facts are made worse by the escape of her killer." Lost in thought, he stared into the crowd, then he winced, shook his head and continued. "To add to our misery is the news dozens of individuals, including many children, became afflicted with a strange illness through the night. Sadly, the weak succumbed to the malady."

Bronwyn swallowed hard. It had to be the same sickness infecting Isla. If not for Alaura, it might be his child's death he mourned. But Isla had recovered. He cleared his throat and scanned the Throne Room. Everyone whispered to the person nearest them. He glanced at Farlan. What had he witnessed while on duty on the castle wall over night? They locked eyes but dared not share their thoughts in a room filled with others who waited to pounce on a shred of evidence.

"Silence." Lord Val folded his trembling hands on his lap. "We have questioned many individuals, but many more will be sought to fill in the missing information. A public inquest will take place this afternoon. I promise, the culprit will be found, and justice will be swift.

"Officers, you're to remain here and await further orders from Lord Mulryan. The rest of you, secure your areas of the castle. If anything unusual is found, bring it to me. Lord Landis and I will be in the study." Lord Val rose and left the room. The rest of the lords, except Mulryan, followed.

With the room secured, Lord Mulryan gathered the guards around him. Bronwyn scanned the many faces he had come to know over the years: Sanderson, Captains Tibbins and Greenhill, Sergeants Glawson and Latchford, ten corporals, including Farlan, and many of the forty-five junior corporals.

He watched Lord Mulryan as he waited for the guards to gather and be silent. The lord, with his feet squarely planted on the stone floor, tapped his thumb on the hilt of his sword. He didn't look directly into the faces of his men, but instead at their boots and their swords.

Bronwyn caught the scent of cinnamon. He glanced at Mulryan a few feet away. Did this smell come from his overnight excursion? The first meal of the day had yet to be served to anyone in the castle. Had it been provided for him where he spent the night? Over the years, he had witnessed Mulryan leave on many occasions and return in the morning. The outings hadn't been suspicious until today.

"Men." Lord Mulryan surveyed the group. "We have failed the lords, Aruam Castle and the people of Maskil. Under our watch a murderer broke through our defences and claimed the life of one of our most respected leaders." He continued in a low, deep voice. "If we had the power to undo the deed, we would in haste. But malicious magic sealed Lady Glynn Dasia's fate. It drained every drop of spirit from her nwyfre."

Nwyfre? Bronwyn had heard the word before but couldn't recall the details. He had once asked Alaura, and she said it to be the life force of all beings. Many thought of it as a person's aura where their spirit dwelt. Those who knew magic held it in higher regard. Alaura had noticed his lack of interest when she mentioned magic and ended the explanation. Now, he wished he'd asked her to continue.

Lord Mulryan pushed his black hair from his eyes. "Today will be one unlike any other. Though we grieve, we must take charge and rout out the murderer who dared cross our lines. Each one of you will play a part in bringing this criminal to justice." His eyes fell on Sanderson. "Immediately after this meeting, I'll meet privately with you and Captains Tibbins and Greenhill. But for now," he spoke to the rest, "it's important we make our presence felt.

"Corporals, those of you who patrolled on night shift, get your men off the wall. They're in a wretched state, suffering from the blind smuir which hung over the castle all night. Give them and yourselves eight hours' leave. Encourage them to eat and sleep.

"Corporals on day duty; recruit from those scheduled for training and double the number of guards on the wall and at the town gates. If you run short of men, meet with Captain Greenhill, and he'll assign soldiers to make up the shortfall. I want every inch of wall scoured for clues. The murderer entered the grounds by some means. Find it!

"Sergeants; the three of you divide up the town and get every available guard and a hundred soldiers on the streets. Once word gets out of Lady Dasia's murder, there's no telling what may happen. Instruct them to keep their ears and eyes open for suspicious behaviour." Lord Mulryan inspected his men, making eye contact with several.

When his eyes met Bronwyn's, he wore a vulnerable expression unusual for the dwarf lord. Did Mulryan seek strength from him? But how could a sergeant bolster a lord? Bronwyn stood straighter, shoulders back, forced a determined expression and placed his hand on the hilt of his sword. The corner of Mulryan's mouth curved slightly. Dwarfs, a noble race, stood ready to face whatever forces challenged them; perhaps Mulryan had forgotten this.

"At 13:00 hours, we'll regroup at the guardhouse." Mulryan adjusted his stance and stood straighter. "The inquest is scheduled for 15:00 hours. If you have anything to report, I'll be in my office or the study. Are there any questions?" No one spoke. "Let's get to work then."

Bronwyn glanced at Farlan. "We'll talk later."

Farlan nodded and headed to the outer wall to relieve the men under his command.

Bronwyn joined Sergeants Glawson and Latchford to plan their duties for the day. He struggled to accept the unbelievable news that intruders had murdered Lady Dasia. If she could be killed within the protective fortifications of the castle, then everyone within the walls lay equally vulnerable: the lords, the guards and their families. He thought about Isla and Alaura alone and defenceless in his quarters. The night had passed safely for them. He had stood guard to protect them if trouble had arisen. If Glenn Dasia had united and a mate shared her bed, would she be alive today? Her mate would have functioned as her personal guardian as Bronwyn had for Isla and Alaura. Perhaps the law forbidding lords to unite contributed to her demise.

15

The Maze of His Nwyfre

"ALAURA!" BRONWYN espied her amongst the mass of people outside the castle entrance. Her face brightened when she saw him.

She waved, then wended her way around the citizens of Maskil to come face-to-face with him.

"How are you feeling?" He held her hands as gently as he would butterfly wings, surprised she allowed him to do so.

"Better." She glanced at the boisterous crowd, many shoving to be next in one of the several lines entering the castle. "Did you check on Isla?"

"I saw her for a moment." He leant forward to ensure she heard. "I apologise for insisting you stay in my quarters yesternight. I couldn't have kept you safe otherwise without leaving Isla alone."

"No need to apologise. In my irrational condition I needed a friend to guard my safety." She held his gaze. "I'm grateful I had you to do so."

"Alaura, I'll always protect you." The corner of her lip curled into a smile, but she refused to let it blossom across her mouth. Before she pulled away, he had to change the subject. "Are you attending the inquest?"

"It's too incredible to miss. Poor Lady Dasia. When I heard the tragic news, I knew at once I must attend."

"You'll need to get in a line and be searched by one of the guards."

She glanced at the men frisking everyone who entered. Their hands touched every part of the body searching for concealed weapons. "This is my first inquest. I don't know the protocol."

"It's for everyone's safety, including your own." Certainly, she wouldn't let a stranger search her but request him to do so. His fingers tingled against her skin at the thought of touching her in places a male caressed to arouse their mate.

She nodded timidly. "Do I have to go through one of those entrances or..." she stared at him, looking for the trust they had grown over the years, "can you...can I go through this door and...you perform the search?" Her grip on his hands tightened.

Shame washed over him. He couldn't take advantage of his position. She wanted to be treated with respect; he'd honour that. "I'm supervising but sure, I can perform the search if you prefer."

"I'd feel... I mean I trust you won't take advantage of your station."

"I never do." He released her hands and pointed to her feet. "May I have your boots, please?"

She slid off her footwear, and he checked each boot.

"Turn around."

She complied, and he guided her arms into the air. He patted down each one, then ran his hands over her sides and back. To his surprise, she wore his tan-coloured shirt. It hung loose about her shoulders and hips. A black belt held it snug around her waist. It felt strange yet enchanting. When he wore this shirt again, he'd think of her and her captivating body wrapped in the same material.

He had performed hundreds of routine weapon searches on both men and women. He zipped through each as if he explored a horse for broken bones. But Alaura wasn't a horse or any other woman. His pulse pounded at the mere thought of exploring places he had only dreamt about with the woman who ignited his blood like no other. He wished their first intimate encounter didn't have to be like this, but the search had to be performed, if not by him by one of the other male guards on duty. Thoughts of another man touching her body urged him forward.

Going under both arms, he reached to her front and placed his palms below her neck. He had smelt her before but never like this. His air passages filled with her scent, and every pore gulped to drink in her warmth. His hands slid to her breasts. Her ripe nipples brushed against his palms, sending a ripple of pleasure through his blood and increasing the heat in his groin. As his training dictated, his fingers slid beneath each breast to make a thorough search, and she gasped.

Continuing the search, he caressed her abdomen and hips.

"Spread your legs, please." It sounded more like a whispered request than an official order. Her legs parted, and his hands slid from her groin to her ankles. Thankfully, she wore trousers today.

When he completed the search of the second leg, he rose and settled his hands on her waist. Her warm fingers came to rest upon his knuckles, and she held them in place. "It was my duty," he whispered into her hair.

"I know." Her soft voice spoke only to him.

"You may put on your boots." He released her and tried to shake the sensations she had created. He knew no woman more enchanting than Alaura of Niamh, and while he considered this search to be his duty, it had provoked profound pleasure.

A shout permeated through the crowd. Two guards wrestled a human to the ground, bound and dragged him away. More people gathered around the entrance, eager to get the search over with so they could enter the castle.

"Sir." A guard came to stand by Bronwyn. "Sanderson requested you to the Throne Room. He instructed me to take over the supervision of these privates."

"Thank you, Corporal."

The guard eyed Alaura. "Does she need to be searched?" He ran his tongue along his bottom lip.

"I've already searched her." He turned to her. "I'll see you inside." He motioned for her to move on.

She caught his open hand, gave it a squeeze, then released it.

ಚಿ ❖ ಚಿ

As Alaura entered the castle and made her way to the Throne Room with the wave of spectators, she replayed the route Bronwyn's hands had taken in the search. She had felt naked as he caressed her body, arousing every nerve and fanning the embers in her blood. She folded her arms across her breasts, still feeling his touch.

She found a seat near the centre of the Throne Room where she settled and savoured Bronwyn's lingering scent as she waited for the inquest to begin. When she washed this morning, she couldn't bring herself to completely remove the odour she had gathered from sleeping beside him. The desire to retain his smell had overwhelmed her and incited her to wear one of his shirts. Fortunately, he had kept any observations of this unspoken. Her cheeks warmed thinking about her response if he had questioned her.

Since he had held her in his strong arms and carried her to his bed the night before, she'd felt powerless against her emotions. While not the first time she wanted him, it marked the first time she'd fallen prey to her desires. The illness had weakened her defences, and she surrendered to the hunger. Seeing him on his knees before her, his eyes filled with concern, made him irresistible. Her gaze had followed his jaw line, then crossed to the lips she longed to kiss. She imagined her hands caressing his bare chest, and without warning they reached for it. Through half-closed eye she watched her fingers draw his shirt tail from his trousers, eager to embrace his naked body. Thankfully, he'd stopped her. But if they'd been alone, would he have resisted? Though wrong to think so, she hoped not.

His scent consumed her when she laid her head upon his pillow. It felt as if she rested in his arms. She had dreamt his gentle hands had removed her dress, and he pressed his firm, nude body against her bare skin. As his sweet kisses warmed her lips, his tender fingers explored every curve of her breasts, drew hearts around her bellybutton and edged their way closer to the softness between her legs. She had surrendered to her desires and had dreamt away the night.

She couldn't have guessed the simple act of attending an inquest would draw them closer, but it had. Dozens of others lingered near, yet it felt as if they stood alone. When his hands caressed her breasts, he had quivered with excitement. The sudden movement had triggered unfamiliar sensations, and she had gasped. The memory stirred impure thoughts. She allowed them to infiltrate her being, wash through her veins like a flood down a mountain side.

Without warning, a person dropped onto the wooden bench beside her.

"Can you believe this?" Catriona huffed in exasperation, adjusted her blouse and straightened her skirt over her lap. "I've never been so embarrassed in my life. They should have female guards to search females if they want us to attend public inquests."

Alaura ushered Bronwyn from her thoughts. "Are you referring to the weapons search?"

"Of course! Those guards are having a field day out there. And a few of the women. Pah! Two girls giggled and said they'd leave so they could be searched again! Imagine. Such immaturity. The man who searched me took his good ol' time. I swear he gave my breasts an extra squeeze for boyish fun! They're not weapons, and nothing is hidden beneath them!"

She sat up straight and focussed on her friend. "I'll tell Bronwyn."

Catriona shot her a look. "That they mistook my breasts for weapons?"

"No! That female guards should be available to search females."

"Did they maul you, too?"

"No, he was an honourable guard. Bronwyn."

"You were lucky. I should have entered at his door." She leant close. "Then again, I'd rather be groped by a stranger I wouldn't have to face again." A peculiar expression crossed her face, and she sniffed Alaura's shirt. "You smell like...like your friend you say you seldom see but often speak of. Certainly, you didn't gather his scent from a quick search."

She shrank in her seat. Although Catriona missed many things, she often had an insight that surprised her.

The Throne Room soon filled to capacity, and guards shut the doors to prevent more citizens from entering. A trumpeter stepped on a raised platform near the thrones and played the familiar tune, signalling the arrival of the Lords of Aruam Castle. Everyone stood.

Alaura searched for Bronwyn and found him near one of the exits at the front of the room. He watched the lords make their entrance and didn't see her. Through bobbing heads, she spied on him, noting how he stood firm with the serious expression he wore whilst on duty. But she knew him in a different light, with a smile that lit up his face and eyes that teased her to reflect the same.

When the signal sounded, the citizens sat down.

Lord Val raised his hand for silence. A peculiar aura surrounded him. Alaura sensed an illness but without a closer examination, she couldn't be sure. Dark rings beneath his eyes suggested a restless sleep.

She studied the other lords. They, too, behaved unusually reserved for the day's inquest. Lord Nevell toyed with the metal pin in the belt buckle securing his supertunic. His eyes swept around the room as if not seeing anyone in particular; no, he scanned the area as if wondering where he sat. The healer was a wise man, not one to belittle tragic events.

With the doors and windows secured, the heat rose inside the room. After yesternight's sweltering temperatures, she wished they permitted air circulation.

Lord Mulryan's movement caught her eye. He tinkered with the metal decorations on his scabbard, then unfastened a leather strap securing his sword and re-buckled it. His hand, constantly moving from one to the other, kept his attention except for the odd time he gazed towards the window as if watching the sun rising.

A person walked down the centre aisle and their small breeze delivered a distinct spicy odour towards her. They must have cooked food before attending the inquest.

She saw Farlan at the front of the room. He safeguarded an exit on the opposite side of Bronwyn. The two guards made quite a pair. Though Farlan measured much taller, they were oblivious to their physical differences. Both men had an eagerness for shenanigans, wore their uniforms proudly and remained loyal to their duties. She had nothing but respect for Farlan.

The captain of the guard held a position near him. The two measured the same height. Farlan's hair, neatly cut and combed, shined with a rich brown, the colour which might have painted Sanderson's before the grey invaded. She thought Sanderson intimidating, but respected his leadership. Gruff better described him.

It felt extraordinary to find such familiarity amongst former strangers. She hadn't gone out of her way to make friends with those in authority at the castle; it happened naturally because of her relationship with Isla. She sighed, feeling safe surrounded by those she trusted and one, she believed, who'd do anything for her.

"Citizens of Maskil." Lord Val disturbed her thoughts. "You have heard by now fiends have murdered Lady Dasia in her sleep." A roar in the crowd forced him to pause. "The ruthless murderer has yet to be apprehended. We are using everything at our disposal to gather evidence and bring the culprit to justice. During this inquest, we give you, the fine people of Maskil, the opportunity to convey your thoughts and offer information which may aid in a swift arrest.

"The individual responsible for the deadly deed used evil magic to destroy Lady Dasia's spirit. The lethal weapon was magic!"

The noise of the clamorous crowd echoed off the stone walls. Alaura cast a worried glance at Catriona. Over the past few months, guards had discouraged the use of magic within the town. It made little sense to her. Magic, like any craft, could be beneficial when used for good. Still, teachers instructed their apprentices to be careful of when and where they performed their spells. And, if possible, refrain from revealing the fact they practised magic.

"Magic is the root of the evil!" Lord Val raised his voice for the benefit of those in the back of the room.

Alaura gasped. How could he, an illusionist, say this? He excelled in the craft. Did he refrain from using magic, or were lords permitted to practise freely? A strange urgency sparked in her belly, and the urge to escape as if a henchman threatened to grab her from behind tore at her. Another pang of fear erupted and sent shivers down her spine. She had a desire to shout out but didn't know what to say.

"Lady Dasia's death must be avenged!" cried Lord Val. "Does anyone have information to share which will help bring this ruthless criminal to justice?"

"I saw strange things, sparkling lights, smoke, flitting about the castle last night!" shouted a citizen. "Sure as there's yesterday's ration in slumgullion, magic created it!"

"Toss the magic-users in the dungeon!" hollered another. "Use every tool in the hand to learn their secrets!"

Alaura sank in her seat. She had general respect for the citizens of Maskil, but what they said sounded ridiculous and frightened her. How could they condemn every person who used magic? Others made suggestions and offered their opinions on how to flush out the murderer. As their voices rose and the atmosphere became more chaotic, she wished she had stayed at her dwelling.

The strange sensation expanded in her stomach, leaving goose bumps on her skin. Her breath quickened and thoughts not of her making urged her mouth to speak. *Magic-users are evil! Look at the one in front of you! She's the murderer!* She slapped her hand over her mouth. Surely, she wouldn't say such things.

A force from behind yanked her from the bench, dragging her over the backrest. In desperation, Catriona grabbed for her, but missed as others pushed and shoved. In a flash, she was lost from Alaura's view.

"Look!" A large human held her by the back of the shirt. "A magic-user! She murdered Lady Dasia!"

Alaura wriggled to break free, but the strong man held her firmly. The mob clamoured, and she scarcely heard her voice as she screamed at him to let her go.

"She's guilty!" hollered the crowd.

Alaura felt helpless in the face of the madness consuming the room. The man thrust her into a mass of swiping hands. They poked, slapped and kicked her as the force of the people propelled her forward. A great shove landed her on her hands and knees in front of the lords.

Bronwyn rushed forward and pulled her to her feet. She clutched him and tried to shelter herself from the insanity. In defiance, he faced the lords. "They're wrong, My Lord! Alaura did not murder Lady Dasia!"

"How can you be certain?" Lord Val glared down at him.

"She stayed with me last night."

"All night?"

"All night. My daughter fell ill. She tended to her needs."

"She stayed in the castle? Under the same roof as Lady Dasia? Do you swear she remained with you the entire night?"

"Yes, My Lord. She slept next to me. I'd have known if she'd left my bed."

Goodness! Alaura wished he hadn't said that. No one could know they shared the same bed. They'd assume other things, and assumptions could beget danger; if the news reached South Ridge, Bronwyn would be hanged for violating her.

A man in the crowd yelled. "She's an evil witch! She's guilty!"

Bronwyn looked around the room. Alaura studied his strained face; he appeared as shocked as she by the confrontation. When their eyes met, his harrowing expression escalated her fears.

"Is she your mate?" asked Lord Val.

"No!" She shook her head. They couldn't think this; no one could because of the repercussions.

"She's a trusted friend," said Bronwyn.

"Is she loyal to you?"

This time, they answered together. "Yes!"

"What do you have to say?" Lord Val scowled at her. "Did you murder Lady Dasia?"

"No, My Lord. I could never do such a thing. Bronwyn speaks the truth. I remained in his quarters all night tending to his daughter. I never left her side." She cowered under the lord's intense stare and held tighter to Bronwyn.

"You're fooling us!" Lord Landis leant forward and peered at her. "Perhaps you used your magic to trick this sergeant, slip from his quarters and complete your deadly deed!"

Lord Val glared down at Alaura. "Did you trick him with magic?"

She shook her head wildly. "I didn't cast a spell on Bronwyn! I didn't murder Lady Dasia! You have to believe me!" The rage grew in his eyes and swelled the veins in his neck. She sensed heat from his body even at this distance.

"My Lord, Alaura is innocent! I eagerly place my life in your hands for her defence." Bronwyn wrapped an arm around her and pulled her closer. "I beseech you, Lord Valmour Efren, see past the accusations. Search your inner self to find the truth. You have the power to see what others dismiss."

Lord Val snapped back as if struck by the speaking of his full name. Had people reduced him to the abbreviation for so long, he no longer recognised it? Did he believe Lord Valmour Elfren to be another person? His pale greyish-green eyes became fixed on her. She felt them upon her skin as if he reached out and touched her. His cold gaze numbed her senses and before she had time to defend herself, he weaselled his way into her nwyfre.

Gripped by the intensity of Lord Val's stare, she felt helpless to stop him from invading her thoughts. He forced his will upon her and searched for the source of her magic. He gasped, and her legs grew weak. If not for Bronwyn's arm wrapped around her, she might have collapsed.

She's guilty!

A peculiar voice echoed in her head. Who spoke the deadly words? Not Lord Val.

"Alaura of Niamh, I sentence—" Lord Val clamped his hand over his mouth, and his eyes grew wide.

He dug deeper into her life force and neared her meadow, the sacred place where her magic flowed. She tried to stop him but fell under his powerful spell.

Kill her!

Once again, the unfamiliar voice sent shivers through her body. Where did this person hide, and why did he order Lord Val to kill her? She wanted to run, but her legs stood frozen in place.

She is innocent! Lord Val argued with the strange voice, fighting it as he searched Alaura's private thoughts.

"Alaura of Niamh, I find you—" Again Lord Val forced his mouth closed.

She tried to hold back the lord's energy force, but he overran her defences. He trespassed into her meadow where her magic cascaded down glimmering stones and pooled within banks made of sweet coneflowers, asters and white trilliums. She watched in horror as he drank from her spring and gathered her magic to use for himself.

Lord Val took command of his voice. "Alaura of Niamh, I find you innocent!"

She buckled from the sharp withdraw of his energy force. It left her faint, and she clung to Bronwyn to steady herself. Pain raced across the lord's face as if he now fought an intruder in his life force.

Lord Val leant forward and glared at Bronwyn. "Get her to safety. Secure her in your office." When Bronwyn hesitated to move, he snapped, "Now!"

Alaura complied with the force pulling her from the Throne Room. She stumbled blindly along the castle halls, fearing she'd slam into the floor before being permitted to stop.

Bronwyn halted and gripped her shoulders to steady her. "You're trembling." He pulled her into his arms. "You're cold, freezing. Alaura, you are as pale as if death has snatched you."

She wrapped her arms around his waist and buried her face in his shoulder. Sharp pain raced through every limb and gathered in her core. The agony grew and with it a chill that threatened to freeze the blood in her veins.

"You're safe," he whispered. "I won't let him harm you."

The heat of his breath upon her neck and his strong arms holding her enabled her to speak. "You couldn't have stopped him if he wanted to." Her voice quivered, and she wept. "He acted possessed."

"Things could have turned out worse, but you'll be fine."

She shook her head. "He trespassed to forbidden places. He scoured my spirit and stole from my spring. I submitted only to save my life. His strength, his anger overwhelmed me." She sobbed louder. Surrendering to his arms, she wished he could erase the awful memories of an unwanted man in her most private thoughts, the most sacred place of her being.

"What do you mean? Did he cast a spell on you?"

She nodded and pressed her cheek against the rough material of his uniform vest.

"What did he do?"

"Bronwyn, he...violated me."

"How?" He pried her from his embrace and held her to face him. "I didn't witness anything."

Her trembling hands tucked her hair behind her ears, and he helped dry her tears. "He...he touched me in intimate places," she began, embarrassed by the fierce encounter. "He's a powerful illusionist. His energy force trespassed into my nwyfre, my life force and...and he saw my inner thoughts...my inner most pleasures, dreams and fears." The tears fell again, and her strength faded. "He besmirched my magic spring! He dipped his goblet and stole what he pleased!"

"But..." His face twisted in confusion. "Alaura, I don't understand magic like you do. I don't understand what he did." He pulled her back into his arms. "Does it hurt? I mean... Does it leave a wound? Do you still have magic?"

"It hurts... It aches. It steals my breath. My magic feels displaced." Her tears fell in steady drops onto the shoulder flashes of his vest, soaking the two yellow triangles signifying his rank as sergeant. "I feel a void, a weakness as if my energy is exhausted." She squeezed her eyes closed, reliving the attack and the feelings it generated. A guttural wail escaped her lips. "I feel dirty! I can't make it go away!"

"What can I do?" He held her tighter. His eyes welled with tears as he struggled to keep her from collapsing. "What can I do to help you?"

She pressed her body against his, feeling every muscle, every contour. She wanted to climb into his skin and let him cleanse the filth from her meadow. "I wish you could remove his foul energy and replace it with your positive nwyfre, but you can't!" She clutched his shoulders and braced herself as her legs threatened to give way.

"Alaura!" He held her steady. "Please, let me help. It pains me to see you in such agony."

"You have no training! You can't do it!"

He cupped her face in his hands and gazed deep into her eyes. "Let me try. I'll do whatever you ask. Give me a chance, Alaura. Please, let me help you!"

She grasped the back of his hands still pressed against her cheeks. She tried to control her emotions, but Lord Val's negative energy created a whirlwind of reactions consuming her senses with a throbbing ache. Bronwyn didn't understand nwyfre; how could he attempt to cleanse her?

Still, she couldn't resist the kindness radiating from his being. She wanted to surrender to him, to relinquish her body, her mind and her nwyfre to him. He secured her in his grip, eager to ease her pain. His charisma beckoned her forward, and she cautiously peered into his life force. There, she found a calmness that soothed her trembling. His hands, warm against her skin, steadied her nerves and after a moment, she breathed deeper. Better able to gather her thoughts, she ventured deeper in his nwyfre and allowed him access to hers. He lay open to her in ways she could never have imagined, and she found herself in a warm secure place.

"Take what you need," he whispered. "I give it freely."

She peered further, and a gentle hand guided her through the maze of his nwyfre. Shy at first at what she might find, she paused to appreciate the many strands of energy caressing her spirit. They washed through her veins and healed a small part of the damage the lord had caused. Going deeper, she caught her breath; Bronwyn did have magic! While untrained and ancient, it felt as powerful as hers. She gazed upon the natural flow of his spring. Surrounded by towering hemlock, it babbled betwixt two large granite stones and pooled beside a clump of luscious ferns. His magic emanated purity and innocence. She knelt on the bank and absorbed the positive energy radiating from his virtuous magic. The ache in her head that threatened to bring her to her knees subsided, and she took a deep cleansing breath.

She sensed Bronwyn smiling, and she looked back to see where he had gone in her nwyfre. He touched her memories of long ago, seeing her as a child in Petra. The time had come to separate before he discovered too much about her life. Gently, she withdrew her spirit from his life force, nudging him from hers as a meeme ushered a child off to bed.

The cold stone walls of Aruam Castle came into focus, and she shivered. She pulled him near and rested her head on his shoulder. His strong arms wrapped around her, and his soft breath fell upon her neck. "Thank you." Her voice sounded weak, but she felt stronger.

"I wish only to do more to help you heal."

She held him tighter and his heart beat against her chest. The rhythm kept time with the blood flowing through her veins and for a moment, she let them sing together. She wanted to tell him many things, but fear for his safety and for her own, stopped her. Though she didn't want to let go, she knew she couldn't stay.

"Bronwyn, I can't go to your office. Beathas is better able to heal me further. And I'll feel safer away from the castle. May I go?"

"I'll take you myself." He gripped her hand and led her from the castle.

16

Pledge to Unite

THE GUARDS on the Maskil town wall watched a horse kick up dust on its approach to the gate. The rider reined in the stallion as he neared the six men defending the entrance. They saluted when they recognised their superior.

"Sergeant, out for a ride?" The dark-haired human casually glanced around the country side as if it were a lazy Sumortide day.

"It's fine weather for one." Bronwyn had no intentions of revealing where he'd gone. "I trust all is well in town."

"A bit of rumpus at the castle. Otherwise, everything's quiet."

"What sort of rumpus?"

"The lords charged Lady Dasia's murderer. They dealt out the punishment without delay, right at the inquest."

Who had they found guilty? Was the person as innocent as Alaura? He quelled the anger threatening to invade his thoughts. Alaura rested safely; nothing else mattered. She'd receive quality healing in Beathas' care. He wanted to stay by her side, but Beathas told him Alaura needed respite.

In a few days, Bronwyn, you'll be able to see her again, she had said. *For now, it's best she recuperates in the silence of the cottage. You have done your duty.*

"Do you know the name of the one charged?"

The guard shook his head. "Been stuck here and on the wall all day, sir, so I'm no witness. Just know it's a hauflin."

He reined his horse forward. At the livery, he gave the animal to the stable hand and made his way to his quarters. He found the halls strangely quiet, amplifying the growling in the pit of his stomach. Not until the return trip from Moon Meadow had he realised he hadn't eaten the evening ration on the previous day or broke the fast this morning. The past twenty-four hours had ignited a whirlwind of emotions, making him forget about food.

Keying the door to his quarters, he stepped inside. He'd make a few sandwiches, then find Sanderson to brief him on the events that occurred after he rushed from the Throne Room with Alaura. As he pulled the bread from the bag, he detected movement out of the corner of his eye. He whirled, drawing his sword to attack the intruder.

"Farlan! What are you doing here?" He sheathed his sword. His friend's head drooped, and he sat on the floor beside Isla's bed with his back against the wall. His large frame slumped forward. If not for his shoulders rising and falling and the occasional movement of his hands hanging over his bent knees, he would have sworn he slept. "What's wrong?"

Farlan's hands flipped up, then down. His body shook.

His stomach churned, and he forgot his hunger. Bracing himself for the news, he sat on the edge of Isla's bed. He rested his elbows on his knees, clasped his hands and glanced at his friend. How long had he sat here, waiting, perhaps for his return? Pumpkin seeds lay scattered about as if Farlan had thrown a handful against the wall. "Has this anything to do with what happened in the Throne Room?"

Farlan's head bobbed up and down, but he continued to stare at the floor.

"Are you going to tell me about it?"

"I couldn't stop them." Farlan's hoarse voice shook.

"Couldn't stop who?"

"The lords...the guards...the people. They acted like beasts of another plane." He caught his breath and looked up. His red, wet eyes bulged from his flushed face. Blood seeped from the wounds around his eyes and mouth and mixed with his salty tears. "I couldn't stop them."

Bronwyn pulled back. He thought about getting the healing kit but sat frozen in place. "What did they do?"

"They murdered him." He caught his breath. "They...they destroyed him. Everything good is gone."

"At the inquest? The hauflin?"

He nodded.

"Who did they find guilty?"

Farlan banged his palms against his forehead. "Liam's das!"

He recoiled. *Impossible!* "Are you certain it was him?"

"They dragged him to face the lords. He begged for his life. The crowd kept shouting he murdered Lady Dasia. I tried to reach him. But..." Farlan threw his head back and hit it against the stone wall. "I couldn't. Lord Val...he...he drained his life. Right there! I fought to reach him. He was innocent. I know he was innocent!"

Bronwyn's eyes swelled with unshed tears. An innocent man destroyed for the sake of finding a person to blame didn't belong in Aruam Castle.

"They decimated his body." Farlan choked on his spit. "The people stomped him. They chanted and stomped his poor little body. The guards didn't stop them. A few joined in." He wiped his face with the back of his sleeve and coughed and sputtered. "Sanderson tried to regain order, but chaos filled the room."

"What did the lords do? They should have taken control of the situation."

"Nothing. They sat on their over-stuffed thrones and watched the spectacle. Lord Val..." Farlan gritted his teeth "appeared indifferent to the life he took. It pleased him as if he had taken care of business." Spit flew from his mouth as hate consumed his features.

"And Mulryan?"

"He sat there and did nothing as if in a trance or stupor. All the lords except Lord Val acted as though they thought of other things."

Bronwyn rubbed his rough hands over his face. He wanted to erase the day and start again, but he was no wizard.

"How am I going to face Liam after witnessing his das' murder? It's my duty to protect the innocent. I failed." Farlan stared, desperate for an answer. "There's an ache I can't ease. I can't get the image out of my head. His voice, begging for his life. The blood. The insane joy the citizens relished in as they crushed and disposed of the body. I can't—" He caught his breath and stared in terror. "If you hadn't stepped in, they'd have killed Alaura instead."

Pain tore through Bronwyn. Farlan's revelation ruptured the security he felt living within the castle walls and the town. "No, I wouldn't have let it happen."

"You couldn't have stopped them. They acted mad. Insane!"

"Then I would have died trying." He tried to steady his hands, but the thought of Alaura being drained of life and her body tortured beyond recognition overwhelmed him. Though he had recently left her, he wanted to run to her and reassure himself of her safety.

"I don't know who to trust anymore." Farlan locked his jaw. "Everyone there today had the chance to stop it, but no one did. Tibs," he growled, "watched as if he enjoyed a good show at the theatre. He pushed a guard towards the mayhem, encouraging him to join in. I hate him."

The loathing in his voice surprised Bronwyn. He didn't trust Captain Tibbins, but he didn't hate him.

"If he makes captain of the guard, I'll relinquish my rank!"

Bronwyn eyed his friend. Anger fuelled his words. "Sanderson will never allow Tibs to claim his office." He put up his hand to stop any comments to the contrary. "You may disagree with Sanderson about everything, but he can be trusted."

"Captain Greenhill is Tib's pawn. He does whatever he's told. He's spineless. You're the only one who'll stand up to either of them. The other two sergeants are controlled by Tibs. I've watched them enough to know."

He couldn't disagree with him. He'd watched the alliance grow over the years, but he hadn't felt threatened until today.

"You're the highest-ranking guard who doesn't question Sanderson's authority." An odd expression crossed Farlan's face. He evaluated him as if seeing him with new eyes. Then he scanned the room as if he tried to piece together a mental puzzle. When he finally spoke, his flat voice shocked Bronwyn. "You're the only non-human with a rank higher than private."

"That's not true."

Farlan shook his head. "Tibs sent Corporal Stephens on a quest last month, and he hasn't returned. A human filled the elf's position. Stephens was the last non-human corporal. And the junior corporals aren't officially recognised by the lords; you know that."

Bronwyn scratched his head. He couldn't be right. What could be gained by having all ranking personnel one race? "Farlan, if this is true, why didn't we notice before now?"

"Because we see everyone as equal. A dwarf life is as important as a human, as important as a hauflin." Farlan swallowed hard. "And now, you're the last one."

He shivered. The history of the town of Maskil placed all four races—dwarfs, hauflins, elves and humans—on equal ground. He'd felt safe as a dwarf living amongst humans.

"Tibs wanted you to go on a quest so your position could be filled by a human."

The words pulsated in Bronwyn's head; could they be true? Thinking back over the year, about two dozen guards accepted quests. He'd have to check his records to be certain of their race, but he believed all were non-human.

"He won't stop until...until you're gone."

He shook his head in disbelief. "You're wrong; you have to be. I'm certain the commotion over Lady Dasia's murder has us thinking like this. We'll see things clearer in the morning."

"And Alaura? Will she see things as clear as she had this morning when she woke beside you? I saw the terror in her eyes when you rushed her from the Throne Room. She may never return."

Bronwyn hung his head. He felt powerless to help the ones in need, as well as deal with the possibility his career as a castle guard would soon end. This was his life; he knew nothing else. Farlan's assumptions had to be wrong. For his sake and for Maskil's there had to be another explanation for this madness.

What could he do next? Sanderson would tell him not to let anger cloud his thoughts. Act, don't react. Take command of the situation.

"Farlan, are you slated for duty tonight?" When he nodded, Bronwyn said, "I'll schedule another to take your place." He walked to the water closet and retrieved the healing kit. He extracted a cloth and poured a cleansing solution on it. The human grabbed his arm when he bent to clean the blood from his wounds.

"Don't you see, Bronwyn? It doesn't matter what we do."

"It does matter. We can't lose hope." He pulled his arm free and wiped the blood from the cuts above Farlan's eyes. "There has to be more than what we see."

"And what if there isn't?"

"Then we'll need all our strength to conquer the evil invading our home. We must be wise, stay alert and recognise those loyal to the castle. We can't abandon our post. If we do, then all is lost."

"Sanderson *had* tried to intervene but got caught up in the mob." Farlan winced in pain as Bronwyn cleaned and bandaged his wounds. "After things settled, I found him on the floor coming to his senses. He had gotten knocked unconscious and missed most of the action."

"You two have your differences, but Sanderson is loyal to the castle, Maskil and his men. He'll never steer you wrong. If I'm..." He caught his breath. "If I'm not around, go to him with your concerns. Confide in him."

"You'll always be around." Farlan placed a firm hand on his friend's shoulder. "I'm not the only one watching your back."

He knew this, but it comforted him to hear it. He had many friends amongst the guards who would eagerly risk their life to save him. After he finished tending the wounds, he stood. "My shift is almost over. I'll be back after I pick up Isla at Mum's. Together, we'll tell her what happened. We'll leave out the details."

Farlan frowned. "She's going to ask questions. She's a smart girl."

"I can't protect her from everything."

Bronwyn left his quarters and headed for his office. Taking a deep breath, the familiar warm air of the castle filled his lungs and for a moment, he forgot his destination and the tragic events of the day.

Giving his head a shake, he tried to focus on the task at hand. His best friend needed his support, and his men needed strong, confident leadership.

Isla stole glances at Liam, who struggled with his emotions. Her best friend couldn't believe his das was gone. She couldn't either. She'd seen him only a few days ago, making jokes about lizards and baby boots, and promising he'd help them build a shelter for the stray cat they'd found. Now, it felt like she lived in a fantasy world without him, one that was taking her best friend away.

Liam rested against the table in the storage room of the Forest Bakery and Herb Shop. She stood beside him, avoiding eye contact but wanting to be near him. His meeme in the front of the shop said good-bye to her das and family. Soon, they'd board a coach that would deliver them to Wandsworth where other family members lived.

She scanned the many shelves holding ingredients needed to create the wonderful aromas pervading the bakery. The room, lit by one small window, felt cramped. She'd sat here many times, reading or completing her lessons. It felt good to be around so many raw materials. The sugars, spices, flours and herbs mixed together to create an unforgettable smell. It enticed and conjured feelings of family and security.

"I won't forget you." His shaky voice broke the silence. "I promise."

She bowed her head. "Neither will I you." Seeing his hand dangling from his trouser pocket, she reached for it and intertwined their fingers. "I used to be sure of things, but I don't know anymore."

"You can be sure of me." He touched her cheek. "I'm a man now. I must take care of Meeme. When she's okay, I'll be back for you."

She gazed into his brown eyes. They appeared red from lack of sleep and from crying, but she saw in them the same strength she heard in his voice. "I wish things could be different." Her eyes welled with tears again. "I'll miss you."

Hesitant at first, he put his hands on her hips and leant towards her. She stepped closer and wrapped her arms around his waist. His arms encircle her shoulders and pull her near. He was right; he grew up fast eating oatmeal raisin cookies. At thirteen, he was more of a man than a boy.

They had hugged before, but those hugs had celebrated a triumph of some sort. Today, with only a few minutes to say good-bye, this hug felt different. In it, she tried to convey all the emotions she held for him. She pulled him closer and rested her head on his shoulder. "I don't want you to go."

"Meeme thinks it's best." He shivered. "She doesn't feel safe in Maskil after what happened."

"Das will protect you."

"Meeme won't listen to reason."

She held her breath, wishing she didn't have to let go but without warning, he pulled away and held her at arms' length. He acted unsure but given the circumstances, she couldn't imagine why. He held his right hand in front of her with the palm up.

"Isla of Maura, with the fires burning in my blood for you, I offer a pledge to unite."

She stared at the palm. Did he offer because of his leaving, because of his sorrow and the thoughts of missing her? Or did he truly believe his blood burnt for her like it would for no other? Could he honour such a pledge made at this age? Could she?

He withdrew his hand and turned to leave. She grabbed him and turned him around. She held his hand in place and laid her palm on it. His skin felt warm against hers.

"I accept your offer to pledge for my blood burns for you. I don't think I'll ever find another who makes me as happy as you do. I pledge to unite with you, my best friend." The words may not have been the same as what others spoke during a pledge, but they came from her heart. For the first time since his das' death, she saw a smile. "I don't want anyone but you."

He stepped closer and held her by the shoulders. Leaning in, he tilted his head and gazed into her eyes.

She recognised his intentions and met him halfway. He didn't need a Be-still Spell or to steal their first kiss. She'd give it freely. She closed her eyes and pressed her lips to his. When they parted, she wondered about the unfamiliar sensations the kiss had created.

"Then we're pledged." He pulled her into his arms. "I can't tell you when I'll return, but you'll always be in my thoughts regardless of where I am."

"You'll be in mine, too." She buried her head in his shoulder, fighting back tears. Hearing footsteps nearing the room, she clung tighter, knowing a family member approached who'd tell them the time had come to leave. His masculine scent filled her senses and branded its mark in her life force.

"Liam," said her das. Sadness filled his voice. "Your meeme is waiting."

After one final squeeze, the two separated. She couldn't stop the tears and ran to Bronwyn, burying her face in his chest. He held her with one hand and gathered Liam with the other, hugging them both. "It's not forever. You'll see each other again. I'm sure of it."

Bronwyn led them from the room to the shop. He guided Liam to his meeme's waiting arms. After a few more hugs and good-byes, the Jenkins family left.

Liam closed the door, and a wretched feeling erupted in Isla's chest. The terrible thought she might never see him again walloped her. She wanted to run and hide, but everyone watched her.

"Honey, why don't you take her upstairs?" Maisie rested her hand on her son's shoulder.

"No, Mum. Isla and I have an important task to complete." He gathered his daughter in his arms. "We'll see you tomorrow." He held Isla's hand and guided her out the door and through the town gates. They walked in silence, exchanging glances now and again. About a mile away, on the road to Moon Meadow, they met Farlan. He led them into the woods to a peaceful meadow overlooking the Shulic River.

Isla looked down at a narrow hole dug into the ground. "What's this?"

"It's a grave," said Bronwyn solemnly.

Farlan picked up a sack and carried it to the hole. With the gentleness of a das carrying his newborn, he placed the sack inside.

"Is it Liam's das?" She clung to his hand, and her insides shivered. She'd never stood this close to a body. A strange odour came from the bundle, and a memory of a woolly animal flashed in her mind. She closed her eyes and tried to make sense out of the warm feelings connected with the smell. She remembered a low murmur but nothing more.

"Yes, it is," said Bronwyn. "We recovered what we could. It was the least we could do."

"Hopefully, this will bring peace to his soul and to those of us who must live with the memories." Farlan, still squatting, looked at her. "I'm sorry we can't do more."

"Maybe you can bring Liam here if he comes looking," said Bronwyn. "Let him know we gave his das a respectable burial, and that we did care."

Isla picked up a grey stone from near the hole. After fingering the granite rock for a moment, she pressed it against her palm and closed her fingers around it. She took note of her surroundings and recorded them in her memory. How far was she from the river? What corner of the Pogwa Mountains could she see? What direction had they taken from The Trail to get here? She'd remember all these things, so she could return with Liam.

17

Moment of Betrayal

ISLA LEANT against the door frame of Bronwyn's office while he searched for a form amongst the papers on his desk. Liam had left two days beforehand, and the ache in her heart hadn't waned. She feared it never would. Her chances of visiting Wandsworth were slim because of the distance and because her das had never ventured farther than the outskirts of Maskil. Still, in a few days, she'd ask if they could go.

The sound of footsteps on the stone floor made her peer into the hallway. Hauflin lord Peadar Tasgall appeared deep in thought as he walked and didn't see her. She sneaked a glance at her das; he continued his search in a cabinet drawer. Slipping from the doorway, she followed the lord.

"Hey."

He stopped mid-stride and turned to face her. "What is your query, child?" Lord Tasgall cocked his head and stared at her. The cloak cascading over his slim shoulders hovered near his knees, concealing his body in a layer of brown brocade. His dark hair swooped across his forehead and disappeared beneath the collar of the cloak. His intense gaze intimidated her.

"I want to know why... Why did you let it happen?"

"Let what to happen?"

She drew a deep breath. Her das had taught her to respect the lords, to speak to the guardians of the castle with appreciation. The wise lords had important jobs. They kept everyone in Maskil safe. But they hadn't kept Liam's das safe. "Why did you let them kill Liam's das? He didn't murder Lady Dasia."

Lord Tasgall sighed sympathetically. "My dear child, I passed no judgement. There was naught I could do."

"But you're a lord. You have the power to control things. You let them kill him."

"I empathise with your loss, but the evidence clearly found him guilty of the crime and deserving of the punishment."

"He couldn't kill anyone. He was a good man." With tears burning her eyes, anger grew inside, and the words spilt forth unchecked. "You're the murderer. You watched them take his life, and you," she dug her finger into his chest, "didn't do anything! Doesn't it matter they killed one of us? A hauflin?"

Lord Tasgall stepped back. "You've been misled, child. I did not witness the extraction of his life."

"You knew they'd kill him, and you didn't have the courage to stop them! I hate you!" Without another thought, she slapped his face. No sooner had she made contact when a force from behind jerked her off her feet.

"I'm sorry, My Lord." Sanderson flung the hauflin over his shoulder. Her feet kicked wildly, and her fists beat on the captain of the guard's upper back. "I'll see to her."

"I understand her grief." The lord touched his palm to his red cheek. "The day traumatised us all." He turned and walked away.

Isla fell limp when Sanderson began walking. As she bobbed up and down with his stride, she caught a glimpse of her das following in silence. Confusion blanketed his face. When he learnt what she'd done, he'd be furious.

Passing through the doorway of Sanderson's office, the captain of the guard gestured for Bronwyn to remain at the threshold while he sat in his chair and plopped Isla onto his knee.

She pushed her hair from her face and looked up at the largest man in Ath-o'Lea. He wiped her tears away with one swipe of his shirt sleeve, then he tugged on the front of her vest to straighten it. In all the years she'd known him, Sandy had never said a mean word to her. Though she sensed a reprimand for her actions, she didn't fear him. She had lived long enough to know most people in her life acted inconsistently and easily gave way to emotional outbursts. Sandy didn't.

"I once knew a young sprite like you," he began. "She abound with spit and fury, too. When she believed in a cause, she never gave up. She stayed loyal 'til the end." He paused. "I didn't mind, but it created a problem." He eyed the young hauflin. "She let the fury get the better of her. I tell my guards, if you're blinded by rage, you miss fine details. They may not seem like much, but they could add up to a story worth hearing." He adjusted her weight on his knee. "I know you hurt. Liam's your good friend. But it doesn't give you the right to slap a lord."

Her das gasped, and she bowed her head. She shouldn't have struck the lord, but he had infuriated her when he said he couldn't do anything to save Liam's das. Why couldn't he? Then she remembered: he said he hadn't witnessed the killing.

With his thick index finger, Sanderson lifted her chin. "You're a smart girl, a little young to understand the workings around here, but I bet if you think about what happened today, you'll be wiser."

Isla stared up at him. She wanted to be wise like him and her das and Alaura. Then she could fix things when they went wrong. "I'm sorry I disappointed you, Sandy. I'll think the next time." She leant in close. "But if he deserves a reprimand and I'm not angry, can I give him one?"

He chuckled. "I'd expect nothing less." He pulled her into his arm pit and ruffled her hair. "Off with you now," he set her on her feet, "before every guard thinks he can sit on my knee for a reprimand."

She walked towards her das, and the fear of a longer lecture unsettled her nerves. When she looked back at Sanderson, he played with the ring finger on his left hand, a habit he did without thinking about it.

"Sergeant." Sanderson eyed Bronwyn. "One reprimand will suffice."

"Yes, sir." He led Isla from the office.

೮೦ ❖ ೮ঽ

Bronwyn led Isla across the Gateway Bridge and headed for the Forest Herb and Bakery Shop. He squeezed her hand, and when she looked up at him, he saw the worry etched on her face. She had struck a lord of Aruam Castle. *Unbelievable!* He didn't know how to discipline her for her actions because of their shocking nature. Sanderson didn't want him to reprimand her, but he felt he had no choice. Her actions were inexcusable. He sighed. His anger worried her. *Shouldn't it?* He released another sigh. Being a das proved to be the most challenging and most confusing position he'd held. Yet, he never considered relinquishing it.

Spotting an empty bench near a shop window where they could sit and discuss the matter, he sat down and gestured for her to sit beside him. He took a deep breath to calm his emotions and gather his thoughts. When he saw tears well in her eyes, he couldn't punish her.

"Isla, I won't lie. I'm disappointed by your actions. Striking Lord Peadar is...is inexcusable." He wiped a tear from her cheek. "But I understand. You're young, and it's difficult to sort your emotions with the recent events. It's difficult for me to cope, so it would be doubly so for you."

"Das, I'm sorry. I never meant to disappoint you." She clung to his hand. "Please, don't be mad. I won't ever do it again. Promise. I'll be good."

"I'm not angry." He pulled her into his arms. "Isla, you *are* good. You're the best child a das could have." He kissed the top of her head and lifted her chin to face him. "Don't ever forget that."

"I won't. I'll try to be wise like Sandy said. I'll fix things instead of getting angry."

"Remember when you do wrong, I still love you. I always will. Nothing you can do will change the way I feel."

"Nothing?" She wiped her eyes with the back of her sleeve. "Nothing at all?"

He kissed her cheek. "Nothing."

"What if I threw a rock and broke the glass?" She pointed to the large shop window behind them.

He frowned. "You'd be in trouble, but I'd still love you."

"What if I stuck out my foot and tripped an old woman walking by with her arms full?"

He gently grabbed her by the front of her vest. "Oh, you'd be in big trouble." He grinned. "But I'd still love you."

She leant close to his face. "What if I took your fenberry jam and dumped it over Mulryan's head?"

"Let me put it this way: you'd be so busy cleaning our quarters, you wouldn't know if the sun shined or the rain fell... But I'd still love you."

"Why?"

"Why? Well, it's as easy as asking you the same questions. Would you still love me if I broke a window, tripped an old woman or dumped jam on Mulryan's head?" Her stare puzzled him, and he posed new questions. "Would you still love me if I accidentally dropped your favourite book into the fire?" She nodded, and he continued. "Would you love me if I lost your precious stones in the river?"

Her expression turned serious. "Yes."

"I see I'm pushing my luck." He chuckled and gave her a big hug. "Isla, it's hard to explain. You must trust me on this. You do trust me?"

"Of course, I do." She knelt on the bench and wrapped her arm around his shoulder. "Do you forgive me?"

"Like a sprite does the moon for shining so bright." On occasions like this, the familiar phrase created by them long ago brought a serious discussion to a happy ending.

Isla squeezed his neck. "I'd do anything for you."

"For you, too."

"Love you."

"And you." He couldn't wish for a more wonderful child, and as Alaura had said, mistakes were an intricate part of growing up. How he dealt with those mistakes made the difference in how she learnt from them.

"Can I be with Alaura today?" She gave him an uncertain stare.

"Alaura's not well. I've explained this to you. She needs a few days to recover."

"I miss her, das. You'd tell me if she was in real danger, right?"

He forced a smile. "Alaura's going to be fine. In a few days, you'll be able to see her."

"Will you take me to Moon Meadow?"

"As soon as Alaura is well. Until then, my parents are happy to have you with them. Your granddas appreciates your help." He stood and reached for her hand.

She jumped from the bench and wrapped her fingers around his. "I'll be a big help. Promise."

He chuckled. "I expect nothing less." His need to see Alaura only grew the longer they remained apart, but she needed her rest. Still, maybe he'd ride to Moon Meadow later and enquire about her progress.

Approaching footsteps caught his attention. It was Catriona. She wore a cloak that covered her entire body, and instead of her usual brisk pace, she walked with a limp. When she neared, it shocked him to see multiple cuts and bruises on her face.

"Catriona! What happened?" He tried to catch her elbow, but she stepped out of his reach. "Are you well?"

"Fine," she said in a hushed voice. She waved him off and scurried away.

Many things ran through his mind as she hurried in the direction of her dwelling. Had she attended the public inquest? If so what had she done while they killed Liam's das? And who had attacked her? He'd visit her dwelling later and seek the answers.

As they neared the bakery, Bronwyn saw his dad adjusting a strap on a horse's harness. Gaven was preparing to make deliveries outside the town walls. Isla would accompany him.

"Good morning, son." Gaven gave Isla a big hug. "And how is my little helper this fine morning? Ready for a waggon ride?"

"Can I steer?"

"You're a little young, yet." Gaven leant close and whispered, "As long as you don't tell your das." He winked. In a louder voice, he said, "We have a surprise visitor this morning. You should run in and see her before we leave."

"Who is it?"

"I'm not telling. She's waiting on you in the storage room." Isla bound up the steps. "Here, hold onto this strap while I go 'round the other side and adjust the cinch." He handed his son the leather strap attached to the harness.

Bronwyn inspected the team of exceptional horses. They'd made deliveries for years and could probably find their way to each stop without a driver. "Who is the surprise visitor?" One of his sisters, Loran or Rhiannon, probably waited inside. With no children of their own, they enjoyed making things for Isla at their dress shop. They often teased him about his little girl dressing more like a boy because she never wore dresses. He didn't choose her wardrobe; Isla preferred shirts and trousers. A dress got in the way of her outgoing spirit.

"Alaura."

His head snapped up. "Did you say Alaura?"

"Yup. She's waited a good thirty minutes. Pull on the strap a bit."

He pulled on the strap as he glanced towards the bakery door. A healed Alaura waited for him inside. He wished his dad would hurry.

"Darn. This doesn't want to fit today."

The horses tugged on the strap and took a few steps forward. He grabbed the bridle to steady them. "Does she look well?"

Gaven glanced up from his work. "Who?"

"Alaura."

"Oh. A little pale, but she said her strength is returning."

The news brought him relief, but he'd feel better when he could see for himself. His dad cursed, and the strap went slack.

"I'll be another minute."

Bronwyn groaned.

Five minutes later, the strap secured, he bounded up the steps, leaving his dad chattering to himself. He scanned the bakery and found it empty, so he walked to the storage room in the back. His nerves fluttered with the anticipation of seeing Alaura again. He wanted her to be well, and he wanted to test the waters of their new-found closeness. Now would she accept a date with him? Thoughts of them together before the inquest as he touched every sensual part of her body, then afterwards as they clung together sharing memories raced through his mind.

When he stepped into the storage room, he disturbed a conversation betwixt Isla and Alaura. It looked serious. He hoped his daughter hadn't caused her more worry; she still suffered from the horrific attack. Isla hugged Alaura and whispered in her ear. He tried to eavesdrop, but she spoke too low, possibly in cant. Before Isla left the room, she threw her arms around his neck and kissed his cheek.

He returned the hug. "Take care of your granddas. He gets sidetracked now and again."

Isla beamed "He's like you." Before releasing him from her hug, she whispered, "Sandy was right. When you think about things, it's easier to fix what's wrong. You didn't want me to tell Alaura how you felt, but I did. She understands."

His body temperature rose. Had she told Alaura about wanting to steal a kiss? His daughter skipped out of sight, taking his courage with her. Bashfully, he gazed at Alaura who sat on a stool next to the table. "Ah...well, it's um..." He stepped nearer. "Children. Isla has a great imagination. She doesn't understand the way...uh, the way things are with adults."

"It's okay. Isla told me how you feel." She smiled, closing the book in front of her. "I feel the same way."

"Really?" Relief washed over him. Maybe Isla had done him a favour after all. "I thought you might, but you wouldn't...You never said anything." He leant closer. "Isla had told me so. I should have believed her."

"She's a keen little girl. It's why I know she'll be fine. She'll miss Liam, but between the two of us, we'll keep her busy." She stared into his eyes.

He hesitated. "Aren't we talking about me... I mean us?"

"We're talking about you and Isla. You're worried she'll be lonely." She patted his hand resting on the table. "In a few days, I'll be well enough to spend time with her. Together we'll see her through this." She squeezed his hand for reassurance.

His gaze fell to the floor. He had assumed wrong. Isla hadn't told her about the way he felt.

"What did you think we were talking about?" She lifted his chin. "What's wrong?"

"Nothing. Isla had worried me is all."

"Liar." She wrapped her fingers around the front of his shirt and pulled him towards the stool. "Tell me the truth."

He tried to look away but became lost in the reflection in her eyes. The light entering the window danced and sparkled in them, teasing him to reveal his thoughts. So much had happened in the past week: the murder of Lady Dasia, the inquest and now Liam and his meeme leaving. The incidents had pushed and shoved him and Alaura in many directions, often with fleeting moments of intimacy.

"I'm not leaving until you tell me." She smiled and held his shirt firmly. "You've been there for me when I most needed a friend. If there's anything I can do for you, I want to do it." She leant closer and tilted her head to look into his eyes.

"I...I'm not good with words...saying things to you." He couldn't resist her smile, her closeness, her scent. They filled his senses and jumbled his thoughts. His gaze fell upon her lips and his mind emptied. He wanted to kiss them.

Her breath caught as if she understood what he wanted. Though ignorant of magic, she froze as if he had cast a Be-still Spell. He leant closer, and her warm body tugged on his skin. Her eyelids drooped as if she prepared to savour whatever pleasures he intended to deliver. The weight of her hand on his shirt drew him nearer until her breath fell upon his lips.

"I can't find it anywhere!" Maisie threw open the door and froze as she saw her son and Alaura in a lover's embrace.

"Goodness!" Alaura shoved them apart.

"Mum!" Bronwyn stepped away from Alaura and straightened his shirt. "We were...talking. Talking about...Isla. Liam. Magic." He fumbled with the words, trying to hide what his mum suspected.

"Don't let me interrupt." Maisie half smiled. "Continue."

The pair exchanged glances. Did his mum expect them to kiss in front of her?

"I have to go." Alaura slid the book from the table and started for the door.

"Don't leave because of me," said Maisie. "I'll be out of your way in a moment. Gaven said he left the delivery list in here. Did you see it?"

"No, I didn't." Alaura moved closer to the door. "I must go. Beathas is waiting for me."

"Then travel safe, my dear." Maisie placed a hand on her arm. "Our door is always open to you."

Alaura left the room.

"I have things to do, too." Bronwyn attempted to leave, but his mum closed the door and stood in front of it. He took deep breaths to slow his racing pulse. He had almost kissed Alaura; his mind could focus on nothing else. "Mum," he gestured at the door, "may I pass?"

"Sit down." She pointed to the stool.

"Can't this wait?"

"It can't. Sit."

He threw his arms up in surrender and sat on the stool. "What's so important?" When she put her hands on her hips, he knew a lecture followed.

"How are things between you and Alaura?"

"They're fine."

Maisie frowned. "You've stumbled your way around that sweet girl for years. You're a grown man, but you're acting like a timid boy. Does this kiss mean you are more than friends?"

"Mum, I'm not talking about this with you." He stood to leave, but she pushed him back onto the stool.

"That's the problem. You won't talk!" She glared at him. "This bashfulness was cute when you were a boy, but now it threatens to keep you from the one who cares about you."

"Mum, I have everything under control."

"As you had control of Breckin?"

The painful memory from long ago resurfaced, and he swallowed hard.

"I don't know exactly what she did to you because you refused to talk about it but from the rumours that circulated, I learnt what your friends and siblings thought happened."

"Mum, I don't—"

She put her hand over his mouth and spoke in a softer voice. "She hurt you in the worse way, honey, but Alaura's not like her."

"I know, Mum." His voice cracked. He could still smell the blooming lilac in the garden where he had let down his defences and allowed the woman he adored lead him into a compromising position. "Alaura's nothing like her. *She's* an evil witch."

"And she has entrapped you all these years, frozen you in the moment of betrayal." She brushed his hair with her fingers. "It's still fresh in your heart because you haven't dealt with it."

"Mum, I want to forget about it. Bury it. Never talk of it."

"If you do, you won't ever be free of it. Don't let her claim your entire life. You've given her more than enough. Take it back."

"There's nothing I can do but forget about it."

"No. You need to tell the one who matters most."

He shook his head and pushed her away. "I won't. A real man forgets such things and moves on."

"You'd lose Alaura to your embarrassment? Isn't she worth swallowing your pride for?"

"Alaura wouldn't understand. We're only friends, after all." She glared at him as if she saw through his lie. "I can't." He surrendered to the ache in his heart. "I want to forget about the stupid, weak-minded, naive fool that bitch suckered!" He clenched his fists, wishing he could strike out at something, anything. Over the past few days, he'd struggled to control his anger. Thinking about Breckin threatened to send him over the edge.

"Why do you blame yourself? She did this to *you!*"

"No! It's my fault. I didn't have the brains to stop her!"

"Why don't you blame your dad, too? He's the one you inherited this bashfulness from. Girls terrified him in his boyhood."

He had no knowledge of this and tried to imagine his dad fumbling for words with his mum.

"I know what you're thinking: he's confident and cocky. But you didn't know him in his youth."

"I can't believe it."

"He hides it well; better than you." She put her hands back on her hips. "When we courted, he told me nothing. I had to ask him out for a picnic. Otherwise, I had to hope he'd happen by while I sat on the blanket with the basket. If not for me reading his mind, none of you children would have been conceived."

He would have laughed if she hadn't described his own methods of courting Alaura. On several occasions he'd tried to ask for her time, but for one reason or another, his attempts failed.

The door opened and Gaven walked into the room. The silence he met stopped him in his tracks. "What?" he asked innocently. "Did you find the delivery list?"

"It's time you had *the talk* with your son about spring birds and twitterpation," said Maisie sarcastically. She walked past her mate and gave him a defiant glare.

Gavin eyed his son. "You're thirty-two years old; a little old for the talk on girls."

"Thanks a lot, Dad." Bronwyn walked away, leaving his dad alone in the middle of the room, scratching his head.

18

One of 51

~~~~~~~~~~~~~~~~~~~~~~~~~~~~

THE SUN cascaded upon the guards securing the walls surrounding Aruam Castle and Maskil. The men's shift began only three hours beforehand, so they were fresh and alert. Sumortide had arrived, but a cool breeze flowed from the north, bringing a needed break from the heat. A cheerful atmosphere permeated the castle despite recent events. The cause lay partly with the arrival of cool temperatures but mostly with the speculation of who would be appointed lord to fill Lady Dasia's position. Posters around Maskil listed the names of several candidates being considered. The selection of the new lord would take place in five days.

Business as usual occurred inside the walls of the castle except in Bronwyn's office. With the door shut, he went through the list of castle guards. The figures he recorded on paper painted a grim picture. Farlan's guess proved correct: Disregarding junior corporals, he held the only rank above private amongst non-humans. The race ratio for the 665 privates equally surprised him. From his calculations, humans numbered 475, creating a majority. Dwarfs came in second at 116 with lower numbers for elves and hauflins, 51 and 23 respectively. If he had guessed at the numbers without consulting his files, he'd never have imagined the extreme unbalance.

He rubbed his forehead. As unbelievable as it was, the numbers spoke for themselves: humans had slowly taken over the position of authority at the castle.

A knock came at the door, and he quickly folded the paper with the calculations and tucked it inside his shirt pocket. He closed his file folders and shoved them into the bottom drawer of his desk. "You may enter," he called out as he pulled his day's work in front of him.

The door opened, and an elf stuck his head inside. "May I speak with you a moment, sir?"

"Of course, Private Kelly. Come in and shut the door." He sat back in his chair and watched the young elf approach the desk. *One of 51.*

"I can stay but a moment, sir. I'm on my way to Sanderson's office with this report." Private Kelly held the paper in front of him. "I am aware this isn't proper procedure... Forgive me, sir. But I thought you'd want to know. She was an acquaintance of yours."

He eyed the private. Who did he speak of?

"Maybe you should read it." Private Kelly handed him the paper and glanced at the door. "But I have only a minute."

Bronwyn scanned the vital information in the incident report and gasped. The coach to Wandsworth had been attacked. The bandits had killed Finola of Mallaidh and another passenger. Gulping for breath, his thoughts went to Liam. "There's no mention of the boy. The woman's son accompanied her on the coach."

"They are delivering survivors to their intended destination. The boy survived and will be placed with relatives in Wandsworth."

He tried to swallow, but the thought of Liam's pain blocked his air passages.

"Sir, it's my duty to deliver this report to Sanderson." Private Kelly held out his hand.

He handed him the paper. "Thank you for bringing it to me. I appreciate your thoughtfulness." The elf walked towards the door. "Again, thank you. I won't mention this to anyone."

The private nodded and slipped out of the room.

Bronwyn ran his hand through his hair and stared at the papers on his desk. They had lost their importance. He closed his eyes and rested his face in his hands. Liam had no one left. The boy had said it himself he didn't know the aunt and uncle who Finola had planned to live with. The poor boy would be devastated. Maybe he could... No. Danger lurked in Maskil for Liam. Was Finola's death connected to Lady Dasia's murder, or was it coincidence? He slammed his fist onto the desk. He had to stop whoever caused these fatalities.

Shoving the chair from beneath him, he stood and walked out the door. He needed air, fresh air. He needed to think. This morning the office area buzzed with activity, leaving him nowhere to hide to find a minute's peace. The North Tower. He'd go there. The tower provided a refuge for Sanderson when he needed to sneak away from the bustling guardhouse. Occasionally, he found the captain of the guard reading or doing puzzles there. But he wanted to do neither. He wanted to sit and think about the events of the past few days.

"Bronwyn." Farlan ran up to him. "Alaura's in trouble. I overheard two guards on the wall talking about her."

"And?"

"She was arrested. They said she tried to run, but the guards dragged her to the dungeon."

"Why?" He grimaced at the thought.

"They didn't know. They heard shouting and looked down from their post to watch." Farlan stepped away. "I have to get back to the wall. The guards said it happened over an hour ago, so she'd be locked up by now."

At first, Bronwyn's feet moved at a regular pace, but as he thought about Alaura in her weakened state in the cold dungeon with criminals, his steps quickened. By the time he reached the top of the stairs leading down to the lockup, he was running. He took the steps two at a time. At the bottom, he came to an abrupt stop as the guard tending the desk stepped in front of him.

"Sir." The guard saluted. "What brings you here in a rush?"

"Alaura of Niamh. You brought her in earlier today." He gestured towards the passageway leading to the cells. "What was the charge?"

The private flipped through the forms for today's arrests. "Here it is." He handed the paper to him.

He read the form. The guards had arrested her for *Unauthorized Use of Magic*. Although vague, it appeared she had used a spell within the walls of Maskil. She'd answer to the charges in five days. If bail failed to be posted and someone didn't step up to act as custodian, she'd remain in the dungeon until that time.

"How much is bail?" He gripped the paper.

"Because this is a serious charge, bail is set at five silver."

A month's wage. "I'll sign for her. Hand me the form to have the money taken from my pay." He quickly filled out the form and handed it back to the private. "Is this a new law?" He hadn't worked in the dungeon for about eight years and remembered only the more common regulations.

"It's an old law we never enforced. Since Lady Dasia's murder, things have changed. The day after the inquest, Lord Landis called an assembly. He instructed us on how to handle some of the more obscure laws in the books. He said in these dire times, things like unauthorized magic use inside the walls of town won't be tolerated. Notices are being posted around town, so there is no excuse." He pointed to a sign on the wall behind his desk.

Unauthorized use of magic within town walls is strictly prohibited. Punishment: three years in the dungeon.

Bronwyn caught his breath. What if they found Alaura guilty? In her fragile state, she might not survive.

"Will you also be her custodian?"

He nodded. As he filled out this form, the guard explained the regulations.

"Do you understand you must know her whereabouts at all times and swear she'll be here five days from now to face the charges?"

"I do."

"And if she fails to appear, you'll lose the bail money and face the charges yourself?"

He stared at the guard. Although he had read the custodian regulations to others, they now sounded ridiculous. He didn't possess magic, yet he'd be charged with unauthorized use? "I do." He handed back the completed form.

"Private Denny!" The guard hollered down the passageway. A guard stepped out of one of the rooms to the side.

"Yes, sir."

"Escort the sergeant to cell twenty-four and release the prisoner into his custody." He addressed Bronwyn. "Explain the custodial regulations to her so she'll be clear about her obligations."

Bronwyn followed Private Denny down the passageway to the cells. Air greeting him from the underground dungeon felt cool on his skin; he had forgotten the temperature dipped this low. He recalled farther into the depths, near where the wall skirted the Shulie River, the dampness rose sharply. Guards reserved those cells for serious criminals or ones with long prison terms. The conditions in the upper cells lacked comfort, but Alaura should suffer no ill effects from her short stay.

As they entered the dungeon, he peered down the aisle leading to cell number twenty-four. He saw a small human with his face pressed betwixt the bars talking with a prisoner. In the dim light of the lanterns, the man's identity couldn't be determined. Then it dawned on him: Dugald, a man who claimed to be Alaura's friend. The man went out of his way to speak with her even when Bronwyn stood by her side. Onlookers who viewed Dugald and Alaura as they stood side-by-side on the street might think they made a wonderful couple. Bronwyn thought otherwise. He didn't like Dugald's shifty eyes, or the way he complimented Alaura, or the way she smiled at the comments. Any time he spoke poorly of Dugald, she rolled her eyes. Although the castle employed the man in some capacity, he didn't trust him. He suspected the slim-built human studied magic.

As he neared, his suspicions proved correct. Dugald stood at Alaura's cell. Her hands were wrapped around the steel bars; his rested upon them. Bronwyn shoved his own hands into his pockets and gripped the yellowish stone Isla had given him. He took a deep breath and organised his thoughts. He'd remain calm.

"Excuse me, Dugald." He stopped beside the man and gave him an authoritative stare. The human measured about six inches taller than him, but Bronwyn stood firm. "I'm here to have Alaura released." He glanced at her. She appeared to be under a great deal of distress. Then he focussed on her hands still held by Dugald.

"Excuse *me*, Sergeant, I am about to do the same." Dugald puffed up his chest and glared down at him. "Since you and the rest of these guards enjoy terrifying young women, I saw to Alaura's safety."

"I'm here now. I'll take care of her." He gestured for Private Denny to unlock the cell. "She won't need your services."

"Let her be the judge." Dugald appealed to Alaura. "I'll see you to your dwelling."

"That won't be necessary." Bronwyn pulled open the cell door and motioned her forward. "Come with me, please."

"And who says she's safe with you?" Dugald released her. "No guards can be trusted these days. They're rude and take advantage of their position."

"You have poor respect for those in charge of your safety." He grasped Alaura's hand and guided her through the door.

"Alaura, what do you say?" asked Dugald. "Would you like me to accompany you to your dwelling?"

Before she had a chance to answer, Bronwyn spoke. "I told you that won't be necessary. She's coming with me."

"Alaura?" Dugald gestured for her to follow him.

Bronwyn stepped between them. When she slapped his shoulder, he looked around at her. "What?"

"I can speak for myself." She stood taller and softened her voice. "Dugald, thank you for coming and providing comfort. I appreciate your kindness."

"Do you wish me to see you to your dwelling?"

Bronwyn waited for her answer. She frowned at him but didn't release his hand.

"Thank you, but I'll stay with Bronwyn."

"Are you positive, my dear?"

She nodded.

"Very well." Dugald glared at him. "If you feel safe with this boorish guard, I'll do as you wish."

"She does." When she squeezed his hand, he kept further comments to himself.

Dugald left the dungeon, and Private Denny followed.

Once out of ear shot, she pulled him to face her. "Jealousy doesn't become you."

"It doesn't feel good either."

"Then let's leave it for those too immature to know it's unproductive."

He didn't answer. Under the circumstances, his actions were justified. Movement to one side caught his attention. A prisoner in the cell next to Alaura's watched them. "Come with me, please. I need to speak with you."

With Dugald out of the way, his thoughts returned to Liam and his meeme. The news would devastate Alaura. His grip on her hand softened. He passed a private, a dwarf, one of 116, leading a prisoner to a cell. The insecurity for his position at the castle resurfaced.

Alaura stumbled as they climbed the stairs.

He caught her. "I'm sorry. I'm walking too fast." He placed a reassuring arm around her waist and guided her to the top. When he turned towards the office area of the guardhouse, she pulled away.

"I want to leave," she said.

"I need to talk with you. It'll take only a minute." He held both of her hands. Her eyes darted about, looking past him, peering down hallways. "What's wrong?" When their eyes met, he thought she might cry.

"I don't... I don't want to see him." Her voice shook.

"See who?"

She leant close. "Lord Val. I can't face him."

Her lips trembled; the same lips he had almost kissed earlier today needed soothing. "Alaura." His voice softened, and he caressed her hands. "He doesn't come down here. Well, not often. My office is not far. You'll be secure there. I'll keep you only a minute, then escort you from the castle."

She searched his face seeking what he thought to be courage to stay. He pulled her hands to his chest, drawing her near. "Trust me."

"I trust you, but others worry me." She caught her breath, and her fingers tightened around his hands. "I'm frightened."

"I understand." He decided to guard the news about Liam and his meeme until she felt stronger. "Tell me what happened this morning. I thought you had gone to Moon Meadow."

"I was on my way."

Someone passing brushed against her, and she shivered. Observing the activity in the hall reminded him of the morning's bustle. It had triggered his need for privacy and the reason he had aimed for the North Tower when he met Farlan. "Come with me to my office. We can be alone." He gently guided her along the hallway.

A moment later, he shut the door to his office. He helped her into a seat and pulled another chair near to sit in front of her. Their knees folded into each other. "So, you were on your way to Moon Meadow. What stopped you from leaving Maskil?"

Her hands wrapped around his as she recalled the events of the morning. "I left the bakery and had almost reached the gates when a woman screamed. In an alley, I saw a large man with a sword about to strike another man. The unkempt man appeared to be a henchman."

"The man being struck?"

"No. The large man with the sword. The woman screamed for someone to save her mate. He was a shop owner. I felt too weak to cast a spell to disarm the henchman, so instead I attempted to protect the shop owner. I threw a Light Spell, blinding the henchman temporarily. I went to assist the woman who helped her mate to his feet. That's when..." She stopped and stared at her hands. "That's when they grabbed me."

"Who grabbed you?"

"Castle guards. They pinned me against the wall." Her voice weakened, and her hands shook. "They recited a law about unauthorized use of magic. They said I'd be taken to the dungeon." She looked up, tears welling in her eyes. "I was terrified. I...I couldn't go to the castle. I panicked. I tried to push them away, escape out the town gates, but they forced me to come with them. I saved the man's life, yet they sought to punish me."

He leant forward and pulled her into his arms.

"What's going on, Bronwyn? When I first came to Maskil, users of the craft practised uninhibited in the streets. I remember watching shows near the theatre. They performed simple spells, ones to hone their abilities. I haven't seen them for a long time."

"There's a law prohibiting unauthorized use of magic within the town walls. Apparently, it wasn't enforced. Circumstances have changed with Lady Dasia's murder. Anyone caught using magic will be charged."

"What happens if I'm found guilty?" She withdrew to see his face.

The truth of the answer stuck in his throat. His mouth tried to move, but it froze as he gazed into her frightened eyes. He wiped away her tear with his thumb. "You won't be. I'll personally see to it." His thumb lingered near her lips. He longed to kiss them but hesitated. Instead, he leant forward and pressed his cheek against hers and savoured the softness of her skin. Her fingers brushed his lips, awakening sensitive nerves, then caressed his cheek. Their warmth stirred sensations he wished to satisfy. He pulled her into his arms again, resting her head on his shoulder. She wouldn't spend three years in a dungeon.

"I want you to warn your friends, your magic user friends, immediately. Tell Catriona. I can help you, but I can't protect them."

"Bronwyn." Her voice, soft against his skin, pricked his hairs. "Thank you for being here for me. I'm afraid to think of where I might be if not for you." She pulled away to look into his eyes. "I never expected you to become someone special to me, a friend so dear."

He sighed. The rapture radiating across her cheek bones and into her eyes aroused the emotions that had idled for her all these years. He savoured the touch of her fingers on his cheek, the smell emanating from her skin and the sound of her gentle breathing. "Alaura, I feel the same way about you. In truth." He paused to gather courage. "My blood burns for you. It has for a long time." Her smile confirmed what he thought; she shared these feelings.

Unable to restrain his desires, he brought his lips to hers. The first tender kiss added fuel to the fire raging in his blood. Her soft lips tasted as sweet as dew-soaked clover. The second kiss lasted longer and probed deeper. He forgot where he sat and the tragic events of the past few days.

At first, she hesitated, but then like one who had not tasted food for several days, devoured his lips. Her fingers entangled in his shirt, and she held him closer. Her bosom heaved, and her firm breasts pressed against his chest.

He caressed her shoulders, then explored her back with his fingertips. One hand slid to her belly and traced the line of buttons on the front of her dress. He quivered when she massaged his thighs, inching closer to his buttocks. He pulled nearer. Through hazy vision, he realised they occupied his office. He kissed her again, cupping her face and stilling the urges to unbutton her dress. Every bone in his body wanted to be alone with her in his quarters.

When their lips parted, she pulled him into her arms, planting tender kisses on his cheek, his ear and neck. Their breathing fell into rhythm, and it felt as though they drew the same breath. Exhaling at the same moment, their energies mixed, were gathered again and shared.

She mumbled something, but he couldn't make out what she said. Her grip held fast, and he thought she might never let go. He listened closer when she spoke again in a low voice.

"I want you. I'll always want you."

Although he didn't want her to pull away, she did. With eyes filled with unshed tears, she stared at him. "I'll think of you always, Bronwyn Darrow. Regardless of where life takes us, you'll always be dear to me. Promise me you'll remember this."

"Where life takes us? Alaura, what do you mean?"

"Promise me."

"But—"

"Bronwyn, please."

"I do. I promise, but—"

"I must go. Beathas will be worried. And..." she glanced at the door "I shouldn't be here."

Reluctantly, he rose with her in his arms. He wanted to talk more, but he'd wait until later. "I'll escort you to the town gates. Can I see you tonight?" As he spoke, he opened the door to find Lord Mulryan staring back at him.

"What's *she* doing here?" Lord Mulryan glared at Alaura.

"She's with me." He stepped forward, keeping himself between Alaura and the lord.

"This is a restricted area. Given her craft, she's not permitted here." Lord Mulryan pointed to the exit. "Get her out of here."

"Does this mean Lords Val, Tasgall and Nevell are also banned from this area? They use magic?" He braced his jaw. Challenging a lord meant going against protocol. Still, he didn't understand the banning of magic within Maskil. Though he had no use for it, he knew many who did.

The lord eyed him. "Are you questioning our security regulations?"

"I question the legitimacy of this law which bans unauthorized use of magic within the town walls. I've served this castle for fourteen years, spending three of those working in the dungeon, and I have never arrested anyone for breaking this law, though I saw many citizens use magic. Why now?"

The lord searched his memories. "The law has always been on the books. These magic users have taken advantage of our good nature. It's time they're put in their place."

"Many of these magic users are our friends and family." He couldn't remember Lord Mulryan's family, if he had one but surely, he had friends who practised the craft.

"Piffle. We don't make exceptions because of personal relations. This creature," he pointed at Alaura, "can be charged as equally as a stranger if she defies the laws. And you," he dug his finger into Bronwyn's chest, "are loyal to this castle, not to her and her sorcery. As a dwarf, your personal honour is at stake. It's your duty to arrest her if you witness such an act. Do I make myself clear?"

Bronwyn glanced at Alaura. Their worlds were colliding, leaving them as helpless observers. Still, something gnawed at his instinct. This law, which had supposedly existed for years, felt wrong. Magic and the sword intertwined, and both played an intricate part of Aruam Castle and Maskil. His parents' business thrived because of those who practised magic. The shop had operated long before his birth. If the original laws banned magic, why did the business survive? Why did so many users of the craft live here?

"You're wrong, My Lord. This law can't exist. It didn't exist when Maskil came to be, and it doesn't exist now."

Lord Mulryan leant back and gawked at him. "Sergeant, you cannot decide which laws to apply and which to ignore. You'll do as you're ordered and that's final."

"I won't." He gripped Alaura's hand as much for courage as to reassure her. Its warmth helped clear his mind and steady his nerves. "This is wrong. I won't pretend it's right. In the history of Maskil, magic played a significant role." He remembered this from his lessons more than a decade ago. He had forgotten the fact until now. In the back of his mind, he heard Glynn Dasia's voice. She had tried to warn him about this unseen threat. He hadn't felt the disruption in the energy, the threat upon his spirit she spoke of, until now. "Magic built Maskil as equally as the sword. To say our founders banned magic is a mistake. To say it has no place in Maskil will lead to more unrest, more chaos. I can feel it; it's in the air. We need magic if—"

"Sergeant, mind what you speak. Your words could be considered treason."

"No, they speak the truth."

Lord Mulryan grabbed him by the front of his vest and jerked him forward. "Listen to me." Their faces were so close, the lord's breath fell upon his cheek. "Dwarfs like us maintain a high level of honour and obedience, or they don't remain in this castle. Don't let your ignorance of this law and your lust for *that*," again, he gestured towards Alaura with his chin, "make you do something you'll regret. You're a good man, but she's leading you down a trail you shouldn't tread. Do I make myself clear enough now?"

He swallowed hard. Maybe he had overstepped his bounds. "Yes, sir."

"Good." Lord Mulryan released him. "I'd hate to rip that insignia from your uniform for something as senseless as this." He turned and walked away.

Bronwyn released his breath but jumped when he saw Sanderson standing five feet away, staring at him with his arms crossed. An unpleasant feeling erupted in his stomach. He feared Sanderson's reprimand more than the lord's. He doubted he'd be sat on his knee and spoken to as kindly as Isla had been earlier in the day. "Sir." His mouth went dry. "I was about to—"

"Step into your office." Sanderson pointed to the door.

Bronwyn cast a concerned glance at Alaura as he released her hand and walked into the room with Sanderson hard on his heels. The large man slammed the door in her face without giving her a second thought.

಩ ❖ ೞ

Alaura stared at the slab of wood separating her from Bronwyn. She wanted to run from the castle but feared she'd put him in an awkward position with his superiors. She hadn't asked him to argue her point, yet she felt responsible for the trouble it brought.

The thick wooden door absorbed most of the conversation taking place behind it, but it couldn't contain everything said in Sanderson's booming voice.

"You let the half-breed steal your senses again!"

Alaura stepped back. Sanderson spoke frankly in his own authoritative way.

"This has gone on too long! She's destroying your career!"

Was she? Had he extended himself past the acceptable position because of her? It shocked her that he'd talk to a lord in such a manner but since she didn't know castle business, she believed the disagreement was typical. Bronwyn's career meant everything to him. A dishonourable discharge would be devastating.

"Is Sanderson reprimanding Bronwyn?"

Alaura jumped. She turned and found Riagan standing beside her. She disliked the dwarf but for the moment stayed put.

"Bronwyn deserves better than this." Riagan stared sorrowfully at the door and then at her. "He's a good man who'll rise in the ranks, maybe even to captain of the guard...if nothing in his life plays against it."

The door flew open, and Sanderson stared at the startled women. His eyes settled on Alaura, and he glared down at her "If you care for this man at all, do what's best for him instead of thinking of yourself." He pushed them aside and walked away.

Alaura wrung her hands as she peeked in the half-open door and saw Bronwyn sitting in a chair with his head down, the same chair she'd sat in while he comforted her. They had endured much together, had an intimacy she'd wished against but regardless of the affections they held for each other, it had to end. Her inability to commit to a relationship jeopardized his position as a guard. She hadn't realised it affected his work in a negative way; he had never said anything. She wore the blame for remaining too long in Maskil. She should have made the painful decision to leave long ago. The hurts would have healed by now.

She stepped away from the door.

After moving several feet, Riagan caught her arm. "Aren't you going to console him?"

She shook her head. "I'm going to do what's best for both of us." Pulling her arm free, she hurried away.

19

The Aroma of Old Age

"BRONWYN."

He jumped at Riagan's voice.

"How can I make you feel better?" She knelt before him.

"Riagan, not now. I've got things on my mind."

"I heard. The door isn't thick enough to hold back Sanderson."

He looked at the closed door. "Where's Alaura? She waited outside."

"She left. She said she planned to make things right for both of you."

"What did she mean?" A strange odour entered the room. Did Riagan's perfume cause the stink?

"I don't know. It must have to do with what Sanderson said to you. She listened to the entire conversation with her ear pressed against the door."

He rubbed his forehead. The captain of the guard came off sounding gruff. What he said didn't reflect how Bronwyn felt. "Sanderson's comments were offensive. No wonder she left."

Riagan tut-tutted and shook her head. "But you should have heard the words she spoke to him. They made his ears turn red." She massaged the back of his calves.

He couldn't imagine Alaura saying anything rude to Sanderson. The unusual smell filled his nasal passages, and he felt lightheaded. What did she wear?

"She threatened Sanderson," continued Riagan. "She told him she controlled you, and at any time she could take you away from the castle."

He considered the idea and guessed it to be true. Alaura need only ask, and he'd follow her anywhere. But would he leave his position at the castle? He didn't think so. No amount of woman magic could seduce him into leaving his post. A tingling sensation arose in his stomach, and a warm feeling spread throughout his limbs.

She slid her hands up his legs. "Alaura's not the right woman. You need a lover who enjoys an encounter with a powerful man. You need a woman who's all dwarf." She eased her way between his legs and moved her hands to his thighs. "You're under a tremendous amount of stress. Let me ease it." She breathed on his neck and nibbled his skin. "I can bring you pleasure you've never experienced before." She moved closer to his face, kissing his chin then the corner of his mouth.

"I'm not interested." As he spoke, his voice softened, and irresistible sensations consumed him. The seductive aroma filling his being overwhelmed him. For a long time, he had chased after a woman, and now a woman desired to catch *him*. His eyelids sagged. If he didn't know better he'd swear his brain teetered on the verge of sleep whilst his body responded to Riagan's sensual touch.

She pulled herself closer and drew him to her mouth.

Strange lips enticed him to forget his duty and surrender to pleasure, but a hint of doubt clouded their true intentions.

When they parted, his senses struggled to take control. The fog dispersed, and shame washed over him. Although every manly nerve in his body wanted to claim this woman, his heart refused. "You'd give me your body though my blood does not burn for you?"

"Again and again," she whispered soft and low. "I'm the woman you need. You'll see as time passes." She held his chin and pulled him to face her. "We're alike, you and I, more than in our physical appearance. We both serve the castle we love. We are loyal subjects."

He studied her face. She appeared flawless except for two small round bruises, one on either side of her neck. The lines and features familiar to his race radiated on her perfect appearance. In her eyes, he saw the fullness of life every dwarf had, a hardy happiness which had carried them through centuries of harsh life. The roundness of her nose could be compared to his sister's, ready to be turned up in defiance. The ruddy texture of her lips contrasted against her earthen-like skin tone. Her ears, slightly pointed on the top, reminded him of the nobility of his line. They grew thicker than a human's and certain individuals might think them crude, but other dwarfs considered them elegant and superior. Unlike any other race, female dwarfs had the unique thin line of hair stretching from their sideburns to mid-way down the chin. Riagan trimmed hers perfectly. He ran his finger along one side. An attraction to a female of his race happened naturally. They shared a history.

History? Every being, every place had a history and in a dusty room, an institute preserved it, similar to the laws. The archives preserved the laws of Maskil. Anyone could access them with permission. But Bronwyn, a sergeant, didn't need permission. He could see for himself if a law existed that prevented citizens from using magic!

Riagan moved nearer to his lips, preparing to persuade him further.

He held her at arms' length. "This is wrong. It doesn't matter we are the same race."

"Alaura doesn't want you."

He squeezed her shoulders, not wanting to hear those words. "You're mistaken."

"Please, don't go." She prevented him from standing. "I'll do anything. Just don't leave."

This confused him. Her seductive attitude disappeared, replaced by one of desperation. "Riagan, what do you want from me?"

"Please. I beg you. Stay with me." She fell into his arms.

"Stop the games." He pushed her away, went to the door and pulled on the handle. It wouldn't open. He frowned at her, disengaged the lock and left the room.

He headed straight for the archives, ignoring anyone who gestured to talk with him. When he reached the floor of the archives, he glanced down both hallways. No one stood about. He slowed his pace as he approached the door. To his surprise, it lay wide open.

"Good morning, Sergeant." The archivist, the same man who attended the meeting in the Throne Room when Lord Val announced Lady Dasia's murder, sat behind a long desk. Unlike that day, his shirt appeared buttoned to perfection, but he wore the pendant around his neck backwards.

"Good morning." Bronwyn gazed about. Rows upon rows of books and boxes lined the walls behind the elf and his massive desk. Several books stood out for their grandness, but most were average size. To the left of the archivist loomed a generous shelf reaching to the ceiling. Identical blue covers bound these books.

The room contained two round tables with ten chairs around each. Three doors at the far end entered smaller, more private rooms. Each had a window, so those inside could be viewed by the archivist. Two lay empty but the third contained Lord Val, leaning over a book deep in thought.

"If you wish to request material, you must sign in." The archivist pointed to the ledger. "Enter your name, the date and your rank."

Bronwyn inspected the half-filled ledger as he signed his name. To his surprise, Lord Val completed every entry except two. Lord Dirck Landis had signed in two days ago, and Dugald had visited yesterday.

"All books, records, charts and archival material are accessible and can be viewed within the archives. The majority of the material is not permitted to leave this room. A small selection of books can be borrowed overnight. The exception is the books on those shelves." He pointed to the shelf containing the blue-covered books. "They cannot be borrowed, and they can be viewed only with authorization."

"What are they about?"

"Those books contain all the known spells in Ath-o'Lea."

"If they're valuable, you should have them in a more secure place. Not out in the open where visitors can take one while your back is turned."

The archivist picked up a wooden paper weight and threw it towards the books. Before the block hit the shelves, a loud snap filled the air, and the block burst into bright blue flames. "Is that secure enough for you, Sergeant?"

The large snap startled Bronwyn. He glanced at Lord Val to see if he had heard, but the lord paid them no mind.

"Is there anything I can help you find?" asked the elf.

Putting the display of security aside, he thought about what he had come to find. "I'm searching for the Law of the Land book. Or maybe the history of the law book. No, the original Laws of the Land."

The archivist rolled his eyes. "Do you seek material on a particular law?"

He nodded. "The one regarding the use of magic within the walls of Maskil."

The archivist held up his index finger. He left the desk and searched through a row of books. "Aha." He pulled one from the shelf. Laying it out on the desk, he flipped through the pages until he came to the appropriate chapter. He turned the book to let Bronwyn read. "You will find what you seek in this section. You may sit at one of the tables to read at your leisure."

He carried the book to a table and sat down. The section, *Magic and Maskil*, filled only two pages. As he read, the door opened to one of the small rooms. Without raising his head, he watched Lord Val pass. He hadn't spoken to him since the inquest when the lord had ordered him to take Alaura from the Throne Room. With the memories of the malicious assault fresh in his mind, he couldn't risk confronting the lord for fear anger would get the best of him. He'd be in more trouble than he had already found today.

Lord Val passed without noticing him. The breeze created by his robes delivered an unusual odour. From what he could detect, it smelt like a mixture of burning evergreen branches and dried burdock root. After the lord gave the book to the archivist, he left, but the scent lingered.

Bronwyn returned to the book in front of him. After reading two paragraphs on general magic use, he read: *No one other than a lord or one granted permission by a lord is permitted to work magic within the perimeter of Maskil.*

He shook his head and read more to learn the original founders of Maskil had recorded the regulation into the Laws of the Land book. Shaking his head, he couldn't believe the words in front of him. It meant the guards in the dungeon merely enforced a forgotten law. One question remained: How could he free Alaura from the charges?

The faint scent he had smelt earlier attacked his senses again. He peered closer at the text in the book. It appeared old, written hundreds of years ago in handwriting matching the era. He leant forward and sniffed it. The odd scent smelt stronger near the page. Could it simply be the aroma of old age?

Learning what he had set out to know, he closed the book and returned it to the desk.

"Did you find what you sought?" asked the archivist.

He nodded.

"Then you'd say you had a productive visit?"

What was he doing? Taking a survey? "Very productive." Before the archivist returned the book to the shelf, he stopped him. "Lord Val stirred an odour when he exited the room. It's strange. I can't place it."

"Ahh, blasted new glue. It stinks up the entire place."

"This book smells like it, too, and it's old."

"Old, yes, but it sits on the shelf next to new books." As the archivist returned the book to the shelf, he mumbled to himself. "I complain, but no one listens."

From what Bronwyn could see, the books on the shelf adjacent the one he'd read appeared equally as old. Could there be another explanation?

20

One and the Same

BRONWYN RAISED his sword and held it vertically in front of him. He stepped back and allowed the blade to fall midway before swinging it horizontally. When it reached the extent of his range, his wrists twisted and reversed the direction of the weapon in one smooth motion. He repeated the action to give the twenty-five men in front of him time to see the steps he'd taken.

The sergeant ran his favourite drill thrice weekly, taking a different group of men each time and working on skills needed to be a good swordsman. Given his experience with the weapon, his peers considered him the finest swordsman amongst the guards. Bronwyn cherished the distinction and strove to keep it.

"Spread out," he said. "Give yourself lots of room. We don't want to trim anyone's hair today." Movement at the far end of the courtyard caught his attention. Lord Mulryan headed straight for him. *Great! What is it now? Is he going to reprimand me again for this morning's outburst?*

Lord Mulryan motioned at a nearby guard. "Corporal, take over the drill." He pointed a finger at him. "You, come with me."

Bronwyn sheathed his sword and followed in silence.

When they reached the edge of the courtyard, Mulryan stopped. He studied him in silence before he spoke. "I've known your dad a long time. He's a good man. I suppose it's why I've put up with his tenacious son for so long."

Bronwyn cast his eyes to the ground.

"Knowing your family like I do, makes what I'm about to say more difficult."

He braced himself. Mulryan had decided to order him to accept the quest, ignoring Sanderson's recommendations. Thoughts of the provisions he'd need to put in place for Isla before he left flooded his mind. Official papers already existed to make Alaura her guardian if anything happened to him. Still, he needed to discuss things with her. His heart sank as he thought about leaving them both.

Mulryan put his hand on his shoulder as if to brace him for a fall. "There's been an incident on the road to Linden Lake. Bandits attacked a waggon." He paused. "Your dad's."

Bronwyn's mouth gaped open.

"He's alive, but he's not good. A crofter brought him to the Infirmary."

"And Isla?"

"What about her?"

"She had gone with Dad to make deliveries."

"The report mentioned no child."

His breathing became laboured. If not with his dad, where was she? Lost in the forest? Injured? Or... He shook his head to clear the dreadful thought.

"Go to your dad. I'll question the man who brought him in. Maybe he knows more."

Bronwyn turned and ran towards the Infirmary. The steady beat of his heart drowned the sound of his boots hitting the stone floor. Thumping filled his head, and pressure pushed against his temples. As he passed others, he saw mouths move but no sounds reached his ears. He sprinted faster, fearing he wouldn't reach the Infirmary in time. He thought of Isla, alone in the forest. The worst images possible passed through his mind, and he quickly forced them away. He had to find her before darkness set in. His thoughts went to his dad and the beating he had taken. Would he draw his last breath before he reached him?

His mouth went dry. He couldn't swallow. His throat burnt from the exertion, but he didn't slow his pace. He took the steps leading to the Infirmary two at a time. When he flew past the front desk, the attendant yelled at him, but he didn't stop. He frantically searched the rooms for his dad. When he found him, he halted near the foot of the bed.

Lord Layne Nevell looked up from the patient when he rushed in. The attendant followed on his heels. The lord waved away the man and motioned him to come near.

"He's received quite a beating." The human spoke in a smooth, sympathetic tone. "There are several bruises about the head and his midsection. A club or similar weapon inflicted the wounds."

"Will he...will he live?" Bronwyn gasped for breath. He touched his dad's arm and stared at the bruises and cuts on his face.

"He's responding well to treatment." Lord Nevell hesitated, but when Bronwyn waited for more, he said, "But I'm uncertain if he'll fully recover. He took a severe blow to the back of the head. But your dad is a strong man. He has a fighting chance." Nevell brought the small white dish he held to Gaven's nose. "He gathered these herbs. He has an eye for quality and harvests only the best. Your dad plays a vital role in my ability to treat my patients."

His parents' herb shop made deliveries to the castle, but he hadn't known to what extent. He assumed the Infirmary depended on various shops in town.

"I dispatched a messenger to notify your mum," said Lord Nevell.

"Has he awakened since being brought in?"

"He mumbled a few words but has been incoherent since he arrived. Rest is needed to aid healing. This herb will help him do so."

Bronwyn reached over and gently guided the dish of herbs away from his dad's nose. "I think I'd like him to wake."

"Sergeant, sleep is best."

"My daughter travelled with him."

Lord Nevell stood upright. "No one informed me of this fact." He placed the herbs on a nearby table.

"I hope he can tell us what happened, and where Isla is."

Lord Nevell assembled several herbs on the table and set out another white dish. "I'll gently nudge him awake but if his body refuses, it's vital he sleep."

"I ask only that you try."

The lord mixed the herbs, then brought them to Gaven's nose. He moved the dish in a circle to stimulate the aroma of the plants. With his hand, he waved the medicine into the nasal passages.

Bronwyn watched and waited. If his dad couldn't provide clues to Isla's location, it made his task much more difficult. His dad's chest rose as if he gasped for breath. Then it settled. Should he stop the wakening for his dad's sake?

"The man who brought your dad in didn't mention a child." Lord Nevell interrupted Bronwyn's thoughts. "If I had known, I'd have acted accordingly."

"I know."

Gaven's head moved from side-to-side. He opened his mouth for a big breath of air.

Lord Nevell kept the dish near his nose. "We can keep him awake only a short time."

"I understand." He leant close to his dad's ear. "Dad, can you hear me?"

Gaven slowly opened his eyes. He stared off into the distance as if confused by his whereabouts.

"Can you tell me what happened? Where is Isla?"

"Isla?" Gaven's voice trailed off. His eyes found Bronwyn, and he stared at him. "Isla."

"Where is she?" He gripped his dad's hand, urging him to answer.

"The waggon. A gnome." Gaven closed his eyes. "Run, Isla." He choked on his spit. When he managed to catch his breath, he glared at his son. He grasped his hand with the little strength he had and drew him near. "Keiron."

Bronwyn's eyes widened. What did Keiron want with Isla? "Dad, did Keiron attack you? Please, hold on." His dad mumbled inaudible words, then slipped into unconsciousness. "Dad! Dad!"

Lord Nevell came to his side of the bed, pulled Bronwyn off Gaven and held him by the shoulders. "He can help you no further. He's too weak."

He clasped the lord's forearms. It horrified him to think of Isla with Keiron. The man had inflicted unimaginable mental and physical abuse upon her. It had taken months of his and Alaura's continual care for her to come out of her shell. With her back in the hands of that thief, she'd face the abuse all over again.

"Who is this Keiron?"

"A thief. A vile, ruthless criminal."

"Why would he want your daughter?"

"Because...because... I don't know."

"What is their connection?"

"Isla spent the first five years of her life with him, but I'm her legal guardian. In all sense of the word, I'm her das."

"Keiron is her blood sire then." Lord Nevell released his hold. "He has returned to claim what he believes is his."

"She's my child. He has no right to her."

"Bronwyn." Maisie rushed into the room and into his arms. "How is he?"

"He's resting, Mum." He hugged her tightly. His oldest sister, Molly, came in behind her. He guided his mum to the bedside.

Maisie went to Gaven and hugged his chest. Bronwyn watched in silence. His mum kept the family together with her determination and courage, but the source of her strength stemmed from his dad. The same held true for him; his dad would be lost without her. They had met in their late teens and together became a force to be reckoned with. He learnt from them how two people who were meant for each other could overcome all obstacles to be together. It didn't matter how small or how large the problem, the fire they carried for each other always saw them through. He had asked his dad once what attracted him to his mum. His first comment joked about her beauty. Then he got serious and said, *A man knows when he's met his best friend, son. He also knows when he's met his match. When they're one and the same, he's met his life mate.*

Molly slipped her arm around Bronwyn's waist and rested her head on his shoulder.

He pulled his sister near. "He's going to be okay. He has to be." He wanted to stay and support his family, but every minute spent here meant one more minute not knowing Isla's fate. After a few moments, he pulled Molly aside. "I have to go."

"Where?"

"To find Isla."

She gasped. "She was with Dad. Where is she?"

"I don't know. The person who found Dad didn't mention anything about a child. She..." His voice cracked. "She's missing." He gripped her hand as tears stung his eyes. "I think Keiron took her."

"What would he want with her?"

"I'm going to find out. I'm taking a company to search the area. If she's not there, we'll track the thief. We'll find her."

She pulled her brother near and kissed the side of his head. "I know you will. May the forest nymphs bring you a swift return."

"Sergeant." Lord Mulryan stood at the entrance. "Come with me." He nodded at the rest of the Darrow family.

"It was Keiron," said Bronwyn as soon as they entered the hallway.

"Keiron Ruckle? The hauflin who stole the research maps from the castle several years ago? Isn't he Isla's dad?"

He nodded. "But I'm her legal guardian. He has no right to take her."

"The Law of the Land grants you possession." Mulryan motioned him down the hall and towards the exit. "I questioned the man who brought your dad in. He found no sign of a child at the attack site." He paused. "If your hunch is correct, then Isla was the target, not your dad." Once out of the Infirmary, Mulryan headed for the guardhouse. "The men are preparing to leave. It appears we'll need a few more than I anticipated."

"I'm leading the search party."

Mulryan glanced at him sideways. "I expected nothing less." They entered the guardhouse and found Sanderson and several other men amid preparations.

"My Lord, we're almost ready." Sanderson stood upright.

Bronwyn felt his stare, but the captain of the guard didn't say anything to him. Remarks made during their earlier quarrel replayed in his mind.

"I'll need six good men for this mission," said Lord Mulryan.

"Sir, I believe these two guards will suffice to investigate an attack on a citizen." Sanderson stood next to two privates.

"There are new developments indicating additional men are needed." Mulryan gestured for Bronwyn to stand beside him to appear in front of the men he'd soon take command of. "You four over there. Come here."

Two dwarfs, a human and an elf joined the small group.

Lord Mulryan continued. "A twelve-year-old girl travelled with Gaven Darrow in his waggon when the attack occurred. She's still missing. We believe a notorious thief, Keiron Ruckle, is behind the crime."

Sanderson shot Bronwyn a concerned glance. He rubbed his chin, and let his gaze drift around the guardhouse.

"This hauflin man is ruthless. What makes this more difficult is the girl, the sergeant's ward, is his blood daughter. We believe Keiron attacked the waggon to capture her." He put a strong hand on Bronwyn's shoulder. "But the law recognises this man as her dad. We'll do everything in our power to reclaim her. But your mission is two-fold. I want the thief brought in at all cost. He's a menace to castle security. It's time to end his escapades."

The man in charge of the livery entered the room. "Sir, the horses are ready."

"We need a few more," said Sanderson. "Saddle seven horses with provisions for a week."

"Make that eight." Farlan came to an abrupt stop at the guardhouse door.

Sanderson and the corporal stared each other down, each waiting for the other to say something to cause a disagreement. Bronwyn had witnessed many senseless spats between the two and hoped one wouldn't erupt here when calm heads were needed. Sanderson's stance eased. He nodded at the livery hand. "Eight." He motioned the men to the tactical room where a large map covered most of one wall.

Bronwyn surveyed the map of Ath-o'Lea; its immense size astounded him. His small daughter being lost out there made it vast.

"Here is where the attack took place." Sanderson pointed to a position on the map. "Given the location, Ruckle has only a few options. He can double back and head towards Ellswire, but he'd have to pass within view of the front gates. He can continue north, through Moon Meadow and onto Petra. Or he can head for the Foothills towards Colgan Pass. Or," Sanderson dragged his finger through the forest, "he might try and bushwhack a trail to connect with the road to Ellswire. If that's the case, you'll have no problem following him. Sergeant, is there anything else we should know?"

Bronwyn stepped forward. "Keiron's not alone. My dad mentioned a gnome, but I'm sure there's more. The scoundrel's not a coward, but he finds safety in numbers."

"Men, we're dealing with a slippery cuss who'd sooner have his throat cut than surrender," said Sanderson. "Don't let down your guard. The welfare of an innocent girl depends on the success of this mission. Use any means necessary to bring the thief back to Maskil: dead or alive, it matters not."

In a gesture of support, he rested a hand on Bronwyn's shoulder and in a low voice said, "Bring Isla home. Whatever needs to be done, do it."

Bronwyn slid from the saddle and studied the hoof and waggon patterns. "Men, scout the edge of the trees to see if they headed into the forest." He imagined the path his dad had taken to reach this point, the deliveries along the way and the possible stops to gather herbs. From his calculations, the bandits had a six-hour head start. Speaking to settlers living along the trail, he learnt no strangers had passed through on the way to Maskil today, at least none fitting the descriptions provided. The deep Shulie River lay to the west. It meant Keiron had headed north or east.

"Sarg! Over here!" Junior Corporal Sawney Cronin poked his head out from behind a bush. "I found a sign."

Bronwyn and Farlan followed him to a small clearing behind a thick clump of evergreens where they spotted more than a dozen manure piles.

"Sarg, the reins of five horses were tied here." Sawney pointed to several trees with chafed bark.

"Keiron has plenty of company." Bronwyn hadn't expected that many attackers.

"And of various races." Sawney drew him near, and they squatted to study hoof prints. "The horses wear shoes of similar size, but they leave imprints at different depths. See this." He pointed to an imprint in the soft ground. "This one over here is deeper, indicating a heavier rider. Perhaps a human weighing about 180 pounds. Or two could have ridden one horse. The first hoof print created less of an impression. The small rider weighed perhaps fifty to sixty pounds. Maybe the hauflin. The rest are mid-range. Maybe dwarfs or elves or small humans."

Bronwyn studied the imprints, trying to absorb the knowledge his scout imparted. He didn't have a lot of experience tracking in the forest. He had spent most of his time guarding walls and buildings and chasing criminals within Maskil. Since becoming sergeant, he'd seen even less action on the streets.

Sawney picked up a round dropping from two different manure piles. "Watch this, Sarg." With one in each hand, he squished them between his thumb and fingers. One squished, but most of it remained intact. The other broke up into large clumps. "This one is fresher. The horse relieved himself shortly before they left the area. The other is about twelve hours old. This means they expected your dad to come this way and had waited for him."

"So, they arrived before dawn?"

Sawney nodded. "They didn't build a fire. I say they lay back and waited."

Bronwyn stood and surveyed the area. His dad had a routine. He made five trips a week outside of Maskil, and on each day he travelled a specific route.

The bandits knew the approximate time his dad would pass this spot. But if Isla was the target, how did they know she'd be in the waggon? Had they watched for weeks waiting for their chance? Or did they know on this day she'd travel with his dad? But, how could they? He didn't know himself until yesterday. With Liam's meeme gone, Alaura recovering at Beathas' and Farlan supervising the wall, it left no other person to watch over her while he patrolled. Keiron couldn't have known all this.

If Alaura had left Maskil when she had planned, his dad would have passed her, probably picked her up. Given her condition, he might have delivered her to Moon Meadow. It would have changed his plans. Maybe Isla would have stayed with Alaura, leaving his dad alone in the waggon.

He shook his head to clear his thoughts. This had to be coincidence. The guards hadn't arrested Alaura to keep her from catching a ride with his dad and changing his route. It'd mean the guards who arrested her had... Coincidence, nothing more.

Alaura's image caressed his thoughts. Did she safely arrive at Moon Meadow? He hoped she'd stay there tonight and into overmorrow. He wished he could send her a message. She'd want to know about Isla. She'd want to know about Finola and Liam, too. He'd tell her all about it as soon as he returned. Until then, he wished for her to remain at Moon Meadow. He sent his wish into the air as if fairies would carry it to her ear.

"Sergeant." Private Hamish Elkin, an elf, stomped through the underbrush. "There's a trail leading east. It's well-trodden, but not wide. Travelling will be single file."

Bronwyn regarded the elf: 1 of 51. "Good work, Private. Mount up men. Let's see where this trail leads."

21

Hoof Prints Dotted the Road

THE EVENING air cooled, and the sun sank behind the trees. A few clouds drifted through the sky but nothing of any size to prevent the crescent moon from casting a gentle glow upon the landscape. The earth settled into a tranquil nap to rejuvenate from the day and to allow nocturnal creatures to tend to their livelihood under the cloak of darkness. The forest breathed a relaxed sigh. All was as it should be.

Anxious energy shot through the air, awakening slumbering fairies and disturbing the quietude of the woods. As strangers approached, nerves stood on end, and creatures hid or prepared to defend their domain. Waiting in the darkness, they held their breath as danger arrived. The laboured breathing of horses echoed from the shadows. Sprays of white, foamy spit flew from their mouths as they released the oxygen-stripped air. The squeaking of leather against leather beat the same rhythm as the hooves stomping the ground. Their riders kicked them, spurring them forward into the night.

The hauflin on the lead horse dug his heals into his stallion and jerked the reins. The scar stretching from his left cheek to his nostril penetrated his scowl.

Behind him in the saddle, Isla held onto his waist for dear life. She had almost fallen off more times than she cared to think about. The first time, she had deliberately let herself go. She had jumped to her feet and ran into the woods. The hauflin had caught her and tackled her to the ground. When he had her under his control, he broke a branch from a tree and whipped her with it. He stopped only when he had appeased his anger despite her shrieks of pain.

Her buttocks and lower back ached from the beating, but she held on and absorbed the agonising pounding of the saddle. She had nowhere to run for safety if she fell off here, in the middle of the forest. They had travelled so far, she doubted she could find her way home. Her only hope lay with her das rescuing her.

Thinking of her das, an ache grew in her chest and moved to her throat. She missed him. She wanted him to hold her, to make it safe. Tears filled her eyes and though she fought to hold them, they fell. She buried her face into the back of the hauflin in front of her. Why had this stranger taken her away from him?

She welcomed the moisture plugging her nose. It blocked the stench coming from the hauflin. He smelt dirty and stinky but oddly, she sensed a familiarity with the odour. She had to be wrong. Her granddas didn't know him, though he had barely time to yell at her to run before being struck with the club.

Isla cried harder. They had killed him. They had beaten him right in front of her as a strange creature held her by the hair. She had screamed at them to stop, but they only laughed. She swung at them, kicked and screamed louder, but no one came to help her granddas. He lay in a heap near the waggon when they dragged her into the trees. She kept yelling at him, but he wouldn't get up.

Onward they went for hours. The horses pounded their way through the forest, and branches whipped her legs. She absorbed the sting. It didn't matter. Ache and pain numbed her body.

The horses broke free of the trees, and Isla scanned the area quickly. They came to rest on a road wide enough for two waggons to pass. She peered into the darkness, hoping to find a person to help her, but the area was deserted. No dwellings lay nearby to run to, but then she doubted her numb legs would carry her far.

The riders gathered the horses in a circle for a short break.

"Yew know what to dew," said the hauflin in front of her. "The castle guards will pick up yar trail, so be quick. I don't want them to catch yew any time soon."

"That won't be your problem," the human spat. From the tone of his voice, Isla didn't think he liked the hauflin. "I hope this satisfies you?"

"Damn right it does," said the other man, a dwarf like her das. Dwarfs were an honourable race, but this one lacked the virtue. "Our debt to you is paid in full."

The hauflin chuckled. "Nice doing business with yew, boys. Maybe we'll meet agin."

The human and dwarf entered the forest directly across the road from where they exited the trees. Isla feared the hauflin might be right. Her das and anyone who came to rescue her would trail them and not her. As they disappeared into the shadows of the foliage, the horse below her turn. The hauflin kicked the animal, and it charged forward. A second dwarf and the strange creature that had held her by the hair followed. She wished the beast had gone into the forest with the others. He was nothing like she had seen in Maskil or Moon Meadow.

The road allowed the horses to travel faster and smoother, and the trail leading to Linden Lake quickly disappeared in the distance. By the time the horse slow, exhaustion had set in. When the hauflin pushed her from the saddle, she fell into a soft mound of grass. There she lay, not wishing to ever move. The horse walked away, and the others dismounted and removed saddles. She wanted to watch, but the aches and pains induced a rest and teased her to sleep.

"Now that you have her, what are you going to do with her?"

The voice belonged to the dwarf. She wanted to learn their plans, too, so kept her eyes closed and her mind awake.

"One can do amazing things with children if they take the time to train them properly."

Isla didn't know what the hauflin meant.

"You going to leave her there?"

A long silence followed, but no one came near her.

"Does it matter?" asked the hauflin.

Leather straps slipped through buckles, lids were removed and spoons clanked against the inside of tin cans. Sleep threatened to claim her several times, but she fought against it. If they said anything, she wanted to hear it.

"I'll take first watch," said the dwarf.

"Wake me for second," said the hauflin. "Reese, you're last."

A long silence followed before the rhythm of snoring settled over the campsite. Footsteps approached, and she froze. The dwarf stood over her longer than she expected, leaving her time to conjure horrible thoughts. Then his strong arms lifted and carried her to a soft grassy place where he draped a blanket over her. She opened her eyes and he stared at her, not smiling nor frowning. The darkness made it difficult to see the racial features he shared with her das. Silently she wished he was her das.

He settled a few feet away from her head, taking up a position under a tree where he'd guard the campsite. Maybe the dwarf possessed a little honour after all.

She closed her eyes. She'd sleep now. Her body felt too tired to argue further. She snuggled into the blanket and before any other thoughts entered her mind, snoring erupted.

‰ ❖ ′

For Sergeant Bronwyn Darrow and his seven men, the night passed at an agonising pace. He believed they'd overtake Keiron and his band of thieves by morning. He was wrong. About a thousand yards from the attack site, the rough path joined a well-trodden route heading southeast.

Still feeling they could overtake Keiron if they didn't stop to rest, he pushed his men to travel the entire night. Exhaustion had set in by the time they entered the road at the first signs of dawn. Sawney, who led the troops, slid from his horse and steered it to a roadside stream. He removed its bridle and let it drink. The rest followed.

Bronwyn remained in the saddle and scrutinized one direction then the other. It appeared to be the road between Maskil and Ellswire. If so, then Keiron didn't go right towards his home town; he went left.

A hand touched his leg; Farlan stared up at him.

"I'll take the horse to drink," said the corporal.

The dwarf wanted to keep moving, but the human didn't budge.

"They need a rest."

Reluctantly, he slid from the saddle. His legs buckled when his feet hit the ground. He'd have collapsed if not for his grip on the pommel and Farlan grabbing his arm.

"So do you." Farlan waited until he steadied himself, then guided the horse to the spring.

Bronwyn shook the stiffness from his legs and walked in circles to work out the kinks. He often rode in training and for pleasure, but he'd never sat in the saddle this long. He suspected the others felt the same.

"Men, we'll rest here for thirty minutes. Eat if you can." He continued to walk, staring at the dirt as he did. Many hoof prints dotted the road, making it impossible to trace the same ones they had followed all night. He saw a pair of boots in his path and stopped.

"Here." Farlan handed him a flask of water.

He unscrewed the cap and drank. The cool water soothed his dry throat. His friend held out an apple, and he accepted it. Together they scanned the empty road.

"I'm sure this leads to Ellswire," said Farlan

"I thought the same."

"Then we know which way they didn't go." He scanned the edge of the forest on the opposite side of the road. "What are the chances they crossed and kept going?"

"It'd be easier to take the road."

"But is it wiser? He's going to use every trick to get away."

Bronwyn released a heavy sigh. It felt as though he shrunk a size when he released the anguish and worry he had harboured all night. Tears welled, but he swallowed them. He had to keep his senses clear. Farlan's large hand came to rest on his shoulder.

"Damn him for doing this to her," said his friend.

Bronwyn gestured towards Sawney who walked along the forest's edge. "He thinks like you. He's wondering if they crossed and kept going."

"Do you think there's another hidden trail beyond those trees? Like the one at Linden Lake? That trail isn't on the map at the guardhouse. All sorts of travellers could pass by Maskil without detection."

Bronwyn scratched his head. Surely a castle patrol had stumbled upon the well-worn path over the years. "When I get back to Maskil it'll be added." He pulled his map from the pouch on his belt and opened it. Then he refolded it, leaving the area of concern visible. He drew-in the hidden trail for future reference. "If I'm right, we're here."

Farlan peered over his shoulder to see where he pointed. "If Keiron crossed and went into the woods, he'd head for the Shulie River."

"There's no visible horse trails. It'd be rough going." He finished the last bite of his apple and tossed the core into the ditch. "If there's a trail hidden in the forest," he pointed to the opposite side of the river, "they could be in Wedgemore in about two weeks. From there, they could head in any number of directions. They could go to Wandsworth, get lost in the city." He swallowed hard. "I didn't have time to tell you this yesterday, but..." He took a deep breath. "I don't know how to say this except to just come out and say it."

Farlan folded his arms and waited.

"Finola's dead," he half whispered. Farlan's face lost all expression, and he stared off into the trees. Both had endured several horrific events the past few weeks. Tragic news no longer shocked them.

"How?"

"Bandits attacked the coach, killing her and another passenger."

"And Liam?"

"He's being delivered to Wandsworth to live with his aunt and uncle."

Farlan walked away, returning to his horse to stroke its neck. His friend still held himself responsible for the death of Liam's das. This only added to the guilt.

"Sarg." Junior Corporal Cronin stopped beside him. "I found a trail into the forest."

Bronwyn followed him to the trees and listened as he explained.

"Two of them entered here. I followed it for about two hundred feet. There's no sign of a defined trail, so they're bush-whacking."

"Only two?" He knelt for a closer view of the hoof prints.

"Yes. If I had to guess, the human was one of them. The prints are fairly deep for this one." Sawney pointed to a track near his foot.

"And the other?"

"It's difficult to say. If your daughter is riding with the hauflin, she adds weight to the horse. I can't tell if this is a medium-sized being or two smaller riders."

"The question is: Did Keiron choose the easy path or the one he had to make?"

Sawney remained quiet.

"The thief will want to travel with speed. Once he entered Ellswire, tracking would be near impossible." Bronwyn looked down the road. "In about six days, he'd feel safe. Using logic, he'd travel the road." He peered into the forest. "But he's a tricky bastard with twisted logic. If he spied on Isla in Maskil, he knows who I am. He knows I'd think he took the road, making cutting a path towards Wedgemore logical."

"Either way you size it up, Sarg, one choice will be right and the other wrong."

He eyed the dwarf. "Would you hazard a guess?"

"I'd rather give you the facts and let you decide." Sawney pulled a sapling near. "The travellers broke this tree not more than four hours ago. Discolouration has begun to set in. This type of tree keeps it's freshness for about three to four hours." He released the branch and it snapped back into place. "If they're breaking a trail, they'll be slower than those who follow them. They might stop to rest. We could overtake them within eight hours. Then we'll see who we're following. If it's not the hauflin and your daughter, we can question them and possibly learn Keiron's planned destination.

"If we choose to follow the road, we may not catch-up with them for days. They might leave the road and enter the forest, and we may not see their trail. Either way, if we don't learn we're following the wrong horses until we reach Ellswire, we'll be weeks behind these travellers." Sawney pointed to the broken trail.

Bronwyn weighed the information. Regardless of which logic Keiron used, Sawney's facts pointed in only one direction. This should have made it easier to choose the path they'd take, but fear of making a mistake caused him to hesitate. One path took him to his daughter, the other away from her. "Sawney, I'm glad you're with us."

"Glad to be of service, Sarg. I know how important this is to you." He stood and adjusted his scabbard belt. "I have a brother about the same age as Isla. We'd be devastated if he had been taken."

"Thanks." Bronwyn reached out and shook the scout's hand. "For everything."

22

His Dark Blue Eyes

ONE BY one, Isla's senses awakened. The pain in her legs and buttocks greeted her first. The bad dreams dissolved into one, and she opened her eyes. The tree branches overhanging her sleeping spot blocked the morning sun but didn't hide the ugly scowl of the hauflin who peered down on her. She trembled, remembering the events of yesterday. He must have sensed her fear because a stupid smirk lit up his face.

She breathed easier when he walked away. Sitting up, she pulled the blanket around her. The dwarf who had carried her to a safer location still leant against the tree. He ate bread from a brown bag. He didn't spread anything on it like butter or fenberry jam. He ate it as if a big cookie.

The strange creature which had held her by the hair and forced her to watch the hauflin beat her granddas to death sat on the opposite side of the campsite. She shivered when she saw him watching her. In a meticulous motion, he sliced slithers of apple with a knife, placed them on his tongue and drew them into his mouth. The colour of his short, thick fingers appeared unlike anything she'd seen on a being. The putrid green resembled stains from squashed peas. His hair lay flat against his scalp as if a year's worth of dirt weighed it down.

The eyes frightened her most. They stared at her as if gawking into her head and reading her thoughts. The cold, green eyes, like the colour of the creature's fingers, seldom opened more than half-way. He squinted at the sun though he sat in the shade.

To settle her nerves, she averted her eyes. The dwarf had waited for her attention and held out a chunk of bread. He tossed it to her, and it bounced onto the ground. She picked it up and brushed away the dirt. After taking a bite, she nodded at the dwarf, silently saying, *Thank you.*

As she ate, she watched him and occasionally glanced at the hauflin. The two didn't get along. They sat contently in their own space and didn't make small talk. When she'd eaten the bread, a flask landed in the moss near her. Again, the dwarf made an offering. She unscrewed the cap and drank the cool water greedily.

Without warning, the water vessel flew from her hands. The hauflin glared at the dwarf and threw the flask at him.

"Keiron, I won't let her starve." The dwarf's deep voice sounded fierce. It petrified Isla. "And I won't take part in killing a child if that's your intent."

The hauflin leered at her as if he'd strike her. Instead, he snarled and walked away.

Her hands shook. When the dwarf leant forward and held out the flask, she froze, terrified to accept it. He nudged her arm with it, but when she still refused, he moved closer.

"Take it. Drink your fill." His menacing expression eased, but his coarse voice remained. Then, with his back turned to the other men, it softened. "Take it." His dark blue eyes were familiar and kind and eased her fears.

She accepted the flask and, keeping her eyes on him, took a long drink. She wiped her mouth and handed it back. "Thank you," she mouthed. He returned to his spot under the tree.

No sooner had he settled when the hauflin approached with a dagger in his hand. He grabbed her by the hair and swung.

Bracing herself for the weapon, she felt a sharp tug on her head but no lasting pain. She gawked at the man and saw he held a handful of her hair. He grabbed another bunch and cut it from her scalp as if he cut dry grass to make a fire. She wanted to reach up and protect her head but if her hands got in the way, he'd cut them, too. She braced herself for each sharp tug and slash. Bunch by bunch, her long hair created piles on the ground around her. The hauflin glanced at her as he walked away, revealing the pleasure he'd gathered from his cruelty.

With gentle strokes, she caressed the lots of brown hair on the ground. It had taken years to grow it but within minutes, the stranger had taken it away. Her das and Liam adored her long locks. Both felt far away. Tears welled in her eyes. She might never see either of them again. The hauflin had said it himself: the castle guards would follow the other two into the forest. They wouldn't follow her on the road. She sniffed back the moisture in her nose as the tears flowed freely down her cheeks.

Her head snapped back by a sudden blow, sending her onto her back. She cowered beneath the hauflin.

"Stop the salt water, or I'll slap yew agin!"

Swallowing the ache in her jaw, Isla lay in the bushes, her arms covering her face. She peeked from beneath her bent elbow and eyed the man who now stirred hatred in her spirit. The dwarf had stood but didn't make any attempt to stop the scoundrel. What did he call him? *Keiron.* The name sounded familiar, but she couldn't place it. By no means did he work at the castle in his filthy condition.

The hauflin rolled up his blanket and tied it on the back of the saddle. Then he lifted the saddle into place and secured the cinch. The dwarf and strange creature packed away their gear and prepared their horses for travel.

Isla cautiously sat up, and the dwarf took the blanket and shook it. Her hair flew into the air and settled on the forest floor and surrounding bushes. Picking up a few strands, she held them close to her cheek. They felt soft and smelt like home. She folded them once, then tied them together. Opening her pouch, she slid the knot of hair inside beside the book Alaura had given her... *the book!* She closed the pouch before anyone noticed her discovery.

When she whirled about, she saw the dwarf watching her. He held up the blanket so no one else saw her actions. A peculiar expression crossed his face. She pulled her vest down to cover the waist of her pants and the top of the pouch. The dwarf finished folding the blanket and shoved it in his rucksack.

"Can I relieve myself?" Her low voice sounded raspy.

The dwarf turned. "Keiron, the lady would like to relieve herself."

The hauflin eyed her. "Go, but know this. If yew don't return, I'll hunt you down and beat yew until yor senseless. Yew'll pee in front of us from then on!"

Isla cast a fearful glance at the dwarf, but he shrugged his shoulders and continued packing. She saw a break in the trees nearby and walked towards it on shaky legs. After a minute's travel, she found a hiding place. Her personal business completed, she dug into her pouch and gingerly pulled page one from her book. Her fingers moved slowly, trying to conceal every sound of the tearing paper. Once free, she folded the page and gripped it in her hand. She tucked the book into her pouch and returned to the campsite.

Plopping down on the same spot on which she had slept, she pretended to be sad about the hair. She missed her hair and felt naked without it, so to mourn the loss came easy. When no one watched, she slid her hand beneath a thick mound and deposited the first page of the book. Her task complete, she released a nervous breath. Her racing pulse slowed.

Keiron mounted his horse. "Isla." His rough voice revealed his meanness.

How did he know her name? It rolled of his tongue as if he'd said it before. She had thought for sure he didn't know her.

"Isla! Get over here!"

She flinched. The impatient man sneered at her. Though she didn't want to, she walked to his horse. He reached down to give her a lift and before she could think further, her sore bum hit the saddle, and the horse moved forward.

23

Sundry Species of Dragon

AFTER THREE hours of riding through the forest, Sawney halted the line of horses near a small clearing and slid from the saddle. "Sarg, a fire pit."

Bronwyn dismounted and followed him. "Take a five-minute break," he said to the rest.

Sawney squatted beside a small charred circle. He played with the black embers. "It's warm. They threw water on it to douse it." He dragged his finger through the ash. "It's two or three hours old, but..." The scout become lost in thought.

"But what?"

"It appears the fire burnt for a short while." He held up a stick with a scorched edge. "It's as if they lit it simply to create a seared mark."

"Perhaps they realised the fire would give away their position so extinguished it." He scanned for clues, anything to indicate Isla had come this way. Seeing a brown paper bag, like what his parents used at the bakery to hold bread, he opened it and found a smaller bag inside. He poked in his nose and drew a deep breath. It smelt like his mum's chocolate brownies with a hint of raspberry. He'd know the smell anywhere; no other bakery in town made them.

"They visited Mum's shop and purchased bread and brownies." He threw the bag into the bush. "They're daring." He went to his horse and removed the water flask. He took a long drink, blinking the dampness from his eyes as the sun attempted to blind him. The heat of Sumortide went unnoticed in the forest, but the horrible flies pestered him. He swatted several before they drew blood. His horse's tail slapped back and forth, knocking the insects from its rump. When he saw his men mount, he climbed into the saddle.

An hour later, the eight Aruam Castle guards surveyed the Shulie River. Late Springan rains had filled the wide water course to capacity.

Bronwyn gazed at the sunlight dancing upon the surface. Several miles upstream, on a gentle bend lay Maskil. Many times, he had admired the river and wondered where all the water went. Today, he wished he watched it through the window in his quarters with Isla by his side. His thoughts went to his dad, still in the Infirmary. Surely Lord Nevell had brought him through the worst of it. He'd be home recuperating soon, being doted and fussed upon by his mum in such a way which might amount to harassment.

"Should we give the horses a drink?" Farlan rode up beside him.

He nodded and dismounted. "Private Elkin, can you take mine?"

"Yes, sir." The private led the horse to the river.

Farlan handed his reins to Private Maltby, and Private Dee took Sawney's horse.

Bronwyn and Farlan followed the scout downstream as he tracked hoof prints in the soft mud.

"It's almost as if they want us to follow," said Sawney. "They didn't enter the water or go to higher ground where the earth might be too hard to imprint."

"Would Keiron use them as bait?" asked Farlan.

"Keiron is ruthless enough for anything." Bronwyn continued along the river, searching for any sign of Isla. She was a smart girl; she'd leave a clue behind, wouldn't she?

Sawney's steps quickened, and he went to the river's edge. "They crossed here."

Bronwyn peered across the water to the opposite shore. The sediment gathered in the gentle bend of the river, forming an alluvial bar, an ideal location for travellers to cross. His eyes searched the shoreline two hundred feet away to see if any clues could be seen.

"I'll get the rest." Sawney walked away.

Once out of ear shot, Bronwyn spoke. "What do you think? Are we following the wrong trail?"

"I don't know," said Farlan.

"I feel Isla would have left a clue by now."

"What type of clue?"

He shook his head. "A shoe? A sock? Something. Anything."

"What did she wear yesterday?"

"The usual: trousers, a long-sleeve shirt and her vest. She had shoes and socks on, but maybe she doesn't want to part with them."

"Then what could she leave behind?"

"Nothing." He sighed. "You don't think she's unconscious? Or bound?" He ached to think of his daughter tied and gagged.

"We'll find out soon enough."

He followed Farlan's line of sight to see what had captured his attention. Several large black birds circled downstream. "Scavengers."

"I wonder what they're scavenging." Farlan glanced at his friend. "Probably a dead animal. Or maybe food these fools we're following threw away."

Sawney led the men and the horses along the water's edge. They climbed into the saddle and began across the river. A few of the horses acted skittish when the cool liquid reached their bellies but came under control quickly.

On the opposite side, Sawney scoured the forest line for tracks away from the river. Bronwyn searched for tracks, too, but the circling black birds played on his nerves. A bad feeling erupted in his stomach, and he fought the nervous flutters.

Sawney gestured to a small break in the trees and guided his horse onto the rough path.

Bronwyn noticed this direction took them directly below the circling scavengers that now swooped towards the ground. The knot in his stomach tightened. An urgency leapt into his heart. He restrained himself from passing the scout and rushing ahead to prove to himself the birds didn't circle Isla.

Sawney slowed as he approached a small clearing directly below the birds. He put up his hand in a gesture which meant to prepare for conflict. The guards drew their swords.

A few feet farther and Bronwyn smelt an odd odour blowing on the breeze. He steeled his nerves. Then he saw it. Not far away, off to the left, a body sprawled across a boulder. The bloody human with thick blond hair stretched across the stone as if sun-tanning. Except the gouge marks in his chest meant he wouldn't be going dancing tonight. The fresh meat glistened in the sun.

Sawney saw it, too. He pointed a little farther along to where a dwarf lay face down.

Bronwyn dismounted and walked past the scout to get a better view of the victim. It appeared he spent his last breath reaching for his sword. The man's side lay open, exposing internal organs. Whatever had attacked these men spared no mercy.

"Duck!" Farlan saw the shadow overhead and jumped from his horse.

Private Harlen reacted too slowly. A green dragon swooped from the sky and dug its massive hind claws into the human's shoulders. With a great rush of wings, the creature lifted him into the air.

Over the private's screams, Bronwyn shouted. "Arrows!" He scrambled to his saddle and unfastened his bow. His fingers moved quickly, but by the time he prepared to shoot, the dragon had already climbed high into the air. Several arrows soared towards the target, but only one made contact.

The dragon screeched and dropped the guard. The private struck several tree branches on the way down and made a solid thud against the forest floor. A quiver of arrows flew into the air. Several hit the dragon, causing it to lurch forward. It recovered and soared into the sky. The hand-like fore claws withdrew the arrows as if they were mere thorns. It roared and turned back on its assailants.

Private Elkin dropped his bow, drew his sword and prepared to defend himself. The dragon accelerated on approach, striking the elf with full force. Together they crashed through the brush. When the dragon found his feet, he turned and roared at the other guards.

Bronwyn gripped his sword. He had already lost one man, possibly two, to a dragon unseen to Maskil. He remembered stories from his childhood in which his dad had told of sundry species of dragons flying over the town. Ones familiar with the lords visited for short rest periods, but most flew on, not taking any notice of the inhabitants. Occasionally, aggressive dragons fatally wounded or carried off victims. Bronwyn had never sighted a dragon. Why had they stopped coming to Maskil?

One story his dad told spoke about a group of young soldiers camped outside the town walls on field exercises. A green dragon attacked at dusk, killing four and spiriting away another. Had the dragon in front of him come from the same species? Certainly, its fierce behaviour drew similarities. Its green, iridescent scales glimmered in the sunlight as it lashed out with its long snout. Thick layers of plates covered the body except for the head and abdomen. They fit together like slate shingles on a cottage roof. The soft scales beneath its neck folded like the shirt collar worn beneath a suit of armour. Pale green spikes protruded from above the eyes and ran the length of the neck. Did they bend like grass, or were they stiff like swords?

With the long-forgotten story of the attack now fresh in his mind, he advanced. A translucent wing lashed out, and he ducked to avoid the strike. He attacked the beast's shoulder, but his sword came to an abrupt stop. He pulled back and swung again with the same result. The scales covering the dragon were as strong as steel.

The green dragon twisted and struck out with its powerful tail. It grazed Private Rorie Critch, flinging him to the ground. The full strength of the tail walloped Sawney and catapulted him into the trunk of a maple tree. The dwarf flopped to the ground, unconscious.

Farlan raced to the front of the dragon and swung at the throat. The dragon raised its large wings and the great rush of wind threw everyone off balance. It grasped the opportunity and lashed out at Private Dee. Its powerful jaws ripped the human's arm from the body. The private swayed from side-to-side, then slumped to the forest floor.

The beast's large shoulder muscle jerked sideways, clobbering Farlan who smashed into the ground as the sword flew from his hands. The dragon whirled about and flashed its menacing yellow eyes at him. With one of its large hind claws, it grasped the corporal in the midsection.

Bronwyn watched in horror as the dragon rose with his friend in its grasp. He gripped his sword tightly and rushed towards the beast. At full speed, he raced up a small hill, jumped onto a boulder and leapt into the air. He snagged the empty hind leg of the lizard and began striking its underbelly with his sword.

The dragon pitched forward and shrieked. A greenish substance dripped onto the sword. He stabbed the creature repeatedly until Farlan's voice changed. The dragon had released him. He let go of the lizard and fell twenty feet into a clump of ferns, rolling to break the impact.

A great rush of wings overhead compelled him to jump up and prepare for another attack. Instead, the dragon flew to the tree tops, then fled south.

Bronwyn shoved his sword into his scabbard and rushed to Farlan who rolled in pain, clutching his side. "Stay still!" He forced his friend onto his back and opened his vest. Lifting the shredded uniform shirt, he gasped at the opening. "Stay here!"

He ran to his horse. "Check the wounded!" He jerked the healing kit from his pack and hurried back to Farlan. His hands fumbled with the equipment. He found the cleansing solution and struggled to get the top off. "This is going to hurt." *That sounded stupid.* "I have to clean the wound. Farlan, stay still."

In his rush to help, he spilt half the bottle of clear liquid over the wound. Farlan bolted from the shock. *Damn! Calm your hands.* He pulled out the bandages. He'd need to use every roll to contain the gash. "What the...!" He froze as a great larva the size of a banana wriggled from the wound.

"What is it?" Farlan watched in disbelief as the green larva slithered away from the cleansing solution to the safety of his dry stomach. It twisted and turned itself in the hollow of the belly button as if trying to re-enter the body.

"I don't know!" Bronwyn grabbed for it, but it slid from his grip. The slimy creature squirmed for another opening.

Farlan twisted beneath it. "Get it off me!"

He dove for the larvae but again, he couldn't get hold of it. It scuttled towards Farlan's face. "Shut your mouth!"

Farlan slapped his hand over the lower half of his face. When the creature slipped to the ground, Bronwyn grabbed his dagger and stabbed it. He held it up and dug the end of the weapon into a fallen tree trunk. Both watched in amazement as the larva struggled against the steel.

Bronwyn wiped his chin with the back of his hand and took a deep breath to calm his nerves. He pulled the clean dressing from the sack and covered the gash. "Hold it steady." He unrolled the bandages and slid one end under his friend.

"I didn't know dragons hunted this close to Maskil." Farlan closed his eyes as if to absorb the pain.

"Neither did I. There's a lot we don't know." He pulled the bandages snug. When Farlan winced, he loosened them a bit. "Is it too tight?"

He shook his head.

"It's the best I can do here." He buttoned his friend's shirt and vest, then surveyed the clearing. "I didn't expect this." He'd seen two of his men fall; they were probably killed. He needed to check on the rest. "Can you walk?"

"With help."

He eased Farlan to his feet and supported him. They made their way towards Private Critch, who tended to Sawney.

"He's out cold, Sergeant, but he's breathing." Rorie Critch wiped Sawney's face with a damp cloth.

Bronwyn spotted Private Dee sprawled in the bushes and flinched at the horrid scene of the guard's internal organs spilling to the ground. Easing Farlan down against the tree beside Sawney, he went to Private Garret Maltby who talked with Elkin. The elf had taken a beating but had no life-threatening injuries.

"His arm is broken, sir." Private Maltby secured the damaged arm with a sling. "Otherwise, he's fine."

"And you?"

"I'm good, sir. A few bruises, I suspect."

"Get him ready to transport."

Bronwyn made his way through the low bushes to Private Harlen. As he suspected, the human lay dead from the fatal fall. He had lost two men already, and he hadn't caught up to Keiron, yet. The bastard would pay for this! He wanted to bury the men here but didn't want to linger in case the dragon returned. Besides, their families would want the bodies returned for a proper send off.

Searching the sky for signs of the green lizard, he found only the scavengers who would feast on anything left behind. He approached the stranger who lay face down in the dirt. The dragon had put an end to the dwarf's running. Seeing the hand outstretched for the fallen sword, he tried to imagine the stranger's thoughts whilst being attacked from behind. What notions raced through his mind while death chased him?

He used his foot to flip the body to its back and recoiled when he saw the horror in its eyes. They stared into the sky as if the last breath hadn't made it all the way to the lungs. Bracing his nerves, he reached down and closed the lids to hide the horrendous story of death.

Searching the carcass for clues to Isla's whereabouts, he slid a small brown sack from the belt around the bandit's waist. Several copper, silver and gold coins rested inside; a fair amount of money for any man. In his chest pocket, he found a folding knife. Searching further, he discovered a bar of flint, a whetstone and twine.

Seeing a pouch attached to the belt, he unclipped the hasp and peeked inside. Next to a deck of cards, he found a folded piece of leather. It felt soft and well worn. He spread it out and discovered a detailed map of all the lands in Ath-o'Lea. He easily located Maskil, the road to Ellswire and the hidden trail Keiron had travelled from Linden Lake. His eyes scanned the place names surrounding his hometown. One name he read twice, dumbstruck by its existence.

The Caverns of Confusion? The prophecy had originated there, a mysterious place of legend and myth. To the best of his knowledge, no one had found the caverns. Why did this dwarf have a map showing the trail to them? Studying the map further, he found several named locations he'd never seen on a map before, including Knavesmire, a mythical place found only in story books. Far more keeps, towers and castles than those familiar to him dotted the landscape. Did they exist for this dead man, or did they only haunt his imagination?

He folded the map and placed it in his own pouch. He took the coins to give to Sanderson who'd divide them amongst the families of the dead guards. It wouldn't replace their lives, but it'd provide a small amount of financial aid.

He left the dwarf and went to his companion sprawled across the boulder. A quick search of the human turned up no valuable clues but several coins. He went to help Rorie gather the horses.

"How's Sawney doing?" he asked.

"He's awake. I think his leg's broken. I put a splint on it." Rorie steadied the horse in front of him. The attack had made it skittish.

"Damn," said Bronwyn under his breath. Losing Sawney meant he lost an excellent tracker.

After helping secure the dead to their horses, he stood beside Farlan as the corporal struggled to climb into the saddle. After two attempts, Farlan's strength failed, and he rested his forehead against the leather seat. "It's a long way up. I don't have the strength in my arms."

Bronwyn called to Rorie. "Can you give us a hand?"

With his help, he got his friend in the saddle. Farlan swayed slightly, but with one hand on the reins and the other gripping the pommel, he nodded to indicate he'd be fine.

By mid-afternoon, the men were resting on the road between Maskil and Ellswire. Relieved of their bridles, the horses drank and grazed freely. Bronwyn helped Farlan to the base of a shady tree. Blood seeped through the material of Farlan's shirt, and he added more bandages.

A silence fell between them as they sat together sharing their food.

Halfway through the ration, Bronwyn spoke. "You know what you need to do."

Farlan eyed his friend. "It doesn't make it any easier."

"You're in no shape to ride let alone fight. As senior rank, it's your duty to see the wounded reach Maskil. You should be there by 18:00 hours if we judge our position correctly. Can you make it?"

Farlan regarded the road to home. "I'm sure we can."

Bronwyn stared at him, battling the emotions swelling inside. In one instance, he wanted to ensure his men arrived safely at the Infirmary but in another, he wanted to continue the search for his daughter.

"As long as you get me in the saddle, I'll make it," said Farlan. "Sawney and Elkin are in fair shape. A few broken bones is all. They're strong enough to keep us going."

Bronwyn's thoughts drifted to the road ahead. The ride towards Ellswire would be gruelling. It'd be days, perhaps weeks, before he returned to Maskil. Alaura's predicament sprang to mind; she'd face the charge of her arrest in four days, long before he'd return.

"Farlan." His voice became urgent.

His friend looked at him with renewed energy. "What?"

"I had forgotten about Alaura."

"What about her?"

"Her arrest. Remember?"

Farlan nodded. "What happened?"

"They charged her with using magic inside the town walls without permission. She faces the charges in four days. I'm her custodian. I'm supposed to be there."

"I saw the signs go up around town. She could get three years!"

He swallowed hard. "You'll have to take my place. Can you do it? As soon as you're able, find her. You need to know where she is. You'll have to inform the clerk in the dungeon of the change." A sudden rush of helplessness invaded his thoughts. "I can't have her spend three years in the dungeon."

Farlan rested his arm across his friend's shoulders. "I'll see to her. I'll use whatever authority I have to make damn sure she's not found guilty. If I have to, I'll recruit the ol' man's help. He'll know a loop hole to keep her free. The last thing he wants is to have his best sergeant sitting outside a dungeon cell for three years."

Bronwyn half grinned, but the worry remained. His exhaustion added pressure to his nerves already strained by the loss of Isla. The uncertainty of his dad's condition only added to his stress. Casting a sideways glance at Farlan, he wondered if *he* had the strength to survive.

A few short weeks ago, he had felt satisfied; he lived the life he wanted. Now, the fear of losing everyone he loved the most played havoc with his heart.

"I'll take care of Alaura," said Farlan. "If I have to, I'll unite with her before she faces the charge."

Bronwyn stared at his friend with a lowered brow.

"They won't put a corporal's mate in the dungeon unless she's charged with murder."

"Why?"

Farlan shrugged. "It's written in the book of protocol. I learnt about it last week when Corporal Murphy used it to free his mate."

"I've read the book from cover to cover, and I didn't know that."

"You must have forgotten it. I consulted the book. It's there."

"Did you find it in my copy? The one Sanderson gave me years ago?"

"They're all the same."

"When you get a chance, check my copy. You won't find it." The books supposedly contained the same information. If Farlan proved correct, *he* could unite with Alaura to protect her if he returned to Maskil in time. He felt uneasy thinking about Farlan and Alaura uniting even if only to save her from the dungeon. Still, he trusted Farlan to take care of her, and when he returned, the three of them would make things right. "I don't think Selina would like your plan."

"It's not Selina I'm worried about." Farlan gave him a nudge. "It's the dwarf whose blood burns like a thousand volcanoes for Alaura of Niamh that concerns me."

He couldn't help but smile. Alaura would be his mate in time. Remembering that he needed to provide an official signature to transfer his custodial right to Farlan, he pulled out a piece of paper. "Alaura doesn't have a lot of friends in Maskil. She has the most contact with

Beathas, but I haven't seen *her* in town for..." he tried to think of the last time but couldn't, "ever. Alaura trusts my family and you."

Farlan coughed and clutched his side. After clearing his throat, he took a deep breath.

Bronwyn waited, giving him a moment to rest. "There's almost twenty gold coins in this sack. I'll tuck it into your saddle bag. Give them to Sanderson for the families of the deceased. I'm going to write this down, but I want you to hear it. As soon as you're well enough, I want you to fill my position—"

"Whoa!" Farlan put up his hand. "I'm not taking your rank."

"You'll be acting sergeant until I return. I need a man I can trust, and there is no one I trust more in my office than you." They stared at each other. "I want you there. You know my routine. You're the best candidate. Anyways, Sanderson will need a guard he can trust in my position."

"You're coming back. This is temporary. I'll protect your position by serving in it, but as soon as you pass through those gates, it's yours again."

"I'd expect nothing less." He reached into his chest pocket, pulled out a folded piece of paper and handed it to him. It seemed like weeks ago he had calculated the number of guards for each race though he'd done it only yesterday morning. "Give this to Sanderson. He needs to know."

Farlan unfolded the paper. His eyes squinted in confusion as he read the numbers. "Are these accurate?"

"You were right. Humans are taking over command at the castle." He studied his human friend. Farlan had always been loyal to him and the castle. Their lives now depended on that trust.

"I don't know how other humans feel, but it doesn't reflect my idea of a balanced society," said Farlan. "I love Maskil because it's unique, a place where people of four races come together to work and live." He folded the paper and tucked it into his chest pocket. "I'll make sure no one sees this but Sanderson."

"Thank you." Bronwyn rubbed the stubble on his chin with the back of his hand. He hadn't shaved for two days, and the roughness of a beard had taken root. He imagined it might be quite thick before he arrived home again.

"Regardless of race, you'll always be my friend." Farlan didn't mince words. "And our little girl out there," he paused to catch his breath, "she's got a part of my heart that won't feel right until she's home."

Bronwyn glanced at the guards gathering their things and getting ready to mount. He wanted Farlan and the others to arrive before darkness settled the land. Every passing hour put their lives at risk. He finished the note and gave it to him. "Make sure Sanderson gets this. He'll be able to handle the custodial change, too."

Thinking of Alaura, he wondered what message to send home to her. He pulled another piece of paper from his rucksack and in the finest handwriting he could muster, he composed a letter. The brief note expressed his concern for her health and well-being, as well as his hope for a quick return. When it came time to sign it, he fumbled. He wanted to sign it, *Your Adoring Mate*, but thought it too forward. *Sincerely, Bronwyn*, didn't say enough. He settled on, *Yours affectionately. Bronwyn*. He folded the paper and handed it to Farlan.

"Give this to Alaura? Tell her I'll see her as soon as I return."

"She'll assume as much." Farlan put the note in his chest pocket.

He rolled another thought around in his mind. What if he didn't return? "Farlan, if I don't come back, can you...can you see to Alaura? Tell her—"

"Tell her yourself. She'll be waiting for you."

"But what if—"

"I don't want to hear about *what ifs*." Farlan grabbed him by the front of his vest and glared at him, desperation clouding his eyes. "You're coming back. Don't ever give up hope. It'll keep you alive when the odds are against you. Every sunrise, I want you to renew yourself. Think of it as a fresh beginning where the events of yesterday can be soothed in the twilight. There is power we don't understand when darkness gives way to light. I've felt it many times. It's as if fairies are flirting with the air we breathe, poking us with needles to see if we're still alive. Breathe it in. Let it wash away your fears."

This puzzled Bronwyn. His friend had occasionally commented about the twilight but never with this much vigour. "Where did you get this idea?"

"My sister." He bowed his head. "At the orphanage, she'd take me outside in the morning light and tell me stories about our mom. I don't remember her, but my sister did. Our mother died a few short years after my birth." He took a shallow breath. "My sister told me magic danced in the twilight. She told me to look to it for strength. The last day I saw her, before her new parents took her away, she led me outside before the sun rose. She told me all the hope one needed could be found in the twilight." His deep expression revealed the tormenting memories. "Each new day I hope I'll find her. And now, I'll also hope you and Isla will return."

Bronwyn listened quietly. His friend didn't often talk about his life at the orphanage or his sister. "I'll keep it in mind. It'll give me strength when I need it most."

Farlan fumbled with a leather bracelet, one of three he wore made by him and Isla. "This is a loaner." He tied the bracelet around Bronwyn's wrist. "You have to bring it back to me."

"Promise, I will. As swiftly as I can."

"I'll be spittin' mad if you don't. It's my favourite." A sly smirk caught the corner of his mouth.

Ten minutes later, the small caravan of wounded guards began towards Maskil. The three made a pitiful sight as they dragged the dead behind them. With a little luck, the tired horses and their riders would reach the town gates in two hours. Bronwyn would mark the time and know the men had arrived home. Turning his horse, he led his two remaining healthy guards towards Ellswire.

24

Chocolate on Raisins

EVERY MUSCLE in Bronwyn's body begged for rest, yet he pushed onward. He and the two privates had ridden at a lope for two hours. Along the way, they had stopped at two campsites Keiron might have made. Neither offered any clues. Because of the decoys, he figured they had added about ten hours to their travel time. It meant Keiron could be anywhere from sixteen to eighteen hours ahead of them. Almost a full day.

He checked his watch: 18:12. Farlan and the others would be at Maskil by now. They'd be receiving care from professional healers and informing Sanderson of the events since leaving the castle. Their time in the saddle had passed.

The road before him changed almost instantly from a well-groomed surface to an uneven one. Although he had heard about work crews from Maskil maintaining the road for 15 miles, he'd never travelled this far away from town to see it. The Trail to the next town would be passible, but the going would be slower because he'd need to watch for protruding rocks that might injury his horse, fallen trees and sections that might be washed out by heavy rains. From his point of view, a waggon could easily pass through, but it would be a bumpy ride.

A stone pillar about six feet tall marked the start of the ungroomed trail. When he passed, he glanced back to read the engraved lettering that ran from top to bottom: 15 MASKIL. He guessed they wouldn't see another smooth road until they neared a populated area.

Turning to face forward, he espied horse tracks leading into the trees. He hesitated to stop, thinking the site held no traces of the bandits or Isla. There'd be hundreds of similar tracks between here and Ellswire. Still, he couldn't pass it by. He slowed his horse and signalled for Privates Garret Maltby and Rorie Critch to halt. "Third time lucky." He managed a grin and dismounted.

"Let's hope." Rorie swung his leg over the rump of the horse and dropped to the ground.

Garret did the same and looped his reins around a branch to secure the animal.

Bronwyn led the way into a small clearing tucked into the forest twenty feet from the road. "They didn't try to hide their camp."

"Probably simple travellers then." Rorie searched the right-hand side of the fire pit.

Bronwyn did a half circle on the left, and Garret came up the middle.

"Look at this." Rorie held up an empty can. "Who'd eat canned worms?" He released it as if it contained poyson.

Scanning the rough-looking campsite, Bronwyn saw a crude fire pit and several patches of soft grass. He walked along the edge of the clearing, stopping at a mound of dry moss, a perfect spot for a small person to bed down. His eyes searched the perimeter. *What's this stuff?* He bent down and picked up a handful. His fears proved correct; long brown hair slipped through his fingers. Glancing around, he saw it hanging from nearby branches and scattered on the forest floor. He pulled a bunch to his nose and smelt it. *Isla's hair!*

"What do you have there, Sergeant?" Rorie came beside him.

"Isla's hair." His eyes flashed at him. "This is her hair."

Rorie scratched his head. "Why would they cut her hair?"

He steadied his hand. They had only cut Isla's hair. It didn't indicate they harmed her.

Garret lifted a piece of garbage from the fire. "Beans. They must have eaten them cold because the pit hasn't contained a fire for a long time."

"A fire would be risky." Bronwyn ran his fingers through the piles of soft strands. What did Isla look like with short hair? Given the amount on the ground, they had cut it close to the scalp, like a boy's cut. "They're disguising her."

"What do you mean?" Rorie squatted beside him.

"We're searching for a girl." Bronwyn grabbed a mound of hair and shook it. "With short hair, they could pass her off as a boy. She's already wearing trousers and a shirt."

Rorie reached for the pile of hair in his hand and extracted a piece of paper. "What's this?" He unfolded it. "A page from a book." He handed it to him.

"A *Trail of Hope*." Bronwyn read the title. "It's Isla's book." He turned it over in his hand, examining it for clues, anything that would help him locate her but found nothing.

"She's a smart girl." Rorie rose. "She's leaving clues they wouldn't see in places they won't look."

"This tells us she's well and is keeping her senses about her," said Garret. "It can only work to our advantage."

Bronwyn stared at them. Isla *had* given them a wise clue. The book contained many pages, more than enough to guide him to her. He folded the paper and placed it in his chest pocket. He gently picked up several long strands of hair and held them to his nose until Isla's scent filled his senses. Tying the locks together, he tucked them into his pocket beside the book page.

An hour later, he halted the men. They had been travelling hard for two days and needed a rest. As the other two guards curled into their bedrolls, Bronwyn sat by the fire, staring at the page from the book. He had already read it twice, trying to extract further clues. Isla had given him a summary of the book about two weeks earlier as she tagged along while he inspected the castle walls. The main character left a trail of pages for her das and brother to find after she had become lost.

The worrying exhausted him; he needed sleep. He pulled a blanket over him and lay near the fire. The burning wood snapped and sent little flairs into the darkness. The warmth and the song of the flame seduced him into dreamland where anxious dreams awaited.

೮ ❖ ೞ

Keiron dropped from the saddle and shoved the reins into Isla's hands. "Take it for water."

Isla obeyed. She guided the horse to the spring, slipped off the bridle and let it drink. Falling to her knees, she bent next to the animal and drank eagerly. The water quenched her thirst but did nothing to curtail her craving for food. She had eaten her last full ration with her das three days beforehand. Besides the bread the dwarf had given her the previous day, she had received only a cup of beans. Now with the sun high overhead, the pains in her stomach became louder. The hollows beneath her ribs ached.

The dwarf had tried to give her food, but Keiron intercepted each attempt. She believed he wanted to starve her to death. He'd be wise to keep her alive if he sought a ransom for her return. But why would he seek money from her das? A castle guard's wages couldn't even buy her a pony.

She pushed herself from the water and ran the back of her hand across her mouth, then her fingers went through her short hair. It felt strange. Her thoughts drifted to the piles of brown strands at the campsite they had left yesterday. She took a deep breath, closed her eyes and hoped her das had found the page tucked within the mounds. *Yes, he did.* She had to keep telling herself this. Moisture pooled behind her eyelids, but she forced it to stop. If Keiron saw, he'd hit her again. She had to be strong like her das. She had to stay calm and be wise like Sandy. But to be strong and wise, she had to have food.

Resting against the grassy bank, she knew the call would soon come to mount. The men only stopped long enough to water the horses. They were in a hurry to reach their destination but hadn't said a word about it.

Hearing movement beside her, she looked up to see the dwarf lead his horse to the spring. Tam, as he called himself, appeared gruff, but she sensed something different about him. At first, she thought his resemblance to her das made him stand out from the other two but in many ways, he was unlike her das. His shaggy beard covered half his face, and his dark brown hair hung to his shoulders. His untidy manner didn't compare to the grunginess of the hauflin. *He* stunk like a horse that had rolled in pig manure and slept in it until Sumortide ended; Tam had but a mild odour.

Tam removed the bridle from the horse's head to allow it to drink. With the animal settled, he dug into his pocket and pulled out a biscuit.

She had tasted many types of biscuits in her life, but even the worse tasting ones filled an empty stomach. Her mouth watered. She rubbed the top of her legs, and her hands trembled; they craved to hold the food.

To her surprise, he tossed the biscuit on her lap. She quickly turned to see the hauflin. He dug into a saddle pack and didn't notice the offering of food. Looking back at Tam, she found him staring off into the forest, eating his own biscuit. She cradled the food in her hand, and a pang of fear stirred in her stomach. If she ate it, would Keiron beat her? If she didn't eat it, she'd surely die of starvation.

With a sly glance, she again observed the hauflin. His search in the saddle bag kept him busy. She put the biscuit between her teeth and took a large bite. The dough rolled around in her mouth as if chocolate on raisins. She'd never tasted a sweeter biscuit. Guarding her mouth, she took another bite. Sensing Tam's movement, she glanced in his direction and found him watching her. She shoved the last bit into her mouth and chewed slowly, savouring the taste. Crumbs stuck in her teeth. She extracted each one and enjoyed them one more time as she rolled them over her tongue.

"Isla!"

She jumped to her feet. Had he seen her? She whirled around and stared at the hauflin.

"Get over here!"

She caught her breath. If she didn't go, he'd beat her. It was his only method of communication. Her arms, legs and backside ached from the bruises. Although she felt dizzy, she forced her feet to move towards him. She must have risen too fast because her head swooned, and she collapsed to the ground. She tried to stand up, but the dizziness kept her on unsteady knees.

"Get up!" ordered Keiron. He clenched his fist and shook it at her. "Stop arsin' around."

Isla pushed herself to her feet but failed to rise. Her arms buckled, and she fell in the bushes. She shivered though the hot sun beat down upon her face. When she looked up, she saw Tam hovering over her.

"Are you satisfied, Keiron? Three days with no food and scarcely enough water has taken its toll. What good is she to you now?"

Keiron strode to Isla, grabbed her by the front of the vest and jerked her to her feet. "If yew fall agin, I'll beat the sense out of yew."

When he released her, she fell backwards, but she didn't hit the ground. Tam supported her from behind.

"Let her go." Meanness filled Keiron's voice.

"So you can beat her again?" Tam shook his head. "A man cares more for his dog than you care about your daughter."

Isla's eyes flashed, and she felt a rush of energy. "He's not my das! My das is coming for me." She glared at the hauflin. "And when he finds *me*, he'll kill *you*!"

"Keiron, you told me *you* were her dad." Tam tightened his grip on her. "But it makes sense now. No man in his right mind would treat his child as you have."

"I'm her das! Not that dwarf who stole her from me! She's my blood!"

Tam grimaced at Isla. "Your das is dwarf?"

She nodded. "He's an honourable man. Nothing like this scoundrel!"

Keiron punched her in the face. If not for Tam holding her, she'd have crumbled to the ground. Keiron grabbed her by the vest and jerked her from the dwarf's arms. "If that honourable man ever catches up with me, yew'll see what I do with thieves." He threw her back at Tam. "Since yew've taken a likin' to her, tend to her." He smirked. "But if yew use her for yer pleasure, I want compensation."

The scoundrel walked away, and the scowl etched on Tam's face frightened her. How would he use her? Why did Keiron claim to be her das? Her das, her blood das, had died long ago. At least Bronwyn thought so. Tam lifted her into his arms and carried her to his pack. He dug inside and pulled out an apple and a chunk of green cheese.

"Eat." He shoved the food into her hands. He rose and grimaced at her.

Isla didn't see a hint of satisfaction from winning the argument with Keiron. But then again, perhaps he didn't consider this a victory. Now he had a burden and possibly a brewing conflict with the hauflin. Tam gathered his horse and bridled it. Before she finished the last bite of green cheese, he pulled her into the saddle behind him. She wrapped her arms around his waist and felt his large muscles through the dark green material of his shirt. Laying her cheek against his back, she closed her eyes and imagined him to be her das, strong and honourable. While Tam may not have consider it a triumph, she felt safer in his saddle than with the one claiming to be her das.

25

I Must Be Plain Stupid

"**WE HAVE** seen them." The human steadied his horse. The handsome young stallion appeared anxious to run.

"Did they have a child with them?" Bronwyn sat back in his saddle and questioned the stranger. He seemed friendly enough. The other human, smaller in stature, remained quiet.

The stranger nodded. "The four of them made a curious group."

"When did you see them?" He tried to steal a glimpse of the clothing the men wore, but flowing cloaks concealed everything, including their swords, if they had any.

"Let me see." The stranger thought over the answer.

Bronwyn gritted his teeth. This man considered his words far too much before he spoke them. Maybe the other man spoke faster.

"Ah!" The man raised his hand in the air and stuck up his index finger. "It was after we stopped for a ration. Or, I should say, after we started again... Yes! It was then."

Bronwyn locked his jaw. The stranger obviously didn't understand the simple question.

"Maskil," said the large man. "You're guards from there?"

He nodded. "We're tracking these men because they kidnapped the child." Maybe the information would produce an answer faster.

"I have a good friend who's a guard there." The stranger chuckled. "He's lived in the town quite a while. I suppose he'll take root soon. Maybe you know him. Name's McGreggor. He's captain of the guard."

Bronwyn glanced at Rorie. The stranger had to be joking, or he knew nothing about Maskil. For as long as he could remember, Sanderson had held the captain of the guard position. "Maybe you're confused with another town."

"No. No. It's Maskil, I speak of. Ol' McGreggor has been whipping those men into shape for years. He's a respected dwarf who should be known by you men."

Bronwyn inwardly groaned, but he'd give them one more try. "Exactly what time of day did you see this hauflin?"

"McGreggor's a dwarf. I thought I said as much." He shrugged. "I can't recall the last time. Maybe three years ago."

"No!" Bronwyn squeezed his reins. *Be calm. Take a breath.* "The hauflin you passed yesterday. If you'd tell us this, we'll be on our way."

The stranger eyed him. "Your manners could stand improvement. I'll have to speak with McGreggor about this."

He leant forward and glared at him. "There's no McGreggor at Maskil. Sanderson, a human, is captain of the guard. Either you're confused or plain stupid."

The stranger raised his eyebrow. "I guess I must be plain stupid. What's your excuse, Sergeant?" He pulled open his cloak, flipping its edges over his shoulders to reveal the black and grey uniform below.

Bronwyn's breath caught. He had called the Dukedom of South Ridge's captain of the guard stupid. Swallowing hard, he studied Trisham Orme of South Ridge, Petra, Lord Cranton Dunsworth's right-hand man. Given the ties between the towns, Orme knew Maskil's top military personnel. Orme had tested him; he had failed.

"I'm sorry, sir. I meant no disrespect." Bronwyn remembered his training. "You acted incompetent, and I misjudged you."

"Next time, Sergeant, I suggest you think before you speak. Anyone can don a uniform and pretend they are from Maskil."

"Yes, sir." He swallowed to relieve the pressure in his mouth. "The men we follow abducted my child. We've trailed them for three days."

"It makes it more important to you to keep a clear head." Orme tilted his head and raised an eyebrow. "You say this is your child? The child they possess is hauflin, not dwarf."

"She's my adopted daughter."

Orme grunted. "They claim *she* is a boy, a son of this hauflin. But it is a terrible haircut and will draw curiosity."

"The evidence found at one of their campsites indicated it to be so." Bronwyn bit his lip. "Did she look well?"

"As well as can be expected under the circumstances. We, Lord Finley Dunsworth and I, passed by them about noon yesterday, so you are about a day behind them. If they're headed for the Midway Keep, they'll reach it by nightfall tomorrow. From there, it's an eight-day ride to Ellswire. If they head towards Paddy's Hill, you'll have a hard go of it. There are many places they can turn off."

"Thank you, sir," said Bronwyn. "We're glad to hear any piece of information that'll help us."

Lord Dunsworth kept his cloak about him, unwilling to reveal anything beneath. The dark-haired human didn't smile, didn't even appear to have smile lines that suggested a happy person sat beneath the cloak. Bronwyn understood the lords in South Ridge weren't appointed because of their exceptional qualities; they were born into the position. It meant, strength and wisdom ruled as much as weakness and stupidity. What did the citizens think about it? Did the lords command respect or was it given freely?

"What is your name?" Lord Dunsworth's break in silence surprised Bronwyn. He spoke in a well-educated voice, but it lacked conviction.

"Sergeant Bronwyn Darrow."

"Sergeant Darrow, are you new to the rank?"

"No." He saw no reason to explain further.

Lord Dunsworth grunted. "Either your training is lax or you're not sergeant material."

He took the comment on the chin. This lord, who became one only because of his father, didn't have the right to judge his qualifications.

"I'll speak with Lord Mulryan about this," said Dunsworth.

"No need to bother." Bronwyn straightened his back to add an inch to his height. "Lord Mulryan knows I'm more than qualified to hold my position. With all due respect, Lord Dunsworth, you have no right to even hint about having my rank reduced." He glared at the human to add strength to his words.

Orme watched in silence. Bronwyn sensed the captain of the guard didn't feel the same as his lord. Did the large human, who had obviously earned his rank, enjoy taking care of this boy who appeared no older than twenty-five.

"If we were at South Ridge, I would have you thrown into the dungeon for your insubordination."

"But we're not there." Bronwyn gripped the reins and prepared to depart. "We do things a little differently at Maskil. Everyone at the castle earns their rank."

Before the lord spoke again, Orme put up his hand. "My Lord, it's best we put our differences aside for the sake of the poor child they seek." He guided his horse out of the way and motioned for them to pass. "Continue, Sergeant Darrow. I wish you success in your mission."

Bronwyn nodded. The captain of the guard had retained his patience, as would have Sanderson if presented with the same circumstances. He would learn from this. He'd need it if he ever obtained their rank. "I'm sorry for the misunderstanding, sir. May your travels be safe."

Orme nodded. "Good luck, men." He pulled his cloak around him and began towards Maskil. Lord Dunsworth rode next to him.

Bronwyn kicked his horse, bringing it to a jog. Rorie and Garret fell into step beside him.

"Sergeant, I'd never have guessed Trisham Orme and Lord Dunsworth would be on The Trail alone this far from Petra." Rorie glanced back at the pair disappearing from sight.

"You and I both." He slipped into deep thought, trying to recall Sanderson and a lord travelling alone. Orme appeared confident as the only protector of Lord Finley Dunsworth. Perhaps the horrible stories of danger on The Trail held more fiction than truth.

26

Illuminated the Shadows

THE EVENING shadows stretched their long fingers across the road. A breeze carried a spindrift of dust to the edge, then dropped it in the moss. Nature eased itself into the resting period. The winds diminished, and the heat relented. Within seconds the rush of hooves against dirt shattered the simmering silence of the empty road. Iron shoes flicked up chunks of earth, and stirrups bounced against the horses' sides.

Keiron pushed his bay hard, slapping it and kicking it with vigour and vim. It gave everything it had, yet he kept asking for more. Midway Keep lay ahead.

About fifteen horse lengths behind, Tam and Reese struggled to keep up. In spite of their exhaustion, the horses continued at the neck-breaking pace.

With no control over her speed or destination, Isla clung tightly to the dwarf's waist. The rapid pace terrified her, making her fear she'd fall off at any moment. After what seemed like hours, Tam sat back and eased up on the horse. She glanced at the gnome who rode abreast. He looked frazzled and as exhausted as the horses.

The animals slowed to a walk, gulping air and spitting foam from their mouths. Isla relaxed her grip. Her arms ached from the strain of holding on. She shook them to relieve the muscles, then rested them on her lap. Because of the size of the dwarf in front of her, she couldn't see their destination, only from whence she had come.

To her surprise, they passed a tall stone building with a window on each side of the doorway. Metal bars secured the glass like on a jail. A jail? A keep? A dwelling? It didn't matter. There'd be people here. They'd help her. She'd tell them these men had kidnapped her and they'd take her home. Her heart leapt with glee. *Stay calm*, she told herself. *Be wise.*

Tam halted the horse, then gave her an order. "Get off."

She obeyed. Since Keiron had given her to him yesterday, he'd lost the little spark of kindness he had. He only spoke to tell her what to do and when to do it. She slid from the saddle and collapsed to the ground. Her legs ached, weak from days of high-speed travel. As she struggled to get up, Tam thrust his hand in her face; she grabbed it, and he pulled her to her feet. She gripped the stirrup to steady herself while he tied the horse at the hitching bar.

"Isla." Keiron came close to her face. His breath burnt her nose. "I'm going to say this once, so hear me well." He put his arm around her shoulder and pasted on a fake smile. "The folks at this keep don't give a fly's arse who yew is. They'd sooner beat the sense out of yew as me, but I warn yew; keep yer mouth shut. If yew start shooting it off, I'll find the ones yew love and kill 'em. I'll start with the woman yer das lusts for." He winked at her. "There's many a man would like to have a piece of her." He laughed and walked away, but his breath lingered.

Isla tried not to breathe it in. She hated the man like she'd never hated another. Frozen in place, a shiver raced through her stomach. The cool evening wind whirled around her feet, and she wished for it to swallow her.

"Take *him* with you. I'll see about the rooms." Keiron walked towards the building beside the keep.

She watched him go, hoping one of the men relaxing against the structure to jump out and attack him with a dagger. But they didn't. They watched him pass as if just another traveller. When he disappeared inside, she searched for Tam. He stood next to his horse, watching her. He waved her towards the building, and she followed him inside. The gnome had already entered.

"Stay near," said Tam in a low voice. He made his way around the supply store scrutinizing things on display.

Isla had visited the castle keep many times, but this place smelt different. An equal amount of old and new equipment was stuffed in the space. Some of the things reeked. A long display unit down the centre of the building divided the keep into two aisles. On either side, shelves, racks and tables held the items offered for sale. From the ceiling hung larger objects like crossbows, armour, shields, nets, lanterns and long bows.

Tam walked down the right side of the display unit. Isla stayed close behind him. He fingered many items but didn't pick up anything. When he stopped to inspect a dagger, she passed and continued. Reese shopped on the opposite side of the keep, out of view. She slid her hand into her trouser pocket where the next page of her book to be left behind for her das waited. Where could she put it? It could easily get lost in the keep's clutter.

She peeked back at Tam; he moved closer, stopping at the pouches on display. He glanced at her, looked her up and down, and then returned his attention to the items before him. She stepped away, hunting for the ideal spot to hide the paper.

She had reached the end of the room. The centre display unit ended, leaving a path to the opposite side. Natural light poured in from two tall windows. Sundry items—lanterns, candles, flint and firesteel kits, tinderboxes, hand mirrors and folding knives—filled the tables beneath the glass. On the sill sat a miniature statue of a dragon beside a small dish and pestle akin to what Alaura used to mix herbs. Three books similar in size leant against the glass frame.

Glancing back at Tam, she saw him testing the strength of a pouch. As she watched, she slipped her hand from her pocket and reached towards the window sill. Seeing her chance, she tucked the page between two of the books. She left enough of it exposed to catch the attention of anyone seeking such a page.

She shivered when a hand came to rest upon her shoulder.

"What are you looking at?" Tam peered out the window.

"Nothing." She shoved her hands into her pockets. "I thought I saw something fly by." He glanced down at her. She knew he didn't believe her. She blamed her inability to lie on her das. He wanted her to be honest at all times.

"Nothing, eh?" He inspected the table in front of them. "Don't get any ideas of escaping through these windows. They're barred on the outside."

Isla could see the bars. She also saw the folded page sticking out between the books like a red flag waving and saying, *Look at me!* She had to move away before Tam saw it. Slipping from his grip, she stepped towards the next display.

Isla stabbed the piece of meat on her plate and stuck it into her mouth. The first real food she'd eaten in days tasted better than raspberry brownies from her grandmeese's bakery. She chewed each piece as if her last. Given Keiron's sudden bursts of cruelty, he might at any moment rip the plate from her grip and throw it onto the floor. She glanced at Tam beside her on the bench. He ate his meat and potatoes as if he'd eaten better, but the ration in front of him sufficed for now. He ate in silence, as usual, not speaking to her or the hauflin, across the table.

Other customers at the Midway Inn enjoyed a meal, but Isla kept her head low and avoided eye contact. Keiron had reminded her of his threat as they sat to eat. She had no doubt he'd honour it. To her surprise and relief, the gnome didn't eat with them. He didn't like eating near them in the forest, so it made sense he didn't want to share a table with them. She knew he still lingered out of sight. Keiron had told Tam he had paid for two rooms, one for him and the gnome, and one for Tam and her.

"Look what the troglodyte dragged in."

Startled, Isla followed the sound of the voice; a female hauflin stood by Keiron's arm. She wore a dress that hung to her knees and revealed her shoulders. Her dark hair hung loose around her neck. She slowly caressed the despicable man's shoulders, and Isla tried to hide her shock. Obviously, this woman didn't know him well.

"Fran." Keiron continued to eat.

"Got room for one more?" She didn't wait for an answer and pushed him along the bench to make room.

He obliged, moving his ration with him. He now sat directly across from Isla. Her grip tightened on her plate, and she chewed faster.

"Tam." Fran nodded at the dwarf. "Good to see you well."

He nodded and took a drink of yellow liquid.

"Who do we have here?" Her expression softened.

"My son." Keiron washed his food down with the same yellow, stinky substance.

Fran lifted an eyebrow. "You didn't tell me you had a child."

"Yew never asked." He shoved the last piece of meat into his mouth.

"He's travelling with you?"

"Just 'til we get to my sister's. The poor fellow's meeme died and left him alone."

The explanation satisfied the woman, and she cuddled up to the hauflin, making Isla grimace. How could she stand the noxious stink? Surely the burning sensation in her nose would make her run away. She glanced at Tam, but he didn't care either way.

"Do you have free time before you leave?" asked Fran.

Though she whispered in his ear, Isla heard. Keiron gestured for her to get off the bench, and he stood with her.

"Tam, keep an eye on the young fella."

"He's your baby-sitter?" Fran half grinned.

Keiron chuckled as he walked away. Fran followed.

Isla relaxed her grip on the plate and ate slower.

After a few minutes of silence, Tam scraped his plate clean. He took a long drink, then placed the empty mug on the table. His gaze roamed the dingy inn that held about a dozen travellers. "Who was the dwarf with you in the waggon?"

The sound of his voice made her jump. "My granddas."

He eyed her. "Hauflins don't come from dwarfs."

Alaura had told her these facts long ago. "But he's the das of my das."

"You're full-blood hauflin, so a dwarf can't be your das."

She lowered her head. Bronwyn was the only das she'd known. He took care of her, protected her, loved her. The hauflin, Keiron, only beat her. Tears moistened her eyes. No one could replace Bronwyn as her das. "He's coming for me."

"Who? The dwarf?"

She nodded and wiped her eyes. "Nothing will stop him. He'll rescue me. He has lots of friends. They'll come, too."

Tam smirked. "Lots of friends, eh?"

She nodded again, then clamped her mouth shut to prevent sharing more information with the enemy. She'd sat in on enough lectures with her das' new recruits to learn this.

"And who might these friends be? More dwarfs?"

She remained silent.

"Should I be concerned about my health?" He chuckled. "Or are these friends all children?"

"Maybe they are." She put a piece of potato in her mouth.

His smile faded, and he fingered the fork in front of him. "You know," he said, giving her a sideways glance, "Keiron is your das. He told us so."

"No, he's not," she spat.

"Did your das, this dwarf, tell you what happened to your blood das?"

"He told me he was dead."

"Is that what he said?"

"He doesn't lie to me."

"Maybe he said he *thought* he was dead. That's different. He's telling you what he believes."

Bronwyn *had* said it that way. Her throat tightened, and the potato hurt when she swallowed it. Keiron couldn't be her das. He was cruel and dishonourable. Did she have to stay with a das she hated? Could she no longer dwell with Bronwyn?

"I don't know. Maybe he's not your das." He tossed the fork onto the table. "Keiron doesn't care about anyone but himself."

She forced herself to finish her meal though her appetite had faded. Alaura had told her to eat to keep up her strength if faced with difficult times. Alaura had taught her many things at Moon Meadow. Until now, she didn't think her life might depend on them.

ಬಿ ❖ ೧೮

The door to Tam's room swung open and he whirled, drawing his sword from the scabbard. When he saw Keiron standing on the threshold, he returned his weapon to its holder.

The two stared each other down as if on the brink of a conflict. Isla stepped deeper into the corner. The small room with only one narrow bed in the centre didn't provide any place to hide. The last rays of the evening sun kissed the glass on the only window. Light from the lantern hanging near the door illuminated the shadows and flashed in the hauflin's eyes.

"I'll have our orders soon." Keiron closed the door behind him. "Be ready to leave at dawn." He glanced at Isla, then back at the dwarf. "Make sure it doesn't escape tonight." He threw a short chain connected to a shackle on the bed.

"What's that for?" Tam glared at him.

"Use yer imagination." Keiron handed him a key.

"You want me to chain her?"

Isla pulled her hands around her. The thought of being shackled like an animal terrified her.

"Concerned it might get in yer way?" He leered at him. "When yer done, chain her."

"This is wrong."

Keiron stepped forward and held a dagger to the dwarf's neck. "What's wrong is a man who doesn't live for himself."

The evil in his eyes made Isla sink deeper into the corner. Her hands shook and her heart beat faster. If Keiron killed Tam, she'd have no buffer between her and him, her and the gnome.

Tam's face twisted in a knot. He measured a foot taller than the hauflin but held no weapon. "Fine." Spit sprayed from his mouth.

~ 241 ~

Keiron released him with a shove. "If she escapes, it'll be yer blood Reese will savour." He scowled at Isla. "Kill her if she tries to flee." He slid the dagger back into the sheath and chuckled. "If yew've got the stomach for it."

"She'll be here in the morning." Tam put distance between him and the hauflin.

"It wouldn't be the first time yew let a prisoner escape." Keiron clenched his fists. "I'm startin' to think yer losing yer nerve."

"He was boy!" Tam's top lip curled. "I won't kill a child for you, not anyone."

"He was practically a man!"

"He was a terrified little boy." He rested his hand on the hilt of his sword. "Did you have to kill his mum in front of him?"

"I carry out my orders. I don't worry about details."

"Is that what she is?" He pointed at Isla. "A detail?"

The hauflin grumbled as he walked out, slamming the door behind him.

Tam stared at the door as if he wanted to follow Keiron and kill him. But he didn't. Instead, he withdrew the sword from the scabbard and tossed it on the bed. He dug into his rucksack and withdrew a sharpening stone. Sitting on the bed, he dragged the stone along the blade. He spit on the weapon to make the slide more effective, then flipped the sword and repeated the action.

Isla guessed he had perfected the motion over the years. She had seen it many times in the guardhouse. When he finished with the length of the blade, he used a special curved stone to sharpen the tip.

The familiar procedure settled her nerves, but she didn't move from her spot. Tam used the same cleaning and sharpening method as her das, Farlan and every other guard in the guardhouse. Did everyone sharpen their swords in the same manner? Keiron didn't. Neither did Reese. Tam took pride in his weapons. He respected them.

He had also taken the bit from his horse's mouth to let it drink. Her das did that, too, and he trained all his guards to do it. He had been trained in the procedure when he enlisted. She had asked him about it once, and he said, *Do you want to drink with a piece of steel in your mouth? Your horse can save your life. Treat it well, better than you treat yourself. When you need it, it'll be there.*

Tam treated his horse with respect. He cared for it the same way her das taught all new recruits to tend to their animals.

As strange as it seemed, Isla wondered if Tam had once served as a guard at Aruam Castle. If so, why had he left, and why did he wander The Trail with bandits? She wanted to ask him but didn't know how. Thinking about the lecture on *How to Interrogate a Prisoner*, she decided to use the shock effect. She'd word her question in a way that made him think she knew more than she did. Her das had said, *Their expression usually gave away the answer.*

"Tam." To her surprise, her voice didn't shake. He continued to sharpen his sword and didn't look up. She thought of the exact words before she spoke. "How long did you serve as a guard at Aruam Castle?"

He glanced at her. "What makes you think I worked at that hovel?"

She caught her breath; he *had* served at the castle. "You did... It's obvious to me." He was about ten years older than her das. Maybe they served together, but she didn't remember him.

Tam stopped sharpening his sword and studied her. "Who are you?"

"Isla of—"

"No, I mean *who* are you? Or better yet, who is your das, this dwarf you speak of? Does he serve at the castle?"

She nodded. Maybe he would help her escape if he knew.

"In what capacity?"

"He's a sergeant."

He rubbed the back of his hand across his chin. "Your das is Sergeant Darrow?" When she nodded, he released a nervous chuckle. "What in Knavesmire does Keiron want with you?"

"I don't know. Do you know my das?"

"Know him? No. But we've crossed paths." He started to clean his sword again. "He's...something."

"What do you mean?"

"Nothing. You look at him with different eyes than I do."

"He's a good man, an honourable one."

He chuckled. "He's that."

The evening passed, and she had done nothing but sit and watch him clean his weapons and equipment. When he stood and put everything away, preparing for sleep, she wondered if he'd carry out Keiron's instructions. The chain and shackle still lay on the bed where they had been tossed. Tam moved them to the foot, pulled back the blankets and turned to face her.

"Take off your shoes," he said. She removed the footwear, and he gestured her towards the bed. "Lay down."

"On the bed?" If she had the bed, where would he sleep?

"I didn't point to the floor."

She climbed onto the mattress, and he pulled the blankets over her. He picked up the shackle and sat next to her head. "Tell me if this is too tight." He fixed the metal band around her wrist and snapped it in place. "Does it hurt?"

She shook her head. "It frightens me."

His face twisted as if he prepared to drive a dagger into his own leg. "If you need anything in the night, wake me." He secured the chain to the corner post and stood. On the floor beside the bed, he spread his blankets. He locked the door, secured it with a metal bar and extinguished the lantern.

He crawled into his bedroll and by the time he settled, her eyes had adjusted to the dim light. As a dwarf, he also possessed the ability to see as well as her under these conditions. Several minutes passed before she found the courage to ask the question haunting her since her kidnapping.

"Tam, does Keiron plan to kill me?"

A cold silence hung in the musty air. When she thought he wouldn't answer, he spoke in a low voice. "I don't know."

"Will you let him?"

He heaved a heavy sigh. "Isla, the first thing you learn on The Trail is you have to look out for yourself, or you're a dead man. If you're sure you can help another without spending your life, then it's up to you to judge if the person is worthy of your help."

He stared at the moonshine illuminating the ceiling. Strong emotions softened his voice, and when she studied his eyes, she thought they glistened from dampness.

"Trail life is brutal," he said. "At times you can't help the one whose life is worthier than your own and when you can't, nothing matters."

27

Hideous Chunk of Flesh

BRONWYN REINED up as he saw the Midway Keep come into view. They had ridden from dawn to dusk yesterday, but it still left them with nine hours of travelling before they arrived at the supply shop. He halted at the hitching pole, dismounted and secured his horse. Rorie and Garret did the same.

"Keep your eyes open," he said. "They may still be here." He scanned the interior of the shop. A man in the corner looked up from a book, and they exchanged nods.

"Sergeant?" The rugged human came to stand behind the pay counter.

"That's correct, sir. A cool day."

"Could be cooler. Is there anything I can help you with?"

Bronwyn walked to the counter as his men searched the keep. "As a matter of fact, there is."

"Anything...for an Aruam Castle guard."

He liked his attitude, but it didn't appear sincere. "I'm searching for someone. Maybe you saw him here yesterday."

"Many pass through. Business is brisk on The Fork."

"This particular fellow, a hauflin, had travelling companions." He stood straight, shoulders back, hiding his weary bones. "He travelled with a dwarf, a gnome and a hauflin child."

The man raised his brow. "Many people fit the description. Do you have a name, by chance, or know what they bought?" The man's confidence slipped.

"The hauflin's name is Keiron Ruckle." The name stirred emotions in the keeper. "Have you seen him?"

"He wasn't here yesterday." The man thought for a moment. "Hasn't paid a visit to the keep for about two weeks, maybe three."

"But you know him?"

"He's passed through on occasion."

"But not yesterday?"

"No, and I worked all day."

"What about the other two? Did you see a hauflin child with a dwarf or a gnome?"

The human shifted his weight from one foot to the other. "People don't like being spied on, talked about. They mind their business. I mind mine."

Bronwyn leant close and spoke in an authoritative voice. "Keiron Ruckle kidnapped the child we seek. If she entered this keep, I want to know."

"What would Ruckle want with a child?" The owner spoke in a hushed voice.

"We'll learn that when we rescue her."

The owner glanced around the empty shop. "Ruckle's a menace. If he learns I told you anything, he'll be out for my blood."

"Not if I catch him." Bronwyn had a few ideas of what he'd do with the hauflin and in truth, he hoped Keiron wouldn't surrender.

"I didn't see Ruckle." The owner bent near. "But the young hauflin came with Tam and Reese. Rumour has it they're working for him."

"Did they spend the night at the inn?" When the keeper nodded, he asked, "Are they still here?"

"They left at dawn. Headed towards Paddy's Hill." He gestured up the road.

The bell over the door dinged. Everyone turned to see a female hauflin enter the keep. She smiled at the men and made her way down an aisle.

"If I see any uniforms come through, I'll be sure to notify the castle." The keeper's voice rose so everyone within twenty feet, including the female, heard what he had said.

"Thank you, sir," said Bronwyn. "We appreciate your cooperation."

The female approached the pay counter.

"Fran, good to see you." The shop owner painted on a wide smile.

"Sam, you always like to see business walk in the door. As do I." She smiled at the human, then turned her attention to Bronwyn. "Who do we have here? An Aruam Castle finest. I always liked a man in uniform." She dragged her finger along his arm. "Sticking around?"

"My business here is done."

"Such a shame. Dwarfs have such vigour in all the right places." She winked at him.

Bronwyn returned his attention to the keeper. "Again, thank you." He motioned the guards to the door.

They mounted their horses, and Bronwyn directed them towards Paddy's Hill. They passed the Midway Inn at a walk. He checked each face lingering outside the building to find a familiar one, but only strangers stared back. Once out of sight of the buildings, he spoke. "Keiron didn't enter the shop, but Isla did. She came with two men named Tam and Reese. They stayed the night at the inn. At dawn, they headed in this direction, towards Paddy's Hill."

"We know she was there." Private Rorie Critch dug into his pocket, pulled out a piece of paper and handed it to him.

Bronwyn unfolded it. "Page three."

"We almost missed it," said Garret. "I stood in front of it, browsing the many items on the table. Rorie came up beside me and noticed the books on the window sill. It slipped out from between them when he pulled one from the shelf."

"I looked at the books," said Rorie, "because they were copies of *Protocol – The Foundation of Civil Organisation*. It's my understanding copies are not permitted outside the town walls."

"You're right." Bronwyn glanced back at the keep. "All copies are property of Aruam Castle. When we return to Maskil, I'll look into this."

ಌ ❖ ೞ

Three hours later, Bronwyn slowed his horse near a clear trail cut through the forest. A governing force hadn't made it. Those who regularly used it as a short cut between this road, the Lower Branch, and the Upper Branch had. From travellers along the way, he had learnt Keiron had most likely taken this trail.

"It's a long shot, Sergeant." Rorie's voice broke the silence. "Because travellers past this point didn't see him, doesn't mean he didn't go farther and take another trail."

"We have to consider it."

Garret dismounted and led his horse to the ditch. Bronwyn and Rorie followed.

Many hoof prints led in and out of the trail. The recent dry weather made the prints shallow or non-existent. About three dozen feet along, a piece of paper caught Bronwyn's attention, and he rushed to it.

"They did come this way!" He couldn't believe his eyes. Isla had left a clear trail. He now had page four; one page closer to her.

They mounted and began on The Trunk Trail, according to the map Bronwyn had recovered from the dead dwarf after the green dragon attack. An hour later, Rorie's attention stayed more on the forest along the trail than the ground ahead. When Bronwyn looked to see what had caught his attention, he thought he saw movement. He raised his hand to slow down.

"Did you see that, Sergeant?" Rorie pointed to the spot along the trees.

"I saw something shift the bushes."

"Probably an animal," said Garret.

Bronwyn stopped. A breeze blew by his ear, and he cocked his head to listen.

"I hear a noise." Rorie slid from the saddle. "It sounds like singing."

Bronwyn dismounted and approached the trees. The breeze *did* carry a melody. He listened closer but couldn't make out the words. The voice became distinct when he entered the forest. He recognised the song as one of Isla's favourites.

"It's a child's voice," whispered Rorie. He stared at him. "Is it Isla?"

"Why would she be in the forest, singing? If she saw us coming, she'd have run to us."

But it sounded like Isla's voice, or at least similar to it. The deeper they went into the woods, the stronger the voice became. "Let's leave the horses here." Bronwyn motioned to secure the reins. "Rorie, go that way. Garret, circle around there. I'll go up the middle."

The guards spread out, and he waited a moment for them to take up position before creeping forward. As the voice grew louder, the more it sounded like Isla. She often sang the song whilst traipsing through the forest with him. To hear her sing it now made his heart leap. Then he remembered Keiron and the others had to be near. He drew his sword and continued.

About fifty feet along, he halted. He detected a peculiarity in the compelling voice. Isla had sung the chorus twice and each time, she had sang it correctly. Usually she changed one word; instead of saying *she*, she said *he*. A man had originally sung the song and when he sang about his mate, she changed it to refer to hers.

Analysing the singing further, he noticed a stress out of place. Isla had a funny way of saying *wondering*; it sounded more like *wandering*. This voice didn't have that distinction. Did the minor inconsistencies add up to an important clue, or was he putting too much thought into it?

He came to the edge of a small clearing and spied between tree branches. The singing Isla sat on a log near a small fire. His first instinct urged him to run to her but instead, he searched for Keiron and the others. It had to be a trap. Ducking beneath a bush, he wiggled into a position to survey the scene. Isla sat still. Only her mouth moved. He studied her. She appeared clean. How could she stay spotless after all these days on The Trail? No marks bruised her face, and her hair reached her waistline.

The apparition, false image or whatever sat on the log couldn't be Isla. He searched the bushes for the other guards. He wanted to warn them about the danger. From the corner of his eye, he saw Garret enter the clearing.

Bronwyn pushed himself to his feet and readied his sword. He scanned the area but found nothing out of place. A story came to mind of a wood nymph that captured her prisoners by her voice. The powerful creature could match any man, particularly those void of magic like himself.

Garret walked deeper into the clearing and stared at the girl by the fire. "Isla?" She didn't look up and continued to sing.

Bronwyn slipped from his hiding place and stepped into the clearing. "Garret, draw your sword. This is not Isla."

The guard gave a puzzled face but followed orders. "Who is it?"

"The question is: what is it?" He motioned him away from the singing girl. "It's in Isla's image, but it's not her."

"An illusion?"

He nodded. "The real Isla would have run to me by now."

Isla's image stopped singing and laughed out loud. She rose and cast ghostly eyes at Bronwyn. He raised his sword but hesitated to wield it against his precious daughter's image.

Without warning, the image lifted its hand in Garret's direction. A bolt of lightning flashed and struck the guard in the mid-section. Garret screamed in agony, dropped to the ground, twitched violently, then lay still.

Bronwyn charged and swung his sword, but the false Isla leapt to safety. He swung again with the same result. It didn't matter how hard or how quickly he wielded the sword, the image evaded him each time. It pranced around, flipped, then danced onto the fallen log. The smile on its face, the same one he loved, looked menacing.

When Rorie charge into the clearing and attempted to make contact, he discovered the same thing; the illusion played a game. The two swordsmen attacked but couldn't strike their target.

If this creature had magic and couldn't be brought down by a sword, Bronwyn didn't know how to defeat it. He moved around the illusion to put it between him and Rorie, hoping one of them would catch it off guard. They swung together, but the image simply shrank and jumped away.

Once again, the guards stood side-by-side, facing the illusion.

"Any ideas, Sergeant?" Rorie sounded out of breath from the strain of missing with his powerful swings.

"Maybe we should step away. Leave." Would the illusion let them escape? Obviously, it had the power to bring them to their knees. Why didn't it use it?

"This may be the wisest decision you've made, Sergeant Darrow."

His jaw dropped; it knew his name. The masculine voice added to his confusion. "Private, back away slowly. I'm be right behind you." He held his sword, ready to fight. It puzzled him still how this creature knew how to replicate Isla's image and her voice. How did it know her favourite song? "Who are you?"

"I suppose it's only fair to see the face of your foe." A soft light consumed the illusion of the hauflin child, and Bronwyn shielded his eyes as the illumination grew and transformed into a human man.

Bronwyn studied the stranger. Both tall and lean, the blond-haired man towered over him. His thick brow shaded his eyes, rendering them dark and lifeless. Fingers as thin and as ridged as sticks folded together before him. A ring on his right hand held a thick red gem. The stone glistened in the fading evening light. "Am I supposed to know you?"

The man raised one eyebrow. "Perhaps, you do not. A shame really. After all, I will inflict the most grief upon your miserable life." He leered at him with a callous grin. "My only regret is the loss of one so true. She would have made a wonderful addition to my collection."

He peered sideways at the man. Who did he speak about?

"Do you not wish to know the woman I desire, the one you have lost?" The man cajoling him with a smirk.

He couldn't help himself. "Who?"

Alaura.

The voice echoed inside Bronwyn's head, pounding against his temples with such force he thought they would bust open. It resonated down his throat and into his chest and created a pain unknown before. It gripped his heart with dread and for a moment, he thought he might collapse from despair. He bent forward, pressed his palms to his temples and gasped for breath as if submerged under water, then he clenched his teeth. How did the man know Alaura? What had he done with her? He choked back the tears threatening to blind him. The unexplainable grief overwhelmed him, and his body fought to surrender to it and begged for mercy. Was Alaura dead?

The man's smile expanded until it spread across his face and touched the corner of his eyes. A light shimmered around him, and he stepped away.

Bronwyn glanced at Rorie through blurred vision. Although unsure if he could move after the attack, when he gave the signal, they'd run. The magical being possessed power unknown to them.

"Men, don't go. The fun has only begun. Don't you wish to know who I am?"

Bronwyn held back. He did want to know the name of this man who inflicted such despair with the sound of his voice. "Yes," he hissed, drool flying from his mouth and mixing with sweat dripping from his forehead.

The light grew around him, and he raised his arms in the air, then brought them forth. "I am the stuff of legend, myth and lore. I am Maskil's favourite man to blame for everything: from a dead chicken to a dead lord."

Bronwyn braced his legs to steady himself while he studied the stranger. It couldn't be. He was too young.

"Lindrum?" Rorie stepped forward. "You're Lindrum, the evil wizard who's destroying Maskil and bringing chaos to everyone?"

"You flatter me with your praise." He clasped his hands in front. "I wanted recognition, not a glowing report."

Bronwyn placed his hand on Rorie's forearm. "Don't."

Rorie shrugged him off. "His henchmen killed two of my brothers." He raised his sword. "The coward deserves to die."

"Private, put the sword down. It's useless against him."

"Listen to him." Lindrum smiled as a child might smile at a chocolate treat. "He knows of what he speaks."

Rorie gritted his teeth. "We just let him go so he can inflict more misery on the citizens of Maskil?"

"I don't think we have a choice." Bronwyn sheathed his sword and attempted to take a deep breath without sending pain to every nerve.

"Observant, Sergeant. Too bad you are dwarf. I'd liked to have kept you." Lindrum stretched his fingers. "But enough talk. Let's see what mares the night has to offer."

Rorie walked forward, and Bronwyn tried to grab his arm but missed. "Rorie, no! Private, pull back! That's an order!"

The guard ignored him and charged.

Bronwyn drew his sword and raced after him. He halted in his tracks when an invisible force struck him to the forest floor. A burning sensation stole his breath and shook his insides. He struggled to get to his feet, but dizziness overtook him, and he collapsed into the bushes. Through hazy eyes he watched Rorie reach his target.

With a great snap, Lindrum withdrew the light and disappeared.

Bronwyn recoiled in horror when he saw Rorie caught up in the extinguishing beam. A wave of blood spewed from the light's edge when the portal closed, severing the body in two. Half went wherever Lindrum had gone; the other half wriggled on the ground, twisting and turning as nerves fought to find pathways to the brain. Rorie's legs kicked and squirmed. Entrails spilt out and life's liquid flowed onto the ground. A hideous chunk of flesh thrashed in place of the once strong, capable dwarf.

He stumbled away from the horrendous sight. The throes in his stomach twisted and churned. The pressure rose to his throat, and though he tried to shake it, he couldn't. His body shivered violently. Rorie and Garret, both good men, had perished needlessly. Why had Lindrum spared him?

He thrashed through the bushes and trees, stumbling over stumps and mounds of grass as branches slapped his body. He tripped over a rotten tree, only to rise and run again. He had lost all his men; every single one he had started with. In his search for his daughter, they had died. How could he explain this to their families? What gave him the right to live?

Tripping over a fallen tree, he crashed to the ground. His stomach heaved. Rolling to his hands and knees he released the pressure, spilling his stomach contents in one violent motion after another. He coughed and spit and gagged until nothing remained.

Exhausted, he rolled several feet and slammed into a tree trunk where his body twisted from wounded nerves. Images of Rorie filled his mind, and tears burnt his eyes. The dwarf didn't deserve to die that way. He imagined what the other half must have experienced. Did Rorie look around in an attempt to find his legs? Did he die instantly, or did he live long enough to know his fate? Did his tormentor laugh as he struggled to make one last futile effort to live? Bronwyn imagined he did. His heart ached for Rorie. The brave guard die needlessly.

He felt helpless to bring him back. He couldn't help anyone, not even himself, far from home, lost and alone. His men were dead and Keiron had escaped with Isla. His beautiful daughter would suffer unimaginable horrors with a monster who didn't deserve to be her das. The ache in his chest grew, and tears flowed freely. Never again would he hold her in his arms and tell stories as she drifted off to sleep, or see her smiling face beaming up at him when she thought she had tricked him into getting her own way, or carry her on his shoulders through the castle. Her small hands would never again cup his face and tell him how much she loved him. "Isla!" His raspy, broken voice rose into the tree tops where the wind carried it away. "Isla!"

Squirming in pain, thoughts of his dad exploded in his head. Lord Nevell had said it himself; he'd more than likely die. In one day, his mum had lost her mate and her youngest son, *her baby*. His family might move as Finola had. She was also dead, leaving Liam alone. He and Isla were separated forever. Farlan had died on The Trail; he felt it deep in his gut.

Alaura shared his fate in the dungeon. He rolled to his stomach and beat the ground. Lindrum had said he had already lost her. He tried to feel her fingers on his face, the little kisses she had planted on his cheek, but the sensations eluded him. He shook with despair. Her death and the loss of Isla filled his heart with desolation. He lived for them. The deaths of his dad and Farlan pushed him further into hopelessness. He wallowed in the emptiness, slipping into blackness that numbed every sense and drained him of every drop of energy. Dreams of hideous sights and mournful screams haunted his mind.

Isla rested beneath the blanket Tam had bought for her at the keep. While old, it didn't smell too bad. She welcomed sleep after a weary day in the saddle. Snuggling into the earth brought a little comfort, but she wished to be in her own bed in her das' quarters.

What was that? She lifted her head and tilted her ear to the wind. *Das?* He screamed her name as if he stood next to her. She jumped to her feet. *Where was he?* A bolt of hopelessness struck her heart. The pain came so great, she couldn't catch her breath. She summoned enough air to scream. "Das!" The convulsions took control, and she collapsed to the forest floor. Wriggling as pain consumed her, she lost her senses and fell into darkness.

Keiron had jumped up when Isla had, but he could only watch as she screamed in agony. It appeared as if an invisible dagger had stabbed her in the heart. In search of answers, he glanced at Tam.

Tam had also stood and stared in disbelief.

Keiron knelt beside Isla. The look of horror on her face made him cringe. "I got a feeling we ain't gotta worry about the honourable Sergeant Darrow no more." He placed a hand on her head. "Such loyalty is unknown." He lifted her to her sleeping spot and covered her with the blanket. When she twitched, he recoiled and backed away.

28

Here in the Twilight

❦

THE SIX legs of the ladybug moved in unison across the leaf. They carried the red and black bug to the base of the foliage where it joined with the stem. Tiny white aphids worked there in the axil, sucking sweet juices from the plant and creating sugar that ants would harvest. The ladybug feasted on the succulent aphids until a robin swooped down, snatched it and flew off to feed its young.

The rush of wings pushed a breeze across the face of the dwarf lying on the forest floor nearby. A soft cool wind entered his air passages and worked to awaken his senses. Gentle but persistent prickles inside his nose and throat roused him further. He breathed deeper. The first dry swallow forced him to generate spit.

Another cool breeze flowed across his chest, rushing into his nose and ears. The first sound, the settling of the forest floor as its temperature rose in the new day, registered in his senses. All around him, the breeze swirled as if attempting to raise him into the air. The sensation made his eyes twitch, but the burning inside kept them closed.

Prickles in his hands as if they had fallen asleep made the dwarf wiggle his fingers. When a force other than the breeze brushed his cheek, he tried to swat it, but his arms felt like lead weights and remained still. He drew a deeper breath.

Alone and with only the feelings early morning conjured, the dwarf stirred. The soft flush of first light caressed his eyes, and he stared at the branches moving with the breeze overhanging his bed. He lifted his hand and drew it down his face as if to wipe away morning dew and cob webs. He lay still, watching and listening to the peacefulness of the forest.

A bird flew overhead, and Bronwyn followed its trail through the sky. His eyes settled on his left hand, scratched and dirty, and Farlan's bracelet. He stared at the beads, conjuring his friend's voice from the day he had given it to him: *I'll be spitting mad if you don't return it.*

A small smile teased the corner of his mouth. Farlan always sought the good, always hoped while others frowned.

A sharp pain like a pin prick sent his hand shaking. He swung his head around, hunting for the source. *Mosquitoes?* He slapped one on his arm. But the pain came from the back of his hand and no mosquito had sat there. Another sharp pain exploded behind his ear but when he swatted it, he found nothing.

He pushed himself to a seated position and gazed around. The sun still waited below the horizon, but its powerful light crept upon the land. *Each day the sun is about to rise, I want you to renew yourself.* Farlan's words whispered in his head. Here in the twilight, with the ability to imagine things floating in the dense cyan air, did fairies flirt in his nose and poke sleepers with needles? Or was it mosquitoes?

Thoughts of yesterday entered his mind. He rubbed his forehead trying to get them out. If he dwelt on them, they'd drag him into the darkness again. If he had lost everything, what had he left to gain by living?

Let it wash away your fears. Farlan spoke to him as if he sat nearby. *Add doubts to that, Farlan.* Doubts were as debilitating as fears. He drew a deep breath of twilight. As he exhaled, he released the images, sent them into the air to be remembered at another time.

He ran his finger between the bracelet and his skin. He smiled recalling the day Farlan and Isla had crafted the jewellery. She had made one for him, but he told her, *Sergeants of the castle don't wear bracelets.*

Naturally, his words disappointed her. She had said, *I'll wear it for you.* He wished he had the bracelet now. He'd wear it always.

He remembered the one thing Isla gave him he never went without and pulled the yellow stone from his pocket. Each time he needed patience with her, he had gripped it. Each time he needed a clear head to give Farlan advice, he held it. When he needed courage to ask Alaura for a date, he pressed it into his palm. Now, he needed all those things.

He pressed the stone between his hands, and its warmth heated his palms. Imagines of Isla playing with it whilst he dressed for duty flashed before his eyes. She smiled at him, winking as if she knew a secret he didn't. One day when Alaura had almost caught sight of the stone, he retreated, hiding it behind his back. He didn't want her to think he believed in good luck charms. She'd been curious and pursued him. It had become a game, and they had stumbled into the pond together. He'd never forget her smiling face as he helped her from the water. Alaura waited for him at Moon Meadow. This thought energized his heart with hope.

The castle had no better healer than Lord Nevell; he'd ensure his dad survived. Nothing would keep the well-loved man from his family. And Farlan? Well, he never gave up. His strength, determination and unorthodox manner would help him arrive at the castle alive.

Remembering Alaura faced the charges of unauthorized use of magic within the town walls today sent a shiver down his spine. He couldn't help her, but Farlan had made a promise. If all else failed, they'd unite, not because of an inner fire, but out of necessity. Either way, Alaura wouldn't serve three years in the dungeon.

Maybe Lindrum believed he had lost Alaura because of this. If she united with Farlan, everyone would think the same. A sigh of relief escaped his lips. When he returned to Maskil, the union would be dissolved, and he would unite with Alaura.

As long as he lived, there was hope he'd see his family and friends again. He needed only hope to continue his journey.

He stood on shaky legs and stared into the sun kissing the horizon. Within seconds, its brilliant light flooded the land. He closed his eyes and allowed his pores to absorb the energy. It washed over him, warming his skin and raising rough hairs on his chin. A new day had dawned. With it came another chance to live. He would take that and use it until every ounce of light drained from it.

Surveying the landscape before him, he didn't recognise any of it. Noting the position of the sun, the trail he'd followed the previous day lay east, into the light. With renewed energy, he walked towards it and soon found the three abandoned horses. He removed the saddles from Garret's and Rorie's mounts and threw them into the bush. Thoughts of their death tried to invade, but he pushed them aside. He had to stay focussed. His daughter's only hope of rescue lay with him, and he'd never allow her to think he didn't do everything within his power to save her.

Scavenging supplies from the discarded saddle bags, he stuffed what he'd need into his. After releasing the horses from their burden, he smacked both in the rump and sent them into the forest to fend for themselves.

He climbed into the saddle and directed his stallion onto the deserted trail. Alone now, he had to use an indirect approach in rescuing his daughter. One against three were poor odds.

ಬಾ ❖ ಲ

Isla dropped from the saddle and stood limp, waiting for Tam. She stared at the ground with little energy to move or speak. Since she had wakened this morning, an unexplained emptiness consumed her. The strange attack the evening before left her in despair. She sensed her das in terrible danger, had felt his fears and anguish. Though she tried to shake the feeling, it clung to her like horse hair on sweaty skin.

"Take this over there." Tam handed her his saddle bag and pointed to a spot near a tree trunk.

Isla stumbled her way there, then fell exhausted upon the bag. She forced herself to her hands and knees but moved no farther. From behind, strong hands lifted her into the air. Tam sat her against the tree trunk.

"Is there anything you need?" His soft voice matched his concerned expression.

She sank to the ground and curled into a ball. He had nothing to ease the pain.

Tam stood and threw a worried glance at Keiron. The hauflin shrugged and unpacked his equipment.

Tam repeated the same actions as he did each night: spread the blanket for sleeping, ready the food for the ration and remove his boots to air his feet. When he set a cup of beans in front of her, she remained motionless. Food had lost its flavour, and it ached going down. She wanted to close her eyes, surrender to sleep and forget everything.

"If you don't eat, you'll die." Tam rested his hand on her shoulder.

"So."

He peered closer and forced open an eyelid. "What's wrong?"

She didn't answer. The words she dreaded to speak caught in her throat.

"Is it your das?"

She shoved away his hand and closed her eyes. Pain overwhelmed her, and she wept. The hopelessness that seized her the previous evening clutched her in its cold grip. She wrapped her head in her arms and descended into sadness.

Tam left the beans, settled near the trunk and ate. He glanced between Isla and Keiron. She didn't move, and he only stared at her, puzzled.

Before darkness claimed the land, Tam shook her. When she opened her eyes, he pointed to the trees. "If you need to go, go now. It'll be dark soon." He stood and walked away.

The urge to pee had pestered her since they arrived, but she fought against it. To rid her body of the irritation, she rose on shaky legs and walked into the bushes. If stronger, she would have run away. Maybe she'd keep walking until she dropped, or they caught her. She stumbled over a stump and fell to the ground. Though her body longed to remain in the damp ferns, she propelled herself to her feet and pressed on.

Tam glanced at Keiron. "She's lost all hope."

Keiron nodded. "It's a worse feeling than starvation."

They watched her stagger into the bushes, looking for a place for privacy. When they lost sight of her, they returned to their own business.

Isla walked on and saw roots of a great tree ripped from the ground. It created a secluded place behind a wall of dirt, rocks and roots to sit and think. Maybe she'd crawl into its bowels and fall asleep. If they found her, fine. If they didn't after a few days, she'd begin for home. She might never reach it, but she had to try.

Upon reaching the base of the fallen tree, she slipped behind the exposed roots and into its shadow. A hot, sweaty hand sealed her mouth and jerked her off her feet, pulling her deeper beneath the upturned soil. Fear raced through her, awakening her senses. A voice in her ear spoke but she couldn't hear the words.

"Isla." The one who held her pulled her to face him.

"Das." His hand muffled her voice.

"Shhh." Bronwyn removed his hand and pulled her into his arms.

"Das." She couldn't contain her excitement. "I thought..." She threw her arms around his neck, and after a brief embrace, he forced her away.

"We must go. Now." He spoke in cant. "Climb onto my back and hold on."

She would follow him into a raging fire if he asked. Her energy renewed, she wrapped her arms around his neck and her legs around his waist. He moved quickly, low across the forest floor and away from her captors. She tried to judge the time. Usually she took about ten minutes to relieve herself. Tam wouldn't start searching for her until then. Given her state when she left the campsite, he might give her a few extra minutes.

That provided little time to escape, but they'd use every second. She clung to her das, helping to make their travelling faster. When they reached his horse, he flung himself into the saddle.

"Ready?"

She wrapped her arms around his waist; it felt like their rides to Moon Meadow, except their life depended on this horse being fast and sure-footed. "Ready." She pulled herself close, embracing her das, drawing strength from his determination to escape. She didn't understand why she had felt he had died? He appeared healthy and able.

As he reined the horse into the fading evening light, she snuggled into his back. He smelt of sweat and dirt, but a more wonderful odour at this moment she couldn't imagine. His scent soothed her. Beside him, she felt at home, no matter where they travelled. He was her hero, and nothing and no one could change that.

Several miles away, Bronwyn slowed the horse to a walk.

"Das, where are we?" The Midway Keep and Maskil lay along the trail. Since their escape, they had travelled only through the forest, making a path as they went.

"I'm not sure. I'm keeping the waning moon to our left. I'm hoping we'll intercept the road near the Midway Keep." He twisted and brought his arm around her. "If I had taken the beaten trail, they may have caught us by now. This way, they'll first have to find our tracks. It'll take them longer because our feet won't leave a clear path. By the time they find the horse trail, about half a mile from their campsite, we'll have a generous head start." He smiled. "Maybe they won't find it all."

"I hope they don't." She ducked to let him bring his arm forward. "Das?" She didn't know how to ask him. He had always been honest with her, but he hadn't told her about Keiron.

"Yes, Isla."

"Is Keiron my...?" She couldn't say the word. Keiron would never replace him as her real das. "Keiron said he was my das, but he's not. You are."

"Isla, I'm your das." He glanced back at her. "You're my daughter, the one I wouldn't trade for anything in the world. Keiron is your blood sire. Nothing more."

"Why didn't you tell me he lived?"

He sighed. "Truthfully, I thought of him as dead and at any time, I may have been right. In his line of work, death follows like a shadow ready to pounce." He swallowed hard. "I didn't want you to know the things your blood das had done. It worried me you'd think less of yourself. I'm proud of you, Isla. You're a wonderful person. No one can take that away from you."

"I'm not like Keiron."

"And you never could be. Catriona says you're a lot like your meeme. She was a kind and gentle woman. You also had the benefit of a loving family who taught you the difference between right and wrong."

"Did Keiron kill my meeme?" She said it quickly before she had a chance to second-guess herself.

He gazed into the night sky while he considered the question. "From what Alaura and Catriona have told me, he didn't outright cause her death. She died from complications shortly after your birth."

"So, *I* killed her?"

"Isla, *never* think that." He half turned in the saddle. "If Keiron had been a responsible mate, your meeme may have lived. He's the one to blame, not you. He hurt her and made her too weak to survive the birth. No mate does what he did. Mates are loving and caring. One gives their own life for the other."

She buried her face in his back. "I needed to know."

He sighed again. "I should have told you long ago." He paused. "Forgive me?"

"Like a sprite does the moon for shining so bright."

He chuckled and patted her knee. "You're one of a kind, Isla. I'm proud to be your das."

Around midnight, Bronwyn halted. "This is a good spot to rest. The trees are thick enough to hide the horse." He held her hand to guide her from the saddle. "We'll stay until dawn and start again."

He secured the horse in a clump of evergreens, then took a blanket and led her to a soft piece of forest floor covered with needles beneath a pine tree. He directed her to lie between two thick roots, and he rested beside her. The roots were so large, they almost concealed his entire body. He spread the dark blanket over them and pulled her into his arms. When he adjusted the cover, its breeze stirred a bad odour.

Isla squished up her nose. "You don't smell so good."

"Neither do you." He grinned.

"If Alaura smelt us, she'd chase us to the bath with a stick." She smiled. "She might scrub us with a brush to make sure she got all the dirt."

"No doubt she would."

"She must be worried with both of us gone."

He pulled her closer. "I'm sure she's fine."

"I know she is." She paused, thinking about Alaura and him. "Be patient with her, Das. I sense something wrong, but I don't know what it is. She's happy most time, but there are moments..."

"Moments of what?"

"Of sadness." She placed her hand on his cheek. "I love you, Das, but Alaura loves you in ways I can't. Farlan and I think it's time the two of you stop arguing about ridiculous things and figure out that you need each other."

"You and Farlan?"

She nodded. "We planned to lock you together in a room until you settled things, but we agreed no room could contain you both."

He glanced at her sideways.

"We think you need to argue with Alaura in a place where neither of you can walk away. Then you'd have to work things out."

"Locked in a room with Alaura, eh?"

"It was my idea."

"Aren't you worried she might freeze me to the wall or cast a wicked spell upon me?"

She giggled. "She'd never hurt you, silly." His smile grew. It was his Alaura smile; it lit up his entire face and made his eyes dance. As a castle guard, he had to be serious while on duty but when he saw Alaura, it didn't matter, he smiled. This reminded her of Tam. "Do you remember a castle guard named Tam?"

He shook his head. "There's no guard by that name. Why do you ask?"

"Tam, the dwarf with Keiron, served at the castle."

He stared off into space. "I wonder why he left."

"He wouldn't say."

"You asked him?"

"He avoided the question. I think something terrible happened, but he won't talk about it."

"I'm surprised he's told you the little he has. He's a thief. A ruthless bandit."

"He's not all bad, Das. He gave me food when Keiron gave me nothing. When Keiron wanted to hit me, he stood between us. There's good in him."

"Then why does he associate with the likes of Keiron?"

"I don't know, but I think I can trust him."

"Isla, you can't trust any of them."

"But maybe I can trust him a wee bit. More than Keiron and the gnome. They scare me."

He pulled her closer and kissed the top of her head.

She thought about her granddas, and her eyes filled with tears. "Keiron and the other dwarf, the one who went into the woods to make the false trail, they..." She choked on the words. "They killed your das. The gnome held me by the hair and forced me to watch. I screamed for them to stop, but they kept hitting him with the clubs." She buried her face in his chest.

"He's going to be okay, Isla. They didn't kill him."

"What?" She gawked up, eyes wide.

"He was found alive. Lord Nevell is helping him heal."

"He's going to be okay?" She wiped away her tears, and he helped her.

"I'm sure he'll be."

She studied his face. "Why didn't anyone come with you?"

"So many questions." He ran his fingers through her short hair.

"Tell me."

He swallowed hard and avoided eye contact. "Others did come."

"They died?"

"Yes."

"Farlan?" She caught her breath.

"He's at Maskil. He and few others returned to the castle to have their injuries tended to. He'll be fine after a few days of rest."

"But the others died?" When he nodded, she asked, "How many?" When he didn't answer, she insisted. "Like you, I need numbers."

"Four, but don't blame yourself. They knew the dangers. When a guard enlists, he takes an oath to protect the citizens of Maskil as well as the Lords of Aruam Castle. When one of ours is in danger, stranger or kin, we put our lives on the line to save them. I risk my life every day for others. This time, others gave their life for you. Remember their sacrifices, but don't feel guilty."

"I'll remember." When they returned to Maskil, she'd visit their families with her das, so he wouldn't have to do it alone. "Didn't Tam take the same oath?"

"He either forgot it or broke it." He kissed her head. "You need your sleep."

"You need it more to keep your strength."

"I won't be able to."

"Please, Das. I'll lay awake and listen. My ears are more sensitive to sound. If I hear anything, anything at all, I'll wake you."

"What about you?"

"I'll be okay. If I fall, you can carry me. If you fall, we're done for." She placed her hand on his cheek. "Please. Let me do this?"

He nodded. "I'll try. But if you feel sleepy, wake me."

"I will."

He snuggled into a comfortable position, with her tucked in his arms, and closed his eyes. "Do anything for you," he said, smiling.

"For you, too," she said.

"Love you."

"And you."

29

The Honour of a Fellow Dwarf

BRONWYN CHECKED his map. From the route he believed he and Isla had taken from the Trunk Trail, he guessed they'd break through onto the Lower Branch Road at any time. Once on it, they'd speed towards the Midway Keep and reach it before darkness blanketed Ath-o'Lea. He'd feel safer in the crowd. Keiron wouldn't dare attack them at the inn with so many witnesses nearby.

He folded the map and returned it to his side pouch. He reached for the half-empty water flask and took a long drink, then held it out to Isla. She sat in the front so he could hold onto her if she slipped. She had lain awake all night whilst he slept and by morning, exhaustion had taken hold. After consuming the water, she handed the flask back.

"It shouldn't be long now." Reining the horse around a large evergreen, he saw a long narrow clearing. He guided the animal into the grassy area and brought it to a trot, searching the shadows to the left and right. Though certain he travelled well ahead of Keiron, he couldn't shake a dreadful feeling in his stomach. It pestered him since he had come upon Isla and her captures the night before. He guessed the unsettled feeling came from his reversed role: he had become the hunted.

An abrupt thud brought his senses to full alert, and his horse stumbled. Another thud brought it down. As he and Isla fell to the ground with the animal, he saw two arrows in its chest.

"Stay near." He pushed her behind him and drew his sword. The arrows had come from the left of the clearing. He backed away to the opposite side, nudging her along as he went.

"Das, I'm scared!" She clung to his vest.

"I know." He could think of nothing else to say. He felt scared for her. Then he saw him; the gnome rushed from the bushes with a thick club. He stepped in front of Isla and raised his sword. It smashed into the club but didn't break it. Isla screamed, and he turned to see the dwarf drag her away. With a great thrust, he caught the gnome in the arm and sent him to the ground. He turned to face the dwarf, only to find Keiron ready with a sword.

They exchanged several blows before a club slammed against the back of his knee, dropping him to the ground. Pain shot through his joints.

"Stop! Let him go!" Isla struggled against Tam's grip. She kicked and punched, but she proved no match for his strength. "Das!"

The club struck him across the back, knocking the wind from his lungs and driving him to the ground. He rolled and jumped up, but before he could defend himself, the club struck his wrist. His sword flew from his grip. He tackled Keiron and connected with several punches, drawing blood from the hauflin's face.

"Das! Behind you!"

Tam had thrown Isla aside, and both he and Reese jumped onto his back. Isla ran and threw herself at Tam. She bounced off and slammed into the grassy floor.

The five wrestled across the meadow. Bronwyn fought with all his might to take down his attackers but in the end, they overpowered him. A sharp twist of his arm brought him face-first into the dirt. He struggled, but his weary muscles couldn't break free. They jerked him to his feet, twisting his arms in an awkward, painful manner.

"A sad sight!" Keiron picked himself up off the ground, puffing to gather breath. "Tsk, tsk, one of Aruam's finest here with us, far from the protection of his pretty stone walls." He wiped blood from the corner of his mouth. "It's time Isla sees what I do with yellow-back thieves."

"Tam, let him go!" Isla ran towards Bronwyn.

Keiron back-handed her, and she collapsed into a patch of dandelions. "He won't get mercy from me." He punched Bronwyn in the jaw, forcing bloody spit to fly from his mouth.

"No!" Isla jumped to her feet, but once again Keiron struck her, sending her rolling across the weeds.

"Isla, run!" Bronwyn pulled with all his might to break free but stopped when a rope slipped over his head and went snug around his neck.

"Reese, yew've snagged a wild boar." Keiron took the end of the thick cord and jerked it forward.

He fell to his knees and then to his stomach. Two bodies jump on his back and before he could resist, shackles and chains bound his wrists and ankles. They wrenched him to his sock feet and dragged him to a towering elm tree with a trunk so thick he'd need four sets of arms to encircle it. When they had him anchored to it, they stepped back.

"What to do?" Keiron paced back and forth in front of his captive. "I could..." he started but stopped. "Or I could... Naw, it's too humane." He eyed his daughter who stood off to the side, watching and waiting. Blood trickled from her facial wounds, but she didn't run.

"Keiron, let him go!" Isla glared at him.

"Call me das." He smirked. "After all, we're blood. The same nastiness flowing through my veins flows through yers. This dwarf stole yew from me." He clenched his fists. "It's my job to decide the punishment for a child thief."

"I'll go with you without fuss. Just let him go!" She turned to Tam. "Do something! Help him! Please!" But Tam stood still, watching with a glum face.

Bronwyn stared at his daughter with his heart in his throat. She didn't understand; men like Keiron didn't let their prisoners go. An icy shiver ran up his spine at the thought of her watching him be killed. He couldn't protect her from this, though he'd give everything he had, including his life, for her to be spared this horrible scene.

Keiron stopped in front of the dwarf and sneered at him. "It's because of yew she's weak minded." He raised the stick he had picked up and walloped Bronwyn across the chest. The hauflin raised it a second time and struck him across the face, breaking the branch in two. "I'll have to rectify the misbehaviour."

Isla rushed Keiron, but he grabbed her by the scruff of the neck and held her out to Bronwyn. "See what I mean. No respect for her das."

"She's only a child! Let her go!" Bronwyn scowled at the murderous thief.

Keiron laughed aloud. "Sure! I'll send her on her merry way." With his free hand, he punched him in the stomach.

Bronwyn doubled over as far as the chains allowed. Blood above his brow mixed with sweat and dribbled into his eye. Unable to wipe it away, he tried to push it aside by squinting.

"Isla, what say yew finish off this dwarf?" Keiron held a dagger out to her.

Bronwyn gulped. The scoundrel wanted Isla to kill him, feel his life drain away. She stared in horror at the dagger, a weapon she had never held before. When her blood das placed it in her hand, she glared at him. Bronwyn recognised the expression. Hatred had replaced her fear.

"We could leave him here for the buzzards to pick away at." Keiron leered. "After all, they enjoy half-dead meat. Course, if yew did finish him off, he wouldn't suffer for days on end chained to this tree." He crossed his arms and appeared to take pity on the prisoner. "After a few days his stomach'll growl so loud creatures near and far will wonder about the noise. And yew don't want to know how he'll suffer baking in the hot sun with no water. It's a terrible state for any man. But it's up to yew. A quick ending...or days of agony."

She held the dagger, weighing it in her hand, and her face went blank. With one mighty swing, she struck out at the hauflin in front of her.

Keiron blocked her arm, knocking the dagger from her hand. He grabbed her wrist and twisted, pulling her close to his face. "Yer just like yer das."

"Yes." She gestured towards Bronwyn. "I'm honourable."

He growled and punched her in the stomach, then back-handed her across the face. Bending, he picked up the dagger and gripped it tightly.

Isla rose on shaky legs with blood trickling from her mouth.

An unbearable ache rose in Bronwyn's heart for her. If he could, he'd rip the chains from the tree and wrap them around the scoundrel's neck. He wouldn't stop pulling until he severed Ruckle's head. He glared at the man in front of him. "You'll dread the day our trails cross again."

Keiron laughed so hard he almost dropped the weapon. He came face-to-face with him, and with droplets of spit flying from his mouth, snarled, "Our paths will never cross agin!"

An acute sting detonated in Bronwyn's side. He gasped as the dagger drew blood; his blood. The weapon quickly withdrew, and he tried to catch a breath but instead wallowed in throes.

Keiron wiped the blade on the castle guard uniform vest, then turned away. "It's time to get moving," he said to the others. "It'll be dark soon." Seeing Bronwyn's sword lying in the grass, he bent to pick it up.

Isla flung herself at Bronwyn, shoved her hand beneath his shirt and placed her warm palm on the gaping wound. She buried her face in his chest and sobbed. Excruciating pangs exploded in his gut as her hand applied pressure to the wound. He wanted her to stop but couldn't find his voice. The more he braced himself against the pain, the more it consumed his body.

He longed to wrap his arms around her but managed only to lay his cheek against the top of her head. The intense throbbing in his side threatened to take his legs from beneath him, but he held on. He wouldn't die in front of her. He savoured every moment of her nearness, knowing it to be their last. Tears fell as he choked on his spit.

Keiron leered at Isla as she clung to the dwarf. He tried to balance Bronwyn's sword, but the weapon was too heavy. He tossed it into the grass. "Isla!" he shouted. "Say yer good-byes!"

Her wide eyes stared up at Bronwyn. "Stay bent over. Don't fight. It's best he thinks you're dying," she said in cant, gulping on the last word. Tears soaked her cheeks.

"But Isla, I..." He closed his eyes, but water seeped through. Couldn't she see his life slipping away?

"Keiron can't see what I'm doing." She spoke more with her eyes and the movement of her mouth than sound. "I'll keep the bond as long as I can."

He didn't understand until the agony eased. Her warm palm still pressed against the stab wound. The hand which had mended minor cuts in the past now attempted to undo the injuries the dagger had inflicted. "Isla," he whispered, "I'm sorry I failed you."

"You have never failed me, Das. You have given me more than I could have dreamt for." She searched his eyes for what he thought was strength. "Promise me you'll live."

He never made promises impossible to keep. Still he forced a weak smile. "Promise."

Her eyes pleaded with him, and she increased the pressure of her hand. "I'll look for you." She breathed deeply and closed her eyes. Her fingertips danced upon his skin as if she weaved reeds by the pond.

"I promise I won't rest 'till I find you," he whispered. He was now capable of taking shallow breaths without sharp pain exploding in his stomach. "Know it as I stand here, as soon as I'm able, I'll be on my way to you."

Footsteps approached.

"Remember, don't struggle."

Keiron grabbed her by the vest and shoved her towards the horses. He sneered at Bronwyn now slumped forward, half peering up at him. "Sorry, me and my daughter can't stick around to see the last of yer blood drain from that yellow-back body of yers but business before pleasure."

Bronwyn fell limp against the chains, and they dug deeper into his skin. He held himself still to reduce the strain. Each passing moment, he felt better, but he had to appear as if dying...for Isla's sake.

Keiron took one last crack at him, sending his head spinning into the tree trunk. He turned and walked towards Isla. "Shut yer mouth, girl, or I'll shut it for yew."

She closed her mouth but wept uncontrollably. Wiping away the tears, she gazed at him. He absorbed the hurt from the punch but could not keep his daughter's anguish from consuming his emotions.

Keiron grabbed Isla by the hair and pulled her forward. "And if yew know what's good for yew, yew'll stop that salt water." A sword drawn from a scabbard made him spin around, releasing her.

Tam stood in front of Reese, blocking him from reaching Bronwyn.

"I want a taste," hissed Reese soft and slow. "Just a touch." The fingers of his putrid green hands intertwined and caressed each other as if he planned to enjoy a delicacy. His excited voice sounded as if he already tasted the ration.

Tam shook his head, and his scraggly brown hair trembled. "I won't let you steal the honour of a fellow dwarf with your despicable ritual. Let him die from his wounds."

Reese spit. "You can't deny me this pleasure. It's my reward."

Isla dried her face with the back of her sleeve and watched the two stare each other down.

Tam raised his sword, ready to strike. "It's your death we'll witness if you take another step."

Keiron moved to settle the spat. "Reese, there'll be others. Let this guard die by his own means." He glanced at Isla. "Yer pleasure would only save him from a long agonizing death."

Reese snarled at Keiron but obeyed and climbed onto his horse.

Tam drove his sword into his scabbard and threw a quick glance at Bronwyn.

Why did Tam protect him? Bronwyn searched his memories to see if he remembered him from the castle. The dwarf seemed familiar, but he didn't recognise the face. He must have left the service several years ago. Thinking about what Isla had said, perhaps he could be trusted. But why had he helped Keiron kidnap her in the first place?

Tam lift Isla into his arms and climb into the saddle. She settled behind him and wrapped her arms around his waist. Her sad eyes pleaded with Bronwyn. He knew what she wanted: for him to live.

Keiron climbed onto his horse. "This is where we part ways." He grinned at him. "Have a nice day." He snapped the reins to move forward. Reese and Tam followed.

Bronwyn watched them leave. He wanted to rage at his chains, rip them from the tree and race after the thieves but couldn't. He did as Isla had asked and pretended to be a dying soul.

When the horses reached the edge of the clearing, he straightened slightly to catch one last glimpse of the little girl who had weaselled her way into his heart and mind. He vowed to find her and kill the man who caused this misery.

30

Fairies in the Wind

LONG AFTER Keiron led the others from the clearing, Bronwyn battled against the chains. The unbreakable steel depleted any energy not already stolen from him by the massive amount of blood loss. He rested the best he could, not able to kneel or sit, yet not able to stand straight. The shackles dug into his flesh unless he positioned himself just right. His aching body throbbed from the discomfort.

The sun sank low in the sky, stealing light; his only source of comfort. He fought to stay awake and at every sound, he jerked himself upright to see what creature might be hunting. It played on his nerves, and his imagination created movement in the shadows. If an animal did come, the attack would be brutal.

The agony of losing Isla renewed itself, and he whimpered from the heartache. He had failed to protect her from the one person he'd been warned about. Catriona had said Keiron would return. The hauflin told her so when he had left Isla with her, but the threat occurred long ago, and as years slipped by, he had forgotten about it.

He heaved a great sigh, and the dizziness made him slouch forward. He had come so far only to die here alone.

The evening air cooled, yet his left leg warmed, confusing his thoughts and making him think of sunshine. The heat grew so hot it stung. The burning sensation persisted, and he struggled to get into a position to swat whatever had attached to his trousers. When he finally managed to brush the back of his hand against the material, he found nothing there. He tried again, slower this time, and felt a bulge in his pocket. Had a rodent crawled inside? With all his might, he fought to reach it.

After much toiling, he pulled his translucent stone and an odd-shaped piece of steel from his pocket. The heliodor had burnt hot but now, clenched in his fist, it felt warm and tingly. Never had it burnt him. Why did it now? Was it magic? He squeezed with all his might. If any drop of magic the pebble possessed could save him from this fate, he'd use it.

He thought of Isla's desperate plea for him to live and the promise he had made, but he didn't know how to keep it. The shackles were too strong, the chains too secure. His mind drifted to warm days on the Shulie, then to the morning she had given him the yellow stone. Through weary eyes he lost sight of it and blinked several times to clear his vision but only saw a fuzzy yellow blob beside a dark shadow in his palm. He closed his fingers around them and guarded the stone as if it contained all his hope.

The image of the shadow teased his mind, and he fought to remember what else he had carried in that pocket. He opened his palm slowly and stared at what appeared to be a twisted chunk of steel. Where had it come from? Fear of losing the stone from his shaky hand, he wrapped his fingers tightly around the objects.

A few more hours passed, but he journeyed in a state beyond noticing the measurement of time. He had spent his strength pulling and tugging and twisting the chains. Sagging against his bonds, he drifted in and out of consciousness. Sounds touched his ears, but his weakened state prevented him from searching for the source. Whistling breezes, hooting birds and soft thuds mixed together to create a night melody. A warm, moist puff of air fell upon his cheek, and fenberry muffins fresh out of the oven consumed him.

"Bronwyn?"

The wind sang a song with his name and beckoned him to sleep. He took a deep breath and relaxed his body further.

"Can you hear me?"

On the verge of slumber, he peeked inside of dreamland and saw Alaura wearing a beautiful dress and walking in the forest beside him. They paused, and he gazed upon her face, traced her jaw line to her chin and admired the lips he longed to kiss. Leaning forward, he caressed them with his own lips, savouring the scent of her skin. He kissed deeper and...

The wind tugged on his chains, disturbing his dreams of Alaura. The sound of steel against steel bounced off the night air. A voice cursed. It sounded like fairies in the wind arguing over the first to drink from the spring. He licked his parched lips.

A quick jerk of the chain securing his left hand made him almost drop his stone and the piece of steel. He held them tighter. The wind would not claim his only possessions. The fairies continued to argue and fight amongst his chains. They travelled along the links to the shackle securing his wrist. Their soft wings caressed his skin. Did they prepare him for his journey to the Plane of Peace? The fays played with his fingers, teasing them to release his treasure. Their fluttering wings kissed his skin and whispered for him to share.

"What's in your hand?" The imps' chorus of tender voices soothed him, enticing him to share his treasures.

A warm feeling swelled in his blood like the feelings that had erupted when Alaura planted little kisses on his cheek. His grip softened. Their wings fluttered about his fingertips, eager to see his treasure. Then it disappeared. They had taken the steel. He clutched Isla's stone; he couldn't lose it, too!

Once again, chinking sounds as sprites squabbled irritated his ears. He imaged his left foot falling free. Then he moved his right foot without the weight of the shackle. They couldn't deliver him to the Plane of Peace if still chained to the tree. An arm released, and he fell forward. One remaining shackle secured him to this life. He swallowed hard and tears for all those he loved welled in his eyes. The feeling of weightlessness lasted but a second, and his knees hit the dirt. He'd have fallen farther, but the fairies caught him and laid him flat. They smelt wonderful, a mixture of wildflowers, horse and sweat.

"Bronwyn, speak to me."

"Alaura?" He mouthed the sweet name, then choked on his dry throat.

"I feared the worse when I saw you."

The death fairies sounded like the woman he longed for. Their wet, cool wings caressed his cheek, and the coolness spread across his face and down his neck. What were they doing? He forced open his eyes and grabbed the wrist holding a wet cloth. Staring into the face in front of him, his thoughts jumbled. *Alaura? An hallucination?* Worse. Lindrum masked himself as the woman he loved. The hate for the man simmered, and he released a low growl.

"Bronwyn, it's me, Alaura. Why don't you believe your own eyes?"

The site of his bare wrist baffled him. The shackle that bound him to the tree had disappeared. He jerked the woman forward for a better view. In the dim light of a floating orb, he saw in her eyes the sparkle impossible to duplicate by an illusion. "Alaura?"

"Bronwyn, don't you recognise me?"

He released her. "I thought you were death fairies." His voice caught in his parched throat.

She caressed his cheek and came within an inch of his face. "You're very much alive, and I'm going to keep you that way."

He sank back and closed his eyes. His body felt like a lead weight, but he had to get moving. Finally free of the shackles, he had to continue his search for Isla. He attempted to stand but failed to muster the strength to rise off the ground. He moaned as every ache in his body attacked at once.

"Lie still. You're too weak to move."

"I have to. They have Isla." He flopped back onto the grass, helpless.

"You saw her?"

"Keiron has her. I'm going to kill him."

She eyed him with a strange expression.

"I have to go after them." Again, he struggled to reach a seated position, but his body refused. "Help me get up." His determination couldn't be heard in his voice, which was no louder than a whisper.

Alaura helped him to his unsteady feet, then released her hold and let him collapse into the grass. She rolled him to his back and knelt by his side. "In this condition, what good are you if you find them?"

He didn't want to think about that. He wanted only to get underway, do something other than lie here, letting them escape. The dizziness that swept over him when he stood dictated otherwise.

"You need to rest. Sleep will help you heal."

"I can't sleep. I have to catch them."

She dabbed at the wounds on his face with the damp cloth.

"Ouch!" He wailed when she pressed too hard on the cut above his eye. His senses became acute. When she hit the bruise above the other eye, he winced again. "Take it easy. My face feels like I ran into a rampart."

"Oh...? I thought you said you were fit for travel?" She pressed on the cut near his lip.

He moaned and grabbed her hand. "Is this how Beathas taught you to mend the wounded?"

A sly grin spread across her face. "Only trying to get your attention."

"You have it." He released her hand, then a heavy sigh. He couldn't tackle a loaf of bread without help, but every moment he lay here put one more moment of distance between him and Isla.

With the gentleness of a mum cleaning the creases on a newborn, Alaura washed the wounds on his face. Her fingers moved gracefully across his forehead and down the side of his head. It felt strange having her care for him like this, fussing over him as if he was Isla after a fall from a tree. In the dim glow conjured by a Light Spell, he saw the concern in her eyes. He must have looked horrendous after the beating he'd taken.

"They have to stop for the night, too," she said. "You're thinking otherwise, but if they travelled all day, they'd need to rest." She dabbed his eyes and wiped away the dry blood.

He sighed again. "You're right." He should be thankful to be given another chance to kill Keiron.

"Where are the other guards?" She dug into her pouch.

"Dead." When she stopped to study his face, he added, "A few returned to Maskil, but I don't know if they made it."

"They did."

"Did you see them? Did you see Farlan?" He held his breath, waiting and hoping.

"Farlan's fine. He'll heal." She dabbed the cut above his eye again with the damp cloth. "A group of bandits attacked the men before they reached Maskil."

"And?"

"They managed to fend off their attackers with assistance from travellers who happened upon the engagement. Once the bandits dispersed, the strangers escorted them to the castle."

"Strangers? Who?"

"I was told the captain of the guard from South Ridge."

"He travelled with Lord Dunsworth."

She nodded. "They brought the men into Maskil. One of the guards, the elf, was in critical condition. The dwarf had a better chance of surviving."

"And Farlan?"

"He's going to be fine. I spoke with him before I left. He told me about the dragon attack."

"Did you see Dad?"

"He was the reason I visited the Infirmary and found Farlan."

"How is he?"

"He's recovering."

"Why did you come? It's not safe for you here."

She paused, gazing into the darkness of the forest. "I couldn't stay at Maskil, knowing you were searching for Isla. I needed to help."

He sensed another part to the story, but exhaustion stalled his mouth.

She finished applying the ointment and bandages, then moved the magic light to inspect the lower part of his body. "Where did this blood come from?" She pointed to red swaths across his vest.

"A dagger."

"You wiped blood from a dagger on your vest?"

"Keiron did." He shivered remembering the pain the dagger had inflicted.

She hesitated. "Whose blood is it?"

"Mine." His hand rested on the abdomen wound.

She brought the floating orb nearer, and the light illuminated the blood-soaked area. "You should have told me about this first," she scolded. She unfastened his vest and pulled open his shirt. "I don't understand. Why is there so much blood? The wound is closed."

"Isla." He closed his eyes and imagined her tear-streaked face looked up at him, willing him to live. He had promised to do so, though at the time he thought it an impossible promise to honour.

"Her hands?" She washed away the dry blood, tenderly dabbing the wound with the cloth.

"She didn't have a lot of time, but I think she healed the worst part." An ache throbbed where the dagger had entered, but there was no sharp pain.

"She's an amazing little girl."

"Not because she knows magic. Magic alone doesn't make one special."

"I didn't mean it that way." She dried the wound and applied a layer of ointment. "Anyways, Isla's ability to heal isn't magic. It's natural. As natural as seeing and hearing is to us. Many confuse the two and believe it all to be magic, but magic must be nurtured. Like when a gifted artist hones his skill by drawing hundreds of sketches.

"Isla has learnt to use her natural ability wisely, but she didn't have to practise the skill. She possessed the ability to heal since birth."

She sat back to rest. "Bronwyn, why didn't you use the key?"

"What key?"

"The key you held in your hand."

"What did it open?"

Puzzled, she pointed to the towering elm tree. "It unlocked the shackles."

His mind raced. Where had the key come from? "Tam."

"Who?" She leant close to hear his low voice.

"Tam," he said again. "He's the dwarf with Keiron. He must have put the key in my pocket. There's no other way for it to have gotten there."

"Why would he help you?"

"I think because of Isla. She said she trusted him."

Alaura put away her things and pulled her rucksack onto her back. "Then Isla has made a friend who might help her." She stood and doused the Light Spell. "We have to relocate. It's unsafe here with the smell of blood attracting the night animals who feed on carcasses." She searched the ground. "Where are your boots?"

He pointed to the area where Keiron's men had tackled him and removed his footwear to secure the shackles.

After a few minutes of wrestling with his feet to get the boots on, she sat back. "It's no use. Your feet are too swollen. I'll carry them." She fastened them to her rucksack, stuffed his socks inside and helped him to stand. "There's a small clearing about five hundred yards from here where I set up camp."

He steadied himself against her shoulder. After taking a few steps, he stopped. "My sword. Keiron dropped it over there. Can you get it?"

Leaning him against the elm that had once held him prisoner, she retrieved the sword and slid it into his scabbard. Together they stumbled their way into the night. After travelling an agonizing distance, his hobbling developed into dragging feet. He laboured to keep moving.

"A bit farther." She panted, catching her breath. "You can do it."

Her confidence slipped, but he used her encouragement to continue. He was slightly shorter, but he was heavier. His thick limbs and muscles must have felt like a cart-load of building stones upon her nimble body.

Ducking beneath a few branches, they staggered into a small clearing. Evergreens, ash and birch trees surrounded the grassy area on three sides. A six-foot rocky bank added protection along the northern edge. Clover, Alaura's pony, grazed a few feet away.

She guided him to the blanket spread near the rocky bank. Half falling with him, their cheeks brushed as she caught herself.

"Sorry." He moved quickly to steady her. "I didn't expect the ground to be so far away."

"Ground has a tendency to move." She winked and patted him on the shoulder as she rose.

He settled, getting as comfortable as possible with the hard ground pushing against his bruises. She assembled items from her rucksack, then removed a pot and mixed the ingredients together.

"What are you making?"

"Soup." She mumbled a few words whilst her fingers danced in the air. A small glow grew under the pot, and she stirred the contents.

"What kind of soup?" Familiar items, such as potatoes, meat or carrots, hadn't gone into the pot.

"It's a mixture of broth, herbs, spices and water. It'll help you regain your strength. You'll sleep well after eating it."

"Why? Did you put magic in it?"

"I'm using magic to heat it."

"I don't want anything queer in it for a spell-induced sleep. When my strength returns, I'm going after them."

"It's a simple soup that will help restore your strength. You're exhausted. You'll fall asleep whether I add a slumber herb or not."

"Don't use magic to make me sleep."

Under her breath she mumbled, "If you keep complaining, I'll double the dose."

"What did you say?"

"Do you trust me?"

She shot *that look* at him, the one that stated he'd better do what she said...or else! After all these years, and after receiving many of those looks, he still hadn't figured out the *or else* part. It still had the same effect on him, taunting him, luring him into an argument.

"Of course, I trust you." He wanted to debate further, but she'd match him word-for-word until exhaustion forced him to surrender.

She poured the soup into a bowl and held it out to him. "Then be a good boy and take your medicine!" He hesitated to accept. "Do you want me to feed it to you?" She glared at him, wheedling him to eat.

Relinquishing, he took the bowl and put a spoonful in his mouth; it tasted warm and soothing. He'd lost this quarrel, but there'd be others.

By the time he finished the last spoonful, sleep beckoned every sense in his body. He wanted to argue the fact she had put magic in the soup but couldn't manipulate his tongue. Instead, when she unbuttoned his shirt and slid it from his shoulders, he didn't resist. When she grappled with the buttons on his trousers, he hadn't the strength to assist her.

And when she helped him to lie on his good side, the one not torn by the dagger, he merely gave a drunken grin and mumbled gibberish. He thought her skin brushed his forehead, but the numbness of sleep seduced his body to the emptiness of slumber.

Alaura covered Bronwyn with a blanket and watched sleep consume his body. The soup would force him to relax and rejuvenate. She'd make another pot for herself without the slumber-inducing dandelion leaves, but first she had to wash the blood and dirt from his clothing. He mumbled as she turned to leave.

"Alaura of Niamh, you're the woman in my dreams."

She kissed his forehead, then caressed his cheek, wishing on wishes never to come true with the man in her dreams. Pulling away, she set to work completing her tasks before she also crawled beneath the blanket.

With the moon high overhead, she settled behind him. Her fingers danced in the air, and she spoke the words to create the Cloaking Spell. They could rest safely beneath its veil, protected from attacking animals and other night travellers.

Gazing upon the man who lay beside her, she shuddered remembering she had almost lost him. But now, safe within her protection and under her care, he would heal.

She had mended many others under Beathas' teachings. With those patients, she had kept her emotions in check. Bronwyn was different. Panic had claimed her when she found him hanging from the tree as if dead. It took all her will to snap out of the shock and act accordingly. Once she discovered he was still alive, her nerves settled. She took control of the situation and saw he yielded to her demands. She disliked being stern with him, but she couldn't keep her true feelings hidden any other way. Nevertheless, he was a man who needed strict care from a woman who felt passionately for him and who endeavoured only to heal his broken body.

She ran a finger along his shoulder and down his arm, then kissed his neck. Snuggling into his back, she savoured his warmth. Her cheek pressed against the dirt and sweat on his skin. Although his strong odour needed dousing, his familiar scent pleased her. She slid her hand to his belly and pulled herself nearer. He'd never know she lay here like this, so close, embraced as lovers. She felt safe knowing she'd not have to explain herself for seeking such pleasures.

She had never lain with a man in such a manner, and she enjoyed every beat of his heart pulsating against her chest. He slept deeply enough to gather three nights of healing from this one. As she listened to his steady breathing, she thought again of finding him chained to the tree. If she hadn't smelt the odd odour drift in on the breeze while she set up camp, she might not have investigated. She shivered when she thought about the consequences if she had ignored her instincts. By morning, Bronwyn would have been dead.

She slid her hand higher and felt the bulk of his chest. He was a strong, powerful man, yet she had never feared him. When she had slapped him in anger many years ago, she knew he'd never strike her. If only he did not serve as a guard with Aruam Castle, or at least not be so honourable, things may be different. If she was a free woman...

It made no sense to fantasize about a life she could never have with the man of her dreams; it only made her duty more painful.

31

Puffs of White Bubbling Clouds

BRONWYN ROLLED over. When he struck a hard surface, he opened his eyes and saw a rocky bank. Where was he? He whirled around. Alaura sat near a small fire pit, cooking.

"Good afternoon, sleepy head." She smiled at him.

"How did I... How did you...?" He cocked his head as he remembered. Holding out a hand before him, he saw the leather bracelet Isla had given him and marks left by the shackles. He had believed it was a dream, but it *had* happened. Here he sat, alive, with Alaura nearby.

"Do you remember?"

He dragged his hand through his hair and gazed at the mid-day sun. "I thought I died."

"You're far from dead, my friend." She turned the piece of meat in the pan. "Your ration will be ready soon, but first," she lifted a kettle from the fire, "you need to wash." She prepared a basin with warm water and arranged the supplies. "Come. Sit here."

He stood, and as the blanket fell away, his jaw dropped; he wore only shorts! He grabbed the blanket and wrapped it around his waist. His legs shook, but he felt much stronger than the night before. He sat on the rock she pointed to, his face glowing as red as the fire heating his food. When he reached for the cloth, she scooped it up, wrung out the excess water and rubbed soap on it.

"If I press too hard, tell me." With a gentle hand, she wiped around the cuts and bruises on his face and scrubbed his neck. An uneasy expression clouded her features when the wounds around his neck revealed a device had been pulled tightly around it. The marks reminded her how close he had come to death; it reminded him as well. Momentarily lost in thought, her long, nimble finger traced the injury.

"It will heal." His voice, low and soft, tried to reassure her.

As if reminded of her task, she rinsed the suds away. She daubed the soap on his chest and arms. "I've never seen the honourable sergeant in such disarray."

Caught off guard by the motherly attention, he sat rigid as she washed his upper body, then moved to his back. He had lost count of the days on The Trail. He hadn't bathed since leaving Maskil, so he imaged how awful he smelt. It felt great to have the dirt, sweat and blood removed. His skin breathed again. He rubbed the growth on his chin. The coarse hair felt itchy. Most dwarfs preferred beards, but he didn't.

Watching out of the corner of his eye, he studied her face as she lathered soap on his back. She was intent on cleansing his body of the filth he had gathered; Isla had guessed right. He had never had his back scrubbed, so he had no idea of the delight it generated until now. She massaged his aching muscles at the same time, soothing his nerves and relieving his tension. He exhaled and moaned.

She stopped. "Is that too hard?"

"It feels fantastic." He glanced at her. "You're welcome to wash my back any day."

She resumed her cleaning mission. Coming around to the front, she folded the blanket to the edge of his shorts. She caught her breath and tried to avoid the rising odour.

He noticed her reluctance. "I'll wash them."

"It's okay. The smell will be gone quick enough." She soaped his legs and feet, foaming big puffs of white bubbling clouds. "This soap will make a skunk smell like magnolia."

He half grinned. "I smell that bad?"

She winked. "Bad enough that I could find you from this distance last night." She worked the soap around the cuts caused by the shackles. "The swelling has gone down. You'll be able to get your boots on today."

He glanced at his footwear, cleaned and standing by the fire. His socks, vest, shirt and trousers hung on sticks nearby. She'd not only cleaned the dirt and blood from his shirt but mended the dagger hole, too. He wished to wear fresh clothes, but he had nothing else. His extra uniform lay with his dead horse. "It feels good to get the boots off. It's the first time since leaving Maskil."

"No wonder you have sores." After patting dry his feet, she applied plantain ointment to the shackle wounds and infected broken blisters. "You must air your feet for a few hours a day. If you don't, within a month, you won't be able to walk."

He hadn't thought about that but truthfully, he had never encountered these circumstances before. Until now, he had always enjoyed a warm safe bed.

She brought the ration and while he ate, she tidied up the campsite. He relaxed and watched her work. She was efficient and soon had the supplies gathered and packed in the saddle bags. He felt uncertain about travelling with her to pursue Keiron and his men. It could end only in a battle, and he didn't want her involved. He should send her home but if he did, he'd be horseless. Thinking back, Alaura had been the only woman he had fought beside. They had worked well together though practically strangers at the time. Even then he thought her beautiful.

"When you're ready, we'll leave." She placed his clothes beside him and took his plate.

He reached for his shirt. "Thank you for cleaning my things." She turned to face him. "Thanks for everything."

"I'm sorry I misled you yesternight, but you needed a peaceful sleep to heal."

"No need to apologise. I'm grateful you looked out for me. In my condition I was being unreasonable." He winked at her. "I thought you had put something in the soup." Her playful smile grew before she turned away. The last time he'd seen her, they had shared more than a kiss. How did he get back to that place in their relationship? From a cold start, he felt it near impossible.

A few minutes later, with the gear packed in the side bags, Alaura lifted herself into the saddle. The sturdy red-chestnut mare beneath her shook its head, rattling the hackamore bridle and reins and shaking the flies from its flaxen mane. He remembered seeing the pony at Beathas' cottage, and Isla riding it on occasion.

Bronwyn considered her position on the pony. He wished she had waited for him to mount. It would be awkward climbing in front of her. She adjusted the reins, straightened her cloak and slipped her left foot from the stirrup. She pressed against the pommel and left the back of the saddle open as if she expected him to sit there.

"Can you move back a bit, please?" he asked.

"I'll adjust myself once you get up."

He stared at the empty space on the back of the saddle again. She did expect him to be a passenger. "I'm going to take the reins."

"This is my pony."

He didn't want to point out the obvious, but she didn't understand protocol. In his most courteous voice, he said, "I'm the man; I'll take control."

She scoffed at him. "It's my pony. I'll guide her. Clover will respond better to me."

"I've ridden many horses stronger than this. I'm sure I can manage." His patience waned. He wouldn't sit behind this unreasonable woman.

"Clover doesn't respond well to men."

"She's a lot like her owner." He half grinned, but the dilemma of taking control of this mare remained. "Slide back and let me in front. I'm sure I can handle her."

"I'm sure I can do better."

"It's only a pony."

"Clover is not *only* a pony. She's special."

"Why? Is she magical?"

"Are only magical things and beings special to you? Don't you think of yourself as being special?"

It wasn't what *he* considered special, but what *she* did. He had no use for magic. But why else would an old pony be special? This woman, who wielded her magic over things, including him, wanted him to believe otherwise.

"I think you are," she said.

The comment sat uneasy in his gut, and he measured its worth as he beheld her. A single braid pulled her hair from her face, exposing delicate features. Her firm but understanding eyes captured the afternoon sunlight. She revealed no hint of sarcasm, no sign of a challenge, merely the honesty he had come to know over the years.

"Here, I'll help you up." She reached out a hand to lift him into the saddle.

"I'm trained to handle these types of situations. It's best if I controlled the mount. Please, slide back so I can get in front." Surely, she'd listen to reason. After all, this was no silly game like those she played with the children at Moon Meadow. He waited, but she didn't budge. Her stubbornness irritated him. Didn't she understand he couldn't accept the inferior position she offered? A sergeant of Aruam Castle couldn't be dragged through the forest on the backside of a pony with a woman in control!

"While you argue with your pride, we're losing precious time."

He clenched his fist. Her words infuriated him. If she was any other woman, he'd physically remove her from the saddle and take control, but he couldn't do that to her. His inability to treat her as he did other women and put her in her place bewildered him and only frustrated him more. Taking two forceful strides, he drove his foot into the stirrup, grabbed her hand and jerked himself into the saddle behind her. He had grabbed her with such force, he thought she might tumble to the ground, but she regained her balance.

The mare moved beneath him, stepping to one side then the other. It reared, sending its front hooves into the air, then stomped them onto the ground. Its head shook wildly as Alaura tried to regain control. It sprang to its muscular hind quarters, then threw itself forward to buck.

Not having time to secure a grip, Bronwyn flew from the mare and landed on the ground. The aches and pains resulting from yesterday's injuries rekindled and shot through him like an arrow. It took a minute for him to regain his breath and for the worst of it to subside. The sharp pinch in his gut where the dagger had entered reminded him he needed more time to heal. He picked himself up slowly and scowled at the animal. It glared back at him, its ears pressed against its poll.

"Damn it! I thought you said you had control of this old nag!"

Alaura slid from the saddle and stood in front of the mare. She caressed its muzzle and spoke softly to it.

The empty saddle tempted him to climb into it. Then, he'd have the upper hand.

"Come." She beckoned him near.

When he stepped closer, the pony pulled away, flared its nostrils and widened its eyes.

Alaura held her hand out to him, encouraging him to try again. He approached the animal from behind her. When he got close enough, she guided his hand beneath its nose.

"Clover, he's my friend. He won't harm you. I promise."

Her soft voice soothed it, and she held his hand steady beneath its mouth as it smelt and nuzzled his palm. If it bit him, he'd most likely punch the stupid creature.

"That's it, girl. You can trust him. He's rough on the outside, but beneath the gruff exterior, he's gentle."

He eyed her. Did she believe the things she said about him?

"I know, Clover. He's a stubborn man, but he's a good man. He did mount you too roughly, but I'm sure he won't repeat the mistake." She caught his eye as she guided his hand along the muzzle, and across the nose to rest upon the white stripe running down the centre of its face.

Clover tried to pull away, but she held tightly to the hackamore bridle. "It's okay, girl. He's not going to hurt you."

"Is this what you meant by her being special; she enjoys throwing her rider?"

"She doesn't trust men. I found her starved and beaten. Her owner, a man, had abused her. It took a long time for her to heal."

He reevaluated the pony and wished she had brought a sturdy horse. This old nag didn't give the impression it could go far before it needed a rest. "I'm not familiar with this breed."

"She's a Haflinger. They're sturdy mounts. Great for trails and mountains." She released his hand, wrapped the reins once over her forearm and pulled a cube of rutabaga from her pouch. She placed it in his palm, then directed it to Clover's mouth. Soft lips gathered the vegetable, drew it into its mouth where it was chewed with exaggerated movements. Reaching once again into the pouch, she pulled out a brown bandana and tied it around his wrist.

"That's Isla's! Where did you get it?"

"She had left it at Beathas' cottage. I brought it with me for her scent." She held the bandana to Clover's nose. Its nostrils flared, and its head bobbed. Hairy ears stood straight and twisted forward as if listening for a distant sound.

Alaura moved behind him, took his hand and rubbed it against the muzzle, then along the cheek and back to the nose. It sniffed his clothes then his neck. When the pony nuzzled his cheek, he leant back.

"It's not going to bite, is it?" Clover sneezed, sending droplets of moisture over his face. "Ah! The orc's curse!" He wiped the wetness away with his free hand.

Alaura giggled. "Clover is starting to like you." She returned his hand to the nostrils, so it could sniff the bandana again. "Isla, Clover. We must find Isla." After climbing into the saddle, she reached for his hand.

He patted the mare's neck and shoulder, eased his foot into the stirrup and hoisted himself up behind her. The pony moved beneath him, but she calmed it. Unsure of where to put his hands, he reached behind and held onto the cantle.

"Hold onto my waist. You'll have better balance." She glanced at him as she adjusted her weight.

"I'll be okay."

"Are you sure? I don't want to have to pick you up again."

He was unsure if he trusted her playful smile. "Let's go!"

Shortening the reins, she made a clicking sound from the side of her mouth and with her leg, signalled the mare to move forward. Clover's walk turned into a steady lope as she made her way past the trees surrounding the clearing.

Bronwyn found his seat with the rhythm of the pony, but each time it dodged a branch or a root or changed direction, he lost his balance. At times, it took flight, shaking its head in the wind as if it had caught the scent of a predatory animal. Only when the mare had to manoeuver around an obstacle did it slow its pace, merely to begin again at a heart-pounding speed. Throughout all this, Alaura never faltered. She stayed as steady as Clover, bending and leaning at the right moments.

After almost falling off twice, he heeded her advice and held on to her. He wrapped his arms around her waist, pulling himself near. She acted as his anchor in the shifting sea he found himself riding upon. Soon, they bounced as one, leant together when Clover lurched in another direction and balanced upon the saddle as they sped forward. They travelled faster, more efficiently and left far behind the elm tree which would have overhung his grave.

32

A Treat in Your Pocket

BRONWYN DISMOUNTED. His legs ached, but otherwise he felt rather well overall. Resting on a large rock, he watched Alaura tend to Clover. For its size, the pony had performed exceptionally well. It had travelled faster than his horse, and already they had covered the distance he and Isla had journeyed the day before. It also had a remarkable ability to follow a scent.

Alaura didn't want to exhaust the mare, so she ran Clover for one-hour intervals, then cooled her out with a thirty-minute walk. Still, they had made impressive time.

She passed him the saddle bag. "There's flint and firesteel in the small pocket."

"I'll get the fire started." He made a bundle of birch branches, added handfuls of old-man's beard and small twigs, then lit it. By the time the flames enveloped the fuel, Alaura had set to work preparing the evening ration.

"I don't have a lot of provisions, but it'll do for a few days." She emptied the canned stew into the pot and added water to increase the volume.

He felt guilty eating her food. "I could go hunting."

"Let's wait until we need to."

With the ration consumed, he sat next to the fire and cleaned his sword.

She sat a short distance away, cross-legged with a book on her lap, flipping through the pages until she found what she wanted. As she read, her arms stretched out and her fingers danced in the air. She repeated the motion. Did she practise a spell?

This marked the first time they were alone together without an emergency pressing on their day. More often than not, he delivered Isla to his parents' bakery and left before Alaura picked her up. Most days, she was gone by the time he returned in the evening. Occasionally weeks passed when he didn't see her. Yet, like the sun behind the clouds, she lived within his world, and at any moment she might appear to brighten it. During the times they shared, someone else, usually Isla, Farlan or a family member, had always been present. Now, with all the time in the world, he didn't know what to say to her. His blood burnt for this woman but in truth, he didn't really know her.

"What are you thinking?" She looked up. "It's hard for me to concentrate with you staring."

He quickly diverted his eyes back to his sword. "I'm wondering what you're doing. Practising a spell?" His neck warmed, and he feared his ears turned red.

"As you practise to hone your skills and to keep them sharp, I must practise."

He dragged a rag across his blade. "I practise every day because I love it."

"I love trying new spells." She smiled. "It's like finding a treat in your pocket."

"Can I help you with anything?" He bit his lip. He didn't possess magic and she knew it. "I mean, if you need a subject to practise on, I'm here. Not that I want to be turned into anything...unless you can turn me back. And I'm not interested in being a target for a fire ball or anything else."

She laughed. "You're not interested in being turned into a pixie or cuddly kitten?"

"Not really." He watched her consider his offer. "Is there a spell that takes two people?" He wanted to learn more about her and prove to her they were compatible. If he showed an interest in the craft, it might impress her.

"I'm not sure." She flipped through the book. "There's one I've wanted to try for a long time but didn't know who to ask." She closed the book with her finger saving the page. "But I'm not sure how it'll work because you're untrained."

"We could give it a try." His confidence faded. The person she desired not only possessed magic, but the skill to wield it. This reminded him of their stark differences. Then he thought about those kisses in his office and her hands on his buttocks, pulling him near. He'd let her turn him into a kitten if she did that again!

"I suppose we could," she said finally. "After all, if it worked, it might help us."

"How? What is it?"

"It's called the Transfer Spell." She came to sit beside him. "The spell creates a magical bridge between two people. It allows one person to send an object to the other person."

"As in from here to there?"

"Yes, and if we stood in different rooms. The more it's used, the stronger the bridge. Eventually, the two people could be hundreds of miles apart and they might be able to transport items."

"Wow! Small and big things?"

"Whatever can fit in the hand."

"So, I could hold my sword and send it to you?"

She hesitated. "Not exactly. Because you're untrained, you wouldn't be able to work the spell. But I could send the sword to you. It would transfer from my hand to yours."

"You mean...because I don't possess magic?" He saw in her eyes she meant this.

"Maybe this isn't a good idea." She stood.

He grasped her hand. "I want to try." She hesitated still. "Not possessing magic doesn't bother me. I live by the sword. It's all the magic I need. I'm interested in learning more because of you. If you could send me an object when I'm in need, it can only help us both."

She sat back down. "Are you sure?"

"Tell me what to do. If it doesn't work, it'll be a good laugh if nothing else."

"Magic is serious. Can you be serious about the spell?"

He eyed her. She knew better.

She opened the book and placed it flat on the ground, then dug into her pouch and extracted three small packages. "Kneel here." Once in position, she knelt in front of him.

The light from the fire flickered in the strands of hair framing her face, creating a warm orange glow. Her eyes caught every spark of light and twinkled like sunshine on Shulie River. He sighed as she carefully measured the ingredients and placed them in a small dish. To this, she added lukewarm water. She stirred until the mixture became thick and sticky.

"May I have your right hand?" She took it and flipped it over so the palm faced up. She supported it from below and studied it. "Your skin is thick." With her free hand, she traced the deep life lines, circled each callus and touched each finger.

Her caress made his skin tingle with warm sensations. Her fingers, long and thin, fondled every space of his palm. It appeared as though she was studying it, committing it to memory. He leant in close enough to smell her odour, an intoxicating scent of sweat, herbs and wood smoke.

Using a spoon, she plastered half the magic mixture on his palm. She stirred three times, smearing it over his skin, as she mumbled secret words to ignite the spell. Occasionally, she glanced at the book to confirm the recipe.

The mixture created a warm sensation in his body; or did her closeness cause his temperature to rise? He watched her movements so closely he had a perfect view of the valley between her breasts and the soft curves on the edge of her shirt. The campfire generated dancing shadows on her skin, and the heat spread to his groin. At this moment, he'd surrender to any magic she wished to perform on him.

"Keep your hand still," she said. She repeated the action on her left palm. When she finished, she set aside the jar and spoon. "We must join, matching finger for finger."

When their hands met, a strange prickly sensation erupted. His blood grew warmer and his heart beat quickened, yet he still didn't know whether her touch or the magic stirred these wonders.

"Repeat after me, Dodem lopin nisp."

He repeated the Hauflin words. "Dodem lopin nisp."

Then they recited the words as one, pressing their hands together and staring into the other's eyes.

"My hand is getting hot. Real hot!" He winced from the pain but didn't separate from her. "Did you misread the spell?"

She shook her head. "This is supposed to happen."

He pursed his lips. The heat became unbearable, yet she never flinched. Could she control the heat because she possessed magic? "Are you sure you have the right recipe?" She ignored his question. He took shallow breaths, unsure of how long he could keep his hand against something as hot as a trivet on the stove.

Finally, she curled her fingers between his and held their hands in the air. The burning sensation subsided.

"We are transfer joined." An uneasy, yet excited expression lit up her face.

She sat near enough for him to feel the heat of her breath on his cheek. If he leant a little closer, he could kiss her, but before he acted, she brought their hands down and released her hold.

He shook his arm, then examined his palm, believing it to be burnt, red hot at the very least. But his hand appeared unharmed. The magic potion had disappeared. "Did it work?"

"Let's see." She picked up a stone and placed it in her palm. Staring at it, she recited, "Travel in air. Travel on land. Transfer this item to his hand."

He grinned at the rhyme.

She frowned. "Please, be serious."

"Did you make up the rhyme?"

"No, it came from a very serious book."

He wiped the grin from his face, but as soon as she spoke those words, it reappeared.

"I can't do this with you staring at me. Turn around." She made a circle motion with her arm. "I'll sit behind you."

He swung his legs around. She did the same, so they sat back to back, leaning against each other.

"Are you ready?"

"Ready." He opened his hand and rested it on his bent knee. She took a deep breath and slowly released it.

"Travel in air. Travel on land. Transfer this item to his hand." She mumbled the words again and inhaled deeply then exhaled.

When the stone didn't appear in his hand after she had repeated the rhyme thrice, he worried his lack of magic made the spell fail. For once in his life, he wished he possessed it if only to make a connection with her. His palm tingled and became warm. A red substance materialized.

"What is it?" He stared at the mess in his hand. "I thought you were sending a stone."

She peeked over her shoulder. "It worked!" She put her hand over her mouth and giggled.

"It's a bog berry!" He rubbed his palm on a grassy edge. "Great! I have a big red dot on my hand. Is this what you wanted?" He held up his hand to show her. The squished bog berry juice stained skin for days. "Is this being serious?"

Her giggle broke into a laugh. "But it worked." She stopped him before he had a chance to rise. "Let's try again."

He glared at her. "What are you going to send me this time? Bat dung?"

She reined in her smile. "How about dirt? I want to see if I can transfer faster."

He rested his back against her again. "Okay, but just dirt this time. Better yet, use those pebbles there by the fire. They'll be easier to clean off." He truthfully felt no anger for her trick. She had merely surprised him by her ability to fool him.

She scooped up a handful of the small stones from near the fire and poured a fine stream onto her hand.

She chanted the rhyme, sounding quieter and more confident. A circle of pebbles materialized in his palm faster than the bog berry had.

It amazed him to be so close to magic and watch it work. The pebbles circled the big red dot on his palm. With the index finger of his left hand, he dragged the top of the circle towards the centre. *Hmph. It looks like a heart.*

"Did it work?" When she saw the way he had changed the shape of the stones, she glanced at him curiously.

He smiled back, then threw the stones into the air to let them rain down upon them.

"You rascal!" She shook the pebbles from her hair.

He chuckled and whirled around to seize her by the shoulders. "Gotcha ya!" He ruffled her hair with both hands, and he lost his balance and fell forward, taking her with him. As he lay upon her, their faces an inch apart, his laughter ceased, and he stared into her sparkling brown eyes. "Do you want to transfer anything else tonight?" Her lips parted slightly as her gaze fell upon his mouth. It delighted him to have her with him like this. No one could barge in hunting for a delivery list. He leant forward and prepared to kiss her.

She put her hands on his hips and shoved him off.

He watched her rise, puzzled by her actions. Why didn't she kiss him?

She went to the ingredients and utensils used to create the Transfer Spell and packed them away.

He stared in confusion. "I guess we should get our rest if we want an early start," he said slowly, wondering if she'd offer an explanation for the quick dismount. She didn't.

He glanced around for a comfortable spot to sleep, a place to shelter him from the cool night air. When they had gone to retrieve the saddle bags from his dead horse, all the food and most of his things, including his blanket, had been either torn apart or eaten. The horse was unrecognizable. He'd have shared its fate if not for Alaura.

He walked to the base of a tree and sat down. The sun had sunk beneath the horizon and soon, it would take the lingering light with it. As he adjusted his position, she spread her blanket near the fire and folded it to create a cover. To his surprise, she produced another blanket and unfurled it next to her sleeping space. When she finished, she looked up.

"Bronwyn, I'd feel safer if you slept here."

He scrambled to his feet and went to the blanket. Without a doubt, he wanted to sleep next to her. For her safety or for his pleasure, it mattered not.

She went to her bedroll, slipped off her boots and crawled inside. Before she settled, her fingers danced in the air.

By the time he removed his footwear and spread the blanket over him, she faced the opposite direction. He rested on his back and watched her for a long time. If he wanted to, he could reach out and touch her. He sighed and stared up at the stars. It felt good to breathe without pain even if his strength and energy hadn't yet returned. They would, given time.

His right hand twitched as a slight burning sensation erupted, and he studied his palm. In the glow of the fire, the red spot appeared as bright as the summer sun in the blue sky. It wouldn't fade for days. Stretching his hand reduced the intensity of the burning and before long, it disappeared. With the spell in place, he felt wary about being magically joined with Alaura. Were there side effects to the spell?

33

Everyone Who Matters

ISLA MEASURED the time. A day and a half had passed since she had last seen her das. Although she had done her best to heal the dagger wound, she worried he wouldn't free himself from the shackles. If he didn't— *No!* She wouldn't lose hope. She'd done that before, and it had produced the worst feeling in her life. Never gain would she succumb to hopelessness.

They had stopped the previous evening when darkness became thick but since the sun had risen, Keiron was determined to make up for lost time. He had surprised her by not saying or doing more at the rest spot. No doubt, he felt no need since he believed her das to be dead. Though painful, she had to play along.

"On guard!"

Keiron's warning shook her from her thoughts, and Tam's muscles tightened. When she glanced around his arm, she saw two travellers, both hauflin, approach. They looked as dirty as Keiron. She imagined how they stank.

Tam touched her knee. "Stay behind me."

She pushed away his hand. She wanted nothing to do with the man who tried to kill her das. He had a chance to help him, but he chose to serve Keiron. In the past thirty-six hours, she hadn't spoken to him.

"Keiron. Good to see you well." The hauflin on the lead horse stopped fifteen feet away. Lack of washing made his bleak clothes darker. The cloak flung over his shoulders fared no better.

"Likewise, my friend. To yew and yer faithful sidekick." Keiron gestured at the hauflin half-hidden behind the man on another horse.

"Buchans endures." He half turned to nod at his friend. "He's a good man. Trusting."

"We all need a trusting soul to watch our backs, Graple. On yer way to Ellswire?"

Isla leant around Tam's arm to watch the exchange, which to her sounded strained. She recognised the controlled voice used by Keiron, the one he used when he lied.

Tam reached around and pushed her behind him. She was about to slap his arm when an abrupt thud made his body stiffen. His hand fell limp. If not for her holding onto his waist, he may have fallen.

"Reese!" Keiron shouted as he drew his sword and attacked Graple.

The gnome drove his horse past her and attacked the second hauflin. Below her, the mare stepped sideways. The clashing swords made it skittish. Unable to hold Tam's weight any longer, he slipped from her grip and crashed to the forest floor. He rolled onto his back, and she gasped in horror at the arrow embedded into his chest. To her surprise, he didn't appear frightened to die. He acted as if he nodded off to a peaceful sleep.

She leapt from the saddle, gripped the end of the arrow and struggled to pull it free. Placing a foot on his chest, she pulled harder. Finally, the weapon released its hold, and she fell backwards into the bushes. She scrambled to his side and found the wound weeping bright red blood. Lifting her hand, she hesitated. Why should she help a man who fought her das and possibly killed him?

Their eyes met. She wanted to help him; he was dwarf like her das. Didn't he have a family, friends who would miss him? Didn't he deserve a second chance?

"Don't waste your time." His weak voice trailed off.

"Why? So you can escape this life without a reprimand?" She glanced at Keiron and Reese. They battled the hauflins more than fifty feet away. She unbuttoned the top of Tam's shirt and slid her hand upon his chest. Pressing her palm against the arrow hole, she felt blood pulsate past her skin. The arrow had created a deep cavity and had severed several blood vessels. Even if she could heal the vessels, he might not have enough blood left to survive. She had to try.

In truth, she didn't want to be left with Keiron and Reese. She needed Tam to live. She held hope her das had survived the beating but right now, right here, much of her hope lay with the man in front of her. The sound of clanking swords let her concentrate on her healing ability. Keiron paid her no attention while the enemy kept him busy. If he knew she had this ability, he'd use it for himself.

Tam drew a breath and coughed.

"Lay still." Leaning close, she focussed on the wound and found it difficult to heal him. The energy had flowed hot and quick when she'd pressed her hand against her das' wound. The tissues wove themselves together; it was like a dance. But with Tam, her weaving fingers felt thick and heavy. Did her exhaustion make healing difficult? The sounds of fighting ceased. Who had won?

Keiron sheathed his sword and approached. He had cuts about the face and a slash mark above his elbow but otherwise, unfortunately, he looked fine. Reese leant on his sword overlooking the hauflin he had killed.

"What are yew doing, girl? Trying to plug the hole with yer finger?" Keiron stopped to catch his breath.

She gawked at her hand. "I'm applying pressure to stop the bleeding."

"Don't bother. A man don't survive a hit like that."

"Do you have anything to dress the wound?"

He chuckled. "Nothing I'd waste on a dead man." He went to his horse and pulled out a few rags to patch himself up.

Isla leant close to Tam's face. "Do you have anything in the saddle bags?"

He nodded.

She raced to the bags and dug through them to find a sack containing clean dressings and bandages.

When she opened Tam's shirt for a clear view of the wound, a low, mournful cry mixed with an excited sigh disturbed her. She turned to see Reese with his hand over the gash in the hauflin's chest, the one Keiron had called Buchans. He wasn't yet dead, and whatever act the gnome performed made him whine. Surely, it wasn't a healing hand he laid on him. Reese's four fingers spread across the skin, and his palm pressed into the cavity of the sword injury. A faint green glow surrounded his outstretched hand. His expression was one of pure pleasure. His eyes, fixed on the man's face, spread wide open and contained an excitement she had never witnessed.

The hauflin's shrieks escalated, and his expression turned from agony into sheer terror. His cheeks vibrated, and Isla thought his eyes might pop out of his head. Unable to speak, his groans echoed throughout the forest. She couldn't imagine the torture he suffered as the gnome worked his magic on him, taking what the body forbid to surrender.

Tam touched her cheek and turned her to face him. "Don't look."

"That's one thing yew don't get use to no matter how many times yew see it." Keiron looked down at Tam. "It's a nasty habit." He walked to his horse and busied himself whilst the gnome finished his reward.

Isla tried to pull her thoughts together. The gnome frightened her more now than he had before. No one, not even the worst criminal deserved to be delivered to the Plane of Peace in that manner. Reaching for the dressing, she noticed the plants growing nearby would aid in healing. She plucked several from the ground, put them in her mouth and chewed thoroughly. She spit them out and smeared the herbal substance over the arrow hole.

"He'll need more than green spit to survive." Keiron chuckled and went to check Graple's and Buchans' horses.

Tam coughed gingerly. "You know what you're doing, don't you?"

"I have wise teachers." She wanted to wash away the blood but didn't want Keiron to see how the wound had almost closed. After packing the chewed herbs over the half-mended hole, she applied a dressing. "Hold it in place." She guided his hand over the cloth and wrapped a bandage around his chest.

Once again, strange sounds spewed from the gnome. He repeated his ritual on the second dead hauflin. Closing her eyes, she forced her attention elsewhere. Was this what he wanted to do to her das? She caught her breath, and stared at Tam. "You stopped him!"

"Stopped who?" His voice had regained strength.

She guarded her mouth and spoke in cant. "Reese was going to do that to my das, wasn't he?"

He nodded.

She couldn't help herself. She threw her arms around his neck. It would have killed her to witness such an act of inhumanity on her das. It would have meant the end for sure. "Thank you."

He shoved her away and glanced at Keiron. The hauflin still rummaged through the enemy's pack and hadn't noticed the show of gratitude. He gave her a stern look. "Don't."

"But—"

"Don't." He held his hand over her mouth when she wanted to speak again.

She pulled away, confused. Though he had helped capture her das, he wouldn't allow the gnome to steal his essence. She wanted to smile but thought it unwise to do so.

"You're an honourable girl," he said in cant.

"Everyone can be. Each morning the sun rises, we choice whether to be honourable or not."

"Those are your das' words."

"But I believe in them as if they were my own."

He admired her. "Your das would be proud."

"If not for me, he'd be safe at Maskil, not chained to a tree struggling to stay alive." Tears welled, but she didn't let them fall. "It's my greatest pain." She stared at him. "I'd sacrifice my life for his. He doesn't deserve to die out there, all alone. He's a good man, the best. Many love him because of his goodness."

"He *is* a good man. Men like him make other men realise how low they've sunk." He paused and glanced at Keiron and Reese, who discussed a find in the bushes. "Don't give up hope, Isla. A good man isn't down until everyone who matters has lost hope in him."

Keiron strode to his horse. "Isla!"

She jumped at the urgency of his voice.

"Come here."

She took a few steps towards him, then stopped. He climbed onto his horse. Reese did the same. They prepared to leave.

"Isla, get over here." Keiron searched the forest with determined eyes.

"What about Tam?"

"I'm not dragging around a dead man. Trogs consider that bait."

"He's not dead!" She swung around to face Tam. "Don't just lie there! Get up! Now!"

He rose to a seated position, but couldn't rise further. She rushed to his side.

"We don't have time for this." Keiron scowled. "The troglodyte's tracks go right through this area. This is their feeding ground this time of year."

Isla hoisted Tam's arm over her shoulder. She wouldn't leave him behind to be eaten by troglodytes. He stumbled to his horse, almost taking her down. "Hold onto the saddle! Grab it!"

He grasped the pommel but sagged under his own weight.

"He can't ride!" Reese sounded anxious. "Leave him!"

She threw her meanest look at the gnome. "Shut up!" She seized Tam by the shirt. "I'll climb into the saddle and help you up. Okay? Hang on." She pulled herself onto the mare's back. It took a good minute to get him up behind her but once there, he was steady.

"This is ridiculous," hissed Reese.

"Yew, follow me." Keiron pointed a finger at Isla. "If yew can't, we leave him." He kicked his steed to a start.

Isla reined the mare to follow. She had ridden Clover, Alaura's pony, many times at Moon Meadow but felt unsteady on this larger animal.

Tam reached around her and gripped the pommel to steady himself. His heavy breathing revealed his weak state.

"Faster!" The nose of Reese's horse banged the rump of Tam's.

"Kick it," said Tam. When she hesitated, he jabbed his heal into the mare's side.

The sudden movement surprised her, but she kept control of the horse. Unlike Clover, this animal needed more encouragement to move forward. She guessed from the sound of Reese's voice he didn't much like troglodytes, but then who did? She had never seen one, but the stories her classmates told of them terrified her.

34

One Best Friend

THE SUN kissed the horizon and melted into the distant hill. Bronwyn scanned the valley below and the meandering river cutting through it. Besides the wildlife, the area appeared deserted. His stomach grumbled, and he placed his hand over it. The thin soups, bread and vegetables they ate might sustain Alaura, but he needed food with more substance. He already felt the loss of mass by eating the sparse meals, and the constant movement only added to his weight loss. He had become lean but hoped he hadn't lost muscle.

A tingling sensation made him examine his hand. The red bog berry stain glowed as bright as if it had been just squished into his palm. His skin warmed, and he wondered if the burning sensation he had felt the evening before returned. To his surprise, an oatmeal raisin cookie appeared.

He spun around and watched Alaura. She put away the cooking utensils they had cleaned and didn't look at him. Watching her, he spied a smile she tried to hide. He bit into the cookie; his mum had made it. Alaura had held out on him; he didn't know she had cookies.

His gaze returned to the valley, and he ate the treat. To know Alaura could send him anything at any time, regardless of his location, intrigued him. She could send him a note, a dagger, a book...a cookie.

What about things like water, a breath of air or a kiss? Could she tickle her hand and send the feeling to him? What if she slapped her hand or bit it? Could she stab her hand with a dagger and send the wound to him? The tingling sensation appeared again along with another cookie.

He brought his hand to his face and spoke directly to his palm. "Thank you, Great Hand, for delivering me these delicious treats." She chuckled, and he looked at her. In the glow of the setting sun, she appeared more beautiful than he could imagine. The diffused reds and oranges created soft tones on her face, and when she smiled, her eyes glistened. As he ate the cookie, he thought of the day in his office, of her hands caressing his skin and being lost in a long kiss. She had been in a weak state and still dealing with the emotional turmoil of Lord Val's assault.

Her strength and confidence returned, she didn't want him to help with anything. He did anyways. It gave him things to do with her, and he wanted to do everything with her.

She struggled to break a piece of firewood that had half burnt and threatened to fall to the side, so he stepped up and put his hand next to hers. "I'll get it."

"I'm quite capable."

He smiled. "I'm also quite capable of helping." He snapped the wood and threw the end piece into the fire. "I'll get a few more sticks to last the night." He held out a hand to help her to her feet and pulled her up, directly into his arms. Her breath caught as he pulled her nearer. Caressing her chin, he tried to remember how the Be-still Spell worked. He leant forward, but she pushed him away. She slipped from his grip and went to the opposite side of the campfire. "Alaura?"

"Yes?" She poked at the red-hot embers, sending sparks into the air.

"Why won't you kiss me?" He had never spoken so bluntly, but his frustration left him no alternative.

"I don't want to kiss. Can't you respect my wishes?" She released the poker and pulled her rucksack near.

"Why not?" He put his hands on his hips. "If your blood burns for me, why don't you want to?"

"I never told you my blood burns for you."

"Yes, you did. In my office after I had you released from the dungeon."

"You're mistaken. I never spoke those words."

"You might as well have. The smile on your face when I told you how I felt said it all! You kissed me as if you did!" Confusion and embarrassment clouded his mind. He had confessed his feelings for her only because he knew she felt the same way. A woman had fooled him again, but this time it burnt him as if she'd tossed him into a raging forest fire. "You told me I was dear to you and that I shouldn't forget it. Damn it! What did you mean?"

"I did say that, and I said you were special." She pulled a water flask from the rucksack. "And you are."

"Special!" The word rolled off his tongue as if he had licked boot wax by mistake. "That's it?" His voice cracked. "I'm special...like your pony but not your lover?"

"You're my best friend, Bronwyn. Isn't that good enough?"

"Friend?" He slapped his forehead and stepped away. "I'm a friend to you? A stupid, foolish, see-you-later friend?"

"No." She rose and stared at him. "You're not just a friend. I said you are my best friend."

"Whoohoo!" His finger drew circles above his head. "A *best* friend. Doesn't *that* make me feel special? I'm junked together with all your other best friends. I'm as important as Beathas, Catriona, *my sisters*. This makes me feel great!" The sarcasm rolled off his tongue. It protected his senses from the increasing ache in his heart.

"No, you're not!" She struggled to find the right words to make him feel special amongst the hundreds of people she knew.

"You could make me a badge. I can stick it right here." He patted his chest. "Alaura's *Special Friend*. It'll make me stand out. Maybe we can make a flag. Hang it on the damn turret!" He tried to sidestep the flying water flask but failed, and it struck him in the shoulder. "Well, like aged manure, I feel special now! I bet you don't throw flasks at anyone but me!"

She rolled her eyes. "You're so unreasonable. Why do I argue with you? You simply make me angry!"

"It's my special talent."

She was exasperated. "Everyone has friends, Bronwyn, but you can only have one best friend! As the word decrees, there can only be *one* best! You can have good friends; you can have great friends, but only one best!" She took a deep breath to calm her voice. "Let me explain this in a way you'll understand."

"Better make it real simple 'cos I ain't too bright. I mean, I think I'm your man, your lover, the only one you'd kiss that passionately, but I'm just another *friend*. Apparently, you go around kissing all your male friends with that much vigour. How stupid can I be?" He shrugged, still clinging to the sarcasm for protection.

"Stupid is one thing you're not." She took a few steps towards him. "Consider this. Think of yourself as a castle and you have an army that protects you, comforts you and whom you confide in."

He folded his arms. She knew nothing about the workings of a castle or an army.

"Imagine all the people in the army. Everyone is a private. They are generally good people who work their shifts. Their many hands make life easy for you and as the years pass, you get to know them, but you don't know them well.

"From these privates, there are about thirty who go out of their way to give you a hand when you need it. They think of you—the castle—as a person to spend time with. They spend long days seeing to your needs. We'll call them corporals.

"Out of these men, there are eight who are more dedicated to serving the castle—you—and the castle enjoys their company and shares stories of their families and of years gone by. The castle knows they'll stand strong to protect it. They are appointed sergeants.

"From these men, four stand out. They anticipate your needs, they soothe your pains and make you laugh. You depend on their service for many years to come. They are your captains." She paused and came nearer.

He had an idea where this was headed but remained quiet.

"From these four, one man's dedication and commitment shine above the rest. The castle recognises this individual because it—the castle—is always first on his mind. Each day, he's there without complaint. He patches the intricate part of the castle no one else sees crumbling. He sits with the castle when the storm winds blow and when it needs a shoulder to lean on. And when the birds sing, the man dances down its halls, bringing joy to whatever he touches. He does all this without want or need for compensation or recognition. He does it for the simple joy it brings him. The castle knows without hesitation this man is his best, and he is appointed captain of the guard." Her voice softened. "There can only be one captain of the guard, Bronwyn. And there can only be one best friend."

He rubbed his short beard. "So, I'm your captain of the guard?" When she nodded, he stared at the ground. *Great.* She regarded him as she would Sanderson, her servant but not her lover. What rank did her lover receive? Was he her lord? "I should be honoured." Funny, he didn't feel so endowed. He'd rather be a private and ravish those lips, but he had to face reality. She didn't see him as a lover, only as a friend. All they had shared amounted to a platonic friendship, nothing more. His throat tightened, and he coughed when he swallowed.

He turned away, not wanting to look at her. He wanted to run and hide, but that would be childish, immature. Anyways, where would he go? He couldn't walk away and leave her to fend for herself. Their chances fared better if they stuck together.

Walking to the edge of the ridge, he looked out over the valley. A lead weight filled his chest and aimed to drag him to his knees. He recalled a story his dad once told about a man whose blood burnt for a woman he could never have. Living in the same settlement, the man doted on her, opened doors, made her deliveries and helped without complaint whenever she called. But she didn't feel the same way and united with another. The other man received her affection, and the man who loved her most, received her courtesy. They lived apart, yet together year after year. Eventually, the man died never satisfying the thirst for his love. Bronwyn's dad had said, *To see him watch her, knowing the fire burning within, was the saddest of sights. It was as if a man holding in his hand all the riches of Ath-o'Lea and not the ability to escape the cavern which entombed him, but worse, for he beheld the treasures of the heart, yet could not indulge.*

Bronwyn had become that man, the saddest of sights, living with a thirst he'd never quench. Of all the twists life offered, this had to be the cruelest. His eyes welled with tears. They were for him and the man his dad knew. Alaura stepped behind him, and when she wrapped her arms around his waist, he shivered. She caused his pain, yet he didn't hate her.

The warmth of her body pressed against his back reminded him of the intimacy they'd never share. He coughed to clear his throat and choked on his spit. She held him tighter. He looked down at her hands, wanting to rip them from his body, but he hadn't the strength. Seeing his own hand and the red bog berry stain, he wondered if he could get comfort from the Transfer Spell, this bit of magic she had instilled in him. Then he feared what feelings he might send to her. But she had said it: he was incapable of sending her anything. In the end, the ache released him of his cares. He pressed their palms together and entangled his fingers between hers. Feeling nothing, he groped in the dark, hoping to find a light. Then it happened. A stream of warm energy travelled through his blood, relaxing his nerves and easing his pain. The ache in his heart subsided and calmness settled his body.

"Take what you need. I give it freely."

Her voice sang on the breeze. He could never hate her. His blood burnt for her more than a hundred fires blazing in the night. Wherever she went, he'd go. Whatever she needed, he'd give.

 ☞ ✦ ☜

Shortly before the sun dropped out of the sky, Keiron ignited the kindling in the fire pit. Before long, it lit up the darkness. "Isla, stay near the fire." He went to his pack and pulled out his sack of food. "Trogs fear fire."

Reese spread his blanket as near to the campfire as possible without it burning. Once settled, he pulled a can from his pack, removed the lid and ate.

The glow from the flames highlighted features on Reese that Isla wished she didn't have to see. When she realised he was eating canned worms, she gagged and looked away. Her hunger faded as she fought to calm her stomach.

Tam lay with his head near the fire. He had grown weaker as the day progressed and now slept. Keeping him in the saddle had exhausted her, and when they had finally halted, she couldn't stop him from falling to the ground.

"It's time yew accept the facts, Isla." Keiron shoved a spoonful of beans into his mouth. "Tam'll be dead by morning light. Don't know what's kept him alive this long."

She stared at him. "Don't you have anything to help him heal?"

"He's beyond help by regular means."

Surveying the edge of the small clearing, she saw the healing herb grew all around. She went to gather a handful.

"I told yew to stay near the fire!"

She quickly picked the plants and returned to Tam's side. Rolling him onto his back, she opened his shirt and removed the blood-soaked dressing. As she moved to throw it into the bushes, Keiron stopped her.

"Throw it into the fire. The blood'll attract things yew don't ever want to see."

She obeyed. The moisture in the material doused the flame for a few minutes but then it dried, and the fire raged on. She washed the wound, using the cleansing mixture in Tam's kit. The arrow hole still wept blood. Not as much as it did at first, but enough to kill him if it didn't stop.

She put a clump of herbs into her mouth and chewed until they felt soft and mushy, then she spit them out and applied the soggy wad to the injury. With Keiron watching, she didn't dare put her hand on Tam to heal him. She'd do it later. The herbs applied, she added fresh dressing and wrapped the remaining bandages around his chest.

Tam coughed, opened his eyes and stared at her, confused. He struggled to a seated position and took in his surroundings.

"Ay! The dead man rises." Keiron chuckled. "Must be magic in her spit."

Isla dug into Tam's saddle bag and extracted a can of beans. She removed the lid and placed it near the fire. "Lay down." She guided him back to the makeshift pillow she had constructed.

He closed his eyes and released a heavy sigh. She emptied half the can of warm beans into a dish and handed it to him. He shook his head. "You eat it."

She glared at him, trying to make the crossed look Alaura had given her many times when she wanted her to do something for her own good. "If you don't eat it, I'll feed it to you."

He took the bowl, grumbling, "You're worse than a mum."

She smiled inside and settled beside him to eat the remaining beans in the can. When he finished, she gave him bread and a drink of water. By the time he had consumed the food, exhaustion had claimed him. He turned on his side, facing her and closed his eyes. In no time, he snored.

"Reese, yew take first watch." Keiron slid a little closer to the fire and put his head down.

The gnome added a few sticks to build up the flames and sat with his back to it, staring out into the night.

Isla lay close to Tam. She spread her blanket over both of them, for extra warmth for him, she'd say if asked, and slid her arm beneath his shirt. She had intentionally left the bandages loose to get her palm over the arrow hole. Once in place, she relaxed and concentrated. She could remain in this position for as long as necessary to heal the wound completely.

An hour later, before sleep consumed her, she withdrew her hand and pulled the bandage into place. Tam drew a deep breath. The choice to live rested with him. If he had enough blood and desire to see the morning, he would.

35

Blade and Magic

AS NIGHT ended and dawn broke, Bronwyn lay awake thinking about what Alaura had said. She considered him her best friend. What did this mean exactly? His dad had said best friends turned out to be life mates. If he applied this logic, she deemed him her mate, but she didn't have the benefit of his dad's wisdom. He thought about the rest of what his dad had said: *You must match your best friend, then you become life mates.* He didn't match Alaura at all.

She obviously thought this, too. It had to be the reason she considered them merely friends. It didn't matter to him that they came from different worlds, excelled in different crafts and were different races. If only she could put aside these differences. She knew he loved Isla as any das loved a child. Her race didn't matter.

Upon rising, he spoke only the usual courtesies accompanied with morning activities. Alaura showed no desire to carry on a conversation, and that contented him. After their argument last night, he had nothing to say.

He released a tired sigh, realising that only a few short weeks ago he had felt satisfied with life. If Keiron hadn't shown up, the perfect life would still be his. He shook his head. There was no logical reason why the thief returned for Isla. What did a man like him want with a twelve-year-old girl on The Trail?

He thought back to when his daughter had entered his life. Prophecy rumours ran wild, and Catriona had insisted they involved Isla. But the prophecy held no more truth than legend or myth! He pushed the idea from his thoughts and tried to focus on the path ahead.

They had travelled through dense forest for over an hour at Clover's top speed. For the next thirty minutes, Alaura cooled her out, allowing the mare to amble at a slow speed to recoup her breath.

The vegetation's moisture filled his senses, and he admired the vibrant greens of the lush foliage surrounding them. The long slender trunks of the oak, maple and birch trees reached into the sky, their leaves searching for light. They created a thick canopy over the forest floor where ferns, leafy flowers, moss and fiddleheads grew. If he was passing through for another reason, he might stop and admire the beauty. Instead, a gnawing feeling in his stomach pressed him to pose the question he wanted to ask for a long time.

He cleared his throat. "Alaura, I've been thinking." Her muscles tightened as if she anticipated a dreaded question. He leant his chin against her shoulder and asked, "Why do you think Keiron took Isla?" Her muscles relaxed.

"I'm not exactly sure. I have a few ideas, but..."

"But what?"

"I'm probably wrong."

"Tell me. We can be wrong together if we're thinking the same."

"I think...," she glanced back at him, "but I'm not sure; it has to do with the prophecy."

His fears proved correct. If the prophecy held a shred of verity, one detail didn't fit: the foretelling called for a pair of hauflin siblings.

In his mind, he recited the mysterious message: *It is said, Hauflin kin and company shall defeat the menace to Aruam and her subjects. With blade and magic, they'll cool the winds and fire the blood, and four shall live as one.*

Isla had no kin. Or did she? "Alaura, you attended Isla's birth. Did Maura deliver a second child that night?" He waited for an answer, but she didn't appear to want to give one. "I have a right to know."

She took the reins in her right hand and slipped the other into his, pressing their palms together. He felt the warmth of her touch but sensed more. He thought he *heard* her voice. She looked over her shoulder and stared into his eyes as she squeezed their palms together.

Yes.

The word hadn't come from her mouth. Instead she delivered it through her hand like the bog berry. Studying her, he thought she said more and listened intently.

But we must not speak of it.

"Why?" he said in cant. Her ability to communicate through her hand surprised him, but the secret she kept from him all these years made him angry. She should have told him, then he could have safeguarded Isla.

Her voice broadcasted louder, as if she learnt how to channel it better. *It's for Isla's protection. Only a handful of people know.*

"But I'm her das." He felt certain his words came from his mouth, but he sensed they also went through his hand. She gave him an inquisitive expression. *Does she have a brother or a sister?* He didn't speak it this time but thought of his words travelling through his hand and into her blood.

A brother, she *said* slowly, studying him in silence.

What? You started this.

A smile teased the corner of her mouth, and her eyes sparkled. *He's amazing. Absolutely incredible! I'd never have guessed he could work the Transfer Spell like this without proper training. What else he can do? If only he'd stop staring at me with those playful eyes, I'd be able to think clearer. Even with his face cut and bruised he's durn distracting.*

Thanks. You're incredibly distracting yourself.

Her eyes widened, her jaw dropped, and panic raced through her and into his hand.

What's wrong?

You can... No!... Stop! She pulled her hand free. "We shouldn't do this."

"Why?" He wrapped his arms around her waist and pulled himself closer in the saddle. "Shouldn't best friends share their thoughts?" She slapped him, more in play than as a reprimand. He pressed his cheek against her back and breathed in a lung full of her enchanting scent. She wriggled as if she replayed what she had thought and transferred to him. She considered him amazing, incredible and darn distracting. Interesting, she'd think this of a best friend. He grinned. She grew warm and halted the pony.

"We should give Clover a break. We can still walk, but she's carried us a good distance. Dismount, please."

He slid from the saddle and stood near to catch her though he knew she could manage on her own.

She shoved him away. "You can lead."

"Sure... If I'm that incredibly distracting." He gave a mischievous smile and walked past her. She grumbled and when he glanced back, her face flushed red. It felt good to be the one confident in their relationship...if only for a moment. He picked up the trail, and she and Clover followed. The breeze blew their scent into his nose, and he estimated their distance behind him. The horse stank, but Alaura ...well... She smelt like Alaura.

He marched through the underbrush, easily following the trail cut by the three horses. The strides measured shorter than when they travelled in the open. Keiron probably thought he had all the time in the world, since he believed him to be dead.

A few minutes later, he stopped and surveyed the area in front of him. Several bushes, ferns and wildflowers lay crushed from the weight of a creature or creatures. Whoever had passed through had turned the otherwise peacefully setting into a jumbled mess. Scanning the ground in front of him, his eye caught sight of an unusual stick. When he pulled it from the leafy bush, he stared at an arrow.

"There's blood on it." Alaura hunted for more clues.

"But whose?" He studied the foot and a half long projectile. It came from a short bow, similar to the type issued at the castle but crude and cheap. Blood covered the steel tip.

"Bronwyn." She motioned him to a flattened area near the bushes. "A person, possibly the one struck with the arrow, lay here." She pointed at dark marks on the branches and leaves. "They lost a lot of blood." Their eyes met. "A larger being, an adult dwarf, probably, or a medium-size human created this depression, not Isla."

"Tam or a stranger."

"The healing herbs surrounding the impression are lopped off; several are torn from the ground. I think Isla used these herbs to heal someone."

"Maybe Tam? I can't see her helping Keiron or the gnome."

"Unless forced to." She put her hand on his shoulder. "But without her telling them of her knowledge with herbal medicine, they wouldn't know."

"I hope it's not Tam." He scanned the area. "He's the only one she trusts." He followed the path, searching for the source of the scuffle. He stopped when he saw two more sets of hoof prints. These horses came from the opposite direction, towards Keiron and his group. He walked farther. The horses went off into the trees, but Keiron and the others continued along, going where the others had come.

"Bronwyn!" Alaura's voice sounded urgent but not frightened. She stood about thirty feet off the path.

He ran back to her and looked to where she pointed on the ground. The remains of a being mixed with twigs and torn-up moss. The bones had been stripped of flesh. He grabbed a stick and moved the clothing around. The blood-soaked, light brown shirt did not appear to be the same Tam had worn. Or Keiron for that matter.

"Oh my." She leant away. "The smell is vile."

He dragged a black chunk of leather from the bush and held it up at the end of the stick. "What size boot do you think this is? Too small for a dwarf; perfect for a hauflin?"

She grimaced as she studied it. "I agree." She lifted the edge of her cloak over her mouth.

He drew her under his arm, hiding her face in his neck. He poked at another piece of clothing, the remains of a belt, perhaps. The stick flicked the object into her leg.

"Ahh!" She jerked herself from his embrace, half shoving him as she sped away. "I can't stay. The smell is making me ill."

What would be the luck these remains belonged to Keiron? He followed her back to Clover.

She grasped the pony by the hackamore bridle and yanked it along. "There's nothing here but the smell of death. Worse than death. It's evil death. Vulgar! It makes my head swoon."

"Did magic kill that person in the bush?"

She stumbled away from the area. "Not sure. Let's just go." She accepted his arm to guide her away from the scene. After a few minutes, she eased her hand from his grip. "I'll be fine. The fresh air is clearing my head. Thank you."

"Does evil magic always affect you like this? You became ill like the night in my quarters when you tended to Isla."

For a moment, she was lost in thought. "I think you're right." She paused, and her fingers climbed the air in front of her as if walking up invisible steps. "Strange. Why is the foul castle air found here?"

He shrugged. "It smells similar, but not exactly. The smell doesn't affect me like it does you. In Maskil, we have grown accustomed to the stench of heat."

She didn't appear convinced but accepted the answer.

He turned and led the way down the trail. He glanced back at her. "You're sure you're fine?"

"It's as if I didn't feel ill to begin with."

He returned his attention to the path. Alaura was different in many ways. These ways had rubbed off on Isla, making his daughter more like her as time passed. Not only did Isla look for the good in others, but she knew plants and healing ways unknown to him. Not that he minded. Her teachings had made Isla wise, more capable than many children her age. Isla needed it now. Did other mysterious connections exist between the females? Both had become ill from the strange odour. Did it have to do with their hauflin blood?

Clover snorted aggressively, and he glanced at the pony. It pulled on the bridle and threw its head sideways, but Alaura kept it moving. When he passed an aged oak, a great force drove him to the ground.

The unidentified weight knocked the wind from his lungs, making it impossible to yell a warning. Blackness, flashes of red light and shadows blurred his vision as he rolled across the forest floor with an animal on top of him. His sword twisted beneath him and the hilt dug into his side. The rush of wind and his head hitting against the earth blocked his ears, but when he finally came to a stop, he heard Alaura shouting.

Sharp claws ripped at his sides, and he struggled to punch the creature that tackled him. When his eyes came into focus and he viewed the beast, he recoiled in horror. *The orc's curse!* What the heck was it? The man-like creature straddled him and slumped forward as if struck from behind. Seeing his chance, he slugged its face several times with his fist, then kneed it in the groin. It lost its strength, and he grabbed for his dagger to finish it off.

But instead of weakening, the creature pounced on his neck, and with thick scaly fingers attempted to squeeze the life from him. A splat of thick yellow liquid landed on his cheek. It dripped from the creature's mouth and nasal cavity. Another drop landed near his lip and oozed into his mouth. It tasted warm and salty. He spit it out and when another drop landed directly on his tongue, he gagged. More determined than ever, he wriggled and threw one punch after another into the side of the creature's head, but nothing inflicted damage. He lifted his butt off the ground and tried to buck it off, but it only added weight onto his neck.

The creature screeched in pain and released its hold. Its yellow eyes flashed at him, and it snarled, parted its lips and revealed a large pincer emerging from each side of its jaw. As it prepared to lunge forward, a brilliant flash erupted from behind, and it shrieked in agony. It swayed from side-to-side before it slumped headfirst, its full weight falling upon him and its large pincers digging into the ground, one on either side of his neck. The thick yellow fluid oozed onto his skin.

He didn't dare move. He believed the creature to be dead, but the sharp pincers would slice his neck if he tried to slither away. A foreign odour filled his air passages. The smell stung the inside of his nose and stole his breath. He'd fall unconscious if he didn't escape soon. In a cautious voice, he called out.

Kneeling beside him, Alaura grasped a pincer in each hand, then gave a firm tug. They came out of the ground, and she removed them to a safe distance before shoving the creature away. She saw blood on the outside of his shirt and lifted it to see the wounds. "I'll get the healing kit."

He lay back in the soft moss to catch his breath. Scrutinizing the ugly creature beside him, it resembled nothing he'd seen before. He spit the salty taste from his mouth and dragged his shirt sleeve over his lips. "Do you know what it is?"

"A troglodyte." She took a damp rag and wiped the blood from his side.

"No wonder they're stuff of nightmares. They're uglier than the stories tell." He whimpered from the sting of the cleansing solution entering the wounds.

"I'm sure he's quite a handsome fellow to his mate." She pulled strips of dressing from the sack and laid them against his skin.

"His face is one only a mum could love." He looked up to find her watching him. "And a mate, I suppose." He relaxed as she finished bandaging his side.

He didn't like to admit it, but he felt fortunate to have her with him. What he didn't know, she did, and vice versa. When he needed help, she provided it, and when she required assistance, he eagerly gave. He thought back to the many times she had helped him over the years. Although he had seldom asked for assistance, she often completed a task for him, then acted as if she had done nothing. From mending his jacket when he had torn it on a hiking trip with Isla to surprising him with new curtains for his quarters, she had made his life easier without need or want of recognition or compensation. He smiled more since he had met her. His life had become richer with her in it. "We make a good pair, don't we?"

She hesitated to answer.

"I mean, we make a good travelling pair."

"We do. Our individual skills complement each other." She took a second damp cloth and wiped the yellow ooze from his face and neck, then she stood and helped him to his feet. Quietly, she gathered her things and walked towards Clover.

"Alaura." She turned to look at him. A strand of hair fell across her face, and she pushed it aside. "I've assigned ranks to my friends, like you have."

She eyed him with curiosity. "And?"

"I've figured out who is *my* captain of the guard." He gazed at her as she waited for his answer. "You are." Her smile pleased him. "Best friends?" He held up his hand as if in a swearing-in motion.

She put her hand over her mouth but didn't suppress the laugh. He glanced at his palm, saw the red bog berry stain and grinned. "We need only the pebbles to complete my thoughts."

She threw her arms around his neck and gave a great hug. He drew her nearer, wishing to keep her here, but in an instant, she pulled away. She remained smiling as she lifted her hand to his. When their fingers intertwined, he heard, *Best friends.*

36

The Woman Wielding the Weapon

LATE IN the day, after setting up camp and consuming their ration, Bronwyn ran through his regular drills with the sword. It felt good to relieve the stress with a workout. Exerting his body made it easier to think. He glanced at Alaura, who gathered herbs near the edge of the clearing. He had seen her wield a sword; she could stand to learn more about the weapon.

"Alaura, come here for a minute."

"What is it?"

"You're more than generous with your knowledge and skills. I want to share mine with you." He held the weapon in front of him. "I've seen you hold a sword. It looks awkward. You're right-handed, so you should grip it like this." Being left-handed made the position uncomfortable for him.

"I'm not a sword fighter, Bronwyn."

"You may encounter a situation where your life depends on it. You're the one who told me to never turn down knowledge."

She considered her own advice, then stepped forward to grasp his sword. "It does feel better this way." She held it straight in front of her.

He moved off to the side. "To make a firm stance, move this leg back like this...and put the other like this." With her feet in position, he slowly moved his hands in an exercise motion designed for her to handle the sword efficiently.

After several tries, she lowered the blade. "It's heavy. Your sword is not appropriate to my build."

He picked up a fair-sized stick. "What you need is a slim sword, one weighing less than a pound. It's like a long dagger, but you wield it in the same manner as you would a sword. The next chance we get, I'll show you what I mean. Until then," he exchanged the stick for the sword, "you can practise the movements with this."

"I've seen what you speak of." She made her stance and held the stick properly, then went through the motions he had shown her.

Her patterns looked good but needed improvement. "Here." He stepped behind her, put his hands over hers, and guided her swing. He'd never taught a swordsman using this method, but then his typical recruit didn't look like her. "Lift like this. Bend this knee." He tapped her on the back of her leg with his knee. "That's it. Bring it back like this, elevate and then flex your wrists. Bring it forward and follow through with your swing. Don't watch the sword. Look at the target, and the sword will follow." He went through three complete exercises with her before he stepped away.

She repeated the motion.

"Now you have the pattern, speed it up. Put more strength into it!"

She followed his instructions. Each time she worked the pattern, she swung harder. She impressed him with the way she manipulated the sword...stick. Without warning, the stick struck him in the forehead, and he dropped to the ground.

"Bronwyn!" She ran to his side. "I'm sorry. It slipped. Are you okay?" Concern filled her voice.

He lay still with his eyes closed while she grasped his face. He wanted to rub the sting on his forehead but didn't. When she shook him, his grin spread across his face.

The shaking stopped, and she playfully slapped his chest. "Oh, you rascal!"

He opened his eyes.

"You had me worried. I thought I had hurt you."

"You did! That was no biscuit you threw at me!" The concern returned as she rubbed the place of impact where a lump already grew. "I really feel special now." He winked. "First a water flask. Now a stick."

She giggled. "I'm sorry." She leant forward and kissed the lump. "Let me help you up."

He stood and brushed the twigs and dirt from his clothes. The kiss on the forehead surprised him. The fewer expectations he placed on their relationship, the more affection she gave him. If he ignored her completely, would she shower him with love? She picked up the stick to inspect it. "Did I damage it?"

A smile lit up her face as she sat near the fire. "Fortunately, no. It's a solid piece of oak. It's stronger than many things, including your head."

Sitting next to her, he watched her use a knife to remove the bark. When she had it stripped, she notched an area near one end. "Making a place for your hand to grip?"

She nodded.

She struggled with the strength of the wood, and he held out his hand. "Let me help."

She handed him the knife and stick. "I want only a shallow indent to not compromise the strength of the...sword."

He slid the knife through the wood. His strong hands made quick work of it, and he created an indent around the entire stick. "You can play with it to make it more comfortable." He handed it back to her.

"Thanks. Maybe I'll work a piece of leather onto it, so I won't get splinters." She tested the grip. "I didn't know wood was a mighty weapon, but this little stick proved me wrong." She eyed him impishly. "It can drop a powerful dwarf with one whack."

He chuckled. "Powerful, eh?" He reached over, gripped the end of the stick and drew her forward. "I think all the might came from the woman wielding the weapon." A genuine smile graced her features, revealing her most beautiful face.

Later, after he had crawled into his bedroll, he rested on his back and gazed up at the stars. They shone as brightly as a thousand Alaura eyes staring down upon him. Somewhere under the twinkling lights, his daughter also admired them. Tomorrow, or the day after, they might overrun Keiron and rescue her.

Alaura turned beneath her blanket and watched him. The dim light of the crackling fire danced in her eyes. Did she think about Isla, too, or Maskil or home? She seldom mentioned Petra, and when she did, she spoke in a detached manner, as if she didn't want to think of her life there. But he had seen her joy when she lived in Petra. When they shared their memories in their life force, he saw her as a happy little girl. What had changed?

"Are you thinking of Isla?" Her soft voice startled him.

He nodded and turned on his side to face her. "You?"

"I think of what she's experienced since her kidnapping. I wonder about where they are taking her." She paused and reached for his hand. "And I worry we won't rescue her. I'm frightened for her."

He swallowed hard, the apprehension in her voice unsteadying his nerves. In all sense of the word, she had replaced Maura as Isla's meeme. "I worry about these things, but I'm determined to find her. I can't think otherwise."

"I am determined, too."

"We'll find her."

"We will. We will." She squeezed his hand and closed her eyes. "We have to."

He watched her fall asleep. He liked to believe she rested peacefully but knew otherwise. Several times through the night he woke to find her fingers gripping his hand she hadn't released. Though he couldn't see her face in the dark, he sensed expressions of anguish and uneasiness. He did his best to comfort her but deep down, he also needed comforting. During the night, he slid nearer and wrapped his arm around her shoulder. She turned and pressed her back against him. He pulled her closer and found solace as their magical hands embraced.

Sunlight cascaded through the trees and spilt upon the forest floor. Bronwyn sat in lush grass near the water's edge and watched the rising mist of several waterfalls. Splashes of colour spattered from every crack and crevice lining the cliffs. He'd visited this place many times and gazed upon the thin, slippery walk ways. He had once climbed those ledges and had hoped to slip to the depths below. They teased him, waited to see if he would try again.

He rubbed the dampness from his eyes. Maybe he would but for now, he let the mistake eat at him like a worm inside an apple. No one could see his wounds created by the parasite. He sniffed back the moisture in his nose and wished again for help to erase the memory of a dreadful night long ago.

He shook when Alaura sat beside him. *What is she doing here?*

"You asked for help," she said. "What's wrong?"

At a loss for words, he pulled his knees to his chin and looked out upon the water. *I can't tell her.*

"Tell me what?" She moved closer and rested her hand on his arm.

"You won't understand."

"Maybe I will."

He shook his head. *I was young. Stupid. She was a bitch. Alaura won't understand.* He rubbed the water from his eyes. "I don't want to talk about it."

"Bronwyn, if two people can't communicate, their relationship breaks down."

"But I can't. It hurts too much." He dropped his head into his knees. *I let her make a fool out of me. I should suffer for it.*

"Why do you blame yourself?"

He looked at her, not realising he spoke out loud. "I was stupid."

"Did you ever think that *she* took advantage of your bashfulness?"

"You weren't there."

"Then take me to that moment in time." Alaura held up her hand.

"What do you mean? I don't know magic."

"Together, you do." She placed her hand over his palm. "All you have to do is think about it, and I'll see what she did to you."

He tried to pull his hand away, but she held him firmly. *I can't do this. It's too embarrassing.* "Please, let me go!"

"It'll be okay. Trust me." She smiled. "You do trust me?"

He stopped fighting. "I do."

"Then let's do this together. I promise I'll stay by your side."

He nodded hesitantly. Taking a deep breath, he closed his eyes and travelled back to his youth. Flashes of a day many years ago jabbed at him like a blunt dagger. The initial happiness stood stark against how the night ended. He attended the final dance of his senior year in study hall with the girl of his dreams, Breckin Dole. Their first date would be their last. After she filled him with ale, she led him to the garden.

He sobbed as the aroma of blooming lilacs filled his senses. *There, next to the purple-flowering bush, she pretended to care about me. She led me on with kisses and her hands. I'd never kissed a girl before that night. I didn't know what to do. She stripped away my clothes and made me a naked fool in front of the entire class. They hid in the shadows watching everything. She laughed when she told them she was the best actor in Maskil for turning a boy into a man and then into a fool.*

He collapsed into her arms. *I thought I was brave, but I was a fool.*

"No, you weren't." Alaura caressed his hair and coddled him as he wept.

I felt so ashamed I ran and hid. He sniffed back the tears.

"You were an innocent boy, and she took advantage of you." She held him tighter. "Trust me, Bronwyn. I'd never hurt you like that."

He knew this. "You're my best friend."

"And you're safe with me. Don't ever think otherwise." She cleared her throat. "Women have their own ways of dealing with other women who hurt their men. I'll take care of Breckin Dole."

He pushed himself up to face her. The tears on her cheeks surprised him. *She's crying for my heartache.*

"Your pain is my pain."

"What will you do?"

She frowned. "You don't want to know. Let's say, she'll regret the day she caused this misery."

He sat up straighter. "You won't hurt her. I mean, I don't want you to seriously injure her."

"Would it bother you? After all, she hurt you deeply."

"But she didn't hurt me like a dagger or a sword or a fire ball would." His gaze lowered. *She embarrassed me, but I'm alive and well.*

"So, I'll embarrass her so she'll run from the theatre screaming."

He looked at her sideways. "What will you do?"

"Leave her to me. Maybe I'll speckle her face with warts, or make her teeth fall out or maybe turn her hair green. She's an actor. Anything spoiling her appearance sends her into fits." She smiled. "Look at you; worried about well-being of the woman who hurt you." She grabbed the front of his shirt and pulled him near. "You're an honourable man, Bronwyn Darrow. It's only one of the reasons my blood burns for you hotter than any other man who walks Ath-o'Lea."

He raised his eyebrows. *Really?* When she reached up to wipe the water from his cheek, he leant nearer. *Was it hot enough for a kiss?*

She bent forward and kissed his mouth.

He caught his breath and kissed her back. Guiding her to the soft grass, he pulled her near. Her warm hand slipped beneath his shirt and settled in the small of his back, igniting sparks in the lower part of his belly. He fumbled with the buttons on her shirt but found it near impossible to unfasten them with any speed using one hand, his wrong one at that. His awkwardness made him curse, and doubts overwhelmed him. He paused and gazed into her eyes. A dwarf like him didn't deserve an enchantress like her.

"What is it?" she whispered.

"I've never..." He gulped. Would he ever gain the confidence to speak his mind to her?

"Neither have I." She unfastened the remaining buttons of her shirt and placed his hand between her breasts. "We can discover the magic together."

As their kisses aimed to satisfy their hunger, their hands explored warm unfamiliar places. Released from his burden, he savoured the offerings of his best friend. His body quivered as if he watched instead of participated in the joining. When he collapsed into her arms, her gentle sigh of satisfaction deepened his desire for her.

The day faded into oblivion and became morning.

37

A Game of Dare

IS IT morning already? It feels like I went to sleep only minutes ago.

It is. I see the dawn's light.

Can I lie here a few minutes more? Bronwyn yawned.

Okay. Only a few more.

He groaned and stretched his shoulder forward. *My shoulder is stiff. I think it's from the tumble I took with the troglodyte. Can you put ointment on it later?*

I will.

Thanks. What a dream I had. It...well. I shouldn't say anything. She'll get angry. Oh, oh. She might ask questions. It had to be the most vivid dream I've ever had. Wow.

Dream? Goodness, I had a fantastic dream, too! But I can't tell him we... Why am I hearing your thoughts?

Alaura sat up quickly, and he forced his eyes open. "What are you doing?"

"Bronwyn!" She pulled her hand free of his. "We were bridged all night. We..." She stared in shock at him.

"We what?" He flexed his hand. It felt stiff. He pushed himself to a seated position and rubbed his hair. Seeing her frozen in place with a panicked expression made him concerned. "What's wrong?"

She shook her head and moved away. The blood drained from her face, leaving her pale.

"Are you okay? Are you going to be sick? Alaura, say something."

"I'll...be back in a minute." She rushed into the bushes.

"That was something," he said, puzzled. "Not what I expected." He pulled on his boots, then flexed his hand again. He must have slept on it. No. He had slept on his left side and draped this arm over Alaura. He stared at the red dot on his palm. *Damn. If we dreamt the vision together, then... Alaura and I—oh, oh... Then she knows!*

He rose on shaky legs. Although he had planned to never tell her about Breckin, if they had shared the same dream, she knew everything, had witnessed the whole ordeal take place. His stomach churned. Never again could he look her in the eye. His body overheated, and his face flushed. Unlike the time many years ago, he couldn't run and hide.

He froze and cocked his head as he stared at their bedrolls. If she remembered everything in the dream, then she knew how he felt. She understood. They had talked it out. She didn't think him foolish. Humph! His stomach settled. Still, she'd be upset about how the dream ended. He placed his hand on his belly, recalling the quiver he had felt. If best friends shared moments like this, then he should have called her his best friend sooner.

಄ ❖ ಛ

Since Bronwyn had awakened wrapped in Alaura's arms with memories of the vivid dream they shared, neither had said much. *The day passed better this way,* he thought. If they didn't talk, they didn't argue.

By noon, they found themselves on a smooth narrow road, one obviously maintained by a governing force. Tall evergreens reaching to the sky lined the thoroughfare. Little birds whipped in and out of branches, playing a game of dare in front of Clover. The pony didn't mind and only snorted if they passed too close.

Alaura fondly patted the mare on the shoulder. "They're teasing you, girl."

With his hands resting on his lap, Bronwyn observed the scenery and the little creatures popping out of the heavy shadows. Since breaking camp, they had ridden steadily until they came upon the well-kept road about twenty minutes beforehand. He couldn't imagine how far they had travelled, but he hoped they had chosen the right course. Occasionally roads made tracking difficult. Would Keiron go left or right? Fortunately, Keiron and his bandits acted carelessly, and as soon as they cleared the trees, they had steered their horses in this direction.

According to the map, this road took them into the northern part of the Dukedom of Dunakan. It led into the mountainous region and eventually to the desert.

A bird shot out from the trees, and he watched as another followed. The feathered friends, no larger than crab apples, darted in and out of the branches. He waited for them to fly in front of Clover again, but they enjoyed their little dance of beating wings. Chests together, an inch apart, they flapped, rising and falling as if on the breeze. He smiled at their antics. Did they play a game of tag or dance? Up and down they went, fluttering their wings, oblivious to the pair on the pony. When they descended to the ground, he realised the purpose behind the activity. Which of the mating birds was the male?

They didn't come together as he expected. One of them flitted along the roadside with the other in hot pursuit. When he saw the lead bird flip and flutter in front of the other, then dart aside again before making contact, he identified the male: the one giving chase. The courtship continued for another minute before, together, they collapsed to the ground and joined. Amazed by the simplicity of the mating, he sighed. Nature made it look easy.

Alaura had also witnessed the breeding, and when their eyes met, they caught their breath and looked away. He recalled images and feelings from the dream they had shared through the Transfer Spell. They happened as vividly as anything he'd experienced while awake. If he hadn't known better, he'd have sworn they *had* joined. Had the mating birds made Alaura think of it, too?

Tempting a glance, he saw she wore a bashful smile, probably as big as his. His arm encircled her waist, and he placed his large palm over her flat abdomen. It swayed with the motion of the pony. His thumb touched a spot below her right rib cage where a brown, grape-size birthmark had appeared in the dream. Did it truly exist, or had his imagination conjured it? He rubbed the spot to see if he could feel a bump.

She slapped his hand and glared at him. The expression on her face made him laugh, and he laid his forehead against her back. She shook then giggled. She wasn't angry. Nature held more beauty than could be obtained with any riches and reminded its creatures of the simplicity of living if they took the time to see it. He would remember this for the future.

"I guess it's what they mean when they say, *As free as the birds.*" He laughed so hard, tears came to his eyes.

Alaura laughed, too. She put her hand over his, still on her abdomen, and held it there. Maybe she'd promote him from captain of the guard after all.

A few minutes later, she tapped his knee.

"What is it?" he asked.

She directed his attention to a spot farther up the road. "I see a structure. It's relatively high."

He stretched around her to see where she pointed. A stone building poked its roof between the tree tops. It was about three storeys tall. "I think I saw it on the map." From his pouch, he withdrew the worn piece of leather and traced his finger along the road. "There it is. I think it's a keep." He held the map to the side to show her, then returned it to his pouch.

"Shall we go in?"

"Can I steer?"

She frowned at him. "We've already had this discussion."

"But I'm a man. It's awkward for me to ride in on the back." This logic didn't change her mind, so he used a different strategy. "What if they think I'm injured? A criminal might attack if they see a woman with a vulnerable guard from Aruam Castle."

She halted Clover to think this excuse over. Glancing back at him, she scrutinised his face. "Are you saying this simply to get in front?"

"I'm being logical," he lied.

She turned and stared in the direction of the keep.

He waited. *Would she?* She answered his request by lifting her leg over the pommel, balancing in one stirrup and sliding her leg behind him. He helped her into the saddle, holding the reins steady. He fitted his boots into the stirrups and pulled himself forward. This felt more like it!

"Are you ready?" He glanced back as she adjusted her cloak. Clover moved beneath him, and he tried to steady her with the reins. He squeezed his legs, but the mare continued to prance.

Alaura reached in front and took the reins, slapping his leg as she did. "Stop squeezing. She's a delicate animal who responds to a soft touch. You can't yank on the reins or kick her." She worked the leathers in a fluttering motion to calm the pony. "There you are, girl. He'll be gentle."

He looked down at her hands as they performed in front of him. There was more to handling this mare than he thought. It'd be better for him to reach the keep on the back of it than to be thrown from it upon arrival."

"See how I manoeuvrer the reins?" She fluttered them again to calm Clover.

"I do."

"When you want her to move forward, flutter your reins ever so slightly and ask her to walk by squeezing your legs— Whoa! That's too hard!" Clover lurched forward, but Alaura calmed her again. She held the reins in one hand and touched his lap.

Again, he looked down. Her fingers rested awfully close to his groin. Her warmth made his skin tingle as she pressed her hand against his trousers.

"Feel the gentleness of my touch? It's all the encouragement she needs to move forward."

It's all the encouragement I need!

"Do you understand? Your legs are strong, and you don't realise how hard you are."

He chuckled. *I know. Oh, boy, do I know!*

"If you can't control Clover, I'm going to have to get back in front."

He grimaced. After reaching the command position, he wasn't about to relinquish it. "I understand. Gentle. I get it." He felt her stare and glanced back. "What?"

"Get moving." She wrapped her arms around his waist as if she expected him to lose control of Clover and gallop down the road.

⊗ ❖ ⊗

The Upper Branch Keep appeared tidy but smelt as if improperly ventilated. The musty stench made Bronwyn turn up his nose. He walked down the aisle and stopped at the display of blades. He glanced over his shoulder and saw Alaura browsing the clothing rack.

Turning his attention back to the weapons, he picked up a sword a little shorter and much lighter than his own; the perfect size for her. He admired the shiny grey stone in the hilt and the simple design of loops. He gripped the well-crafted weapon in his left hand, turned it in a circle, then balanced its mass across his index finger. It weighed about a pound.

Alaura was right-handed, so he shifted the weapon to his other hand. At first, it felt good, but then a strange feeling erupted. As if same poles of two magnets came together, his hand wanted to reject the weapon. He'd never felt such a sensation.

"Put it down."

He whirled to find Alaura glaring at him.

"Put it down. Now!"

He held up the light sword. "This? It's well-crafted. I thought you..."

She reached over and pushed his hand to the display case. "Let it go."

He released his hold. "What's this about?"

"It possesses evil magic." She shuddered as if shaking rain from her shoulders.

"You can sense that from over there?" He glanced at the keeper, busy with another customer.

~ 339 ~

She shook her head and pulled his hand to his face. "You held it with this hand," she whispered. "It felt as if you sent the bad magic directly to my blood."

"Is the spell supposed to do that?"

"I didn't read anything about it in my book, but when you held the weapon in this hand, I felt the evil. I tried to push it away, reject it, but you held it tightly."

"I felt the strong sensation rejecting it from my hand."

"If you ever feel it again, get rid of the item. I don't know what will happen if you use it."

"Will it hurt you?"

She shrugged. "I'll ask Beathas when we return. Until then, remember the feeling, and do as I ask."

He nodded. The Transfer Spell had become more than either of them had anticipated. He picked up another narrow sword but before shifting it to his right hand, he looked at her. "Good?"

She waved her fingers over the weapon and nodded.

He tested the sword. Though sound, it lacked the quality of the rejected weapon. "What do you think?"

She took it and performed a few movements. "It'll do." She remained still as he strapped the scabbard around her waist.

He stood back and admired her. "You cut a fine silhouette." He winked at her.

"Now it's your turn." She pointed in the direction of the clothing rack. "I've found a few items here you may be interested in." She held up a vest, shirt and trousers. "Are they suitable?"

He shook his head. "My uniform is fine."

"You won't find many respecting it this far from the castle. In fact, it might do you more harm than good."

"My uniform is important to me. It doesn't matter how others view it."

"Yes, it does," she said. "Lawful men respect it. Others think, *There's an Aruam Castle guard far from home. Let's capture him! Let's kill him!*" When he attempted to walk away, she gave him *that* look. "Bronwyn, be reasonable. On The Trail there are all kinds. You're proud of your uniform, but do you want to attract unwanted attention? You're putting your life at risk as well as mine."

He shoved his hands into his pockets. She was right, but he hesitated to admit it. He sighed. "We'll take them."

"You can pick out other garments, but these appear to be the best on the rack for your size." She paused. "But you don't have to take them."

"It doesn't matter. They're only clothes."

She frowned as he walked away. Following him, she placed the clothes, the light sword and the food they had picked out on the pay counter.

Bronwyn leant on the surface next to her as she paid for the goods. Maybe he did need clean clothes, ones not torn by weapons and travel. The vest she had chosen resembled his uniform vest, but had diamonds embroidered on it like Isla's. He remembered the day she had received the vest from his sister. It had made her happy to have one like his. Now, he had one like hers.

"Excuse me, sir."

A small voice interrupted his thoughts, and he glanced down at a timid boy. The elf was around the same age as Isla. "Hello."

"Are you called Bronwyn?"

He raised his eyebrows. "Do I know you?"

The boy shook his head. "I'm to give this to you." He handed him a folded piece of paper: page seventeen from Isla's book. She had scribbled, *Bronwyn, keep – 36 miles – trail* on the top of the page. He passed it to Alaura. They had planned to question the keeper once they paid for their supplies but with this evidence, he didn't wait.

"Bairns. They're always playing around." The large, dark-skinned human behind the counter grumbled. "Foolishness." The keeper glared at the boy. "Mungo, get back to work."

"Wait." Bronwyn put his hand on the boy's shoulder. "Did a hauflin girl give you this?"

The boy squished up his nose. "She said she was a girl, but a boy is what I saw."

He nodded. "Did she come inside the keep?"

"How would he know?" The keeper put his arms in the air, revealing a lengthy scar above his left elbow. "So many people pass through. He's only a boy."

"Did she?" Bronwyn asked again.

The elf nodded.

"Did she come with a hauflin man?" Again, the boy nodded. "A dwarf? Gnome?"

"Both; all three."

"Was she hurt?"

"Her eye was black and green. The dwarf, he dozed on the step. She... The boy had to shake him to move, and when he walked, it was with her help."

Bronwyn grimaced. The only sense of security Isla had depended on Tam. If he died, her fears would escalate. He looked back and found the keeper scowling at the young boy. "Keiron Ruckle kidnapped the child. We've trailed him from Maskil. If you can provide further information, I'd appreciate it."

"What would the scoundrel want with a child?" The shop owner spoke low. "Let the boy get back to work before you bring him trouble you can't imagine."

Bronwyn nodded at the scared child. "Thank you." After the boy scrambled to the backroom, he turned to the keeper. "You know the man we seek. Did he say where they headed?"

The keeper shook his head. "They didn't stay long. They went towards Wirksworth."

"About what time did they arrive?"

The keeper gave this thought. "I opened at six, and they showed up about an hour or two later. Can't say for sure."

"This morning?"

He nodded.

He was only four or five hours behind them. "Thank you." He helped Alaura with the supplies and walked out. After packing the gear in the side bags, he mounted and reached down to give her a hand up.

A rugged man in a chair on the stoop spoke. "Appears the pony's 'bout to buckle under yer weight. I've a hawse out back I'm willin' to trade. It's more fittin' fer yew."

"No, thank you. I'm attached to the ol' nag." He patted Clover and glanced at a second man resting against the wall. Both strangers appeared to have been drudged from a dirty pit.

"Shame. It's a good lookin' hawse." The first man ogled Alaura. "She yer mate?" When Bronwyn nodded, he said, "Yew wanna sell 'er?"

He half grinned. "I'm attached to this ol' nag, too."

"She'd make yew a fair price." The stranger licked his bottom lip.

"I'm not interested." He asked Clover to move forward.

After travelling a distance from the keep, Alaura slapped him on the thigh. "I don't like being talked about in such a manner. You made me appear vulnerable, as if I'm a person to be conquered and possessed. And I'm *not* your mate! Don't mislead others into thinking I am."

"What did you want me to say?" He spoke his next words in a refined voice his elders would use. "*Excuse me, good sir, you're insulting my best friend with your vile mouth. Could you, please, reword your questions in an appropriate manner as to not offend her?*" When she slapped him again, he chuckled. "Be careful. I was offered a fair price for you. I bet he'd honour it if I rode back and told him I had changed my mind."

She pinched him in the butt, and he rose to escape her fingers. "Men such as them make my skin curl. They want only one thing. You should have spoken with respect to my being, and they may have sensed me to be a capable individual."

"I'm not out here to reform anyone." He smiled back at her. "But I will protect your virtues."

"I'm capable of doing that myself."

"So you are, Alaura of Niamh. So you are." He nudged Clover into a trot, hoping once away from the keep, she wouldn't ask to get in front. She didn't. Instead, she wrapped her arms around his waist and lost herself in thought.

An hour later, he halted Clover. "This is a good place for a break. I see a brook for water."

She dismounted. "You can change into the clothes we bought. I'll feel better travelling without a target on my back."

He wanted to keep his uniform but agreed with her logic. This far from Maskil, people didn't respect the castle's colours. Anyone who had a run in with a guard might try to take it out on him. He slid from the saddle and dug the new shirt, vest and trousers from the side bag.

"Hey."

He turned in time to catch a rectangular object wrapped in cloth.

"Take the opportunity to wash before you don clean clothes. You stink." She led Clover to the stream.

His jaw locked at the order laced with a minor insult. Had Beathas taught her to take command, or had she come by it naturally? He shrugged it off and carried his supplies to the brook, then walked a short distance downstream for privacy. At a small pool, he stripped and climbed into the cool water. The foamy bubbles from the soap smelt of lavender. He grimaced. He'd stink more when done than when he started! After lathering his hair, he slipped beneath the water's surface to rinse.

The cool water refreshed his senses and soothed the aches he had gathered since leaving Maskil. It felt good to be clean. His fingers ran over the scar left from the dagger wound. When he pressed on it, a sharp pain shot through his gut, and he grunted. The claw marks of the troglodyte cut above and below the wound, creating a patchwork of injuries. He'd be happy to get back to the castle and take a couple days off to let his body rest and heal completely.

The cool air brushed against his wet skin as he climbed onto the shore. A strange noise upstream made him cock his head to listen, but he didn't hear anything further, so continued to dry himself. He threw the soaked drying rag against a stone next to his tattered uniform. After donning his new clothes, he strapped on the scabbard, then hiked upstream.

Movement on the opposite side of the small clearing caught his attention, and he looked to see what Alaura was doing. He froze when he saw a man standing there, the same man who had rested against the wall of the keep.

The man whirled, revealing a twisted knot in his face. He drew his sword and prepared to fight.

Bronwyn scanned the area quickly, desperate to find Alaura. As he advanced on the stranger with his weapon, he saw her. She lay still on the ground with her shirt ripped open beneath the vile man he had talked to at the keep. Seeing her in the awkward position with the man's face buried in her chest made his blood boil. The surging rage felt unlike anything he'd previously experienced. He raised his sword and attacked, swinging with all his might at the human who stood between him and his best friend.

Although the man fell with the first strike, he swung several times more, slicing him in three pieces. When he scowled at the beast who had violated his Alaura, he released a fierce roar and pounced. He sliced and swung until the man looked like a jigsaw puzzle.

He dropped the bloody sword and knelt beside Alaura. They had beaten her about the face with a club, and blood oozed from several cuts. He felt helpless to erase the dirty deeds the men had inflicted on her. An ache grew in his chest and threatened to steal his breath. Where had the common goodness of all beings gone? Better to be killed outright than violated like this. Alaura stood for the essence of purity, and they had defiled her.

How could he help her heal? Water and soap. It would cleanse her of their filth. He ran to the stream and wet a rag. He found the lavender soap where he had dropped it and returned to her. With the decency and gentle hands of a mate, he bathed her chest to remove the attacker's sweat and spit.

When he finished, he closed her shirt, but several buttons were missing, and the sleeve was torn. Rummaging through her rucksack, he found his tan-coloured shirt, the same one she had worn on the day of the inquest. He wrapped her in it as if his shirt had the same power to protect her as he and his sword. It kept her warm, cradled her as a babe in his arms. Her trousers remained fastened which meant they hadn't gotten too far. He placed a reassuring hand over the buttons. While he lived, no man but he would unfasten them.

When he stood to gather his thoughts and to survey the area, his eyes absorbed the bloody scene surrounding him. Pieces of men lay scattered about as if they had been chopped up and tossed aside like discarded fish heads. Blood stained the greenery, and internal organs glistened in the afternoon sunlight. The smell of the fresh kill entered his air passages and awakened his senses further. As his mind processed what he had done, the speed of his pulse increased. Not only had he killed the two men, in his rage, he had butchered them. His thirst for revenge had taken control and created a monster. A spore of evil infected his blood. The honourable Sergeant Bronwyn Darrow of Maskil lived no more. Life on The Trail had replaced him with a man of necessity.

He stared at Alaura. What would she think if she woke and saw the slaughter? His heart raced. She couldn't see this ugly side of him. He gathered their things in haste, but when he scooped up his uniform, he froze. That which he had once worn as a symbol of honour had lost its importance, its smoothness and its comfort. Winding up, he threw the bundle of clothes as far into the trees as he could muster. He straightened the blue vest Alaura had bought and went to her.

He lifted her into his arms and walked towards Clover. His determined steps made the pony jittery. When he reached for the pommel, it moved away.

"Damn it, nag! Stay still!" The mare stepped away, flared its nostrils and pinned its ears to its poll. He lowered Alaura to the ground and marched towards the animal. He'd punch it silly if need be to take control of it. It lurched when he grabbed the hackamore bridle, but he held it firmly. His anger grew, and he yanked it to face him. Its wild eyes revealed its terror. It expected abuse from a man. He glanced at Alaura. She believed Clover to be a special creature that needed careful handling. If she woke and saw him commanding it like this, she'd be more shocked than by the mess of blood and guts.

"Here, girl." He eased his grip but did not release the bridle. He tried to stroke its muzzle, but it jerked away. "Clover, it's me. I won't hurt you." He managed a stroke along her nose. "That's it, girl. Calm down. We have to get Alaura to safety." He soothed the mare with his voice as much as with his hand. With the pony back under his command, he released it.

Carrying Alaura over his left shoulder, he grasped the pommel with his right hand, put his foot into the stirrup and lifted himself into the leather seat. He positioned her side-saddle in front of him, and her body fell limp against his chest. Cradling her with his right arm, he guided Clover with the other.

By the time the sun sank low in the sky, he had a campsite set up. Alaura rested on her side, wrapped in a blanket near a crackling fire. She hadn't yet stirred, causing him to worry. If she didn't wake by morning, he'd have to seek help. He had done everything he knew, including dusting her nostrils and tongue with what he jokingly called the wake-up herb. He and his dad had gathered the plant on many occasions, but he didn't know how to use it until Alaura taught him.

He fed the last piece of rutabaga to Clover, patted her side, then walked to the fire. The half-eaten ration he had made sat on a nearby rock. He picked it up, stirred the food and sighed. Although he had no appetite, he had to work at regaining his strength lost through his injuries, and he could only do that by eating. Exhaustion was a sneaky creature. One might run for days and not feel tired, but in a moment of weakness, it pounced, draining the energy and dropping its victim like a stone. *Be reasonable.* Those were Alaura's words. *Eat.* He spooned the ration into his mouth. It tasted cold and flavourless. Still, he cleaned the pot. Hunger, like exhaustion was a sneaky fiend.

With the camp secure, he settled behind Alaura. Grasping her hand, he tried to connect with her through the Transfer Spell. He closed his eyes and searched for a sound, a feeling...anything. *Alaura. Can you hear me?* Nothing. He listened for a long time, but no voice came to him. It felt as if he stood outside on a calm night when darkness had not yet completely consumed the land but nothing, not a creature nor a breath of wind, broke the silence. Still, he felt life, vibes of energy floating in the air and entering his air passages. It meant she lived but little else.

He spread both blankets over the two of them, wrapped his arm around her mid-section and pressed her back against his chest. He felt secure with his sword lying next to him and a dagger under his makeshift pillow. For a long time, he watched the fire dance into the night air, sending up small sparks into its heat spirals.

When sleep finally overtook him, wicked dreams haunted him. Like an erupting volcano, blood flowed freely. The rage he had felt when he had butchered the vile men who hurt Alaura resurfaced. He grabbed at the demon but it ran, laughing at him. The evil teased him, wheedling him to follow into the darkness. He stumbled onward and found strange, unfamiliar faces watching him. They belonged to The Trail, deep caves and swamps. He didn't want to obey but believed he had no choice. Without an anchor to cling to, he pursued helplessly.

38

A Sneak in the Night

BY MID-MORNING, Alaura's unconscious state filled Bronwyn with dread. Though she had turned during the night to face him, she hadn't awakened and now, with a slow, cool drizzle dampening the land, he wrestled with what to do. He couldn't return to the keep with her in this condition, and the nearest settlement lay a day's ride away, well past the location Isla had scribbled on the book page. If Alaura needed a healer's attention, then the longer he waited, the less likely she'd recover.

He folded the map and shoved it into the pouch. He cursed himself for his inability to know what to do, then he cursed for what he had done. If he hadn't bathed or changed his clothes, those barbarians wouldn't have gotten their hands on Alaura. She'd be well. He swore out loud. Never again would he leave her unattended whilst on The Trail! She belonged at Maskil, not in the wilds risking her life and well-being. He promised himself when he finally got her to the safety of home, it'd be where she'd stay.

He rested his head in his hands and rubbed his eyes. The sting behind his eyelids had become a common feeling since leaving home— not enough sleep and too much worry. The wicked dreams rekindled, and the anger grew. He should have been wiser, stronger, better prepared and this wouldn't have happened to her.

"Bronwyn."

He bolted upright. "Alaura?" He ran to her side and grasped her hand.

She sat up and looked around, confused, as if she didn't recall what had happened to bring her here. But he remembered; he'd never forget.

"Where are we?" Her voice sounded strong.

"About three hours from the keep."

"The keep?" She bowed her head as she searched her memory. "The keep. Those men!" Her eyes flashed at him. "They attacked me! They came out of the bushes." She rubbed her head. "They struck me with a stick or club!"

"You were knocked unconscious."

"They had hunger in their eyes. The kind..." She buried her face in her trembling hands. "They wanted to—"

"They didn't. I took care of them." He jerked her to his chest and held her. His hand caressed her side, ran down her thigh and back again. She'd feel his hand, not theirs. "They won't hurt another woman." His heart sank when she sobbed. He never wanted her to feel this way, like a piece of meat men sought for pleasure and nothing more. The rage idling on the sidelines flared again. If he had those men in his hands now, he'd tear them apart without a second thought.

Time passed, and while her weeping ebbed, his anger grew hot. He knew he had done the right thing, but he had done it the wrong way. He had crossed the line between honourable men who killed to protect and those who killed for revenge. Take a life to save a life; he had believed this from the moment he picked up his first sword. Now he questioned it.

Without warning, she slapped his chest. "I told you not to speak of me in that manner to those men! They saw me as vulnerable. They might never have followed us if you had spoken about me with respect."

He sank back. Did she speak the truth? If he hadn't reduced her to an old nag and had corrected them when they offered to buy her, would they have come after her? Would they have seen her as his equal if he had spoken about her properly? He swallowed hard. He had even joked about taking her back to them.

"Why did you do that?" She pushed damp hair from her face and stared at him through reddened eyes. "It's not what you believe, so why didn't you treat me as an equal in front of them?"

He didn't know many things, including the answer to her question. He was only a man, not a druid of knowledge. "I don't know," he said slowly, then walked to the edge of the campsite. Had they been in Maskil, he'd have walked on and gone where his feet took him, but he was far from his birth town. Never had he felt more lost.

He inspected the clothes he wore. They were those of a traveller, not an Aruam Castle sergeant. Had he thrown away his principles with his uniform? He shivered when Alaura's arms wrapped around his waist. She rested her head against his shoulder and held him tightly.

"I don't blame you." Her voice fell softly on his neck. "You'd never hurt me. There is no one I feel safer beside."

He released his breath. She may not blame him, but he did. Yesterday he had changed into a person he disliked and disrespected, a man who had no right to be with her. He pushed her hands from his waist and walked to the campfire. "Eat. I'll pack up the gear."

"Let's discuss this." She followed him to the fire.

"Talking's a waste of time." He knelt, grabbed the blankets and forced them into a bundle. "The sooner we get on the move, the sooner we catch that bastard and kill him!"

Within a half hour, he had everything packed and he sat in the saddle. When Alaura looked up at him, he pulled his foot from the stirrup and reached out a hand to help her up. When she hesitated, he said, "Whilst you stand there arguing with your pride, we're losing precious time."

She frowned at him and mounted. Before she settled, he nudged Clover forward. "You're being more than rude today."

"Say hello to the new me. A man who doesn't give a damn!" As he guided the mare onto the narrow road, he bit his lip and swallowed hard. The problem with this new man was he *did* give a damn. Her arms settled around his waist. He wished to enjoy the feelings they had once created, but he no longer deserved the pleasure. A pure spirit like Alaura wouldn't forgive him for what he'd done, and he didn't expect her to try. She had told him her blood burnt for him because of his status, but he no longer could claim to be an honourable man.

After travelling several miles, Bronwyn consulted the map. He determined they had covered about thirty-six miles from the keep. If Isla proved correct, along this area horse tracks would reveal Keiron's route. A few minutes later, Alaura tapped him on the shoulder and pointed. Hoof prints made by three horses led to a partially-hidden trail.

He guided Clover off the road and onto the path. If they hadn't searched for it, they might have missed it. He stopped for a moment and marked it on the map. It would serve as a reference point for their return trip. Adding the extra time for their stop, he guessed Keiron travelled about eight hours ahead of them. His plan for catching the bastard today wouldn't be done.

Extra time meant he had more of it to think about the events of yesterday. Though he didn't want to, the scene by the brook replayed in his mind. The pleasure emanating from the man's face as he defiled Alaura left a stinging reminder of her vulnerability. He had brought those monsters to her with his careless talk and actions. Flashes of his sword striking the men again and again made his left arm twitch. Clover grew uneasy. He patted the mare's shoulder, and his hand trembled.

Resting his tell-tale hand against his chest did nothing to ebb the regret and torment. Alaura's arms tightened around his waist, and he looked down at her hands. Her long, slender fingers crossed his stomach as if trying to hold goodness in...or keep evil out. He wished he could share his regrets with her but if he did, she might never look upon him with the same innocent ideals she once held.

The ache in his heart grew painful. It pushed into his throat, and his jaw became rigid. The pressure extended to his ears and sounds faded away. Beads of sweat formed on his hands, making his grip on the reins slippery. As images flared before his eyes of Alaura lying still in the forest and of the men he butchered, the pressure increased. If he didn't confide in her, his chest might explode. His hand fumbled to find hers, and he pressed the palms together.

After initiating the Transfer Spell, he instantly regretted it. He attempted to break free, but she held him firmly. His spit burnt in his throat as he struggled to find the right words. *I'm sorry.* Again, he tried to escape her grasp, but she tightened her grip. *Let me go!* "Please, let go!"

Bronwyn, you can tell me anything.

"No! I can't!" *I'm afraid you won't...* Something snapped in his gut, and he couldn't take a breath without a sharp cramp exploding in his ribs.

Goodness! Bronwyn, you must tell me! She pressed herself against his back. *You are inflicting this torture on yourself. I feel it!*

"I'm fine. Just let me go!"

"You're not fine. You're suffering."

It didn't matter how hard he tugged on his hand, she wouldn't let go. *I'm the reason those men attacked her? I don't deserve to be her best friend.*

It's not your fault. You don't control the actions of other men.

He glared at her for reading his thoughts. "Stay out of my head!"

"If you'd simply share this with me, we can work it out. I don't blame you."

"But I blame me. If I hadn't acted like an idiot, they wouldn't have followed."

"Or they still might have. You don't know."

"I wasn't there to protect you." *I shouldn't have left her alone.*

"You can't be with me every minute of the day."

"I know better though." *And what I did to those men makes it worse.*

"What did you do?"

He glanced back at her and gazed into her innocent eyes. *I can't tell her. It would change forever how she thought of me.* She appeared confused. *Don't think. Simply turn around,* he told himself. *She can hear everything.* He tried to clear his mind and focus on the trail ahead. If she wouldn't release his hand, he'd fill his mind with emptiness. *Think of the drizzle, the smell of the wet trees. Anything but that.* He drew a deep breath and cringed from the discomfort growing in his gut.

You can't keep it inside forever. Alaura hugged him tightly.

The horrible images of the slaughtered men returned, and she gasped. *Damn it! Stop looking!* "Alaura, let me go!" His attempts at blocking the visions only brought them into sharper focus. The raw flesh glistened in the sun, and blood and entrails splattered the forest floor. The terror in his gut forced him to throw his body from the saddle. She didn't release him until they crashed against the wet road.

He jumped to his feet and ran. From a safe distance, he watched her rise, brushing the mud from her clothes and feeling the tenderness of her elbow that bore most of the impact. When she looked up, he gulped. He only caused her more pain.

"I'm sorry, but you wouldn't let go... I didn't want..." He hung his head. It mattered not what he said. He saw from her expression, she no longer considered him a friend.

"You hurt me more by not sharing your feelings." She wiped her eyes with the back of her sleeve. "If you believe I hate you for what you've done to those men, you're wrong. I'm not as innocent as you think."

He looked up, lost for words. The fall had displaced her cloak, and revealed the dagger strapped to her calf and the one worn on the opposite side of the light sword. If he didn't know her, he might think her to be a thief wearing clothes of The Trail, but appearances were deceiving. She was Alaura of Niamh, a student of magic, the meeme of Isla and the seamstress who worked alongside his sisters. This woman was as innocent as Rhiannon. She wasn't a thief, a sneak in the night, fearless in the face of danger.

"You killed two despicable men who aimed to violate me in the worst way," she said. "If you hadn't killed them, I would have if given the chance. How they died is irrelevant!"

The confession stunned him. Her anger and fear made her say those words, just as his rage had made him kill without mercy.

"As for your boorish comments, you were being a jerk, but they didn't make those men attack me." She came nearer. "Men like them hunt women for pleasure."

"But I was—"

"A jerk! If you think you're the first man to reach that status, you're wrong. I forgive you for being one. Try not to make it a habit."

"But it's not that easy for me. I'll always feel as if I'm to blame. And...," he placed a hand over his stomach, "deep down, I feel a growing ache for the wrong I've done. I'm not... I'm not an honourable man. I'm no longer worthy of you and in many ways, it's you who matters most."

When she laid her hand on his, he jumped. "Bronwyn, you have proven time and again that you're not only worthy, but honourable." She caught his chin as he shook his head in disagreement. "I will never think of you otherwise."

"Alaura, the images haunt my dreams. Every time I close my eyes, they're there. What I've done makes me no different than any other murderer."

"The simple fact this is eating at you like a troglodyte on a fresh kill means you are different. Your conscience is hardest on you. Can't you see that?"

Did she speak the truth? Or did she say these things only to make him feel better? "The scars my actions created on my heart can never be erased."

She brushed a tear from his cheek. "A life without scars is a life unlived."

He closed his eyes and let the warmth of her hand permeate his inner being. If she could forgive him for his deeds, then he was not completely lost. "Will you help me chase the demons from my head?" His gaze swept across her face, hoping she had the ability to ease his suffering.

"I could never refuse my best friend." She drew him into her arms and kissed the side of his head.

For the rest of the day they ambled, following Keiron's trail and sharing the events which had brought them to this point. By the time they made camp for the night, they had come to an understanding that he had acted out of necessity, nothing more. Raw emotions were a force to be reckon with and more powerful than most understood.

Darkness eased its way upon the land, and the fire sent sizzling sparkles into the air. Bronwyn lay in his bedroll watching Alaura slip off her boots. She slid beneath her blanket and turned to face him.

After a few minutes of silence, she spoke. "Are you afraid to sleep?"

"The nightmares were real, as if made of flesh."

"They'll pass with time."

The fire light shimmered against his shirt that she wore, and he reached out to touch it. The reddish glow found her eyes, and they sparkled with life. He *had* done the right thing. He had protected a person more worthy of living than him. He sighed. She couldn't be more worthy if she tried, and he felt honoured to be her best friend. "Alaura, of the many friendships I've enjoyed through the years, I value yours the most. Without you, I'm afraid to think of where I might be."

Her eyes watered, revealing strong emotions stirring inside. She smiled and caressed his cheek. "Without you, I wonder the same about my fate."

She guided his hand to her back and drew him to her breast. Pulling his body nearer, he rested his head beneath her chin. His hand slipped beneath her shirt, slid over the birthmark and pressed against her bare back. Drawing a full breath, he became intoxicated by her scent. Her fingers entangled in his hair as if she'd never let go. In all of Ath-o'Lea where he had felt pleasure, nothing compared to this. He kissed the skin above the shirt button, then surrendered to the essence of her purity. Her goodness washed over him, flushing his veins of the evil spore that had tried to take root. His peaceful sleep restored his faith in himself and all he treasured.

39

Chorus of the Dead

BRONWYN PULLED the map from his pouch. While Alaura guided Clover onto the narrow trail following the river, he marked their route with a pencil. After studying it for a few minutes, he prepared to make a guess at their destination.

"See this dot?" He held the map in front of her.

"The square dot?" She raised a quizzical eyebrow.

"I think it's where Keiron is headed."

"Where is it?"

"The map doesn't say, but the person who marked it obviously sensed its significance. It's about a three-day journey from here." He sighed in frustration. "The only other course is to cross the river and head into the mountains towards Glen Tosh. It's the long way to the city. Staying on the Lower Branch would have been easier."

She rested her hand on his knee. "Don't over think things. Keiron is only a man. He's wily, but I've watched him; he acts on impulse. He has a burning anger that clouds his thinking." She looked back at him. "He's an ugly cuss, soiled by meanness."

He chuckled. "Uglier than a troglodyte." He folded the map and wrapped his arms around her.

"You could say that." The terrain became rough, forcing her to hold the reins with both hands. She guided Clover around a boulder and looked down at the river cutting through the earth ten feet below. "Keep hold. I don't want to lose you," she warned him.

"You won't lose me." When Clover lurched forward, stepping to higher ground, he held onto the pommel for security, but left one hand on Alaura to help her balance.

An hour later, she halted Clover. "She's getting weary. Let's walk a bit."

He dismounted and turned to ease her to the ground. "I'll lead." He patted the mare on the neck and walked in front of it. Looking down at the gully, he guessed the drop to be about two hundred feet. The river, dark in the shadow of the cliff, raced towards the base of the mountain. He glanced back at Alaura. She held Clover's bridle to safely guide the animal along the trail. The two were quite a pair. He couldn't image her with any other pony. She caught him watching and smiled. It was a knowing smile, the kind triggered by warm feelings between two people who have shared more than the average friendship. He winked and turned his attention to the path in front of him.

A few minutes later, he halted and picked up a piece of paper caught in a bush. He unfolded it. "Page twenty-three." He handed it to her.

"She's still well enough to leave clues." She wrapped her arm around his waist and snuggled into his side. "We must be close."

Clover nudged Alaura in the shoulder blade and snorted.

"What is it, girl?" She rubbed the animal's chin.

The pony pranced and threw its head back, making its flaxen mane dance. With its nostrils flaring and ears upright, it twisted in one direction then the other.

He scanned the area. "Do you think an animal is spooking her?"

Clover snatched the page from Alaura's hand, startling her. "Is it Isla?" She stared at the pony.

He peered farther along the trail. After taking a few steps, his eyes grew wide with awareness. *Listen*, he mouthed. The wind blowing into his face carried voices to his ears. He motioned her towards the bushes, scooped up the reins and tied them to a thick branch. Grasping her hand, he bent low and led her along the trail.

ౠ ❖ ౪

Isla ate a biscuit, then took a long drink from Tam's water flask. She wiped her mouth, recapped it and passed it back to him. Sitting on a fallen tree in the direct sunlight, she soaked in the heat. The higher they climbed into the mountains, the colder it got, and she'd take advantage of the sun's warmth. Keiron had vaguely explained the directions to the other two, saying their destination lay about three days away. Their payment awaited them there. She thought about the compensation Tam might receive for delivering her. Certainly, it couldn't be measured in gold coins.

He looked up from his seated position on the ground next to the log and held up an apple.

She took the fruit and bit into it. Sweet juices pooled at the corners of her mouth, and she sucked on the flesh to draw it in. Lately she seemed hungry all the time. She doubted it could be blamed on a growing spell like Liam claimed. Sighing, she let her mind wander and images of her best friend came to her. Did Liam know she had been captured?

Tam coughed on a piece of apple and struggled to clear his throat. He appeared stronger but was incapable of strenuous work.

"Be a shame to make it this far to choke to death on yer food." Keiron smirked.

Tam's recovery had baffled the scoundrel. When he had wakened the day after the arrow attack and began his usual routine, Keiron stared in astonishment. Isla felt as if she had won a mini-battle against the wretched man who called himself her das.

Tam grunted, cleared his throat and took another bite. He glanced up at her, his dark blue eyes calm and reassuring. She sensed he knew she had performed the miracle to keep him alive, but he wouldn't dare say anything. In that way, she trusted him as she would her das, though the two viewed the world differently. Breaking eye contact, she gazed into the distance of the trees on the adjacent highland. She sat far from

~ 359 ~

home, but the scenery reminded her of the Pogwa Mountains. If only these were those peaks, she'd sneak away and find Beathas' cottage.

Out of the corner of her eye, she saw the gnome slip into the bushes. She wished an evil creature would grab him and squeeze the life out of him. Everything about him, from eating canned worms to his terrifying ritual, sickened her. Tam had said a disease or parasite had infected Reese, radically altering him from his normal gnome state. He could be cured by death only.

She finished the apple and threw the core in front of her—one more piece of evidence for her das to find if he still followed. Keiron packed away his food sack, indicating they'd leave soon.

"Isla." The hauflin pulled the strap through the buckle. "If yew gotta go, go now."

Scanning the area, she searched for a place to find privacy. She didn't want to go anywhere near where Reese had entered the trees, so instead she walked farther up the trail and ducked behind the trees. Opening her pouch, she pulled another page from her book. She closed her eyes and thought of her das. As all the times before, she gripped the page and wished it to find his hand. She kissed it and went to shove it into her pocket but stopped. Pulling the pencil from the pouch, she scribbled a note on it.

ജ ❖ ര

Bronwyn and Alaura came to an abrupt stop. They couldn't reach Isla in time before she returned to the others. They had made a wide circle and positioned themselves ahead of them on the trail.

While he scanned the area, he slipped his hand into Alaura's. *I don't think Tam will put up a fight if he sees the other two go down. I think he'll help Isla. I'll kill the gnome. He's a slippery creature, and I'm unsure of his abilities. You disable Keiron with a spell. Have your dagger ready. He's a creature of strength, so if you can disable him, he'll fall easily. If Tam decides to fight, leave him to me.*

Kill them even if they surrender?

They won't surrender. He suddenly realised he talked to Alaura, not one of his men. *What am I doing? She's never killed anyone before.*

I have.

Surprised, he eyed her. *Stop reading my thoughts.*

Then stop transferring them.

Still puzzled, he asked. *You've killed a being before, an intelligent being?*

She nodded.

Where? When? I wouldn't have guessed. When she gave him a strange look, he knew he had sent his thoughts again. *How in the heck does she keep her own thoughts to herself?*

I'll teach you later.

I can't keep anything from you like this. He shook his head. *Kill them. Show no mercy.*

Alaura raised an eyebrow. *Are you sure, Sergeant?*

The title surprised him. *Honour is nothing if I lose Isla. Anything I need to do to save her, I'll do it.*

I understand. I'll do the same. She squeezed his hand. *Let me battle the gnome. He's a creature of magic.*

He appears more dangerous than Keiron. I'll deal with him.

It's because he has magic that I should fight him.

He couldn't get his thoughts around Alaura taking a life. *She talks as if she's trained to do this. I don't understand.*

I am trained for this, Bronwyn.

Damn! The first chance we get, you're teaching me how to keep my thoughts to myself. Then you're telling me about the training you've had. He peered through the bushes at Isla. Keiron was giving her an order. *Okay, you take out the gnome. I'll be there to help as soon as I can.*

From the trees or bushes? she asked.

Huh?

I think we should climb a tree and jump down upon them. We'll be on top of them before they realise what's happening.

Good idea. He fell silent and lowered his gaze. *I don't know if I can do this. I don't want her to get hurt. If they get their hands on her...* He shuddered.

Don't start doubting now. We can do this.

He stared at her. *Listen. If you get Isla, run. Get on Clover and don't look back. They'll never catch that pony with only you two on its back.*

I won't leave you here to die.

He pleaded with his eyes. *Please, go. Get our daughter home.*

She squeezed his hand, and with her familiar stern glare, sent a clear message. *I won't leave you. That's final. We can do this, Bronwyn. Together, we are strong.*

His eyes softened. *But if things go bad and I fall, promise me you'll take Isla and run. Don't fight a losing battle and sacrifice yourself. I can't bear to see you... I want you to live.*

Tears welled in her eyes.

Promise me. He insisted.

She nodded.

Say it!

I promise.

Don't break your promise. I won't ever forgive you if you do. He squeezed her hand for strength. *Are you ready?*

She nodded.

Bronwyn pointed to two trees about fifteen feet apart. *I'll take that one.* He prepared to move away.

Alaura heaved a heavy sigh. *Finley, be damned!*

Huh? She caught him off guard when she pulled him into her arms and kissed him square on the month. She held him so tightly, he couldn't pull away if he tried, not that he did. Her lips held his as if they would never kiss again. When they separated, he stared at her, an inch away, catching his breath. Her smile touched her eyes, and he had no idea of the size of his grin.

She bit her lip, and her gaze swept across his face. Then, as if feeling the urgency, she mouthed, "Go!"

He slipped away, glancing back at her once, puzzled by the sudden need for a kiss. Creeping towards his attack position, he replayed what she had said before the embrace: Finley, be damned? Who was Finley? Certainly, it couldn't be Lord Finley Dunsworth of Petra.

Once he had settled in the tree, he searched for Alaura but couldn't see her. Given her nimble body, she no doubt had beaten him into position. From what he could see through the thick, leafy branches, Keiron led the way; the gnome followed, leaving Tam and Isla last. Tightening his grip on the dagger, he took pleasure in the knowledge he'd give the scoundrel what he deserved.

A hairy, four-legged creature ran down the path towards the small group. Bronwyn watched it go. It resembled a deformed dog with two large sweeping tails and eyes the colour of fire.

"Whoa!" Keiron yelled at his horse as the black animal rushed by. "Cursed devils!"

Bronwyn hid near enough to see the scowl on the hauflin's face. The scar across his cheek added to his menacing appearance. Keiron started again, but his casual expression changed to one of deep thought, as if he wondered about the strange creature that had passed him. Did he recognise it? The man looked from side-to-side as if expecting an attack.

Of all the luck. Why did the creature have to run by at this time? He held his breath. As soon as the thief rode into position, he would drop like a rock. He hoped to attack before Alaura. It'd give him a few extra seconds to silence the bastard before he turned to kill the gnome. He counted the seconds: eight, nine, ten. He dived from the branch and landed on the back of Keiron's saddle.

He brought his dagger down to strike the hauflin in the chest, but it froze mid-way. Before he could pull his arm free from the invisible force holding it, a flash erupted behind him. The horses jumped, and he and Keiron crashed to the ground. He sliced through the air with his dagger but only grazed the hauflin's shoulder.

The thief scowled at him and stabbed with his own dagger.

Alaura had positioned herself on a thick branch and as she threw the magic fire ball at Reese, it gave way. She fell against the gnome, bounced off the horse's rump and tumbled to the forest floor. Dazed, she scrambled to her feet. The blast startled the horses, and they bucked their riders. The terrified animals bolted down the trail as if a banshee gave chase.

Isla smacked the ground hard and Tam landed on top of her, knocking the air from her lungs. She tried to push him off, but he weighed too much. He scrambled to his feet, snatched her from the ground and held her behind him as he drew his sword to fight.

Isla searched for who had attacked the others. "Alaura!" She tried to run to her, but Tam grabbed the back of her vest.

"Stay here!" He raised his sword and prepared to meet the animal that had run by the horses earlier. The fanged creature snarled and jumped at him. He caught it in mid-flight and sliced it in two.

The gnome scrambled out of the bushes and drew his sword. Alaura's hands flew into the air and as they danced, she mouthed the words to a spell. Light grew around her fingers and when it reached its apex, she directed the energy at him.

Reese braced his sword and reflected the power from her spell into the trees. The branches sparked and caught fire. Several small ones exploded and rained down upon them.

From out of nowhere, the dog-like creature tackled Alaura, and they rolled across the forest floor. She stabbed it several times with her dagger before tossing aside the carcass. By the time she rose, the gnome had disappeared. She searched for Isla and saw Tam battling three more of the strange animals. One circled him and leapt into the air behind him. To her horror, it latched onto Isla's arm and dragged her along the ground.

The galloping mongrel released the young hauflin and pounced on Alaura. They wrestled across the dirt and stones until she killed it. Staggering to her feet, she looked up to find the gnome holding Isla with a blade to her neck.

"That distance will do." Reese glared at her.

Alaura froze, horror racing across her face.

Isla jolted forward, and a wicked yelp filled the air. The gnome's grip slackened from around her waist, and he swayed from side-to-side. Isla wiggled frantically and escaped his hold, but when she tried to run, he grasped her hand. He fell to his knees, and she saw Tam standing behind him with a bloody dagger.

"Lindrum's not going to be happy you killed his pet!" Keiron shouted. "You'll never see your sister agin!"

Isla fought to free herself but couldn't. Her face twisted in pain, and she shrieked in agony. Warm air swirled around her and the gnome. As Reese's body jerked forward, his eyes, wide from exertion, ogled her. He tried to speak but his mouth froze open. Pale colours of greens, reds and oranges danced in the air, climbing as the swirling wind ascended into the sky.

Alaura reached for Isla, but her hand slammed into an invisible force. She cast a worried glance at Tam. He tried to kick the gnome, but his foot hit the unseen shield.

The wind continued to swirl, sending the colours higher into the sky. Isla shook from the energy entering her body. She fell to her knees and continued to cry out in anguish.

The rainbow of colours took shape, creating images of various people. They simmered into the air, as heat rising from a rock on a hot day. Released from their prison within the gnome, the chorus of the dead sang into the Plane of Peace.

Alaura gasped and stared in shock. Two familiar faces appeared amongst the freed spirits: Lady Dasia and Finola, Liam's meeme.

When the last life-force escaped, the expression on Reese's face calmed. "Thank you," he breathed. He released his grip on Isla and fell forward, dead.

Alaura threw her arms around the shivering child and held her tightly. A quick movement off to the side startled her.

Tam swung his sword and cut down the beast before it reached the females. With the dying animal squirming at his feet, he prepared to fight another.

⁝ ✦ ⁞

Bronwyn bent his knees and prepared to tackle Keiron, but another of the strange creatures jumped towards his face, sending him over backwards. He thrust his dagger into its chest and cut it wide open. Once on his feet, he drew his sword. "Let's finish this."

"I'm sick of dead men walking," growled Keiron, gripping his weapon.

Their swords came together with a heavy clank. One strike after another weakened the thief's position. Bronwyn forced him near the edge of the gully but didn't push him over. He wanted to draw blood and know, without a doubt, this hauflin breathed no more.

From a nearby tree, a beast jumped onto his shoulders. It drove him to the ground, and his sword flew from his hands. He rolled to his back and punched the mutant dog several times, then pulled a dagger from his belt and stabbed it. He lifted the animal off his body with his feet and threw it into the gully. He grappled for his dagger, but it remained in the dog-like creature and tumbled over the edge.

When he turned, Keiron jumped on top of him. The hauflin's dagger missed its target, and the pair wrestled across the hilly ground. Unarmed and on his back, Bronwyn struggled to gain control of the thief's weapon. He grasped the man's wrist, keeping the cold steal from driving into his chest.

"I should have dismembered yew when I had the chance." Sweat and spit dripped from the hauflin's mouth. "I won't make the mistake agin."

Although overheated from the fight, Bronwyn felt a warm tingling sensation in his right hand pressed against Keiron's head. His grip expanded to make room for the dagger that quickly materialized. "Such chances come but once in a lifetime, and you've wasted yours. I'm taking back my daughter!"

Startled by the appearance of the dagger against his forehead, Keiron's hold slipped. Bronwyn closed his fingers around the weapon and struck the hauflin with his fist. He rolled on top and straddled the man who had turned his life upside down. He raised the dagger and plunged it deep into Keiron's chest four times. As he pulled the weapon from the flesh the last time, a beast tackled him. He killed it, then stood to survey the area. Alaura cradled Isla in her arms. He locked eyes with Tam who stood near them, watching with a blank expression.

Bronwyn glanced back at Keiron whose lifeless eyes stared into the sky. It was done then. The wretched man would never harm Isla again. He picked up his sword and turned to walk towards Tam, then stopped. He searched the area for the mutated dogs he and the others had slain. All had vanished.

"Alaura!" When she looked at him, he pointed to the path leading to Clover. "Go!"

She rose with Isla in her arms, scanning the area for the reason behind his order.

"What is it?" Tam sheathed his sword but grabbed it again when a dog-like beast ran towards the women. He cut it down only to turn and face three more.

A force struck Alaura from behind, throwing her to the ground and knocking Isla from her grip. One of the animals snatched the child by the arm and dragged her away.

Tam turned to save Isla, but four creatures jumped at him, pushing him closer to edge of the gully. As quickly as he fought and killed one, another appeared. They advanced, growling and snapping madly. He held them at bay as he struggled to keep his footing.

Bronwyn chased the beast that dragged Isla. She tried to grab hold of a tree but couldn't maintain a grip. The canine circled back towards Alaura, and as he turned to follow, he heard laughing.

Alaura jumped to intercept the animal, but it turned away. It ran towards Tam, now surrounded by five snarling creatures, then raced in another direction. She raised her hands and danced her fingers in the air. A bolt of energy shot out and dropped the beast to the ground.

As soon as Isla stood, another dog appeared, grabbed her by the back of the vest and dragged her away.

The laughing grew louder, and Bronwyn searched for the source. He believed the person behind the laughing also conjured the mongrels. Then he saw him, the same tall, slender man who had transformed from Isla's illusion near the campfire: Lindrum.

He sheathed his sword. Nothing in his military training had prepared him to defeat or defend against a magical being. Knowledge on how to fight magic should have been standard at the castle. Why wasn't it? The lords were not the only ones who fought battles threatening the stronghold. He searched his memories, sweeping away years of cobwebs to view them clearly. He remembered a story told to him as a boy by his uncle living at Goshen. Uncle Darby spoke about a magic-user who snatched a private's sword from his hands. To protect himself, the private had used a special stone. His uncle said all the guards carried stones for protection, and the more experienced were versed in spells.

But Bronwyn had no stone for protection. None of his men did. Where had the stones gone? He cocked his head. Why hadn't he remembered this story before? He scoured his memories. Many things came to him as he stood in the clearing, things he hadn't thought about in years. Most of them concerned magic, potions and recipes his mum had taught him. Others were his observations of the castle guards. In his earliest years, citizens welcomed them into every dwelling, every shop. They worked alongside the citizens of Maskil, and he dreamt of being one of those men when he grew up. Things had changed drastically. Why hadn't he noticed?

Isla's scream shook him from his thoughts. The beast dragged her in the same circle, past Alaura and towards Tam. The man who had befriended Isla forced his way from the edge of the gully. The immediate danger of him falling to his death passed. The dozen or so snarling monsters surrounding him followed, taking turns snapping at him. He side stepped each one and struck out with his sword. His stance became clumsy as his body grew weary.

Bronwyn studied the fight as he raced towards Tam with the hope of intercepting Isla. Once he seized her, he'd help him. At first, he believed Tam controlled his own movements, but as the dog-like creatures continued to attack, they steered him towards a huge oak. Backing up against it, the thief-turned-ally continued to kill the creatures but as one fell, another came out of the shadows and attacked.

The beast dragging Isla didn't turn as it had before. It ran full speed towards Tam. It leapt into the pack, released the girl and jumped onto Tam, forcing him to stumble backwards into the tree. A bright light flashed, and a piercing snap filled the air.

The sharp sound forced Bronwyn to cover his ears. When the sound and light faded, Tam was gone. Bronwyn searched the tree limbs and the ground before it, but only the pack of dogs and Isla remained. Had the tree swallowed him? Was he dead? Or did the tree contain a portal and transfer him across Ath-o'Lea? He stared in shock. Although he saw it happen, he couldn't believe it.

The animals surrounding Isla disappeared. She stumbled to her feet and threw her arms around the great oak, wailing for the man who had vanished. "Tam! Where are you? Tam!"

Bronwyn turned to face Lindrum. The wizard shrugged, then a slow, malicious smirk spread across his face. His red-gemmed ring sparkled in the sun as he spread his palm and appeared to cast a spell. Keiron's body moved slowly through the air until it dropped at the wizard's feet.

Lindrum's quick hand motion ignited a blast of energy and threw Bronwyn against a tree. His insides jumped and sizzled as if on fire. It stole his breath and gripped his stomach. Dazed, he clutched his head to regain his senses. Finding the wizard, a faint glow shimmered around him. He had initiated the portal, the same one that had sliced Rorie in half. Lindrum planned to leave with Keiron by his side. Alaura screamed, and he whipped around.

A beast dragged Isla near enough to Alaura for their hands to touch, but not for her to grasp the child.

Isla shouted for Alaura and her das as she bounced along the ground.

Alaura jumped to her feet and sprinted after her.

Bronwyn struggled to stand, but the dizziness sent him toppling. Alaura and the mutant dog rushed towards the portal, and his heart raced, but he felt helpless to save her. Lindrum intended to do it again!

A burning sensation erupted in his pocket. He fought to remove it and found Isla's stone. Its shimmering light lit up his hand. The pain ripping through his body eased, and renewed energy propelled him to his feet and towards Alaura. As he ran, the mongrel dropped Isla on top of Keiron. The glow around the trio increased, and he knew it would close soon. The ache in his heart grew and burnt his throat when faced with what he had to do.

With every muscle pushed to the limit, he dashed towards Alaura. In the last second, he threw himself at her, shoving her to the ground. She struggled to break free until he pinned her. Dumbstruck, she stared at him.

He held her firmly as the portal snapped close, and his heart exploded with grief.

She grabbed his vest and shook him. "I could have gone with her! Why did you stop me?"

He gripped her shoulders, trying to hold her steady. "You'd have been slaughtered." Taking a painful breath, he tried to explain. "He waits to see if anyone is foolish enough to follow. Then it's too late." He stared into her brown eyes, hoping for her to understand without him saying more. Her blank stare forced the words from his mouth. "When you're partway into the portal, he closes it; you're sliced in half. He did it to Rorie."

"I might have made it." Her voice shook. She lowered her head and sobbed. "You saved me, but we lost Isla."

He surrendered to an exhaustion he had never felt. He had come so far to rescue Isla, only to fail. If Alaura hadn't been here, would he have foolishly attempted to enter the portal? His throat, dry from the fight, felt parched as the ache expanded and threatened to cut off his air passage. The moisture rose in his eyes, and his energy drained.

He pulled her into his arms and cradled her, seeking comfort in her embrace. Despite their best efforts, they had lost their daughter to a man with unknown intentions. Portals opened and closed across Ath-o'Lea. Lindrum could take Isla anywhere. Their search had no starting point, no trail to follow.

There, in the silence of the trees, they clung to each other and wept openly.

40

A Loyal Man

SANDERSON SAT in his chair and rubbed his chin several times with the side of his thick index finger. Releasing a heavy sigh, he eyed the dwarf sitting across the desk from him. "No need to inform Mulryan. I'll take care of things."

"What about Sawney? He deserves the promotion." Bronwyn had spent the past two hours discussing his concerns with the captain of the guard. Farlan had given him the numbers concerning race and ranks, but he didn't appear troubled by them. The news should have shocked him, but instead he brushed it off. His resignation upset the man more.

Sanderson avoided eye contact and dragged his finger along the stone wall beside him. A pebble came loose, and he fitted it back into place.

"But he won't get it, will he?"

Without warning, the tall man stood and went to the door. "Come with me."

He rose, straightened the vest Alaura had bought him at the keep on the Upper Branch and followed.

They remained silent until they reached the North Tower.

"Shut the door." Sanderson stepped inside.

Bronwyn closed the thick piece of wood and turned to see his superior installing the glass panels which had been removed for air circulation.

"Grab that one."

The room would grow hot in short order with the windows sealed, but Bronwyn lifted the panel into place. Sanderson had never taken him to the tower, always willing to do business in his office. It felt strange being here now, in the captain of the guard's private sanctuary. Everyone knew the rule: *Don't bother me unless it's urgent.*

The room, twenty feet square, contained only a comfortable chair and a four-shelf unit filled with books. Two long windows on each wall lit up the room as if one stood outside.

After securing the space, the captain of the guard rested against a window ledge and folded his arms. "You'll have privy to this information for one reason: I know where your loyalties lie." He looked around the small area. "Do you see this room?"

Bronwyn nodded and took up a position on the next window sill.

"It's a sanctuary. It's unlike any other place in the castle." He paused, scrutinizing him as if waiting for him to read more into his words. "Men have come and gone from this room, men I've trusted. Here we talk without fear."

Puzzled, he looked closer to see if the room held a particular significance. It didn't.

"Men of all races. Men whose loyalties are true." Sanderson paused and released a long sigh. "I'm not going to promote Sawney. He doesn't deserve it. If I promote him, I might as well sign his Missing on Duty papers the same day. And Sawney deserves better."

Bronwyn didn't understand. Non-humans held every rank above junior corporal. Sanderson had to promote other races into authority.

"Do you know why I turned down every recommendation you made for a non-human in the past year?"

He shook his head.

"Captain Tibbins recruited each promoted man and try as I might, I couldn't convince them to refuse the cursed quest." He clenched his fist. "They are compelled to accept. Every one of them disappeared."

"But you're the captain of the guard. You have the authority to change it."

Sanderson chuckled nervously. "One would think." He stared out the window as a guard passed on a nearby wall. "But I don't know what possesses men to do what they do. All I can do is protect my men the best I know how. Sawney's a good man; so are dozens of other non-humans serving the castle."

"What are they supposed to do? Accept the fact they'll never rise above private?"

"You know me better than that."

He thought he did...once.

"There's change in the wind," said Sanderson. "I feel it when I walk these halls. I'm preparing to meet the next challenge. I've assigned fifty-three men to a secret force. Now, fifty-four men." He eyed the dwarf. "These men, mostly non-humans, have special ranks unknown and unrecognised by the lords. Most are corporals, three—four—are sergeants. One is their captain. Each recognises the other, but those outside the force are oblivious to their existence. Sawney is one of those men. Remember this but tell no one."

Bronwyn stared. What possessed Sanderson to create a special force unknown to the lords? "And Farlan?"

"The boy is tenacious, too easy-going, but you've rubbed off on him. He's going to make a good sergeant. He'll make a better captain to the men of this secret force.

"Burkenshaw is loyal to the castle. It's all I ask of any man. It's all I asked of you." Sanderson cleared his throat. "The Laws of the Land are shifting, and I have no control over invisible forces. It's important to focus on the things we can control."

"What if I find Isla next week and returned to my post? Will I be reduced to a private?"

"Stay away. I won't accept your application."

He frowned.

"I can't protect you," explained Sanderson, "and I won't lose you to unknown foolishness. When I'm ready for you, you'll know. While you're on leave, the men of this secret force will recognise you as sergeant but won't address you as such. When you're reinstated, you'll lead them as captain beside Burkenshaw."

"I don't understand the need for a secret force. The lords must realise a negative influence is affecting the castle. Why can't they act?"

Sanderson grimaced. "The lords don't control the castle and her men, Bronwyn. I thought you understood."

"If they don't, who does?"

A serious expression settled on his face. "The lords are servants of the people. They tend to their needs. It's the captain of the guard's duty and honour to care for the castle. It's the highest rank any man can reach."

Bronwyn raised his eyebrows. The highest rank a man can reach? "You're the castle's best friend?" He grinned as he thought of Sanderson dancing down the halls bringing joy to everything he touched.

Sanderson chuckled, and relaxed his stance. "I never thought of it like that but, yeah, I suppose so."

Maybe Alaura knew more about the workings of a castle than he believed. If so, Alaura didn't have a lord, didn't need one. She needed a best friend: him. But if Sanderson ran the castle, then he had the power to make things right. "Why don't you take control of the situation? Make things the way they should be?"

"It's more complex than simply giving orders. Imagine a man trying to control a woman. He knows what's right, but she has her own ideas." He half smiled. "They've gotta work things out their own way. If I used force, things may fall apart in my hands."

Bronwyn knew exactly what he meant.

"There are other powers at play," said Sanderson. "I can't see them clearly, but they're there. The castle shares its secrets, but it's weak. It's as if it's holding its breath until relief arrives." He looked him in the eye. "I've shared this with you because I trust you. You won't let me down, won't let the castle down. For security sake, guard your mouth. Trust no one, not even your woman."

"You have my word."

"Your word is your bond."

"My word is my bond." It was unnecessary to bond him; these secrets would never be shared. His loyalties to the castle felt as strong as those to his family, Isla and Alaura. A strange sensation stirred in his stomach, moved into his chest and caused a burp.

He brushed aside the confusion it caused. "Thank you for taking care of the charges against Alaura. We were unsure of what we'd return to."

"I couldn't have my best guard with his mind in the dungeon for three years, could I now?"

Bronwyn's neck warmed.

"She's the one, isn't she?"

He knew how Sanderson felt about Alaura and his guards uniting. Still, he nodded and tried to hide the smile.

"I figured as much," he said. "When a man looks at a woman as you did the night Alaura walked in to meet with the lords, he loses all control of his senses. It's as if his blood catches fire and every time she comes near, she adds tinder to keep the flames rising. I tried to douse the flame but knew it was like trying to extinguish a conflagration with drunken spit."

He swallowed hard. It sounded like the captain of the guard once had a fire for a woman, one that burnt out of control. "My face looked that dumb?"

"I wouldn't call it dumb. More like daft, dim-witted." An easy smile enlightened the captain's face. "Are you taking her with you?"

"No, she's staying with Beathas."

"She's the kind of woman who'd want to be by your side."

"She probably does," he said slowly, "but I want her safe."

"We'll see how it works for you. Remember what I said about force and things falling apart in your hands." He changed his tone. "Lord Finley Dunsworth dropped in for a visit while you were gone."

"And?"

"He asked about Alaura of Niamh. Seems he has an interest in her, but he wouldn't say how. He asked about you, too."

"Me?" Bronwyn remembered the meeting on the road outside of Maskil. He wouldn't make that same mistake twice.

"He wanted to know about your relationship with her. I told him the truth." Sanderson continued in a flat tone. "You hired Alaura to care for Isla, nothing more. The two of you got along fine as long as you paid her wage on time. If not, she could get spittin' mad."

"Why did you tell him that?"

"I sensed more to the story than he shared. Did she ever mention Finley?"

Thinking back to when Alaura kissed him before they fought Keiron, he believed she had mumbled his name. "She's never mentioned him to me. They're both from Petra. Maybe he knows her from there."

"I'll look into it. Might make a good story."

"I've another story for you," he said. "Do you remember Tam, a dwarf, who served with the castle?"

"Tam Mulryan?" Sanderson sat up and lowered his brow.

"Mulryan? I didn't know his sire's name."

Sanderson rubbed his chin, lost in thought. "He's Lord Laird Mulryan's kid brother. He was a worthy guard."

"He's dead."

"I know. Died about ten years ago."

"No, he died trying to save Isla."

A fog of confusion clouded Sanderson's eyes. "He served with us for about seven years, reaching sergeant. Tibbins sent him on a quest, and he never returned."

"He didn't die on the quest and has wandered The Trail ever since. He worked with Keiron."

"Damn!" Sanderson grumbled. "He was good man. But I had a strange feeling about him. Did he say what happened?"

"I didn't get a chance to question him. Isla had recognised him as a trained guard. She..." His voice cracked, and his eyes filled up. He thought he had control of his emotions but talking about Isla like this stirred the hurt in his heart. Clearing his throat, he continued. "She befriended Tam. She has a way of doing that."

Sanderson placed a strong hand on the dwarf's shoulder.

"In the end, he tried to help her," said Bronwyn, "but in an instant he disappeared. We believe he's dead."

"Tam was a loyal man, a *good* man."

"What happened then? He had the chance to return to the castle. Why didn't he take it?"

"I can't say." He folded his arms and stared out the window as he spoke. "I wondered about him for a long time. He didn't want to go on the quest and told his brother this. Lord Mulryan wouldn't hear of his own kin turning down the offer; it would have disgraced him. The night before he left, I overheard a heated argument between the two. It almost sounded as if Tam accused his brother of being a traitor to all dwarfs. Mulryan defended Captain Tibbins' request for the service."

"What did Tam know that we don't?" Bronwyn recalled another piece of the story. "Did Tam have a sister?"

"She was more ornery than most men. She assaulted the guard at the recruiting office when he turned down her application."

"She wanted to enlist?" He stared in shock.

"When the guard told her she couldn't because of her sex, she proved him wrong and broke his arm."

"What happened to her?"

"When Tam didn't return, she left. Maybe she went to find him; he was the youngest of their kinfolk. Maybe she wanted to get away from Laird; he can be unreasonable."

"I think she's still alive. If my hunch is correct, Tam helped kidnap Isla to gain her freedom."

"Damn shame. Both were worthy swordsmen. She simply needed an attitude adjustment."

Bronwyn stood. "I should get going. I still have a lot to do before I leave tomorrow."

"Remember, this door," Sanderson pointed to the one for the room, "is always open to those loyal to the castle."

"I'll remember." He reached out to shake the man's hand. "It's been an honour serving with you, sir. I hope to again as soon as time permits."

"You're a fine man, Bronwyn. The best sergeant I've had the pleasure of reprimanding." He half smiled and shook his hand. "I'm sure our time will come."

He hated good-byes, and the past two days contained many. Hesitantly, he turned to go.

"Bronwyn."

He looked back and thought he saw Sanderson's eyes gloss over as if he struggled to keep the moisture from breaking free of the ducts.

"No matter what anyone says, you won't regret your decision."

He had believed Sanderson would think otherwise, that he had thrown away a military career by leaving his post to search for Isla. Then again, many things about this man remained a mystery.

41

To Be Where You Are

JORIS HUGGED his brother and slapped him on the back. "I'll watch her." He poked his finger into Bronwyn's chest. "For you." He grinned. "Anyways, I can't imagine another man patient enough to put up with her stubbornness."

Bronwyn chuckled. He'd miss his older brother but knowing he and other family members would watch out for Alaura reassured him as he prepared supplies for his journey. "Has Dad listened to Mum?"

His sibling looked at him sideways. "Does he have a choice?"

They both laughed. Bronwyn had arrived home less than forty-eight hours beforehand, and already he had witnessed his dad grumble at the pampering his mate bestowed upon him.

"I better get going." Joris released him but didn't move away. "Take care, Bronnie. We'll all be waiting for your safe return as well as Isla's." He backed away, took one last look, then left the room.

He glanced around his old bedroom. In his absence, Farlan and Selina had occupied his quarters. He didn't mind. The recently united couple needed a place and, as Farlan said, if he and Isla had returned, they'd have regained ownership of the residence. The union hadn't surprised him. His friend had thought of no other but Selina for more than two years.

Farlan had delivered his and Isla's possessions to his parents' home. His mum had packed them here. He had rummaged through the trunk and sacks, taking what he needed for The Trail. Everything else stayed put.

He fingered the page; the last Isla had left for him and Alaura. As if by magic, the wind had carried it to his hand while they consoled each other after Lindrum escaped with her. He read again the note she'd scribbled across the top: *For you, too... And you.* No one, but he and Isla, understood the meaning of those simple words. They'd carry him through until he found her.

He picked up a small brown sack Alaura had given him. She told him it contained magic. Good magic. Her magic. Anything carried in it stayed dry and undamaged by fire. He folded the page and slipped it inside. When footsteps fell outside the door, he looked up to see his best friend.

Alaura wore dark blue pants, fitted snug at the waist and a white shirt that revealed her subtle curves. Her hair, pulled from her face with a simple buckle, hung down her back. His breath caught in his throat. If a more beautiful woman lived in Ath-o'Lea, he had never met her.

She smiled and leant against the dresser. "Your mum said for me to come in."

"I expected you." He hadn't seen her since the night before but had thought of her all day.

"Did you speak with Sanderson?"

"I did this afternoon."

"How did he take your resignation?"

"He didn't." He glanced up from placing the small sack amongst his travelling gear. She appeared disappointed. "He gave me a leave of absence from my duties."

"So, you still serve the Laws of the Land, honour them as if still a sergeant."

Her expression as she waited for his answer puzzled him. "While I'm not wearing a uniform, it doesn't mean I ignore my duties."

She looked away.

"Why do you think otherwise? You know the value I place on upholding the laws."

She folded her hands in front of her. "I should expect nothing else. You're the most honourable man I know."

"Then why are you disappointed?"

"I'm not." She forced a smile. "My things are prepared. I'll be ready to leave in the morning."

He froze. The moment he had dreaded arrived. He took a calming breath and placed a pair of socks in his rucksack. "Where are you going? To visit a friend?"

She glanced at him sideways. "I'm going with you."

"It's safer in Maskil."

"We'll be safe together."

"The Trail is no place for a woman. You'll only slow me down."

She frowned. "That's nonsense and you know it."

"It doesn't matter. I give the orders, and you're not coming."

"You can't order me around. I'm not one of your men. I'm free to do what I want, and I'm going with you. I'm going to help find Isla!"

He leant towards her. "You're not!"

"I am!"

"I can't be looking out for you while I'm watching my own back. A woman belongs in town, not traipsing across Ath-o'Lea battling crazy wizards and hunting down killers."

"Where would you be if this woman had stayed at home instead of chasing you through the forest? Dead! That's where!" She swallowed hard, and he felt her pain. He remembered the night she found him chained to the tree and left for dead. "You're a strong man, but you can't do this alone."

"I'm going to have to because I won't allow you to come." He looked into her eyes. The light from the lantern danced within them. He found it challenging enough to leave her let alone argue with her to stay.

"You said it yourself, we are great travelling companions."

"Alaura, I almost lost you. Don't believe I'll ever forget that day by the brook. I'm not taking the chance again."

"Am I to stay here and hope each day you'll walk through those gates, wondering as the weeks and months pass, if *I* have lost *you*? That's not fair." She shook away the welling tears and placed her hand upon his shoulder. "I need to be with you."

It didn't sound fair for her, but he wouldn't change his mind. He'd give anything to take her in his arms and sleep the night away. While on The Trail it had been easy but since arriving home, they had slept apart. If he didn't alter his strategy, she'd talk him in to letting her go. "Not fair?" he countered. "Who's really being not fair? I've shared everything with you, and you've pushed me away."

Her expression changed, and she no longer appeared confident.

"Alaura, why are we best friends but not lovers outside of dreams?" When she didn't answer, he continued. "Why won't you let me kiss you, hold you and let the fire racing through my blood ignite the passion that lives in yours?"

When she looked away, he knew she searched for an answer to satisfy him.

"What do you want from me?" He cursed himself for hurting her but deep down, he needed the answers. "I've given you everything! Allowed you into places no other has visited! Still you don't allow me access to you and the places reserved for your lover." Tears pooled in his eyes, but he refused to let them fall. "All I ever wanted was to be where you are, for you to see in me the special person who makes life worth living. I believe I am that person, but you won't admit it. I trust you have never lied to me, but I'm certain you've withheld truths, truths that may set you free from your past."

She folded her arms and brought one hand up to cover her mouth. A tear fell, and she quickly wiped it away. There she stood, once again, struggling with her emotions, deciding on the right words to put him off. He wished this once she'd share her thoughts, the ones on the tip of her tongue, the ones she cloaked in her mind when he searched for them with the Transfer Spell.

"I only wanted to be friends." Her voice sounded raspy. "I told myself we were only friends for Isla's sake. But sensations more powerful—"

"Friends?" His sarcastic tone sliced the air. She always gave the same answer. *Damn her!* She knew how much it hurt him. "That's what we are: friends. So, as one friend to another, I wish you'd leave. I have things to do and you, friend, are in the way."

"It's not what you think."

"What is it I think? Do you care to share my thoughts because be damned if you won't share yours with me!" When she didn't answer right away, he continued. "What's wrong? Thinking of a spell to shut me up? Maybe you should go back to magic school."

"You don't know everything, Bronwyn. You don't know the whole story."

"Of course! I'm a dwarf void of magic. How could I know the whole story? I'm nothing like you. You know everything and if you don't, you make up a tale that fits your—"

"Shut up!" Her bottom lip trembled. "You're a stubborn, overbearing, tenacious man!"

"Is that supposed to flatter me?"

"You're by far the most exasperating man in Ath-o'Lea. If you only knew how much—" She stopped herself cold.

"Was that a bit of truth about to slip out? If I only knew what? Come on, Alaura, what is it you wish me to know?" She clamped her mouth shut and struggled to find the words. He stepped closer. As he held her chin to face him, he stared into her eyes, willing her to reveal more. Why could they be best friends but not lovers? Why could no one think of them as mates? Why had she left Petra? Who was Finley?

He wrapped his arm around her. Drawing her near, he reached for her left hand. Sensing he wanted to bridge the Transfer Spell, she grabbed the material of his shirt and held tightly. Her unwillingness to connect and share her thoughts frustrated him. "Alaura, tell me your secrets."

"Bronwyn, ..." Her eyes filled with sadness, and she looked away. "I can't."

"I didn't think so." He pushed her from his arms. "Get out."

"You're making a horrible mistake. You need me with you. I need... I want to be with you."

"It's you who's mistaken." He stood straight with his hands on his hips. "I don't need you."

"Please..."

She dragged out the emotional *please* as if begging him to change his mind. He had never known her to beg for anything. He shook his head, and she struggled with what to do next. The need to tell him became so great, he thought she might erupt, spilling her secrets before him. Then the pressure subsided, and the saddest expression darkened her face. He thought she might cry, but she didn't. Instead, she stood there, staring at him as if he had told her he'd never return for her. When he second-guessed his actions and wanted to pull her back into his arms, she turned and left the room.

An ache swelled in his chest. Already his arms longed to hold her. It would have been easier if he departed with heart-felt good-byes. Now, his last memory of her would be this stupid argument. He threw a sack of nuts against the wall, and it exploded into the air.

He wanted to leave now, put Maskil and Alaura behind him, but the town gates would be locked in less than an hour. Maybe if he rushed through his packing. No, that was irrational. He needed a good night's sleep before his journey began. It would be foolish to act upon the raw emotions she provoked. If only she had been reasonable and shared her secrets.

Movement at the door caught his attention. Alaura had returned. Unable to suppress a smile, he spun to greet her. Instead of finding his best friend, he found his mum staring at him. He froze. She probably wanted him to race after Alaura and apologise for what he had said, but she didn't take her usual lecture stance. She simply leant against the door frame with a somber expression.

"You'll always be my baby, but you're more man now than your brothers. There's nothing I can do to ease this hurt." She turned and walked away.

42

Heart Made of Pebbles

THE EARLY morning's sun heated the empty cobble street leading to the main gates of Maskil. Bronwyn guided Tam's sturdy horse onto it. From its behaviour, he sensed the well-trained mare once had a thoughtful former master. Needing a second mount, he believed Tam wouldn't mind if he claimed his ride. He also knew Isla would recognise it. If she saw it, she would search for Tam and find *him*.

He and Alaura had studied the large oak that had consumed Tam and found no trace of him. She probed the area with magic. Still no sign of life materialised. She had heard of a spell which entombed its victims within tree trunks and believed this to be Tam's fate. *They're absorbed into the being of the plant and cease to exist*, she'd said.

A hooded person rushed from an alley, startling Bronwyn. When a breeze tossed back the hood, he stared in disbelief. The female dwarf, speckled with warts and adorned with flowing green hair, stopped abruptly. She gawked at him in horror, pulled the hood over her head and ran towards the centre of town.

He watched her go. Was that Breckin Dole, the woman who had caused him such grief? Had Alaura carried out her promise? He nudged the horse and continued towards the gate. Women had ways of dealing with other women who hurt their man. *Their man.* He smiled thinking of Alaura and the night she had referred to him by the phrase.

A warm feeling swept through him. That same night they had joined, in dream only, but it had felt real, vivid, with true images and feelings. On the return trip to Maskil, they had talked little, riding separate horses. They travelled faster, but he missed the closeness they had shared being in one seat; separate saddles brought a distance between them he hadn't expected. Only at night, when they fell into each other's arms to ease the pain of losing Isla, did they touch. During those times, they had bridged the Transfer Spell only once by accident as they slept.

Their dream, as vivid and as real as the previous, placed them near a mountain pool overlooking a town. Urged on by a strange sense of knowing where he headed though he had never journeyed there, he squeezed between two boulders and entered a rocky crest. There, he found Alaura, sitting with her knees pulled up to her chin staring over the valley. His appearance startled her. He sensed a great weight on her shoulders, but she remained silent. Although he encouraged her to talk, she didn't want to.

There's nothing to say about things one cannot change, she said. *All we can do is enjoy the moments we have.* Then she kissed him.

Bronwyn had tried to soothe the unhappiness he sensed but in the end, with the joining complete, the sadness had grown. He held her tightly, feeling powerless to extinguish her fears, ones he felt as strongly as if they belonged to him. Isla had identified the situation exactly: for the most part, Alaura appeared happy, but she suffered moments of unexplained sadness. He should have pressed her to learn more as she had done with him, but he didn't want to deepen her sorrow.

From thereafter, Alaura guarded her hand. She slept with it under her cheek, so the Transfer Spell couldn't be bridged. He had asked her about the fear, but she brushed it off.

He released a heavy sigh and looked at his right hand. The red from the bog berry juice had faded, but the portal to Alaura's hand rested in front of him. He might not be able to send items to her, but he had sent his thoughts.

Pressing the palm to his lips, he mustered his concentration and kissed it. In his head, he recited the words which fuelled the spell. *Travel in air. Travel on land. Transfer this kiss to her hand.* He imaged his kiss being received on her hand with her long slender fingers wrapping around it. The feeling entered her skin and travelled through her blood to reach her lips. He clenched his fist to trap it inside.

Alaura lay out there, sleeping probably. He thought about finding her and apologising for the way he had spoken to her the evening before but knew it was a mistake. Then, she'd again ask to come.

Farlan waited for him at the front gates. He mounted a horse and fell into stride beside him.

"You're not coming." Bronwyn glanced at his friend. Farlan appeared well, but his injury kept him on the inactive roster. He was permitted to wear the uniform and perform light tasks in the castle for a few hours a day to ease him back into service while he healed completely.

"I want to ride a while."

The pair rode in silence for about ten minutes before Farlan halted his horse. He swung one of his long legs over the pommel of the saddle and stared at his friend.

He admired the sergeant badge on his lapel. "The badge looks good on you."

"It'd look better on you." Farlan gazed down the road. "We all have our duty."

"And you?"

"I guess my duty is right here, taking care of the citizens of Maskil and this cursed castle." Farlan chuckled. "Who knows, by the time you get back, I might have this place whipped into shape. I might have the ol' man confiding in me like he did you."

"I wish things could be different, but..."

Farlan shrugged. "The important thing is to find Isla and bring her home. I'll take care of everything here."

"Visit my family while I'm gone. Mum will be expecting you."

"I'll keep an eye on them... Alaura too. I'll see to her. Make sure she's well." He paused. "Did you two have an argument?"

"Why do you ask?"

"She waited at the gates this morning when I opened them. I've never seen her so distraught."

"Which way did she take?"

"Towards Moon Meadow." Farlan adjusted his position on the saddle. "I'm sure she'll be fine."

"She wanted to come. It'd have been easier if she had accepted the fact I wanted to keep her safe. But she's so damn stubborn, it—"

"Like another friend I know!" They chuckled to ease the tension.

Bronwyn wanted to move on, get past the good-bye, but he couldn't tear himself away from the friend he had come to know better than any brother. The horse beneath him shuffled its feet, eager to get underway.

"Listen." Farlan became serious. "I want you to check in now and again. I might need advice on things." He paused. "Send me a message. Let me...let me know you're still out there...still searching...still—"

"Alive?"

"Life's a precious thing. We all need a little reassurance now and again." There was no mistaking the sincerity in Farlan's words.

A warm sensation grew in his right hand, and he looked at his palm. A red spot surrounded by a heart made of pebbles appeared. Without a doubt he knew it to be a squished bog berry. He smiled, relieved her anger diminished enough to acknowledge him. Had she received his kiss?

"Alaura has more than one way to get to you." Farlan studied his hand, puzzled.

He pulled the small pouch from his pocket and dumped the pebbles inside with Isla's book page. Long after the bog berry stain faded, he'd have Alaura's stones.

Farlan flipped his leg back into the stirrup, guided his horse closer and grasped his hand. "Safe travels, Bronwyn. I'll be waiting your return."

"Remember you're not alone in the struggle, Farlan. You not only have friends, but those who are like family." He equalled his friend's handshake.

"Likewise you. You'll never be alone in your journey. The thoughts of many travel with you."

They released their physical bond. Farlan turned his horse and headed for Maskil.

Bronwyn looked back several times, capturing the image in his mind. As he left the sanctuary of the only home he had known, he cast a final glance at the stone structure that kept his family and friends safe. He knew every inch of the wall, the inside passages and tunnels, but he wondered if he would ever see them again.

His thoughts drifted to the fateful day when Isla became part of his life. The same day, he came face-to-face with another female who had touched his being in more ways than he understood. In his memories, he watched her walk confidently into the Private Audience room. A captivating vision and an enchanting scent had swept past her to fill his eyes and cloud his mind. It was as if a spell had been cast.

Tam's horse tugged at the reins, and he realised he was smiling. One day he'd return for Alaura of Niamh. For now, he had to focus on the daunting task of finding Isla. Gathering his reins, he nudged the horse to a jog as he followed the Shulie River south towards Ellswire.

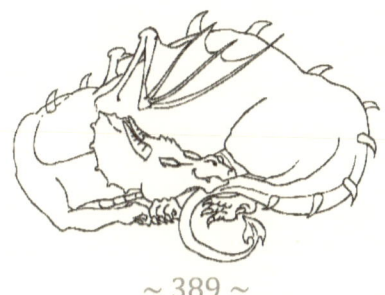

Epilogue

Rhiannon Darrow

Rhiannon Darrow untied a large bundle of chamomile from the drying rack and placed it in a cloth sack. She carried it downstairs to the small table behind the counter of the Forest Herb and Bakery shop. From the time she was young, she had spent many hours preparing herbs for sale. She could identify hundreds of plants by smell alone. While being a seamstress and owning her own shop was her passion, practising the art of herbalism was her duty.

A bell rang, and she looked up to see a familiar young dwarf enter the shop. Through her narrow path of sight, she watched Carbrey. He was handsome and charming, and he often came when she tended the counter.

Leaving the table, she emerged from hiding. "Carbrey, may I help you?"

He smiled. "Rhiannon, it is a pleasure to see you."

She returned the smile. "The pleasure is mine." Heat rose into her neck. "Your mum is in need of supplies?"

"A few." He handed a list to her. "If you have the time."

"It's what I'm here for." She glanced at the list of herbs and gathered them swiftly but not too quickly. When everything was packaged, she placed them in the leather pouch he had brought. "Tell your mum I said hello."

Carbrey paused, his hand on the pouch. He appeared to want to speak but instead released a slow breath. "Thank you. I will tell her."

She watched him leave and when he closed the door, he stole one last look through the glass, then walked away. An odd but familiar feeling surfaced in her chest, one that robbed her from fully enjoying his visit. Once again, their meeting today hadn't quashed the uncertainty.

"He won't wait forever."

Rhiannon jumped and found her mum, Maisie Darrow, standing behind her. "He needn't wait for me." She returned to the chamomile and began chopping it on the block.

"He admires you."

"As much as I admire him, he fails to generate the feelings I seek."

"Sometimes those feelings need nurturing. Learn from your brother."

She chuckled. "Alaura always had what Bronwyn searched for; he only needed to find the common ground." A nagging question resurfaced, and she spoke it before her courage failed. "Mum, why did you encourage their relationship when she is not dwarf?"

A vulnerable expression dawned. "It was my duty to discourage it, but," a soft smile creased her lips and a twinkle lit her eye, "I couldn't deny them their heart's desire. To do so would have condemned them to a life of misery."

"And if I chose a man who is not dwarf?" She held her breath; her destiny travelled a different path than her brother's.

Her mum studied her as if a thousand years passed through her mind. When she spoke, her words weighed heavy. "We shall cross that bridge if it's in your future."

Isla of Maura

Isla of Maura outlined the military vest, pressing lightly so if the line had to be erased, it wouldn't leave an indent in the paper. The curve of the shoulder was difficult. It took five attempts to get it to perfectly match the other one. The black lead moved slowly as she imagined the sun shining on the top of the blue material. In the sunshine was where they had spent their happiest times, and here was where the lightest of touches would accent the glow. She shaded lightly, then used her finger to smudge the colour just right.

A short time later, she sat back to admire her effort. The eyes of her das stared at her as if he would walk across the tower roof and tell her to get ready for bed; they had a busy day tomorrow. Perhaps they'd ride along Shulie River or take a hike to Moon Meadow. She'd ask if Liam could come.

She squeezed the pencil and her eyes fell upon her best friend's image. His smile created an ache in her belly that rose to her chest and into her throat. Tears threatened, but she knew they would not deliver her to her das or Liam. Swallowing hard, she gently set the tip of the pencil on Liam's chin and lightly touched it, shadowing the edge of his jaw with caressing strokes. Recalling the feel of his skin when he brushed against her settled her thumping heart. If she drew breath slowly, she could smell his scent. A smile creased her lips, and the pencil added minor strands of hair around his ears, combing them into soft waves, the same she had done with her fingers when they sunned by the waterfall pool. Her imagination would spend the evening here, safe with the boy she loved.

Bronwyn Darrow

Bronwyn Darrow laid the map flat on the large stone. His calloused finger traced the road from Wirksworth to Little Ram, stopping midway between the towns. In his mind, he thought of the distance from this point to his current location on Blue Mountain. If he continued south west, he'd intercept the trail to Glengarry Keep. Considering the rough terrain ahead, he estimated it would take five days. He'd know he was on the right path when he reached River Blue.

He glanced up at the sky. Clouds were moving in. He had to cover as much ground as possible before dark.

Although it had been risky to travel this far into uninhabited land, the venture had paid off. He had found the hamlet of Drumclog Moss and met the prisoner who had been held at Blackvale Castle for three years. The woman had been released shortly after Isla had arrived, and she provided enough information to give him hope. Isla was alive and unharmed. The woman had said the other prisoners gave her special care, but the terrified child wanted only the comforts of home.

Bronwyn folded the map and slipped it into his belt pouch. He fastened the bridle onto Sorrowsweet's head and mounted. For once, he wished he was a horse, or at least had the ability to graze. Sorrowsweet had plenty to eat at this low altitude, but the season and terrain provided little for a dwarf. He took a mental inventory of the food he carried. If he had one small meal every second day, he'd have enough to reach the keep.

Six days later, he stumbled from the saddle towards red berries that glistened in the sunshine. He fell to his knees and picked the strawberries feverishly, shoving them into his mouth. He had never tasted berries so sweet.

Alaura of Niamh

A voice shattered the stillness of the night. Alaura of Niamh pressed against the stone structure and waited, drawing her cloak around her. The village of Inishmore existed on the edge of Forest of Caucy. The inhabitants were humans and elves and a mixture of both races interbred. Its history of archaic magic and secrecy hadn't brought her to its cobblestone lanes. Instead, the stories of a half-elf who had once been imprisoned at Blackvale Castle lured her to the isolated location.

Her contact spoke about an elder who lived near the centre of the village in an abode carved into a mammoth boulder. The entire village subsisted within the rock with homes carved into or built around stone. Alaura had never seen a place such as this. From afar, the settlement appeared small and insignificant but upon entering, countless knolls transformed into roofs of homes and businesses.

She sneaked down the lane. Moments later, she paused at the base of a ladder leading to an oval door: Elwyn's door. A dim light glowed within the peaceful dwelling. Her contact had said the woman was harmless to those with good intentions, deadly to others.

Sources across Ath-o'Lea had spoken of her fiery temper and her quickness to judge, making Alaura hesitate. This elf, well-versed in magic, may judge her incorrectly. Still, she had to meet with her, gather the intelligence needed to learn Blackvale Castle's secrets. Perhaps good fortune would grant her an audience with the former prisoner. To save Isla from the same prison, she'd ask the impossible.

She stepped onto the first of five rungs, making her way to the doorway slowly. Before she gathered the courage to knock, the door flung open, revealing a venerable woman who gawked at her with more curiosity than concern.

Kellyn Mulryan

"Stop!" shouted the guard. "You can't go in there!"

Kellyn ignored the quackpod and kept running. While drawing water from the well in the courtyard, she had seen Merk Lindrum cross the open balcony and enter his study. He had been absent from Blackvale Castle for several days, and this was the first opportunity to inform him of the tragedy that had occurred to his favourite prisoner.

She reached the door, flung it open and raced inside. Merk stood admiring a painting on the far wall. He glanced in her direction but remained silent.

The castle guard tackled Kellyn to the floor before she could speak, knocking the wind from her lungs. Another guard jumped in to help subdue her.

Kellyn punched, kicked and scratched to break free but ultimately, she became pinned with her arms secured behind her back.

"Our apologies, My Lord," said the guard, as he jerked her to her feet and placed his hand firmly over her mouth. "We'll see she's punished for her disobedience." He dragged her away.

Kellyn clamped her teeth down onto the guard's hand. He grunted and pulled free. "I need to speak with you!" she shouted.

Merk shrugged and returned to admiring his painting.

"Your pet is dying!"

He shot her a deadly glare. "Halt!"

The guards stopped at the threshold.

"Which pet?"

"Isla."

He raised an eyebrow and looked to the side as if to contemplate her answer. "Release her."

Kellyn wrenched her arms from their grip and scowled at them. "Check your ego at the door, dingleberries."

"Leave us," said Merk. The guards exited quickly, and he eyed her. "Dying in what way?"

"You haven't noticed? It began before you left."

He nodded reluctantly. "She seemed disturbed but..." He clasped his hands before him. "Tell me more."

Which path do I take to continue the adventure?

The directions are on the next page.

Which Path Do I Take?

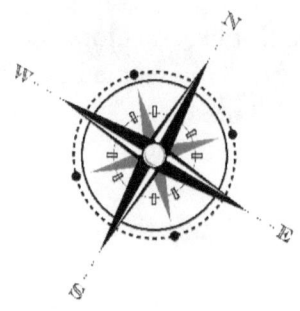

Castle Keepers Series: *Revelation Stones*, book 2

OR to continue reading in chronological order

Mystical Series: Beyond the Myst

Please Note: The four-book Mystical series grew from an exercise of exploring where Willow came from. It ties into the Castle Keepers series, but readers won't be confused if they don't read it. However, if they do read it, magical details will be revealed. Each book is about 100,000 words long, shorter than any book in the Castle Keepers series.

Cast of Characters

The Castle Keepers fantasy series tells the stories of many characters. Some appear for only a short time. Others will appear in all the books.

Characters are listed according to last names to reveal family lines. Female hauflins are listed according to their meeme's (mother's) name, such as Niamh, Alaura of.

Information is provide according to the status when they first appear in the book. For example, Farlan Burkenshaw first appears as a private. Later he is promoted. If family ties are revealed in future books, that information will not be revealed here.

Ailsa, Beathas of: Hauflin, female, sorceress, lives at Moon Meadow

Blomidon: Royal sage at Aruam Castle

Buchans: Hauflin, male, thief, drifter

Burkenshaw, Farlan: Human, male, private with Aruam Castle

Burkenshaw, Saraline: Human, female, sister to Farlan Burkenshaw

Clover: Haflinger pony, mare, companion to Alaura of Niamh

Critch, Rorie: Dwarf, male, private with Aruam Castle

Cronin, Sawney: Dwarf, male, junior corporal with Aruam Castle, scout

Darrow, Bronwyn: Dwarf, male, corporal with Aruam Castle, son of Maisie and Gaven Darrow

Darrow, Gaven: Dwarf, male, owner of Forest Bakery and Herb Shop, lives at Maskil, Maisie Darrow's mate

Darrow, Joris: Dwarf, male, wheelwright, lives at Maskil, son of Maisie and Gaven Darrow

Darrow, Loran: Dwarf, female, dressmaker, owns Sew in Style Clothier, lives at Maskil, daughter of Maisie and Gaven Darrow

Darrow, Maisie: Dwarf, female, owner of Forest Bakery and Herb Shop, lives at Maskil, Gaven Darrow's mate

Darrow, Molly: Dwarf, female, daughter of Maisie and Gaven Darrow

Darrow, Rhiannon: Dwarf, female, herbalist, dress maker, owns Sew in Style Clothier shop, lives at Maskil, daughter of Maisie and Gaven Darrow

Dee: Human, male, private with Aruam Castle

Denny: Human, male, private with Aruam Castle

Dole, Breckin: Dwarf, female, actor with Scintillate Theatre, lives at Maskil

Dugald: Human, male, royal messenger at Aruam Castle

Dunsworth, Canton: Human, male, Duke of South Ridge

Dunsworth, Finley: Human, male, Lord of South Ridge, son of Canton Dunsworth

Ealasaid, Maura of: Hauflin, female, Isla's meeme, Keiron Ruckle's mate, lives at Maskil

Elkin, Hamish: Elf, male, private with Aruam Castle

Fran: Hauflin, female, strumpet, applies her trade at Midway Inn

Glawson: Human, male, sergeant with Aruam Castle

Graple: Hauflin, male, thief, drifter

Greenhill: Human, male, captain with Aruam Castle

Harlan: Human, male, private with Aruam Castle

Jenkins, Liam: Hauflin, male, teenager, son of Mr. Jenkins and Finola of Mallaidh, lives at Maskil

Kelly: Elf, male, private with Aruam Castle

Latchford: Human, male, sergeant with Aruam Castle

Lilja: Dragon, female, magical, guardian of Aruam Castle, missing for years

Lindrum, Merk: Human, male, Lord of Blackvale Castle, illusionist

Mallaidh, Finola of: Hauflin, female, Liam Jenkin's meeme

Maltby, Garret: Human, male, private with Aruam Castle

Maura, Isla of: Hauflin, female, daughter of Maura of Ealasaid and Keiron Ruckle, lives at Maskil

Mongo: Elf, male, boy, works at Upper Branch Keep

Moonsmy, Alfwin: Elf, male, archivist at Aruam Castle

M'Rasnil, Pym: Hauflin/human mix, male, Alaura's brother, son of Niamh and Egan Rasnil, lives at North Ridge

Mulryan, Kellyn: Dwarf, female, prisoner at Blackvale Castle

Niamh, Alaura of: Hauflin/human mix, female, magic-user, daughter of Niamh and Egan Rasnil, lives at Maskil

Orme, Trisham: Human, male, captain of the guard with South Ridge

Parnell: Elf, human, junior corporal with Aruam Castle

Reese: Gnome, male, thief, drifter

Ruckle, Keiron: Hauflin, male, thief, Maura of Ealasaid's mate, Isla of Maura's das, lives at Maskil

Sanderson, Zipporah: Human, male, captain of the guard with Aruam Castle

Selina: Human, apprentice, healer, lives at Maskil

Stephens: Elf, male, corporal with Aruam Castle

Tam: Dwarf, male, fighter, vagabond, drifter

Tibbins: Human, male, captain with Aruam Castle, governs the prison

Wheatcroft, Catriona: Human, female, sorceress, lives at Maskil, daughter of Kathleen and Emerson Wheatcroft

Wheatcroft, Emerson: Human, male, cartographer, lives at Wandsworth, Kathleen mate

Wilhelm: Human, male, royal scribe with Aruam Castle

Lords of Aruam Castle

Lady Glynn Dasia: Elf, female, healer, tends to the basic needs of citizens

Lord Valmour Elfren: Elf, male, healer, illusionist, governs the relations and communications with other settlements

Lord Dirck Landis: Human, male, governs over the justice system and dungeon

Lord Laird Mulryan: Dwarf, male, governs the guards and army

Lord Layne Nevell: Human, male, healer, governs the Infirmary serving the inhabitants of the castle, castle guard and the army

Lord Peadar Tasgall: Hauflin, male, magic-user, governs the education system

The Seasons

In the Land of Ath-o'Lea, there are six seasons that make up one succession. In general, the seasons correspond to the northern hemisphere months as such: Wintertide (January/February), Spring of Leaf (March/April), Springan (May/June), Sumortide (July/August), Harvest (September/October) and Forstig (November/December).

The longest day of the year is called Sumortide Solstice. The shortest day of the year is Wintertide Solstice.

The Castle Keepers Novel Series

Shadows in the Stone

Scattered Stones

Revelation Stones

Healing Stones

Gathered Stones

Origin of the Stones

The Stone Gatherer

Rebellion Stones

Hearthstones

The Lost Journal of Bronwyn Kintale

Castle Keepers Tale Series
fantasy shorts

Destiny Governed their Lives
starring Catriona Wheatcroft

Blade of Truth
starring Bronwyn Darrow

The Pledge
starring Alaura of Niamh

Mystical Series
the series within a series

Beyond the Myst

Within the Myst

H

www.ingramcontent.com/pod-product-compliance
Lightning Source LLC
Chambersburg PA
CBHW030914050726
47498CB00003BA/732